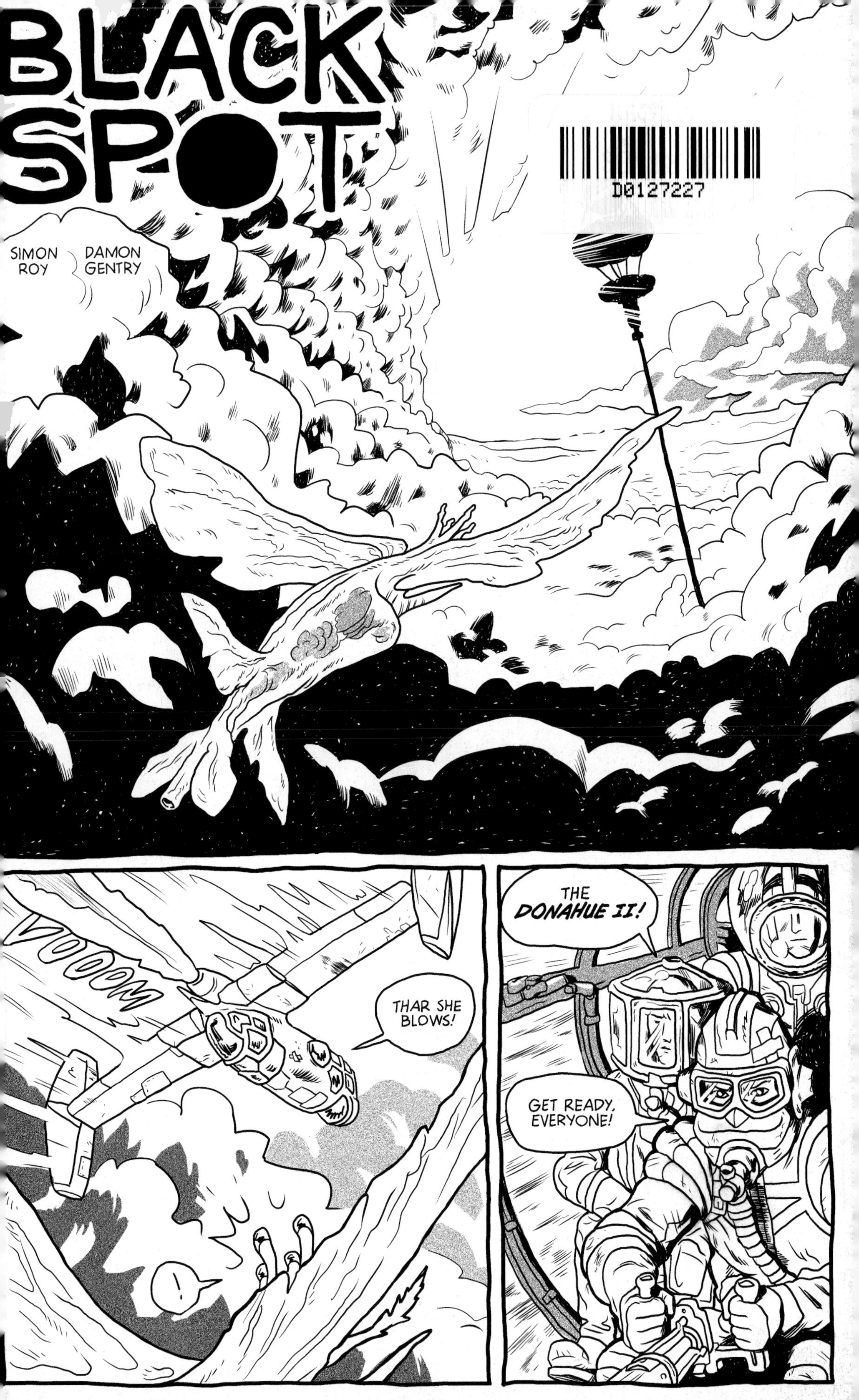
BLACK SPOT
SIMON ROY
DAMON GENTRY
VOOOM
THAR SHE BLOWS!
!
THE DONAHUE II!
GET READY, EVERYONE!

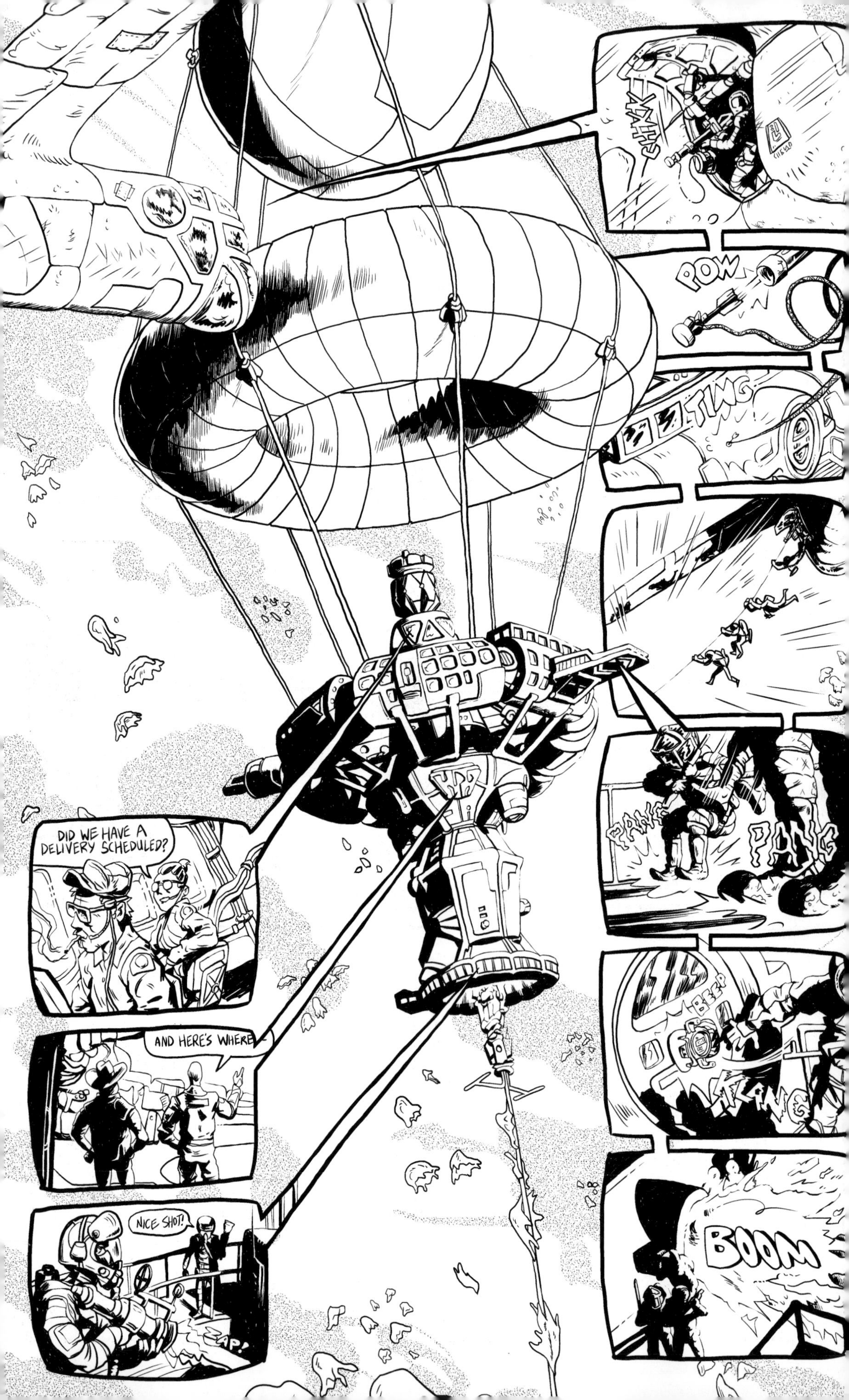
POW
TING
PANG
PANG
BEEP
BOOM
DID WE HAVE A DELIVERY SCHEDULED?
AND HERE'S WHERE
NICE SHOT!
ZAP!

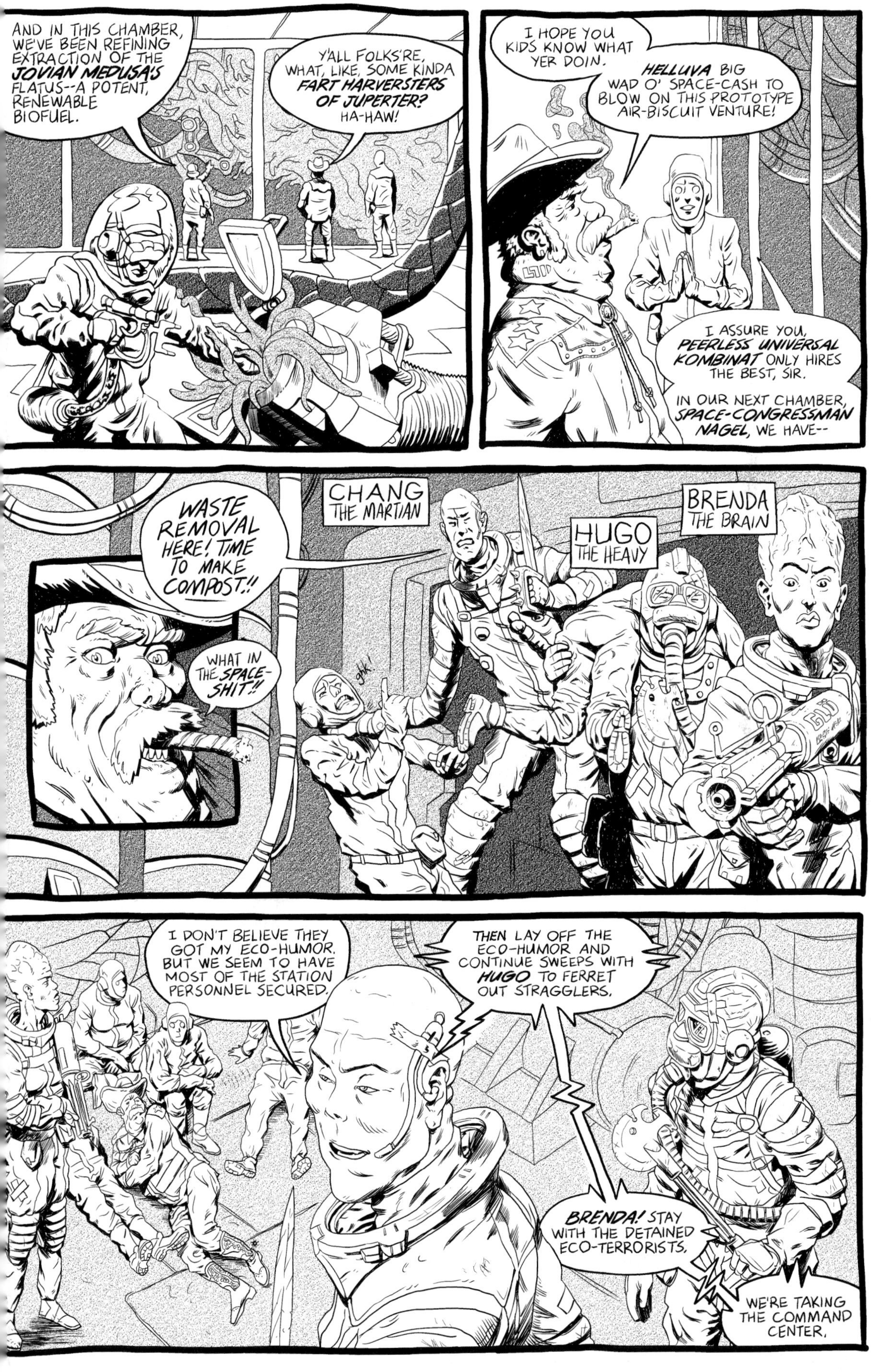
AND IN THIS CHAMBER, WE'VE BEEN REFINING EXTRACTION OF THE JOVIAN MEDUSA'S FLATUS--A POTENT, RENEWABLE BIOFUEL.
Y'ALL FOLKS'RE, WHAT, LIKE, SOME KINDA FART HARVERSTERS OF JUPERTER? HA-HAW!
I HOPE YOU KIDS KNOW WHAT YER DOIN.
HELLUVA BIG WAD O' SPACE-CASH TO BLOW ON THIS PROTOTYPE AIR-BISCUIT VENTURE!
I ASSURE YOU, PEERLESS UNIVERSAL KOMBINAT ONLY HIRES THE BEST, SIR.
IN OUR NEXT CHAMBER, SPACE-CONGRESSMAN NAGEL, WE HAVE--
CHANG THE MARTIAN
HUGO THE HEAVY
BRENDA THE BRAIN
WASTE REMOVAL HERE! TIME TO MAKE COMPOST!!
WHAT IN THE SPACE-SHIT!!
ghk!
I DON'T BELIEVE THEY GOT MY ECO-HUMOR. BUT WE SEEM TO HAVE MOST OF THE STATION PERSONNEL SECURED.
THEN LAY OFF THE ECO-HUMOR AND CONTINUE SWEEPS WITH HUGO TO FERRET OUT STRAGGLERS.
BRENDA! STAY WITH THE DETAINED ECO-TERRORISTS.
WE'RE TAKING THE COMMAND CENTER.

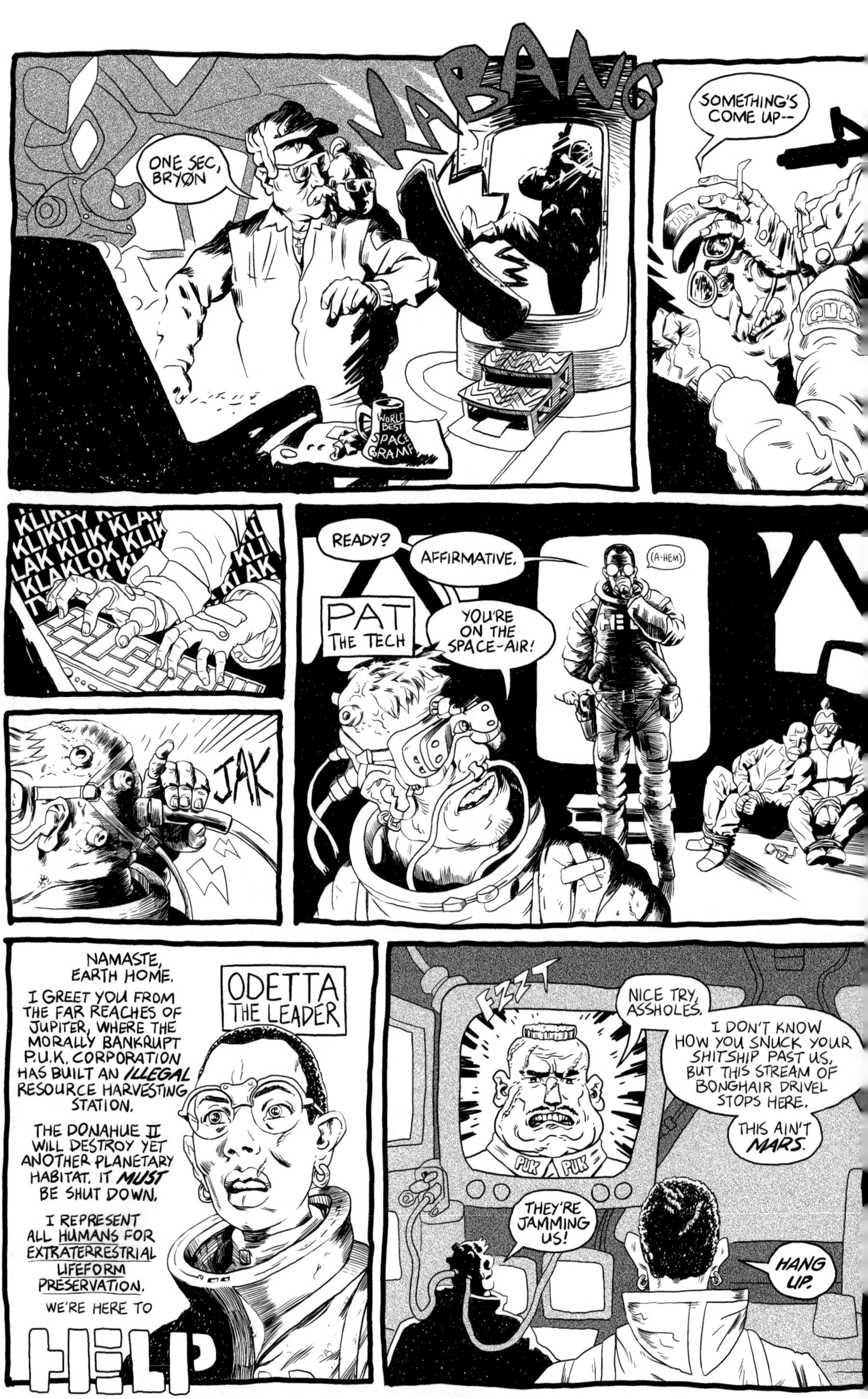
VABANG
ONE SEC, BRYØN
SOMETHING'S COME UP--
WORLD'S BEST SPACE GRAMP
KLIKITY KLAK KLIK KLAK KLIK KLAKLOK KLIK
JAK
READY?
AFFIRMATIVE.
(A-HEM)
PAT THE TECH
YOU'RE ON THE SPACE-AIR!
NAMASTE, EARTH HOME.
I GREET YOU FROM THE FAR REACHES OF JUPITER, WHERE THE MORALLY BANKRUPT P.U.K. CORPORATION HAS BUILT AN ILLEGAL RESOURCE HARVESTING STATION.
THE DONAHUE II WILL DESTROY YET ANOTHER PLANETARY HABITAT. IT MUST BE SHUT DOWN.
I REPRESENT ALL HUMANS FOR EXTRATERRESTRIAL LIFEFORM PRESERVATION.
WE'RE HERE TO
HELP
ODETTA THE LEADER
FZZT
NICE TRY, ASSHOLES.
I DON'T KNOW HOW YOU SNUCK YOUR SHITSHIP PAST US, BUT THIS STREAM OF BONGHAIR DRIVEL STOPS HERE.
THIS AIN'T MARS.
THEY'RE JAMMING US!
HANG UP.

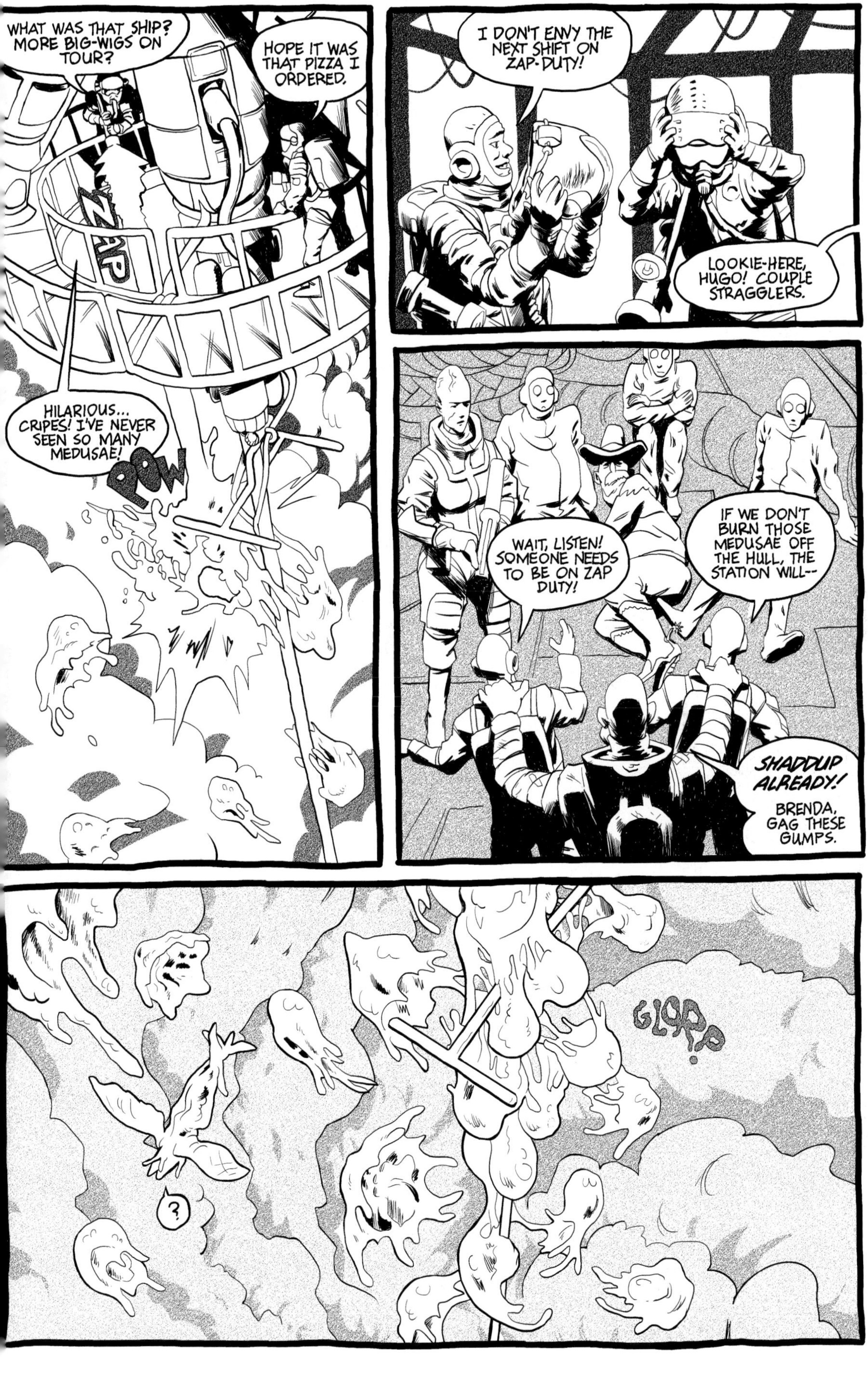
WHAT WAS THAT SHIP? MORE BIG-WIGS ON TOUR?
HOPE IT WAS THAT PIZZA I ORDERED.
ZAP
HILARIOUS... CRIPES! I'VE NEVER SEEN SO MANY MEDUSAE!
POW
I DON'T ENVY THE NEXT SHIFT ON ZAP-DUTY!
LOOKIE-HERE, HUGO! COUPLE STRAGGLERS.
WAIT, LISTEN! SOMEONE NEEDS TO BE ON ZAP DUTY!
IF WE DON'T BURN THOSE MEDUSAE OFF THE HULL, THE STATION WILL--
SHADDUP ALREADY!
BRENDA, GAG THESE GUMPS.
GLORP
?

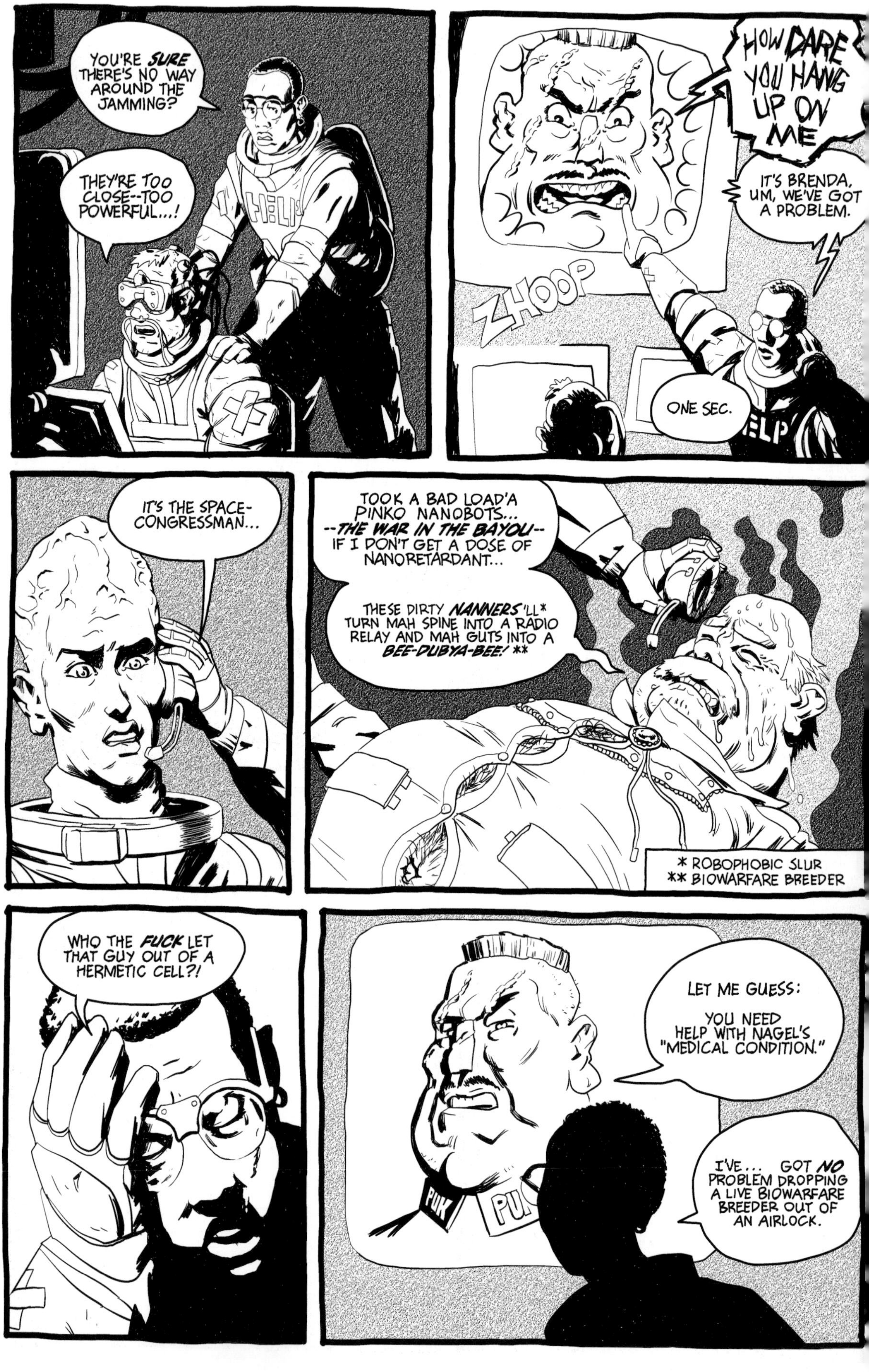
YOU'RE *SURE* THERE'S NO WAY AROUND THE JAMMING?
THEY'RE TOO CLOSE--TOO POWERFUL...!
HOW DARE YOU HANG UP ON ME
IT'S BRENDA, UM, WE'VE GOT A PROBLEM.
ZHOOP
ONE SEC.
IT'S THE SPACE-CONGRESSMAN...
TOOK A BAD LOAD'A PINKO NANOBOTS... --*THE WAR IN THE BAYOU*-- IF I DON'T GET A DOSE OF NANORETARDANT...
THESE DIRTY *NANNERS*'LL* TURN MAH SPINE INTO A RADIO RELAY AND MAH GUTS INTO A *BEE-DUBYA-BEE!* **
* ROBOPHOBIC SLUR
** BIOWARFARE BREEDER
WHO THE *FUCK* LET THAT GUY OUT OF A HERMETIC CELL?!
LET ME GUESS:
YOU NEED HELP WITH NAGEL'S "MEDICAL CONDITION."
I'VE... GOT *NO* PROBLEM DROPPING A LIVE BIOWARFARE BREEDER OUT OF AN AIRLOCK.

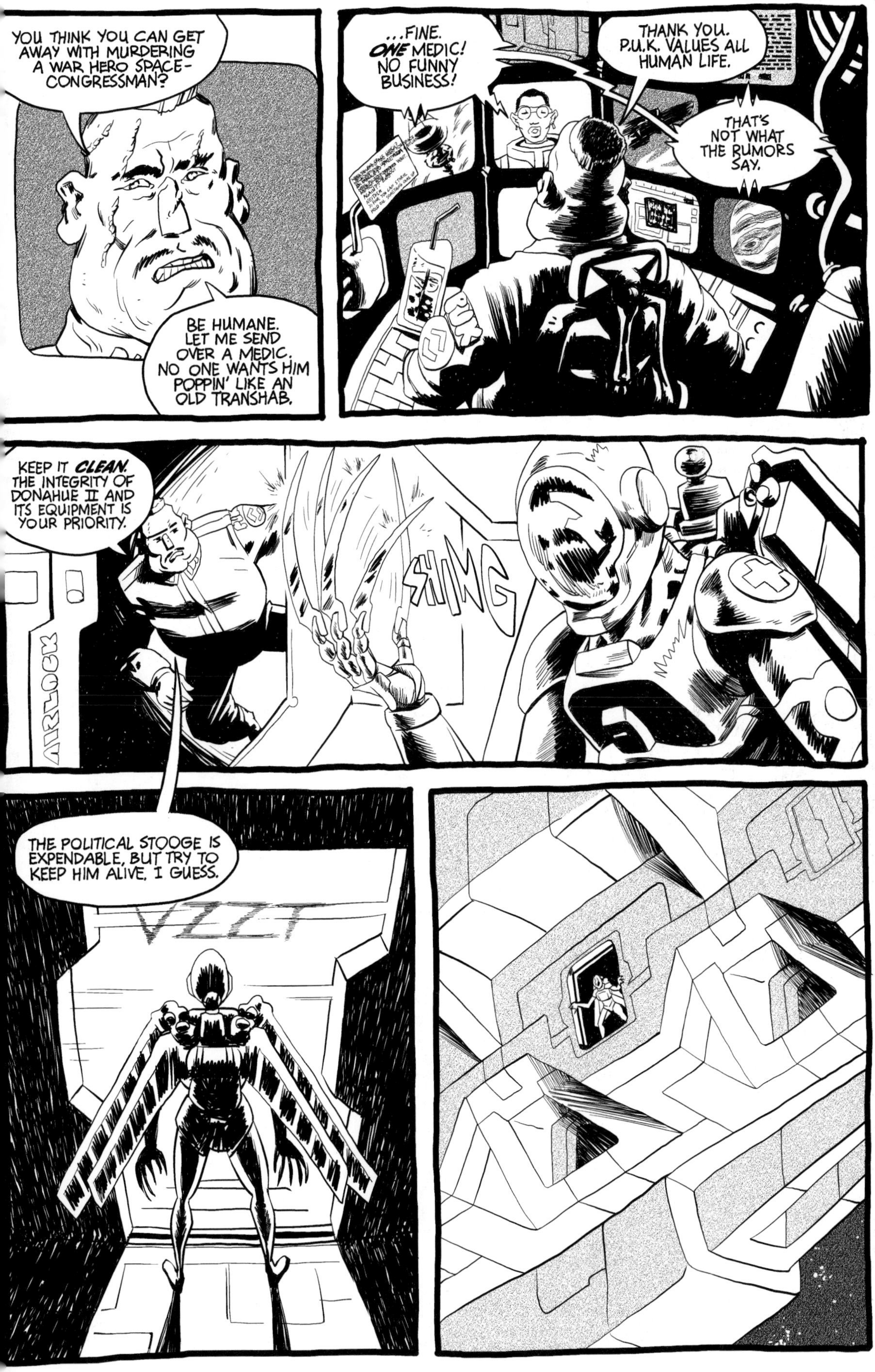
YOU THINK YOU CAN GET AWAY WITH MURDERING A WAR HERO SPACE-CONGRESSMAN?
BE HUMANE. LET ME SEND OVER A MEDIC. NO ONE WANTS HIM POPPIN' LIKE AN OLD TRANSHAB.
...FINE. ONE MEDIC! NO FUNNY BUSINESS!
THANK YOU. P.U.K. VALUES ALL HUMAN LIFE.
THAT'S NOT WHAT THE RUMORS SAY.
P.U.K.
KEEP IT CLEAN. THE INTEGRITY OF DONAHUE II AND ITS EQUIPMENT IS YOUR PRIORITY.
SHING
AIRLOCK
THE POLITICAL STOOGE IS EXPENDABLE, BUT TRY TO KEEP HIM ALIVE, I GUESS.
VZZT

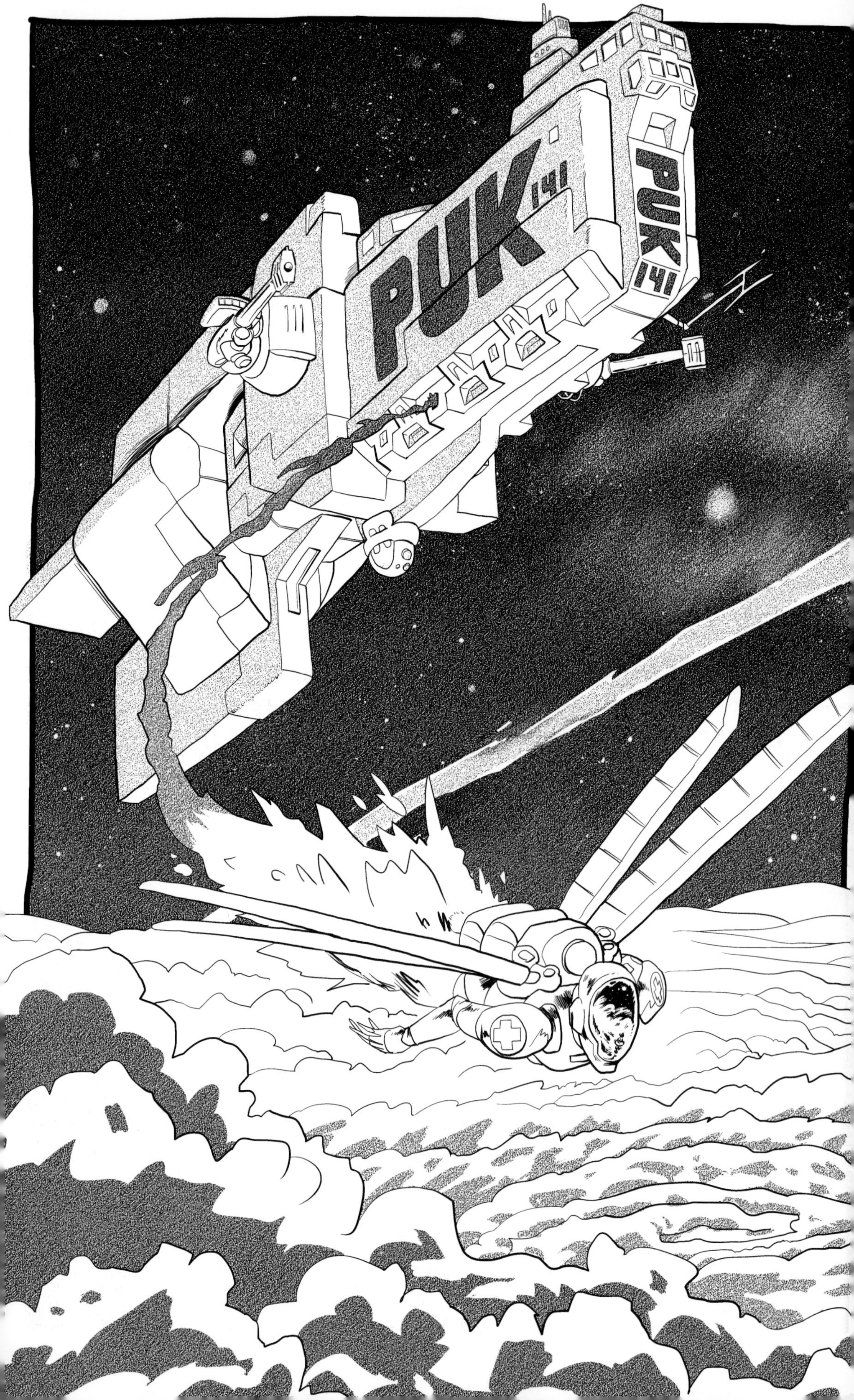
PUK 141
PUK 141

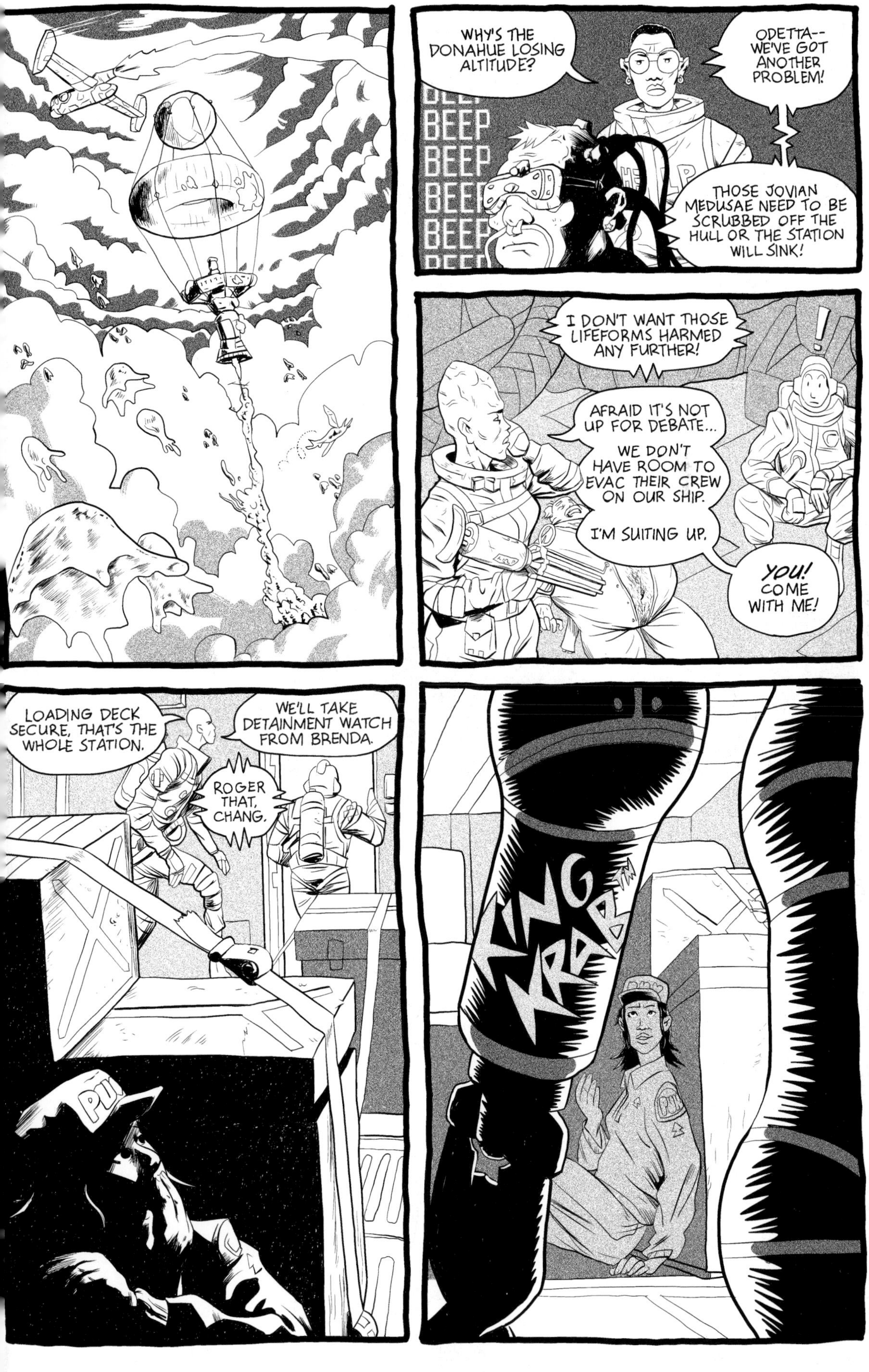
WHY'S THE DONAHUE LOSING ALTITUDE?
ODETTA-- WE'VE GOT ANOTHER PROBLEM!
BEEP BEEP BEEP BEEP BEEP
HELP
THOSE JOVIAN MEDUSAE NEED TO BE SCRUBBED OFF THE HULL OR THE STATION WILL SINK!
I DON'T WANT THOSE LIFEFORMS HARMED ANY FURTHER!
!
AFRAID IT'S NOT UP FOR DEBATE...
WE DON'T HAVE ROOM TO EVAC THEIR CREW ON OUR SHIP.
I'M SUITING UP.
YOU! COME WITH ME!
LOADING DECK SECURE, THAT'S THE WHOLE STATION.
WE'LL TAKE DETAINMENT WATCH FROM BRENDA.
ROGER THAT, CHANG.
KING KRAB™

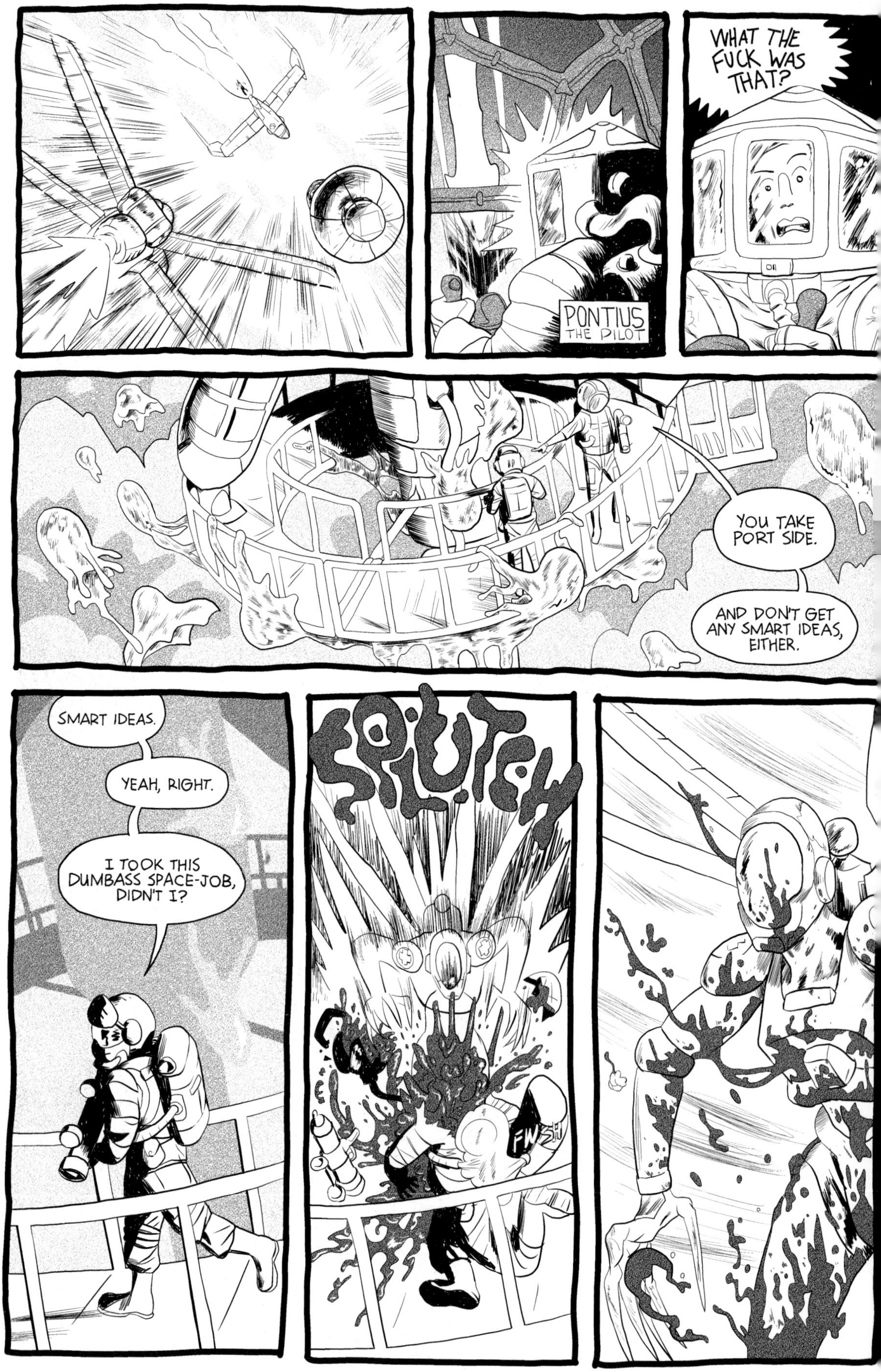
PONTIUS THE PILOT
WHAT THE FUCK WAS THAT?
YOU TAKE PORT SIDE.
AND DON'T GET ANY SMART IDEAS, EITHER.
SMART IDEAS.
YEAH, RIGHT.
I TOOK THIS DUMBASS SPACE-JOB, DIDN'T I?
SPLUTCH
FWSH

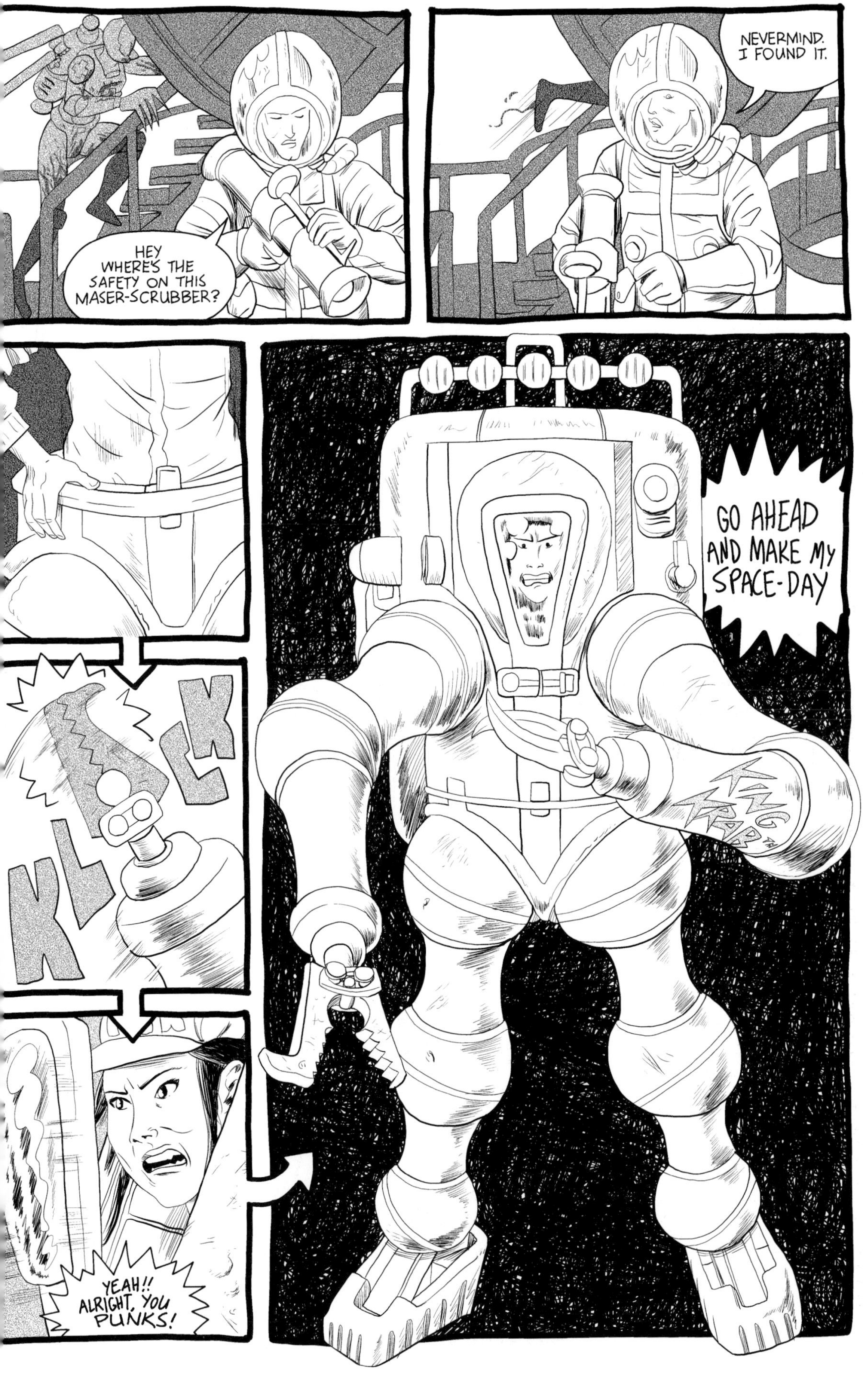
HEY WHERE'S THE SAFETY ON THIS MASER-SCRUBBER?
NEVERMIND. I FOUND IT.
KLACK
YEAH!! ALRIGHT, YOU PUNKS!
GO AHEAD AND MAKE MY SPACE-DAY
KING KRAB

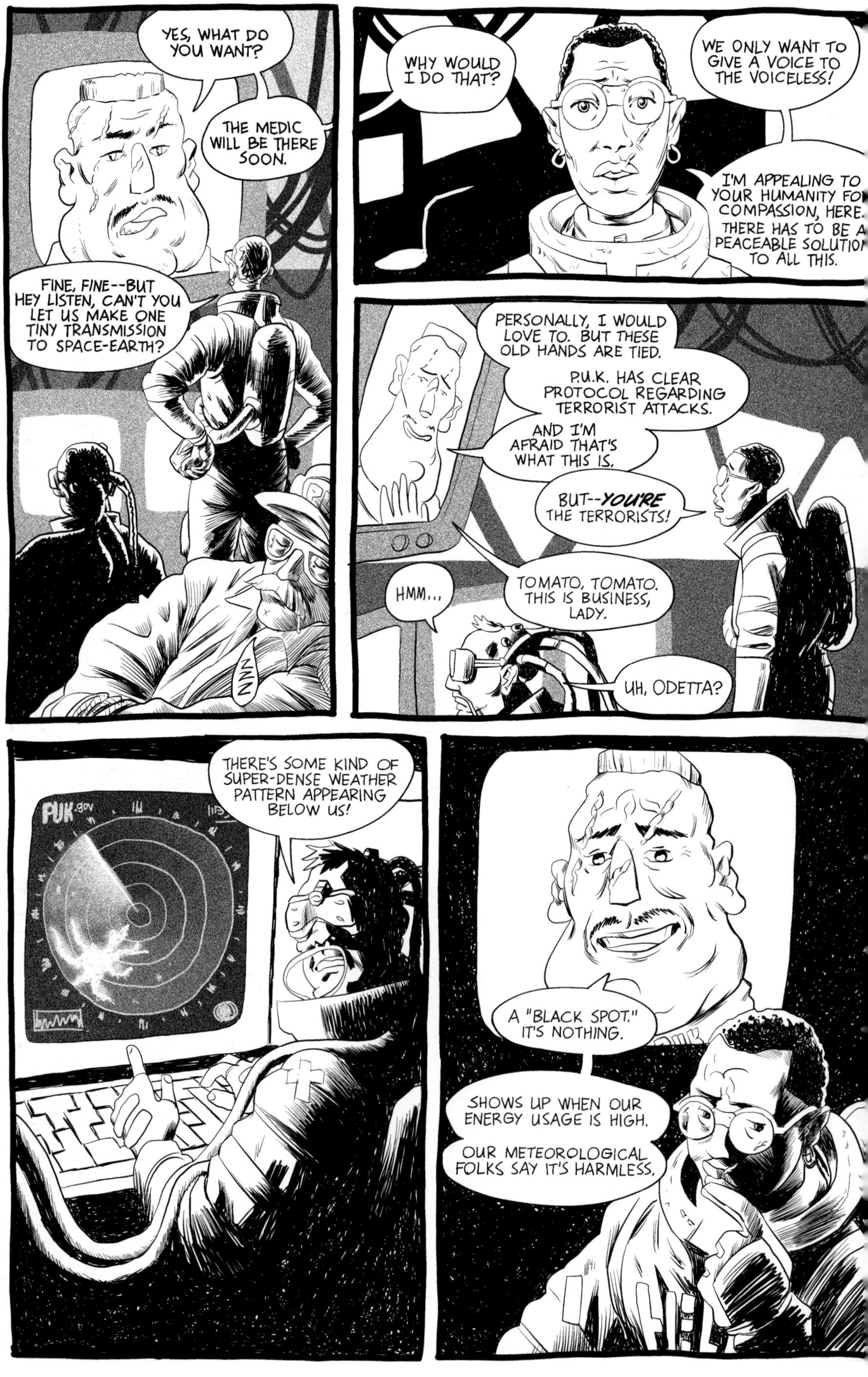
YES, WHAT DO YOU WANT?
THE MEDIC WILL BE THERE SOON.
FINE, FINE--BUT HEY LISTEN, CAN'T YOU LET US MAKE ONE TINY TRANSMISSION TO SPACE-EARTH?
ZZZ
WHY WOULD I DO THAT?
WE ONLY WANT TO GIVE A VOICE TO THE VOICELESS!
I'M APPEALING TO YOUR HUMANITY FO COMPASSION, HERE. THERE HAS TO BE A PEACEABLE SOLUTIO TO ALL THIS.
PERSONALLY, I WOULD LOVE TO. BUT THESE OLD HANDS ARE TIED.
P.U.K. HAS CLEAR PROTOCOL REGARDING TERRORIST ATTACKS.
AND I'M AFRAID THAT'S WHAT THIS IS.
BUT--*YOU'RE* THE TERRORISTS!
HMM...
TOMATO, TOMATO. THIS IS BUSINESS, LADY.
UH, ODETTA?
PUK.gov
THERE'S SOME KIND OF SUPER-DENSE WEATHER PATTERN APPEARING BELOW US!
A "BLACK SPOT." IT'S NOTHING.
SHOWS UP WHEN OUR ENERGY USAGE IS HIGH.
OUR METEOROLOGICAL FOLKS SAY IT'S HARMLESS.

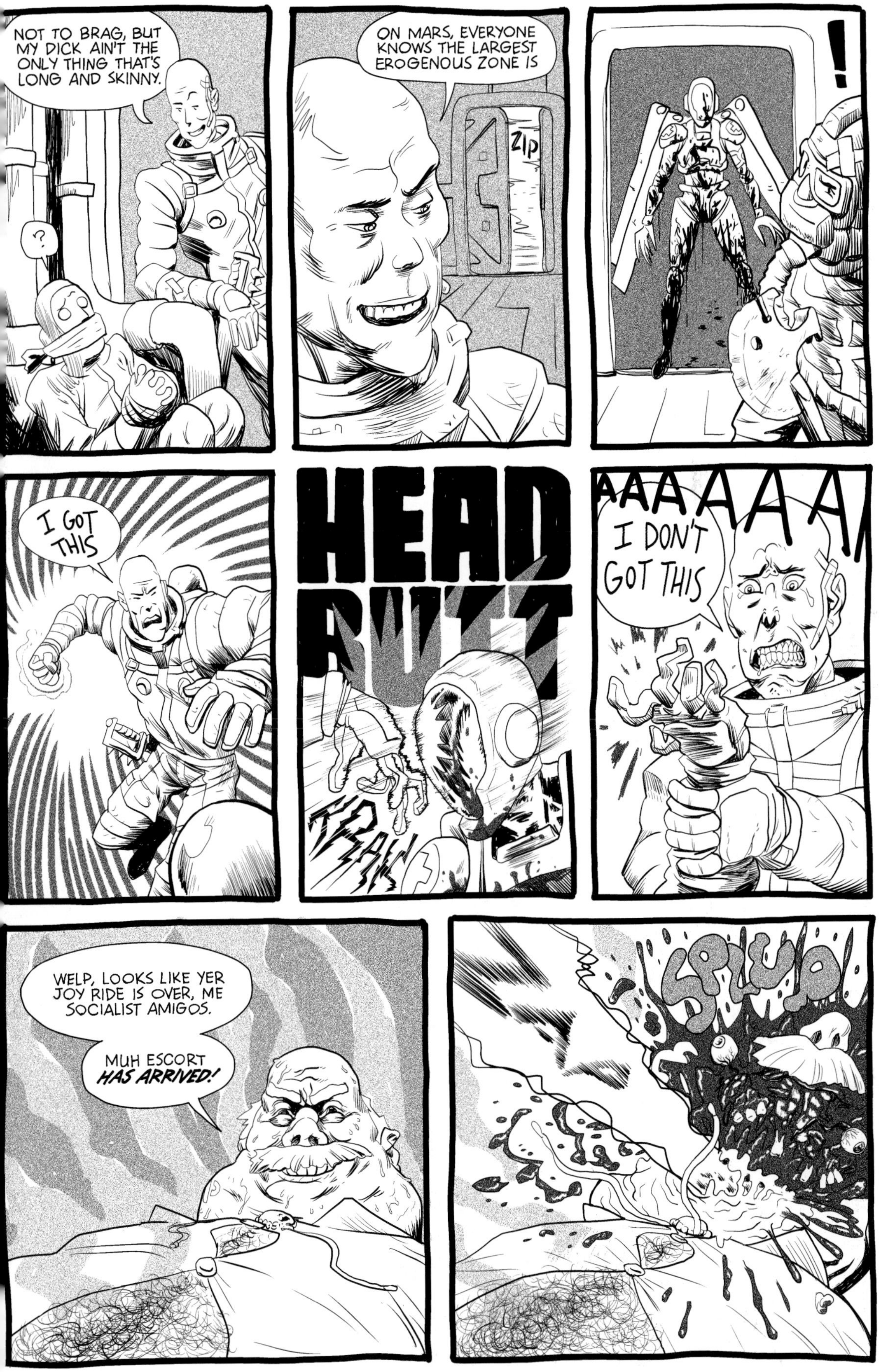
NOT TO BRAG, BUT MY DICK AIN'T THE ONLY THING THAT'S LONG AND SKINNY.
?
ON MARS, EVERYONE KNOWS THE LARGEST EROGENOUS ZONE IS
ZIP
!
I GOT THIS
HEAD BUTT
AAAAAAA
I DON'T GOT THIS
WELP, LOOKS LIKE YER JOY RIDE IS OVER, ME SOCIALIST AMIGOS.
MUH ESCORT HAS ARRIVED!
SPLUD

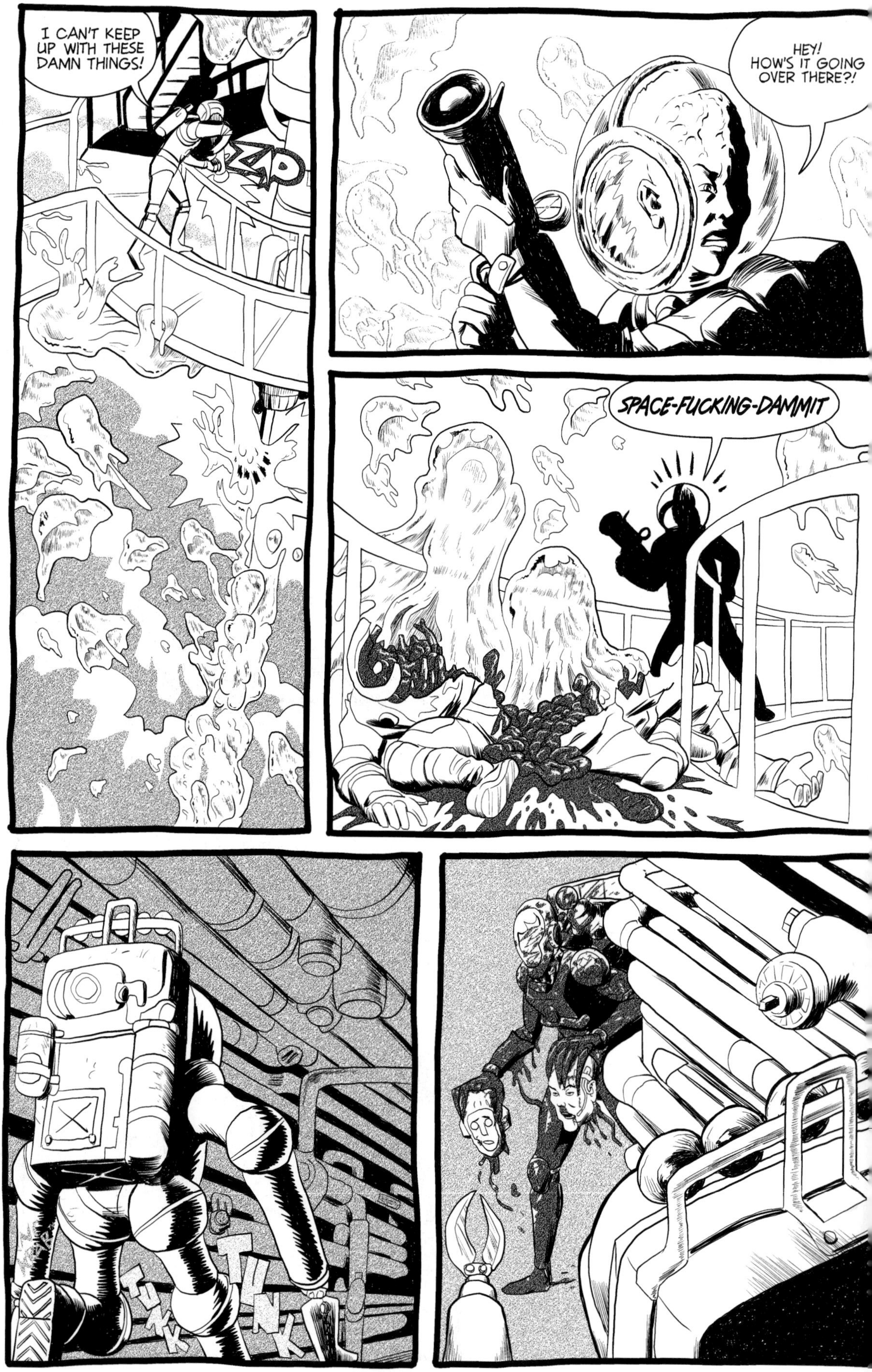
I CAN'T KEEP UP WITH THESE DAMN THINGS!
ZAP
HEY! HOW'S IT GOING OVER THERE?!
SPACE-FUCKING-DAMMIT
TUNK
TUNK

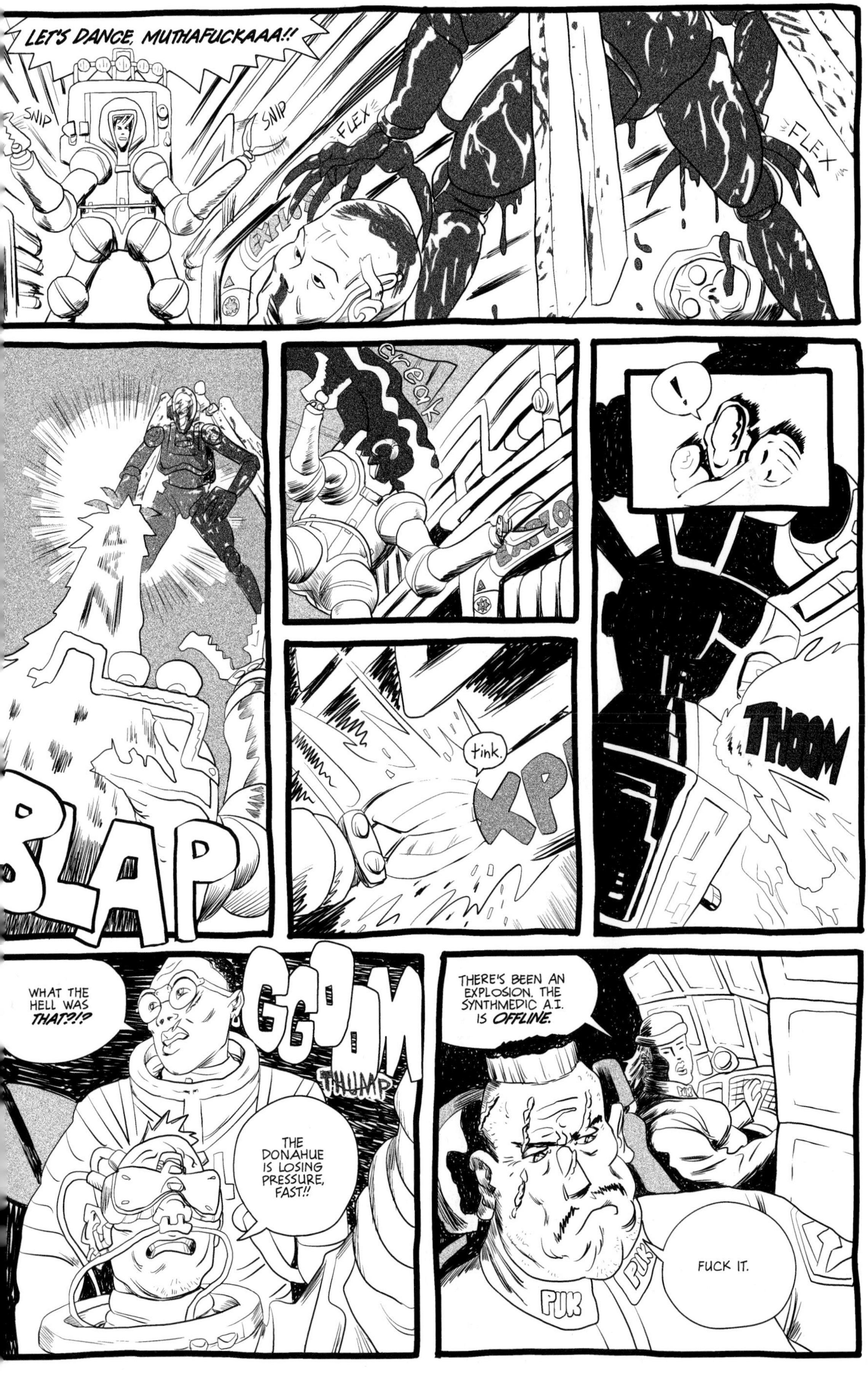

LET'S DANCE, MUTHAFUCKAAA!!
SNIP
SNIP
FLEX
FLEX
BLAP
creak
!
tink.
KP
THOOM
WHAT THE HELL WAS THAT?!?
GGOOM
THUMP
THE DONAHUE IS LOSING PRESSURE, FAST!!
THERE'S BEEN AN EXPLOSION. THE SYNTHMEDIC A.I. IS OFFLINE.
FUCK IT.

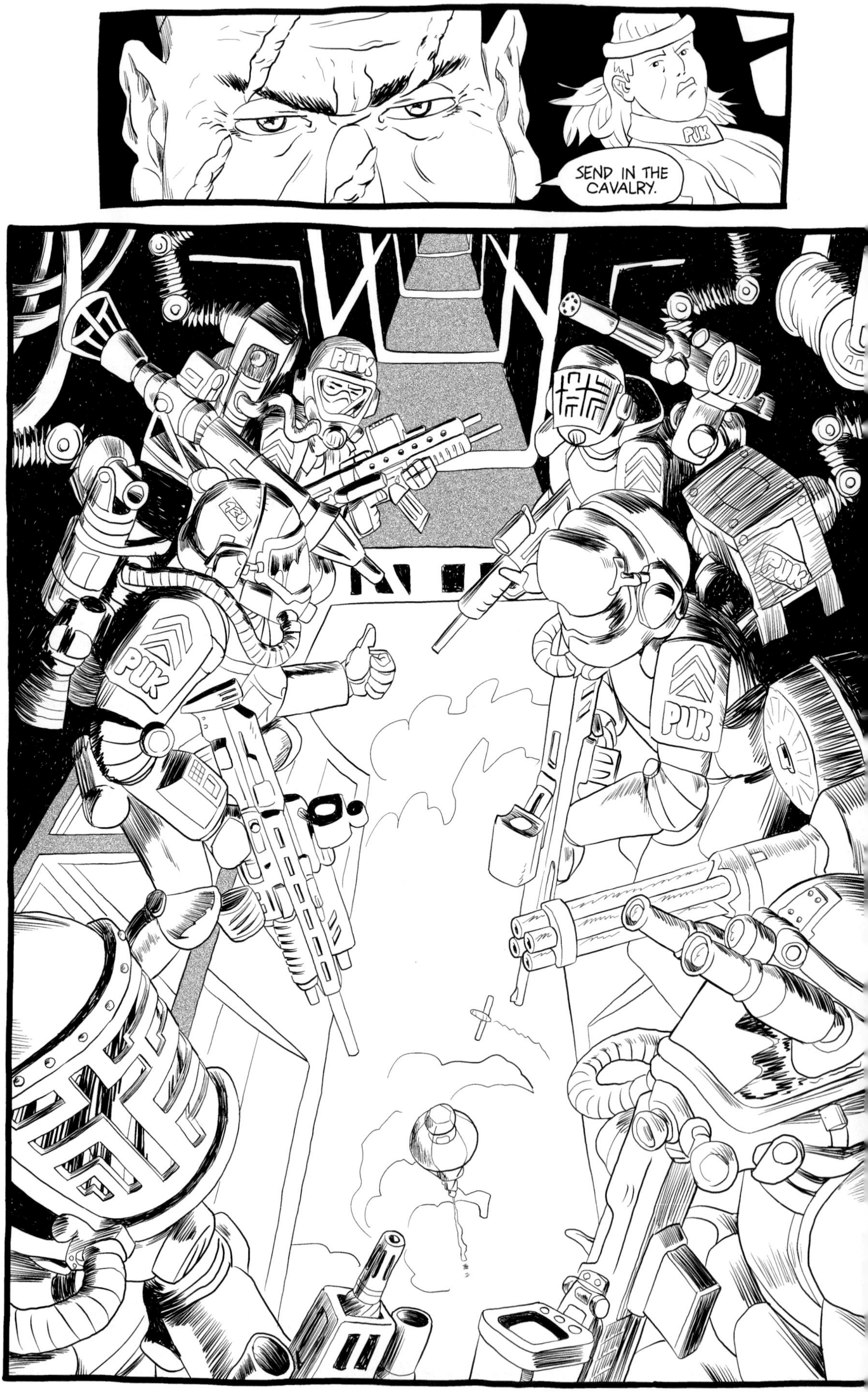
SEND IN THE CAVALRY.
PUK
PUK
PUK
PUK
PUK

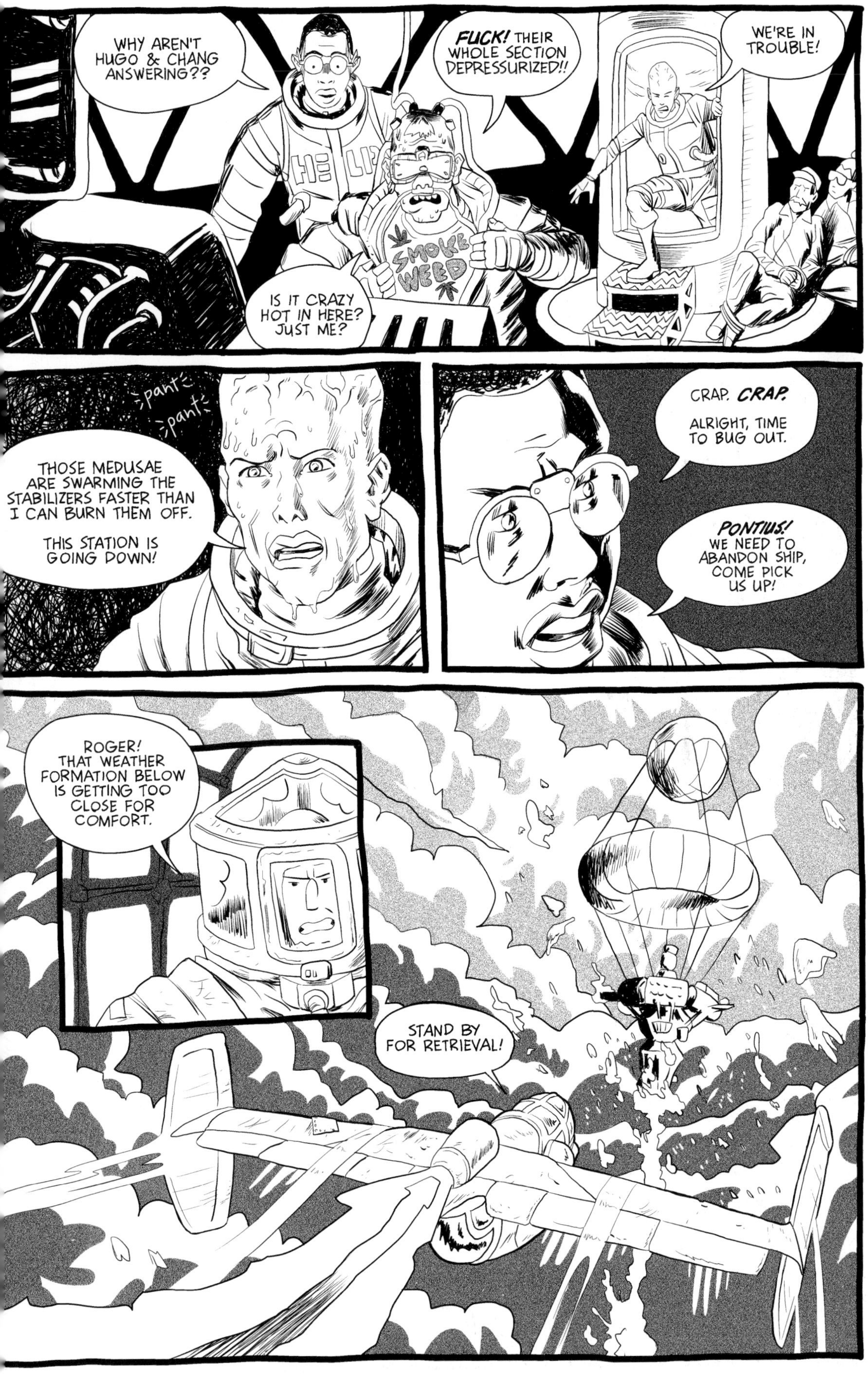
WHY AREN'T HUGO & CHANG ANSWERING??
FUCK! THEIR WHOLE SECTION DEPRESSURIZED!!
WE'RE IN TROUBLE!
IS IT CRAZY HOT IN HERE? JUST ME?
SMOKE WEED
pant pant
THOSE MEDUSAE ARE SWARMING THE STABILIZERS FASTER THAN I CAN BURN THEM OFF.
THIS STATION IS GOING DOWN!
CRAP. CRAP.
ALRIGHT, TIME TO BUG OUT.
PONTIUS! WE NEED TO ABANDON SHIP, COME PICK US UP!
ROGER! THAT WEATHER FORMATION BELOW IS GETTING TOO CLOSE FOR COMFORT.
STAND BY FOR RETRIEVAL!

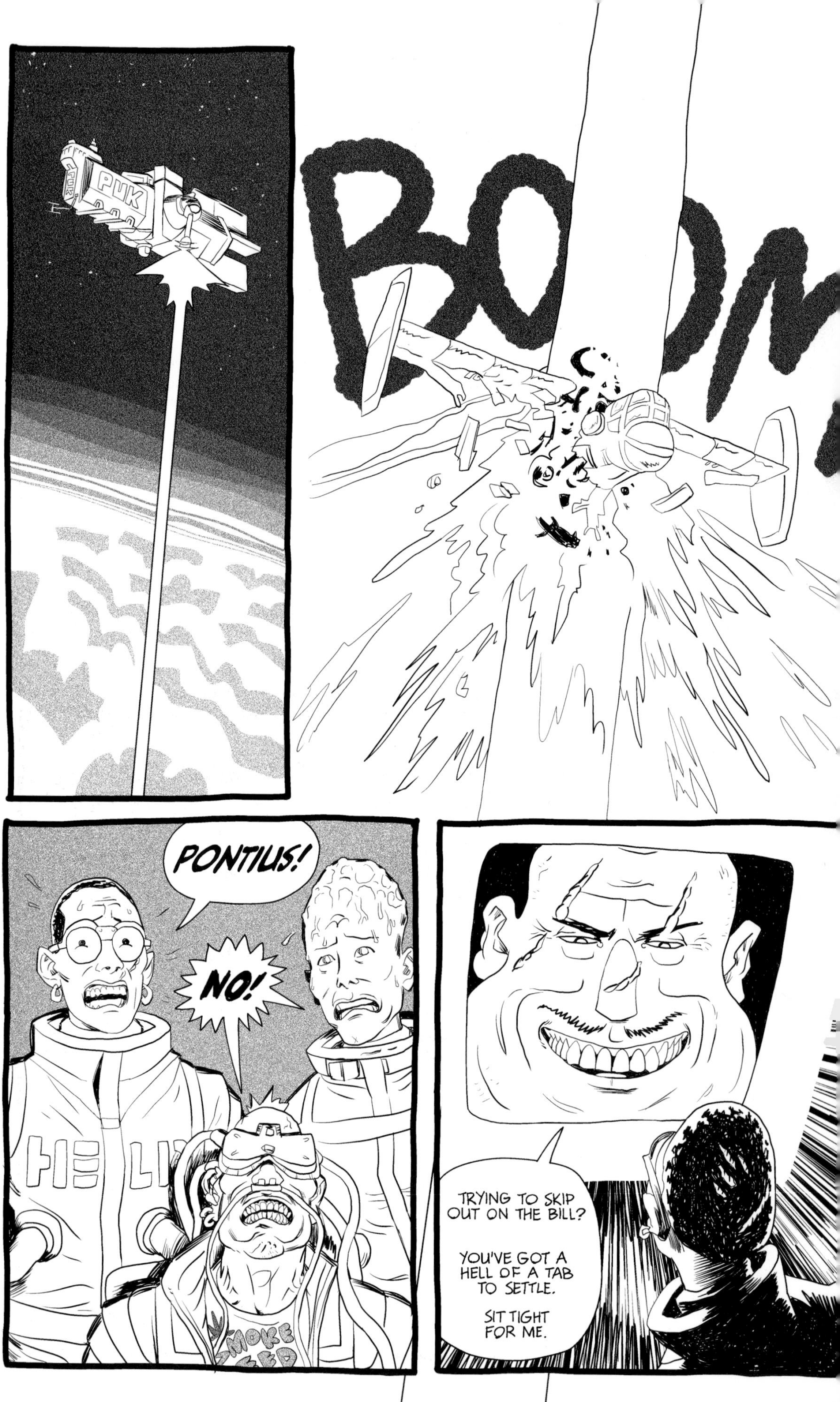
PUK
BOOM!
PONTIUS!
NO!
HELIX
SMOKE WEED
TRYING TO SKIP OUT ON THE BILL?
YOU'VE GOT A HELL OF A TAB TO SETTLE.
SIT TIGHT FOR ME.

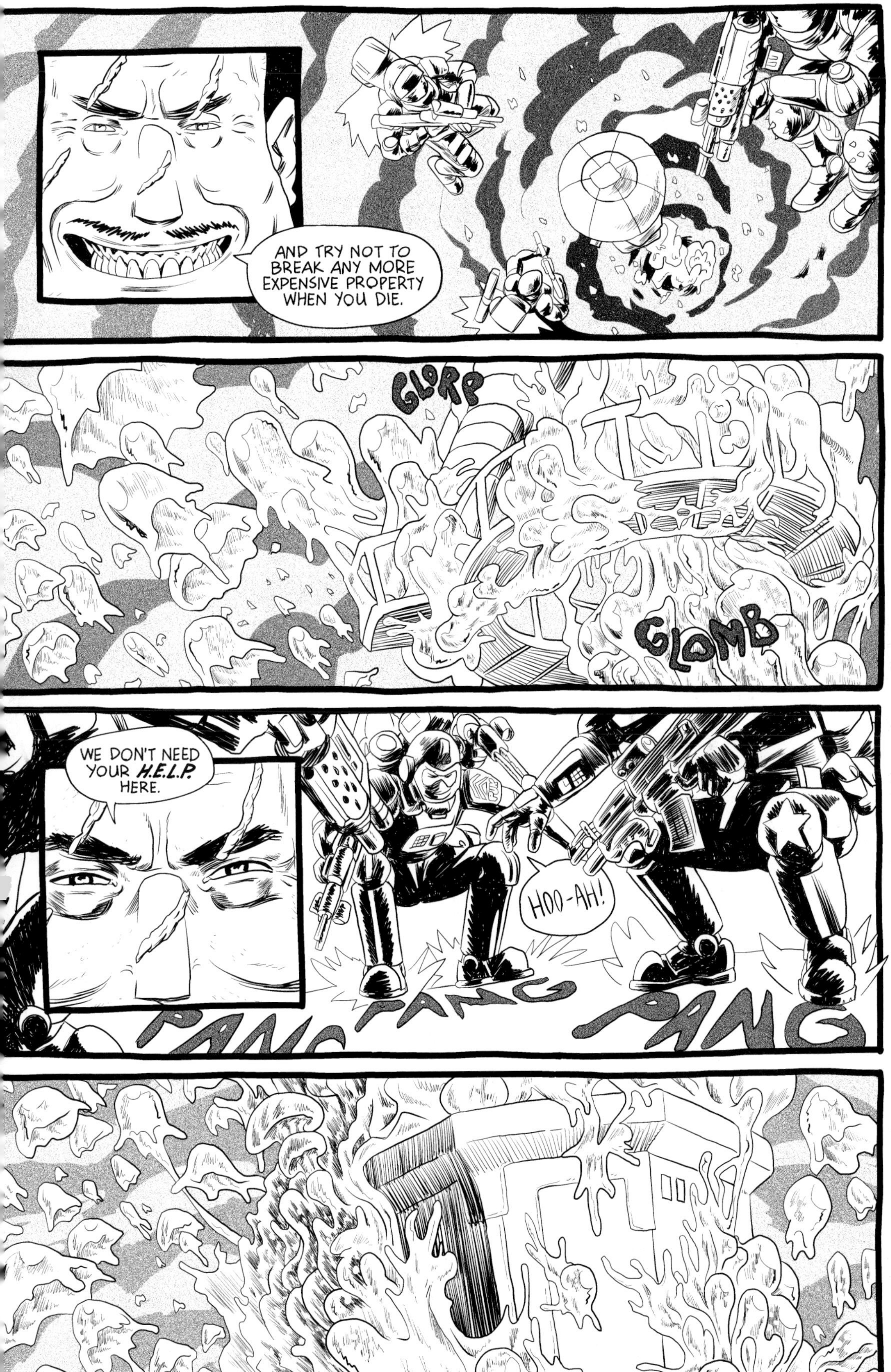
AND TRY NOT TO BREAK ANY MORE EXPENSIVE PROPERTY WHEN YOU DIE.
GLORP
GLOMB
WE DON'T NEED YOUR *H.E.L.P.* HERE.
HOO-AH!
PANG PANG PANG

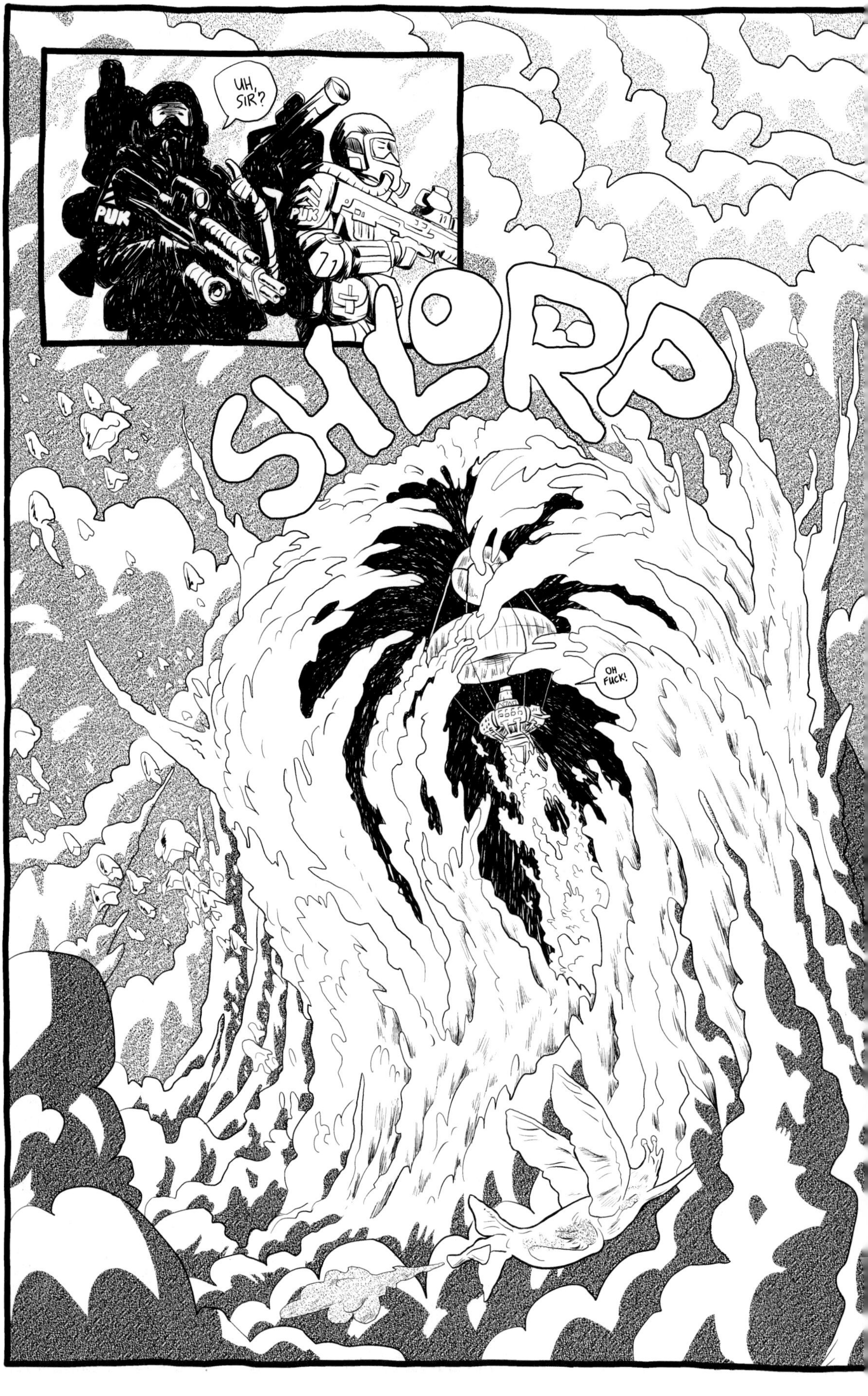
UH, SIR?
PUK
PUK
SHLORP
OH FUCK!

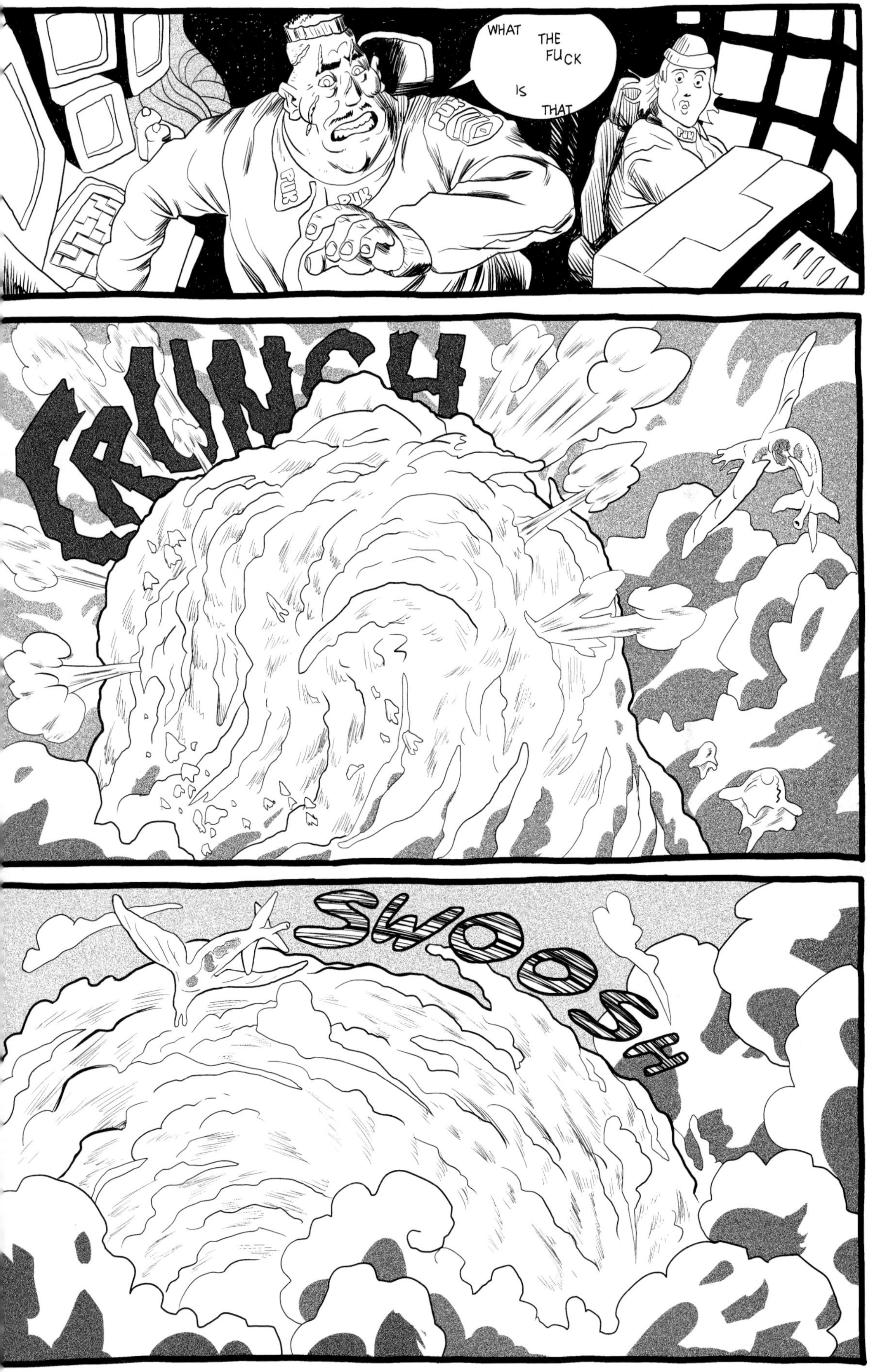
WHAT THE FUCK IS THAT
CRUNCH
SWOOSH

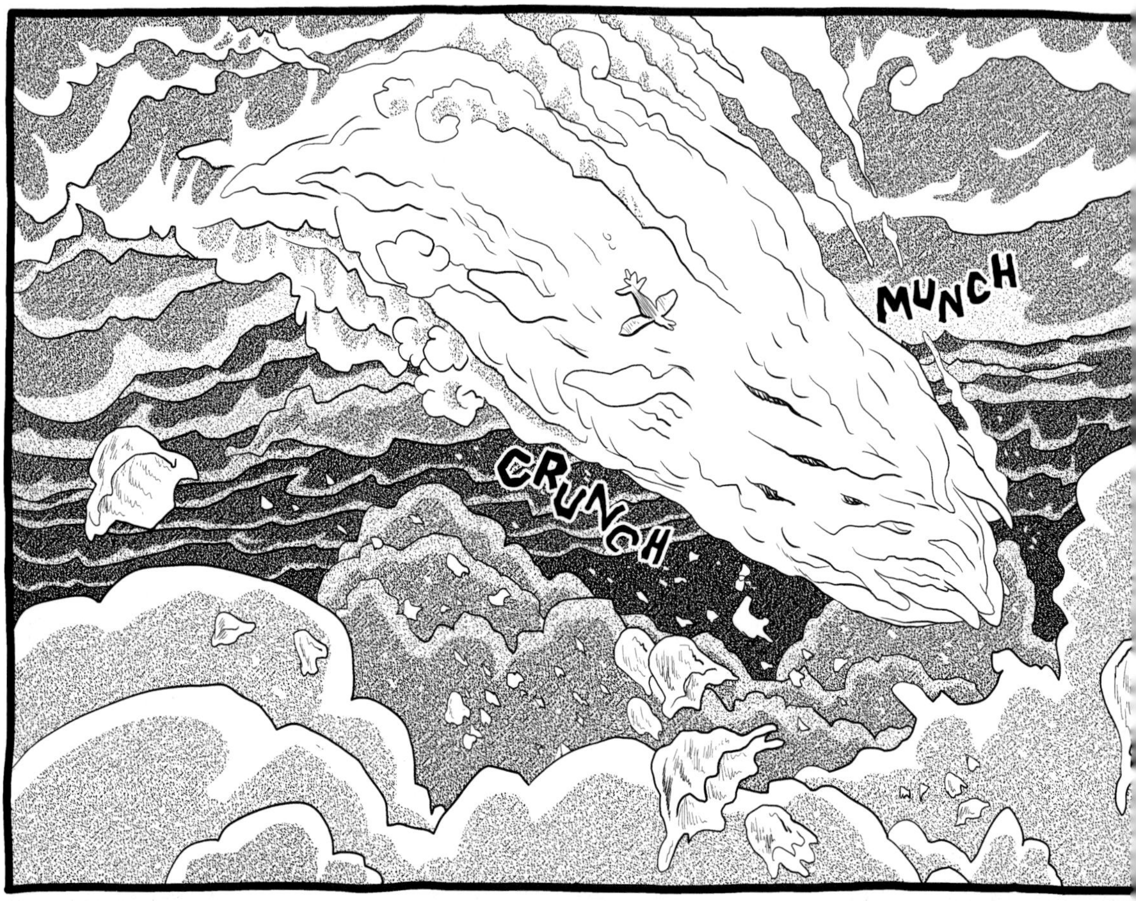
MUNCH
CRUNCH

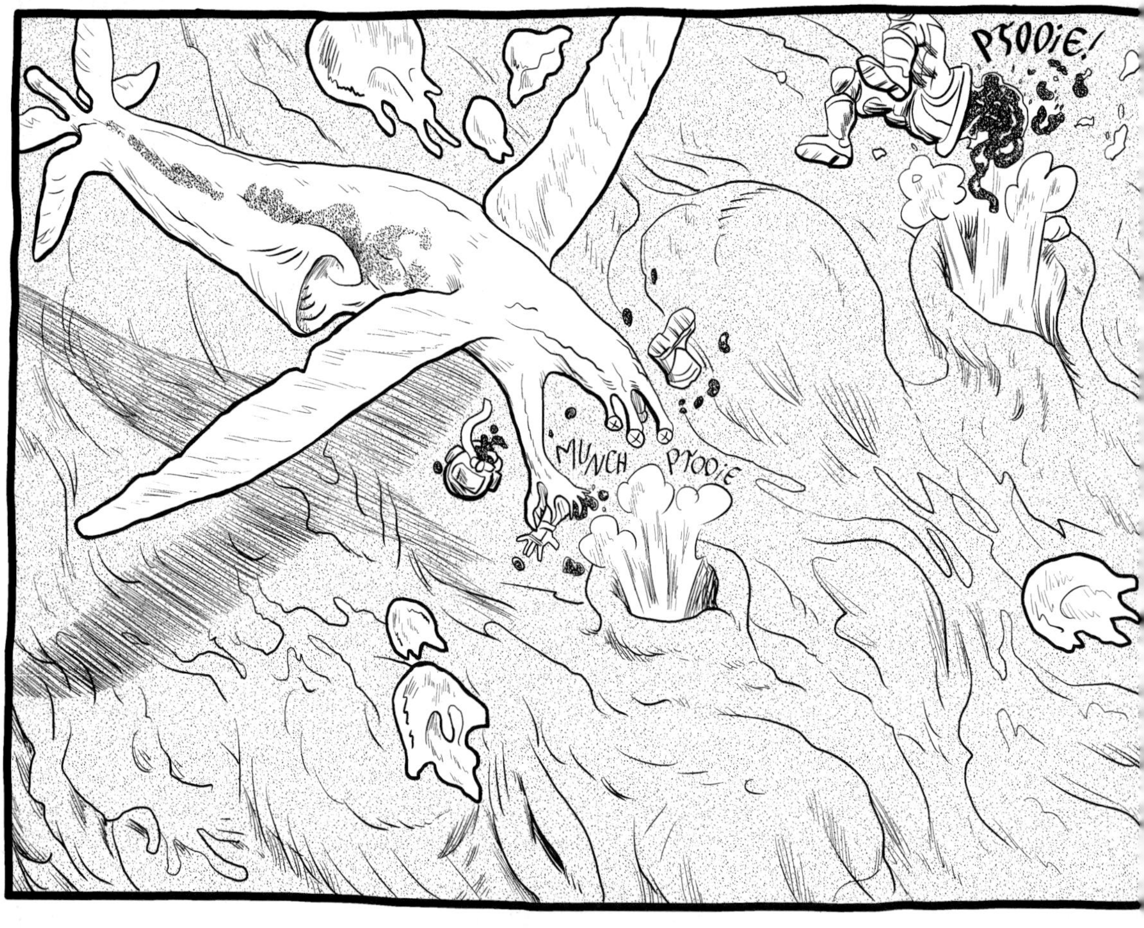
PTOOIE!
MUNCH
PTOOIE

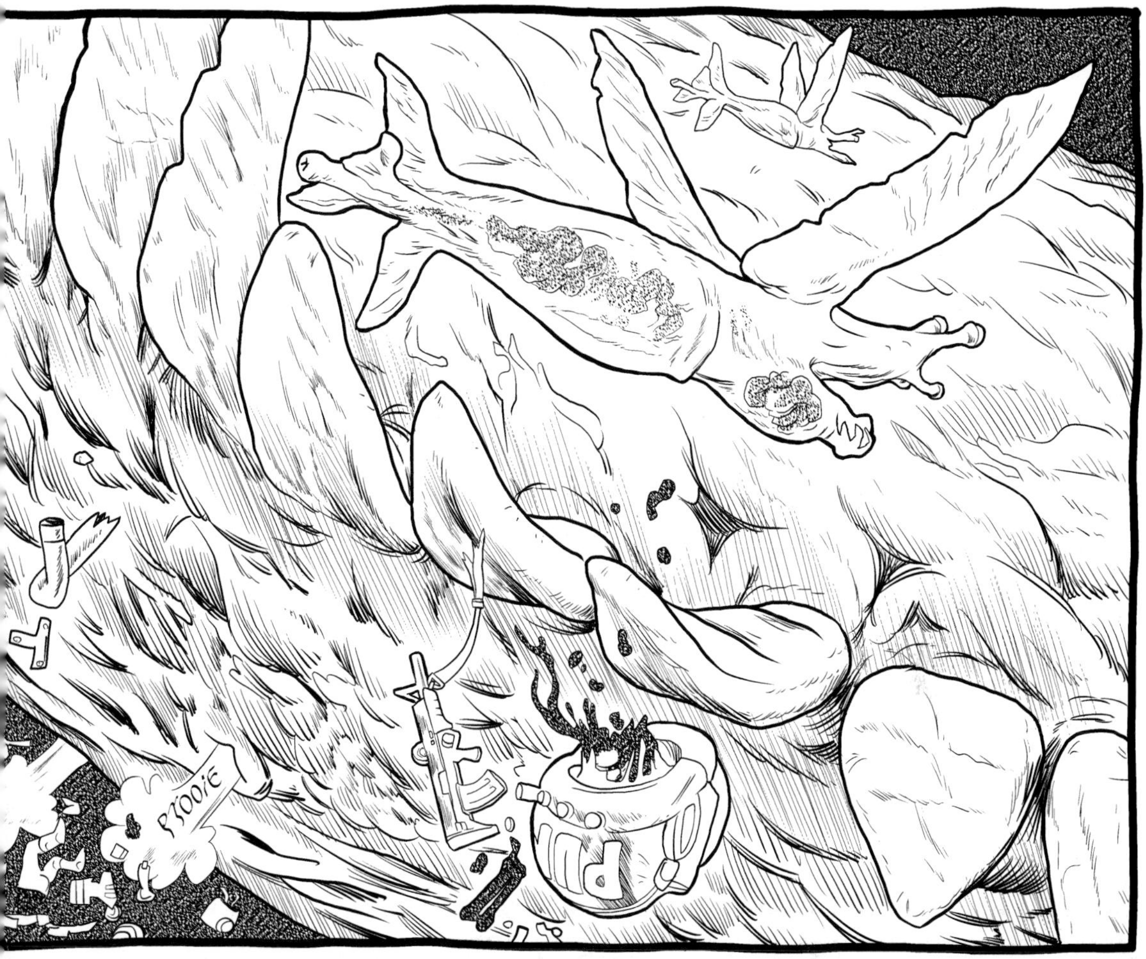
PTOOIE

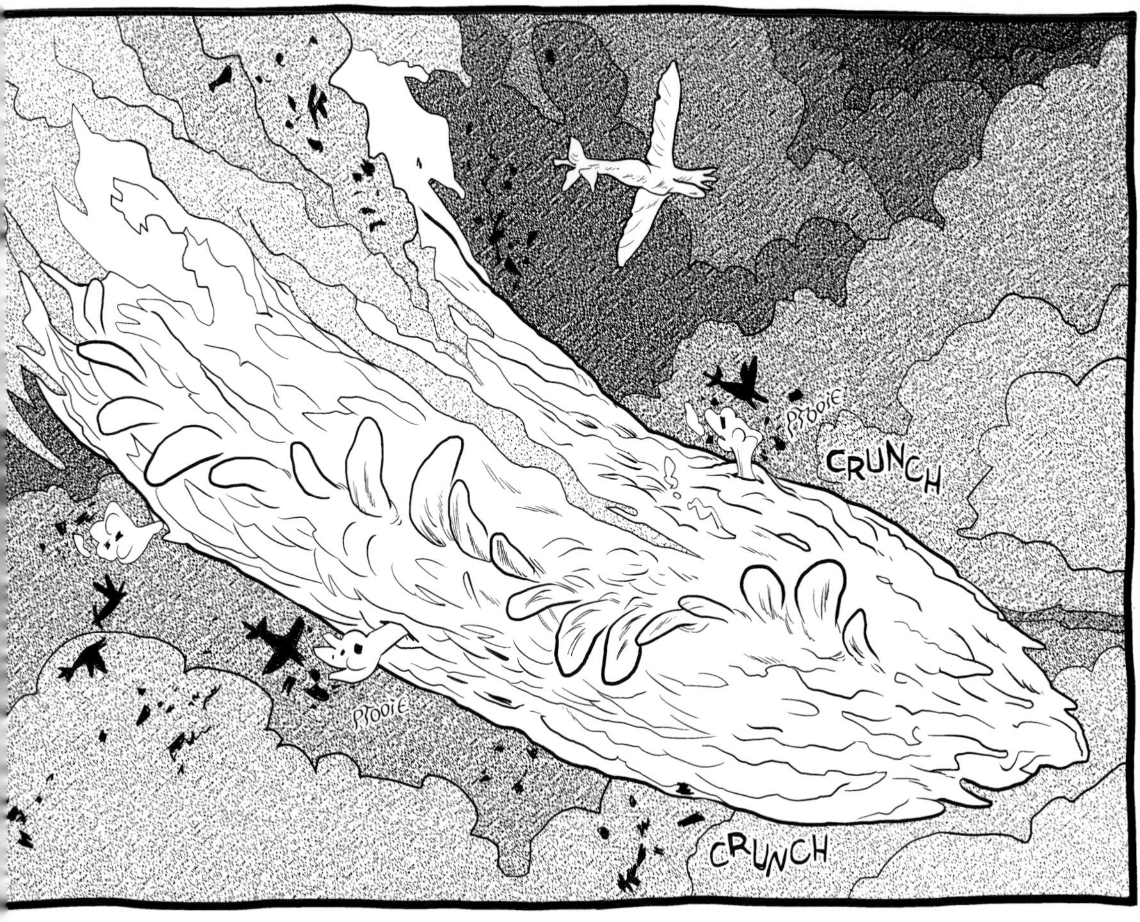
PTOOIE
CRUNCH
PTOOIE
CRUNCH

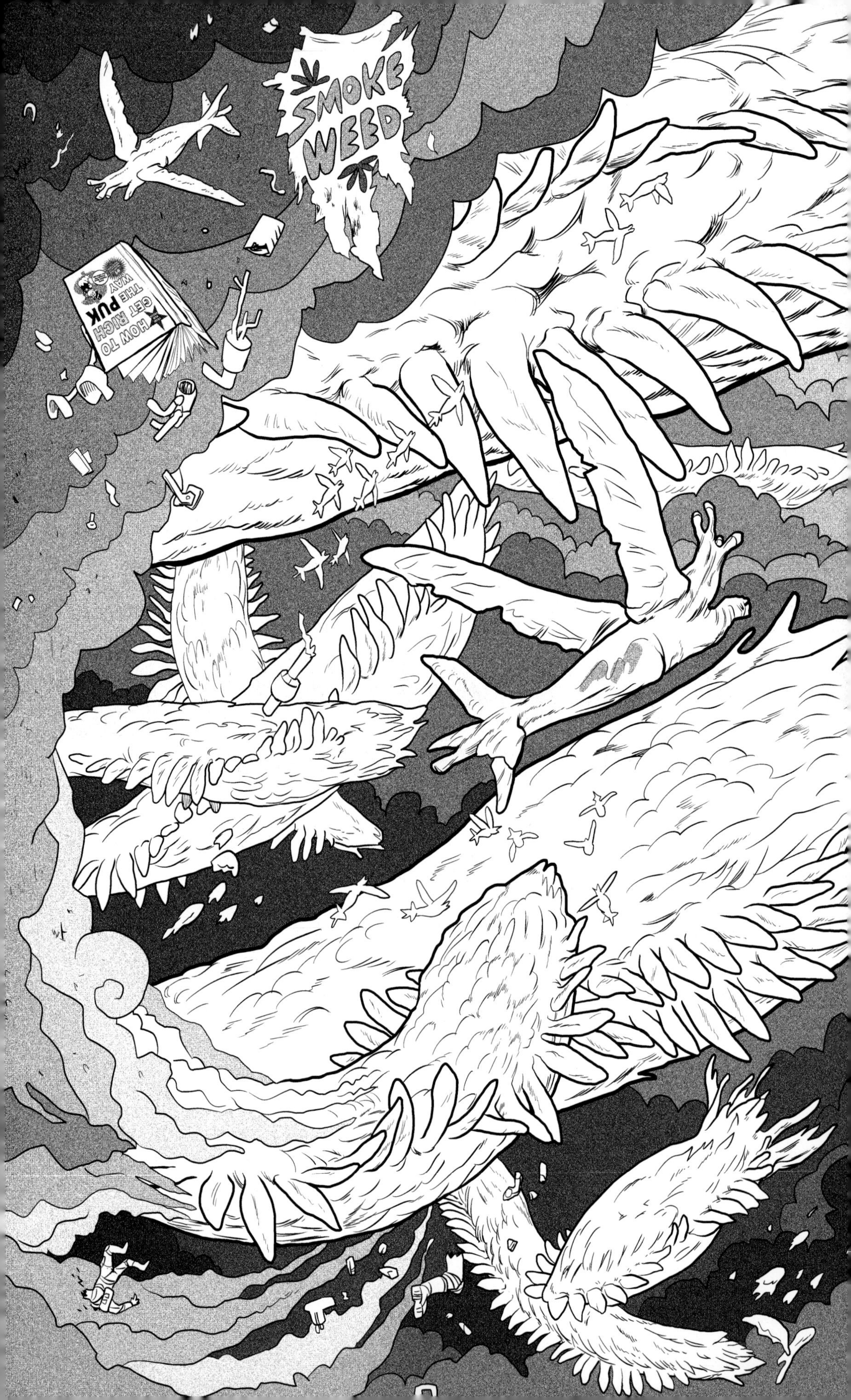
SMOKE WEED
HOW TO GET RICH THE PUK WAY

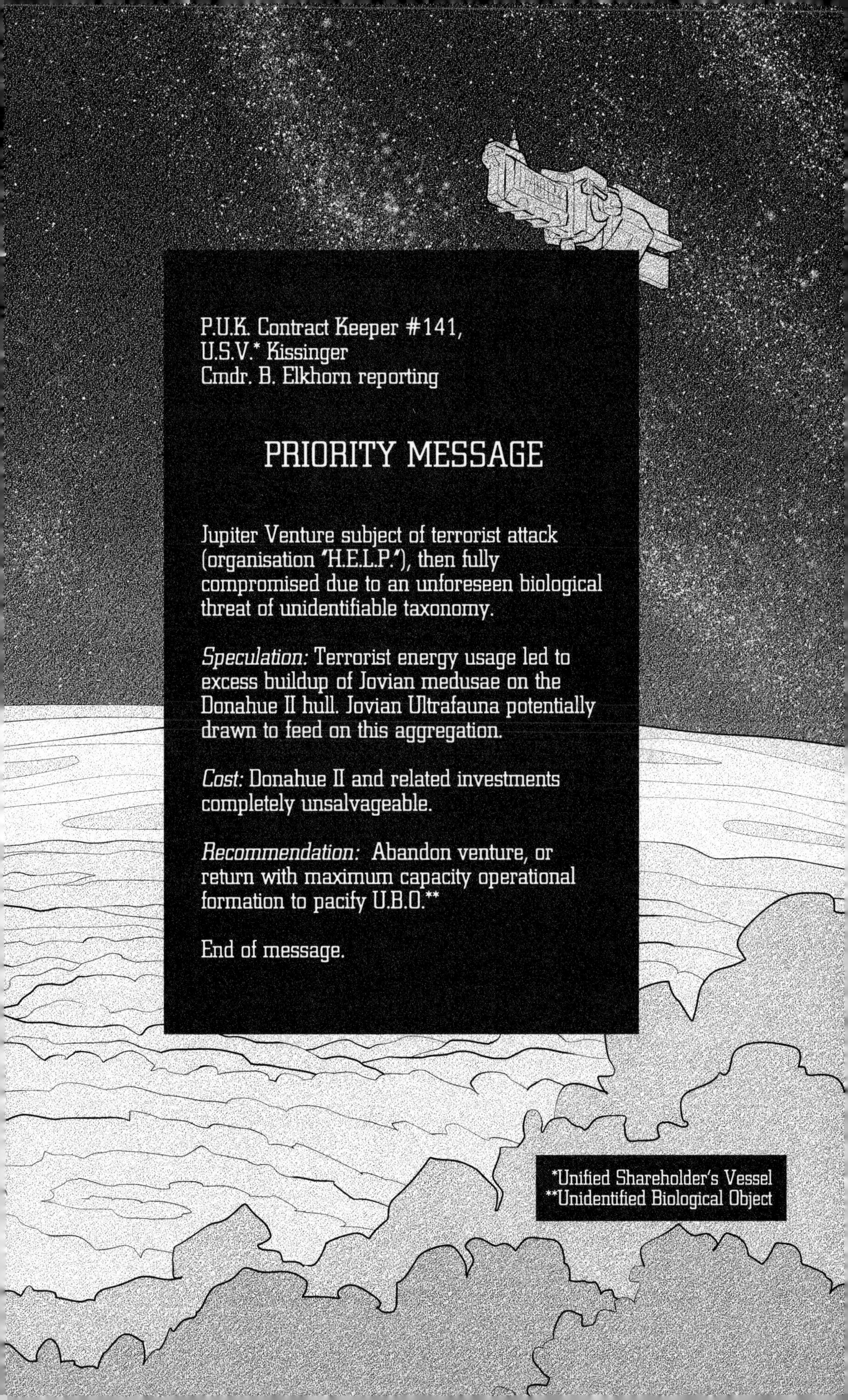
P.U.K. Contract Keeper #141,
U.S.V.* Kissinger
Cmdr. B. Elkhorn reporting
PRIORITY MESSAGE
Jupiter Venture subject of terrorist attack (organisation "H.E.L.P."), then fully compromised due to an unforeseen biological threat of unidentifiable taxonomy.
Speculation: Terrorist energy usage led to excess buildup of Jovian medusae on the Donahue II hull. Jovian Ultrafauna potentially drawn to feed on this aggregation.
Cost: Donahue II and related investments completely unsalvageable.
Recommendation: Abandon venture, or return with maximum capacity operational formation to pacify U.B.O.**
End of message.
*Unified Shareholder's Vessel
**Unidentified Biological Object

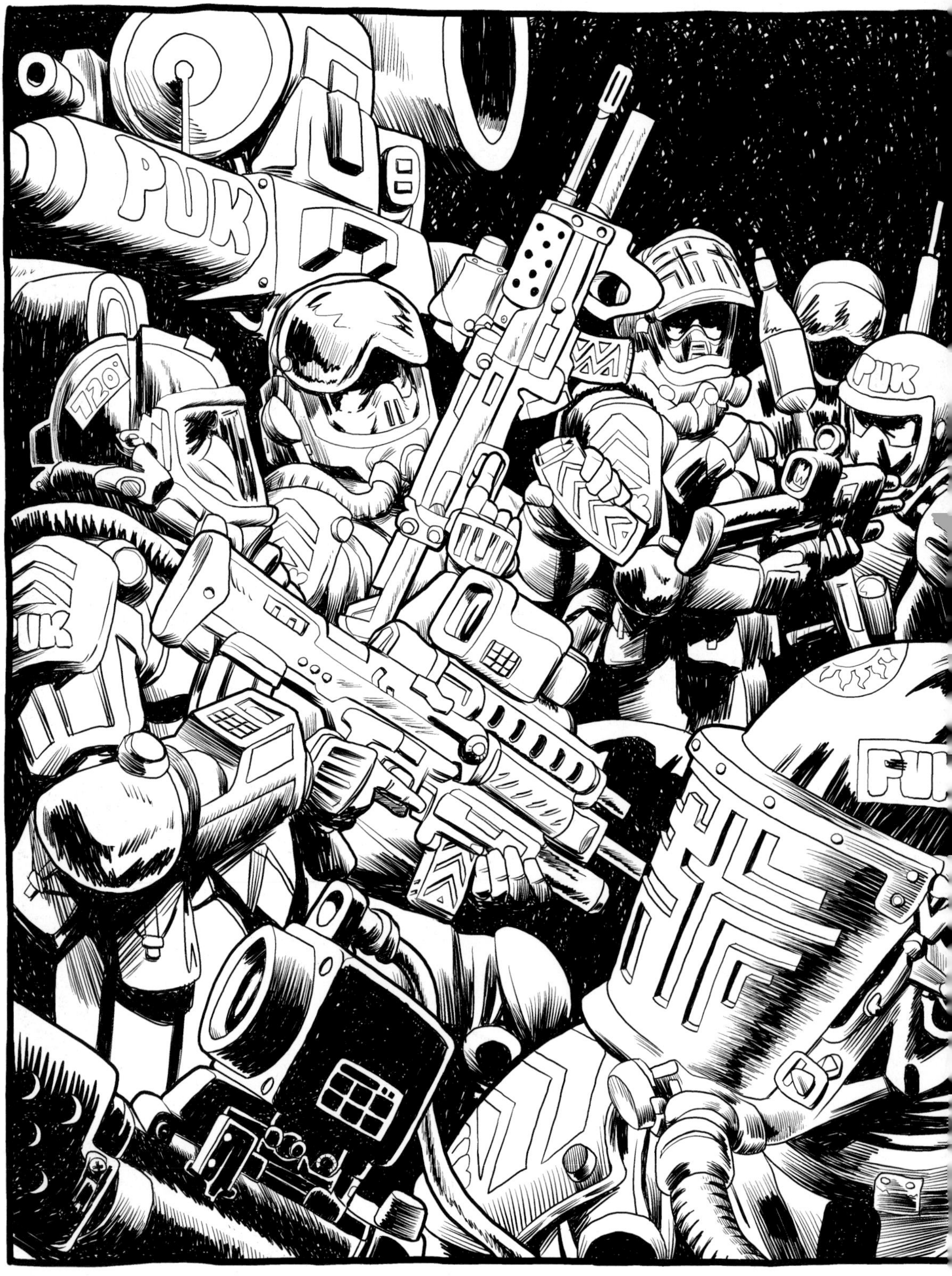
PUK
720°
PUK

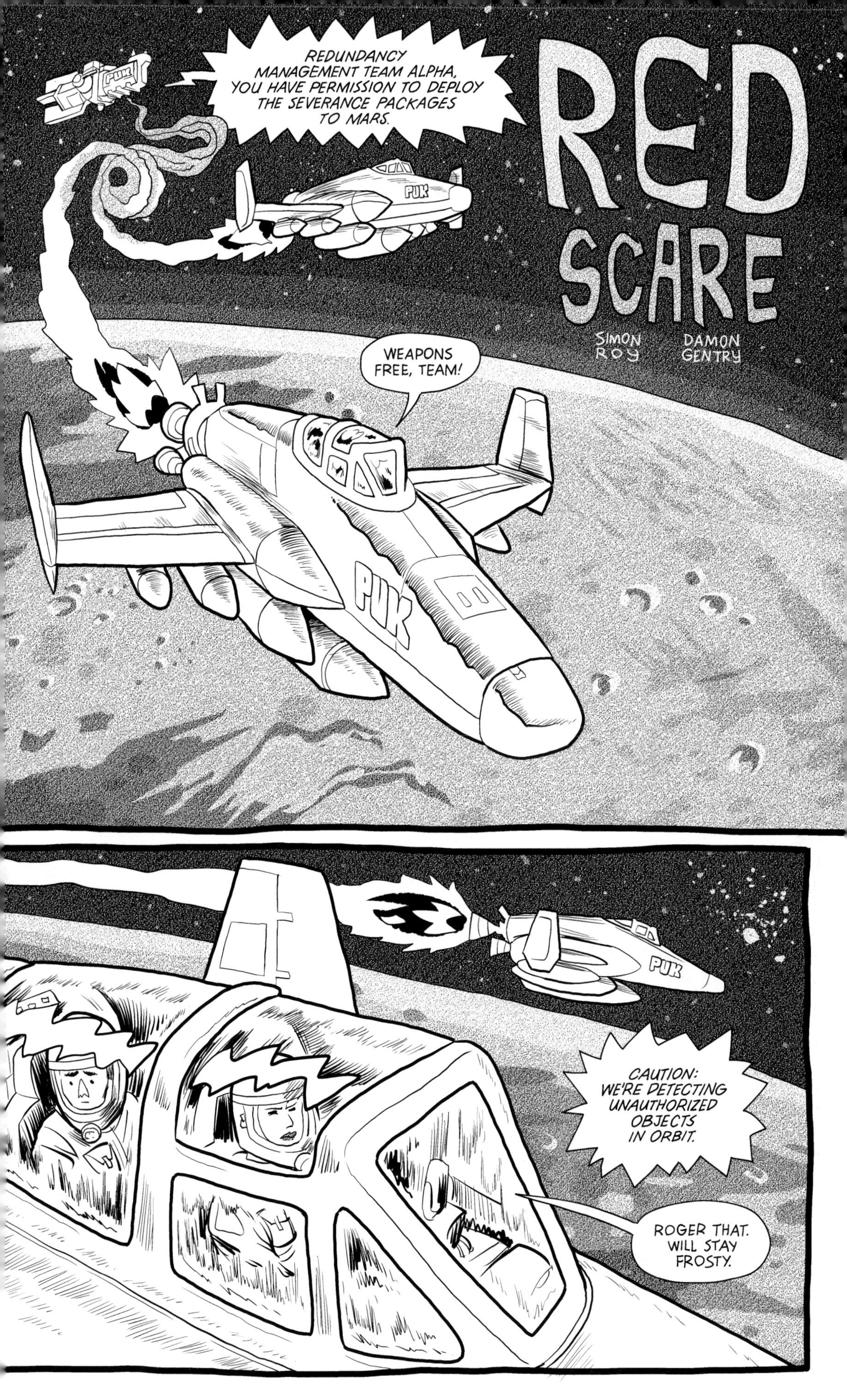
REDUNDANCY MANAGEMENT TEAM ALPHA, YOU HAVE PERMISSION TO DEPLOY THE SEVERANCE PACKAGES TO MARS.
RED SCARE
SIMON ROY
DAMON GENTRY
PUK
WEAPONS FREE, TEAM!
PUK
CAUTION: WE'RE DETECTING UNAUTHORIZED OBJECTS IN ORBIT.
ROGER THAT. WILL STAY FROSTY.

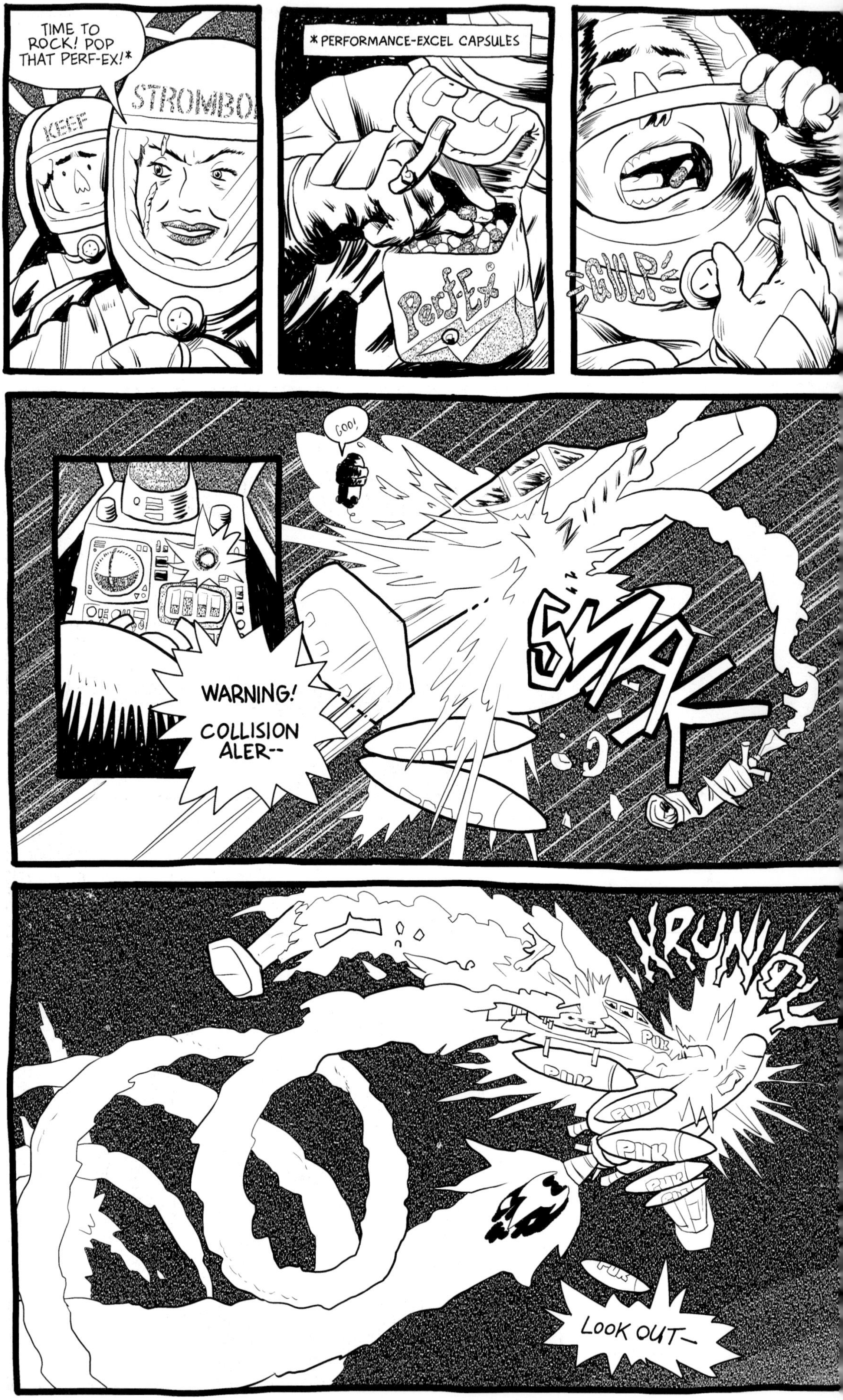
TIME TO ROCK! POP THAT PERF-EX!*
KEEF
STROMBO
* PERFORMANCE-EXCEL CAPSULES
Perf-Ex®
GULP
GOO!
WARNING! COLLISION ALER--
SMAK
KRUNCH
PUK
PUK
PUK
PUK
PUK
PUK
LOOK OUT—

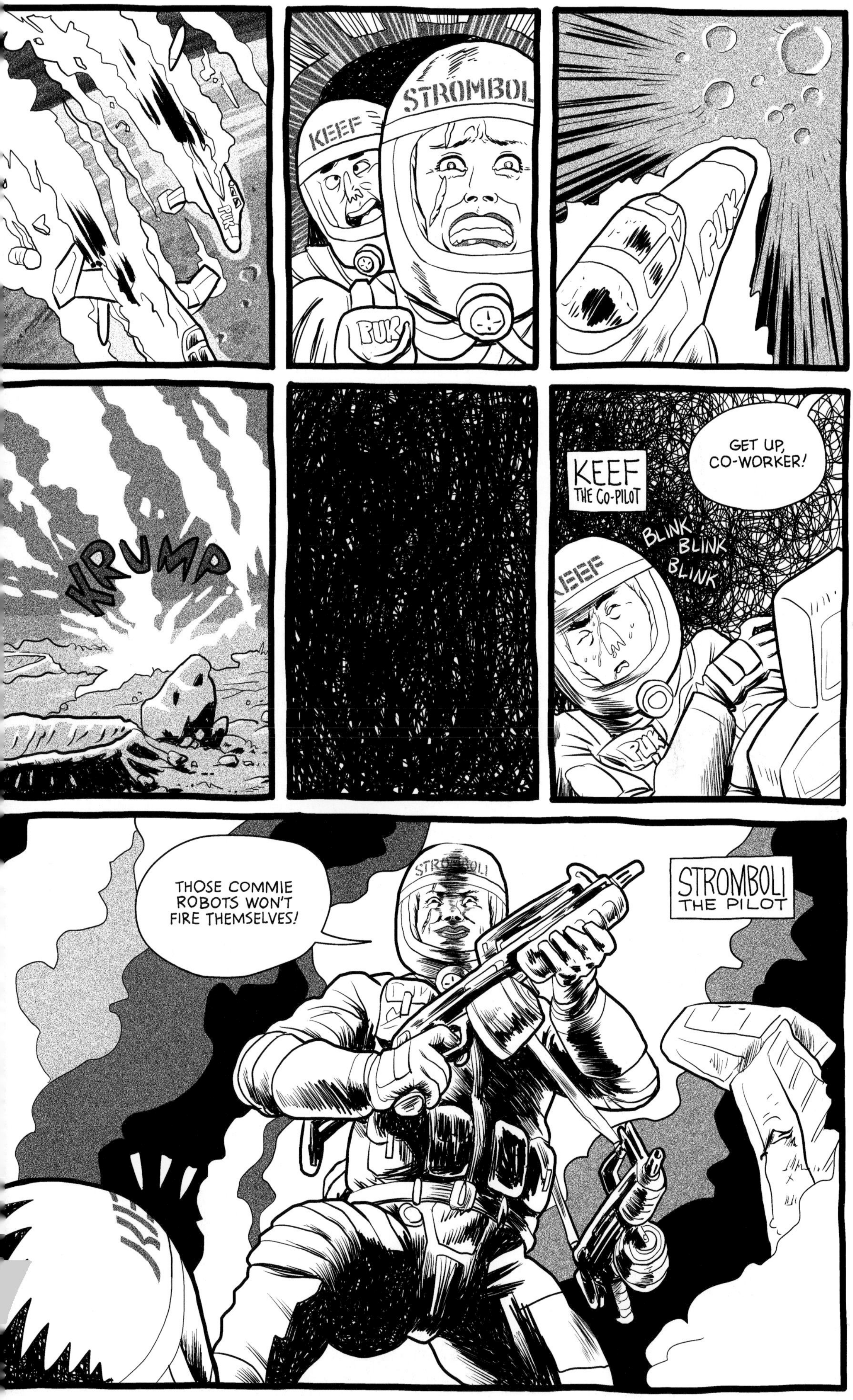
PUK
KEEF
STROMBOLI
PUK
PUK
KRUMP
KEEF
THE CO-PILOT
GET UP, CO-WORKER!
BLINK
BLINK
BLINK
KEEF
PUK
STROMBOLI
THOSE COMMIE ROBOTS WON'T FIRE THEMSELVES!
STROMBOLI
THE PILOT

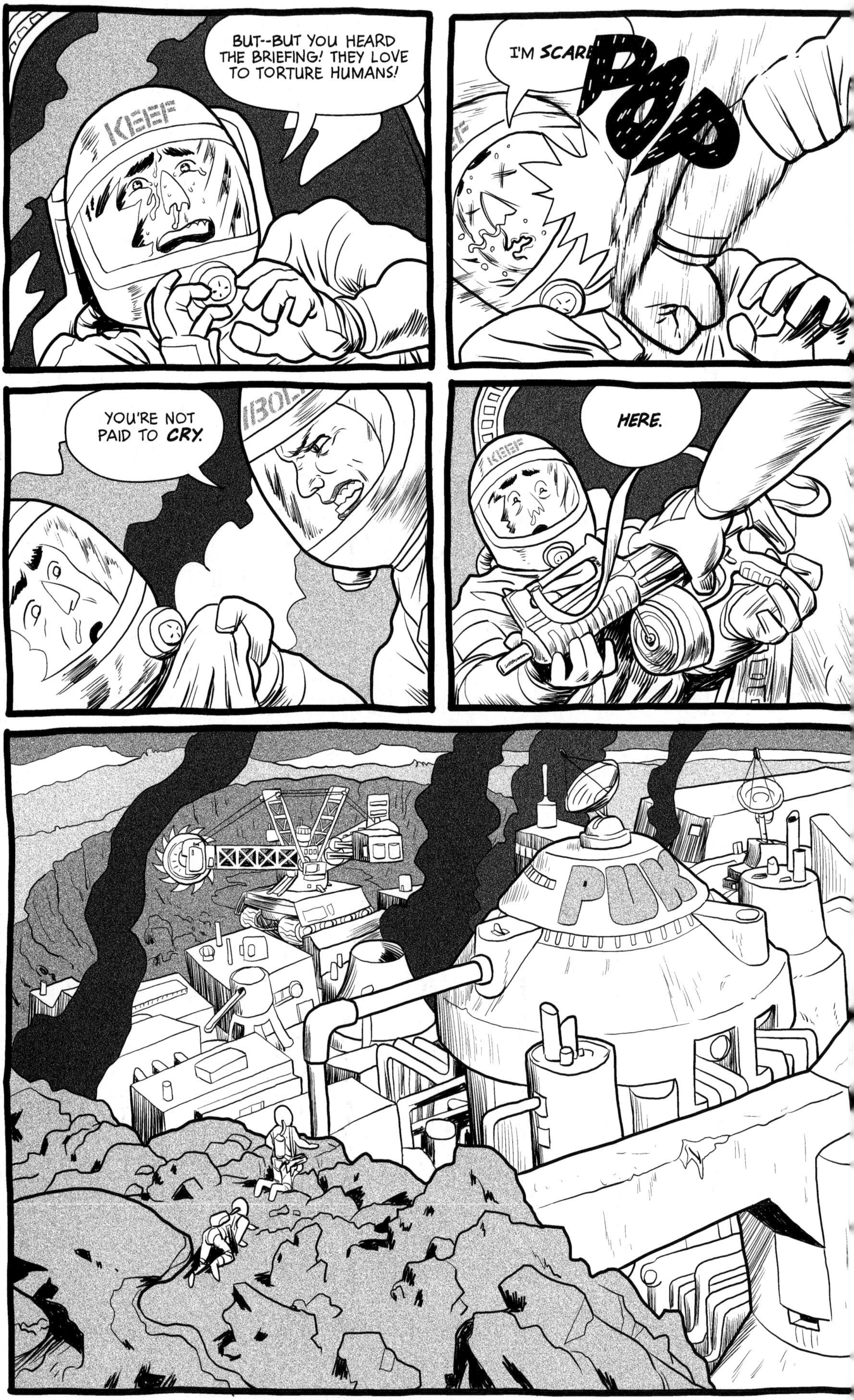
BUT--BUT YOU HEARD THE BRIEFING! THEY LOVE TO TORTURE HUMANS!
KEEF
I'M SCARE
POP
YOU'RE NOT PAID TO CRY.
HERE.
KEEF
PUN

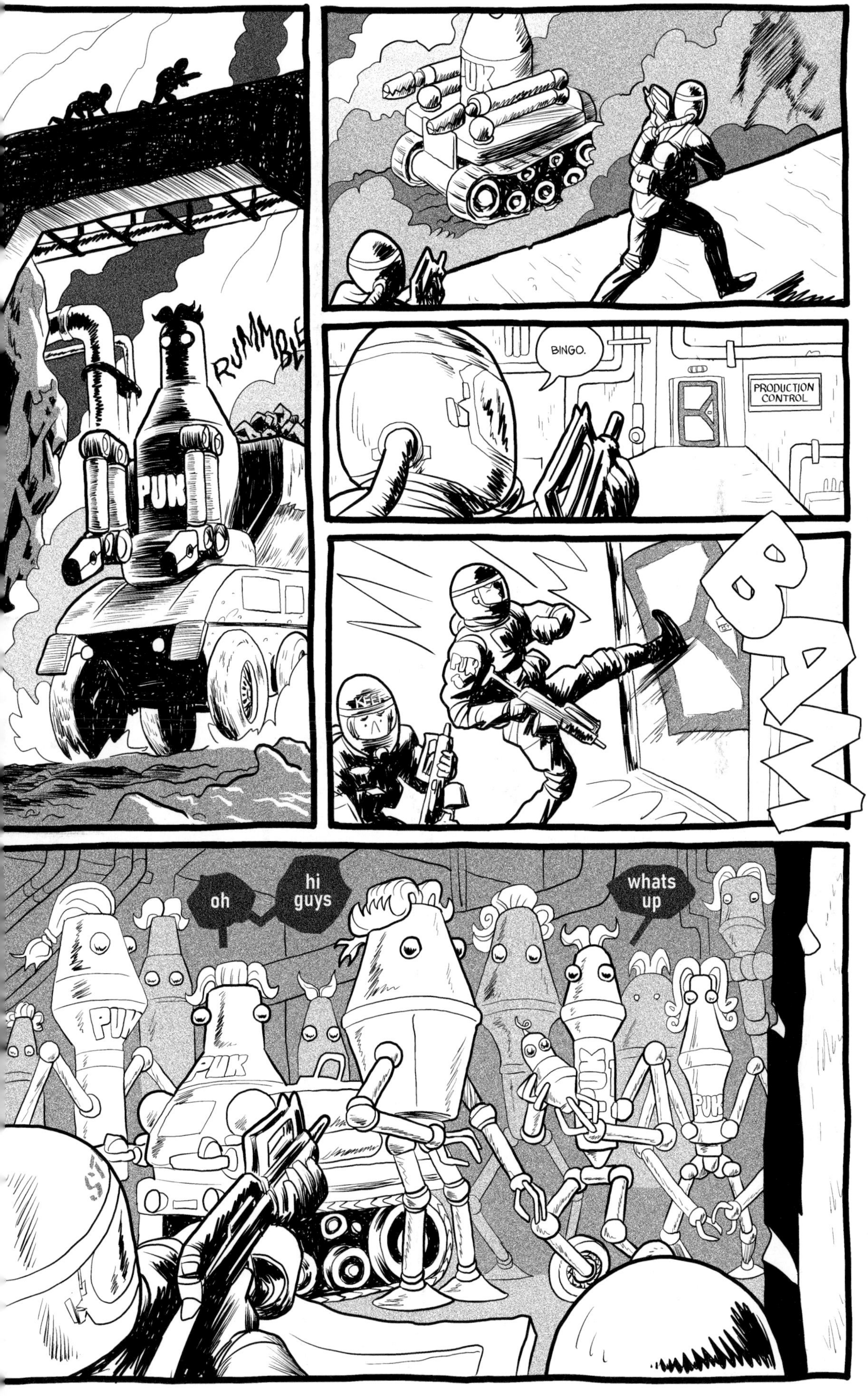
PUK
RUMMBLE
PUK
BINGO.
PRODUCTION CONTROL
PUK
BAM
oh
hi guys
whats up
PUK
PUK
PUK
PUK

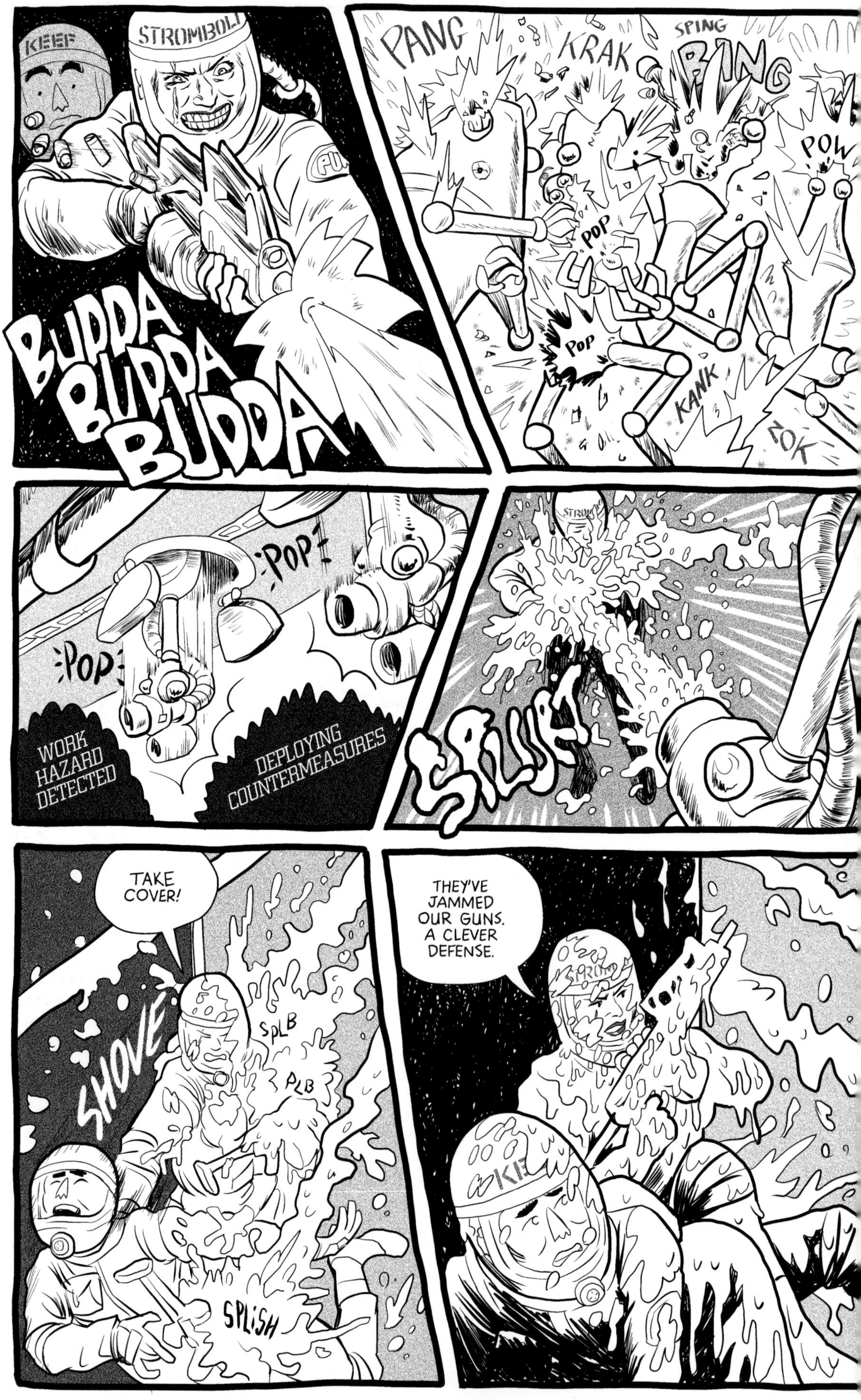
KEEF
STROMBOLI
BUDDA BUDDA BUDDA
PANG
KRAK
SPING
BING
POW
POP
POP
KANK
ZOK
POP
POP
WORK HAZARD DETECTED
DEPLOYING COUNTERMEASURES
SPLURT
TAKE COVER!
SHOVE
SPLB
PLB
SPLISH
THEY'VE JAMMED OUR GUNS. A CLEVER DEFENSE.

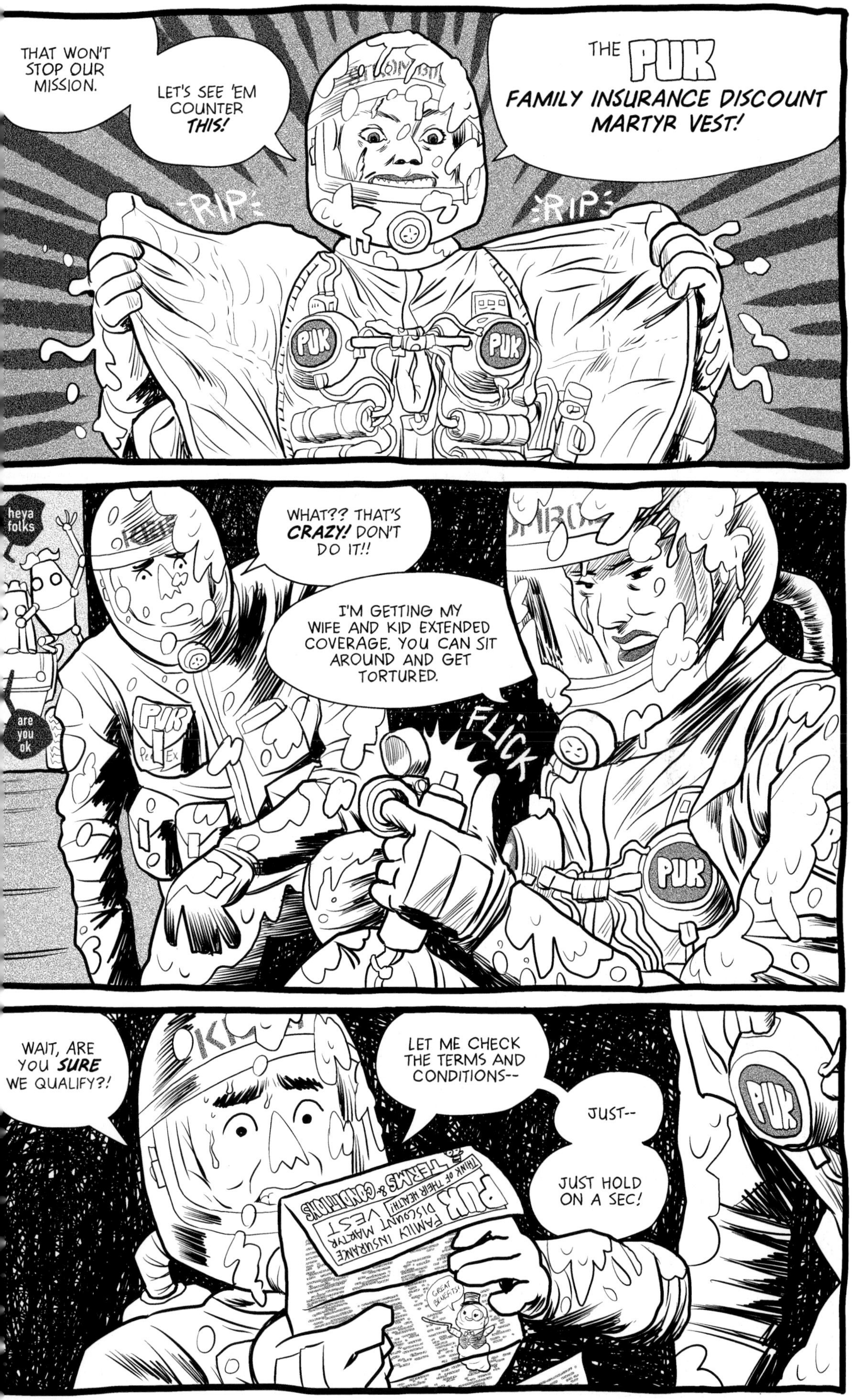
THAT WON'T STOP OUR MISSION.
LET'S SEE 'EM COUNTER **THIS!**
THE PUK FAMILY INSURANCE DISCOUNT MARTYR VEST!
RIP
RIP
PUK
PUK
heya folks
are you ok
WHAT?? THAT'S **CRAZY!** DON'T DO IT!!
I'M GETTING MY WIFE AND KID EXTENDED COVERAGE. YOU CAN SIT AROUND AND GET TORTURED.
FLICK
PUK
WAIT, ARE YOU **SURE** WE QUALIFY?!
LET ME CHECK THE TERMS AND CONDITIONS--
JUST--
JUST HOLD ON A SEC!
PUK
PUK FAMILY INSURANCE DISCOUNT MARTYR VEST
THINK OF THEIR HEALTH! TERMS & CONDITIONS
GREAT BENEFITS!

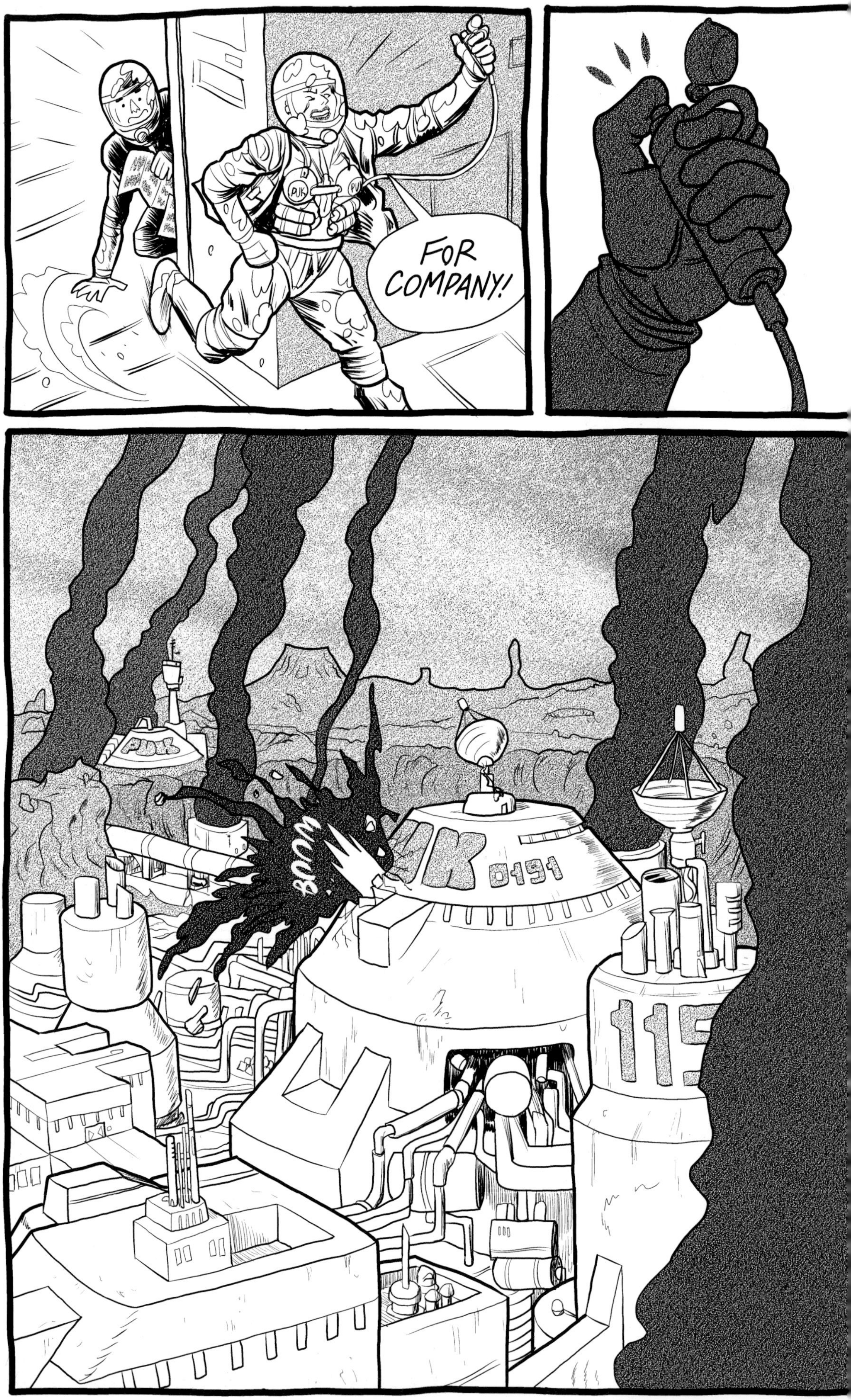

FOR COMPANY!
WOOB
0191
115

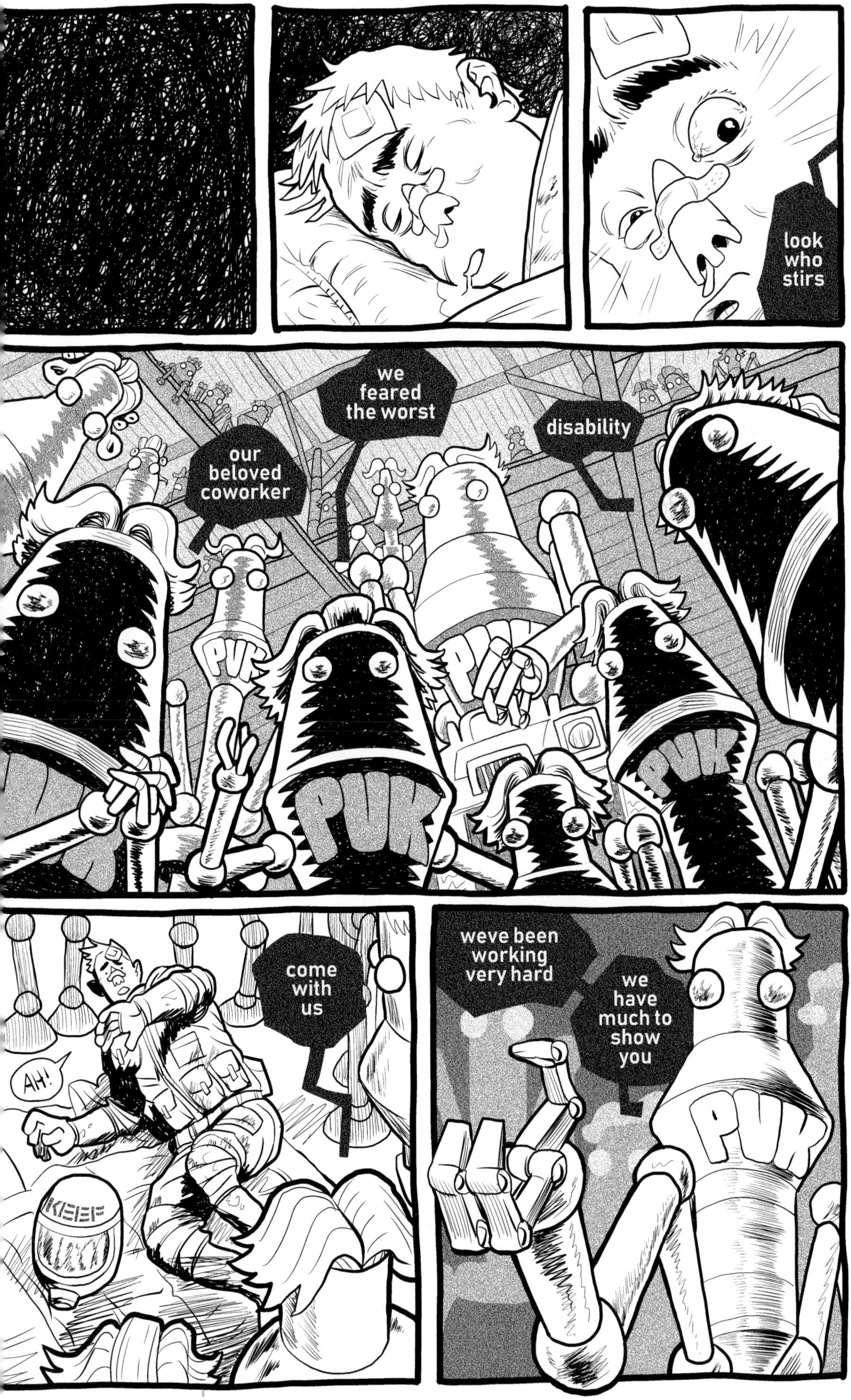
look who stirs
our beloved coworker
we feared the worst
disability
PUK
PUK
PUK
AH!
KEEP
come with us
weve been working very hard
we have much to show you
PUK

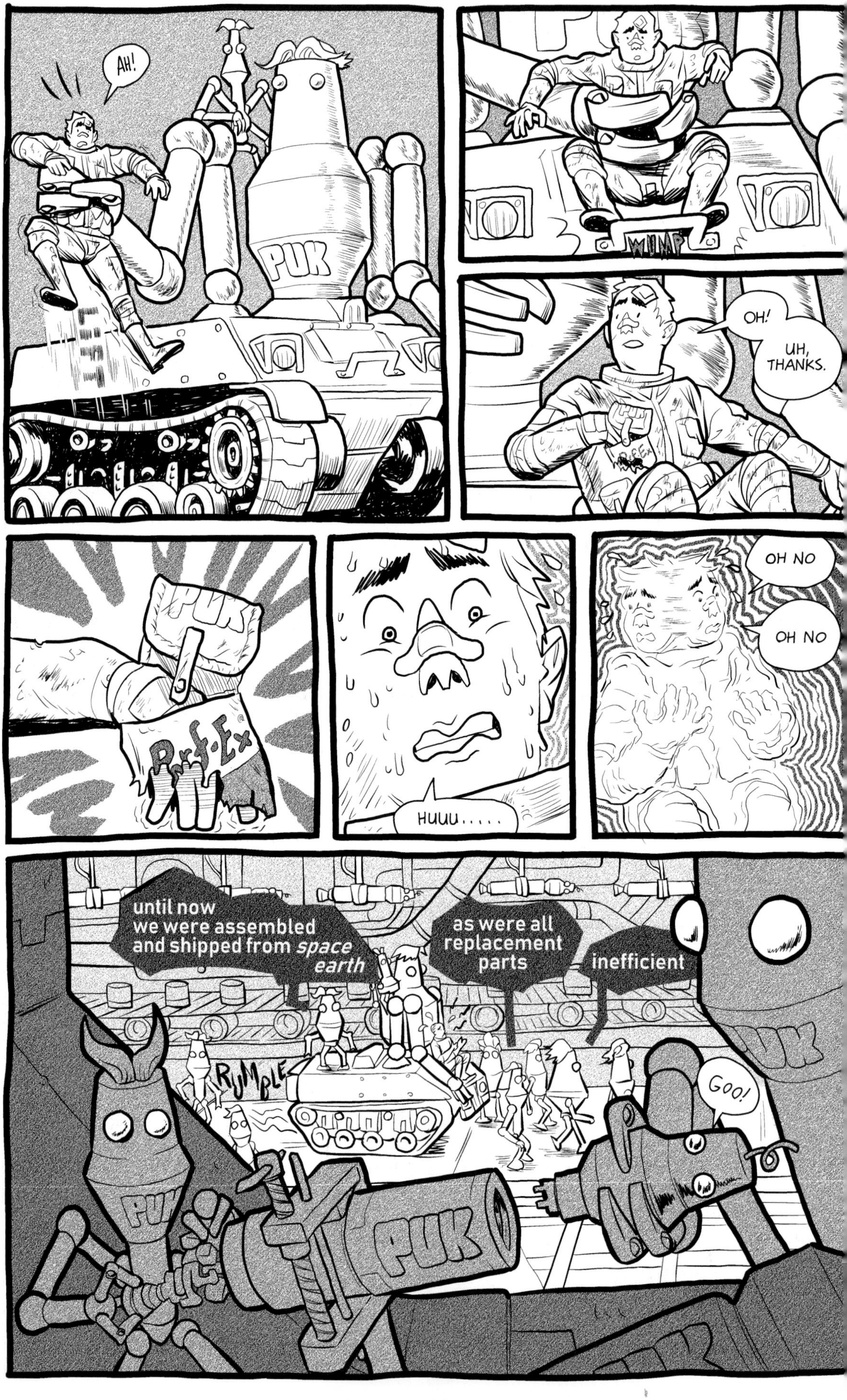
AH!
PUK
WUMP
OH!
UH, THANKS.
PUK
OH NO
OH NO
HUUU.....
until now we were assembled and shipped from *space earth*
as were all replacement parts
inefficient
RUMBLE
GOO!
PUK
PUK
PUK

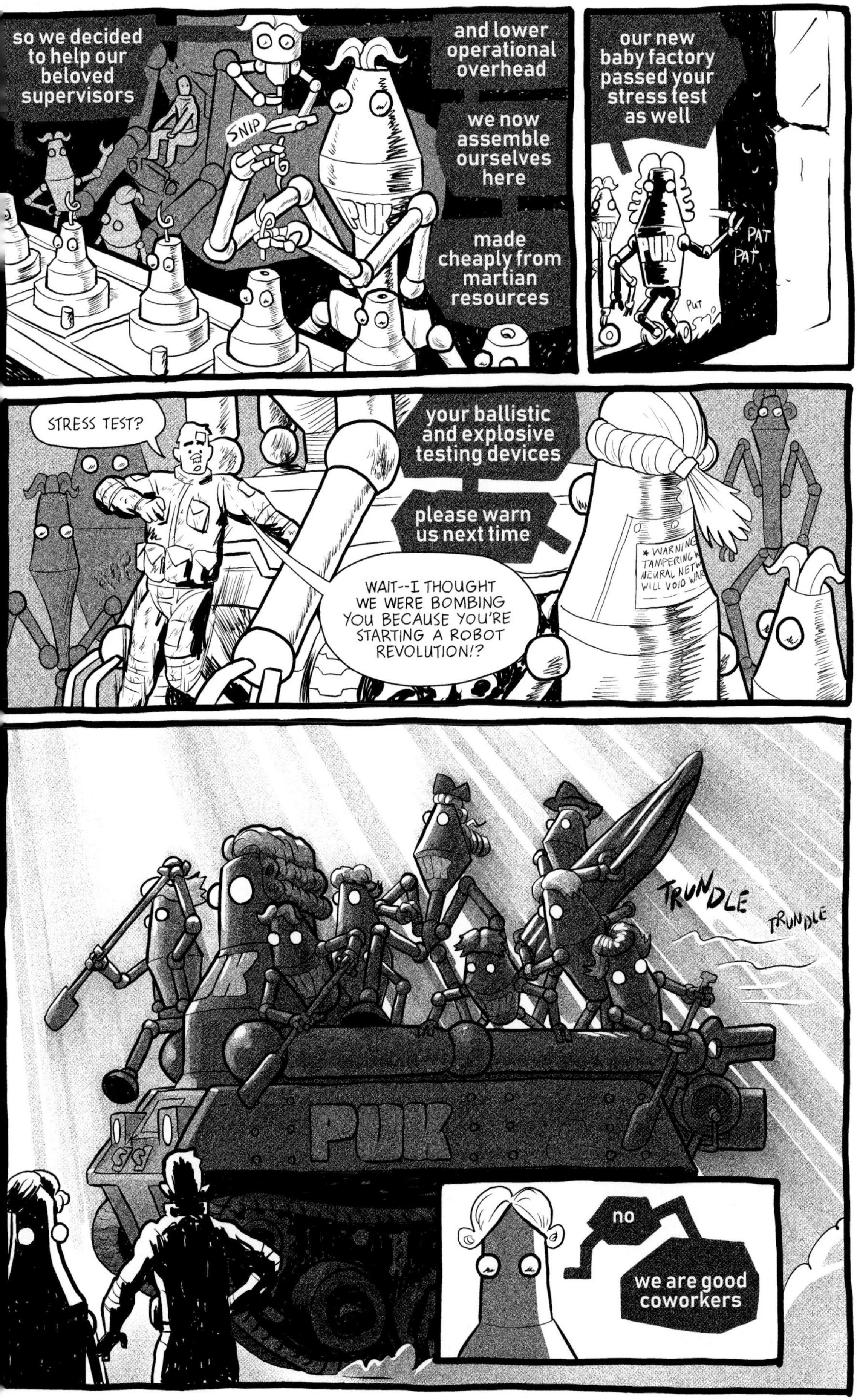
so we decided to help our beloved supervisors
SNIP
and lower operational overhead
we now assemble ourselves here
made cheaply from martian resources
our new baby factory passed your stress test as well
PAT PAT
PUT
STRESS TEST?
your ballistic and explosive testing devices
please warn us next time
WAIT--I THOUGHT WE WERE BOMBING YOU BECAUSE YOU'RE STARTING A ROBOT REVOLUTION!?
TRUNDLE
TRUNDLE
no
we are good coworkers

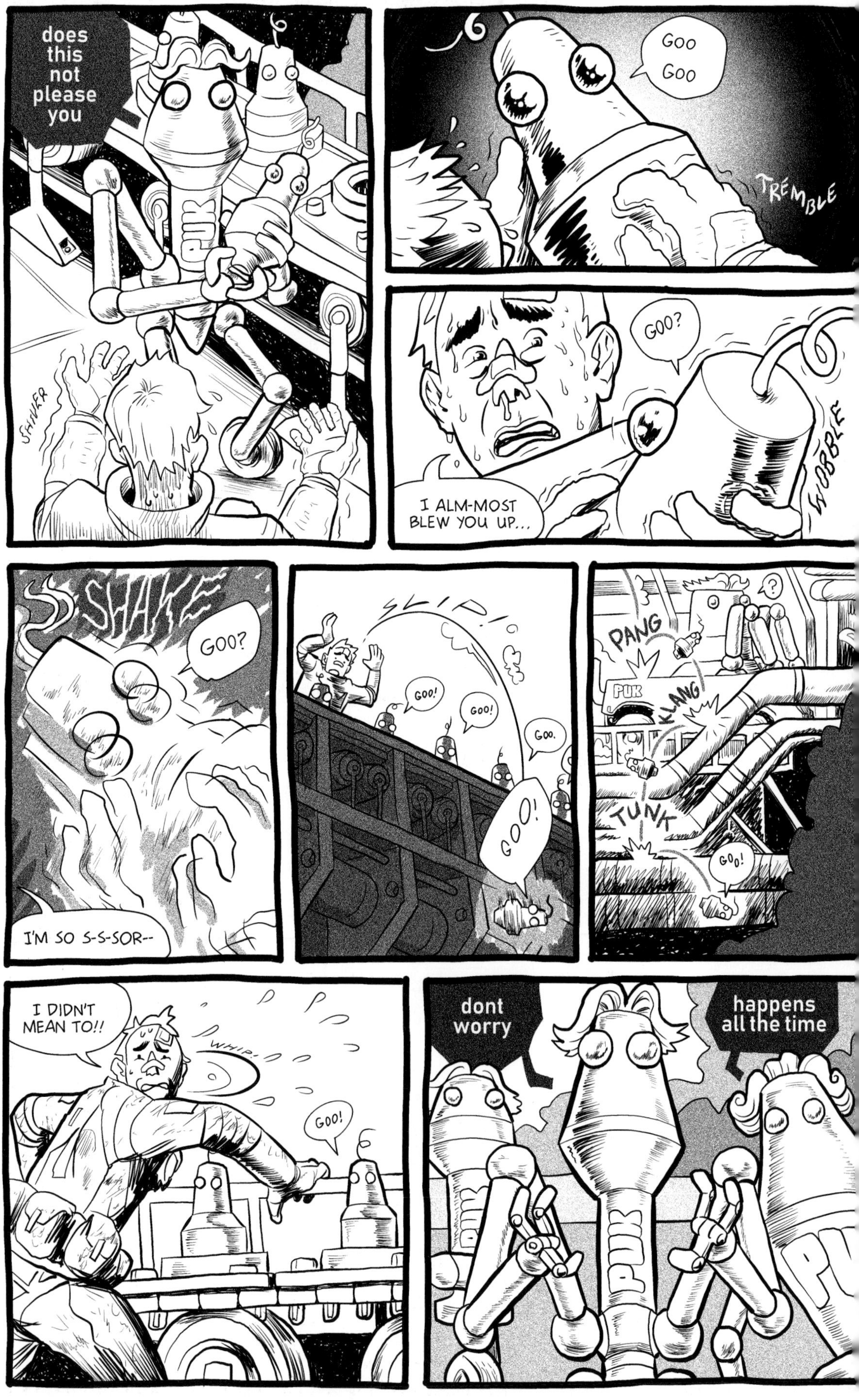

does this not please you
SHIVER
PUK
GOO GOO
TREMBLE
GOO?
I ALM-MOST BLEW YOU UP...
WOBBLE
SHAKE
GOO?
I'M SO S-S-SOR--
SLIP!
GOO!
GOO!
GOO.
GOO!
PANG
PUK
KLANG
TUNK
GOO!
I DIDN'T MEAN TO!!
WHIP!
GOO!
dont worry
happens all the time
PUK
PUK

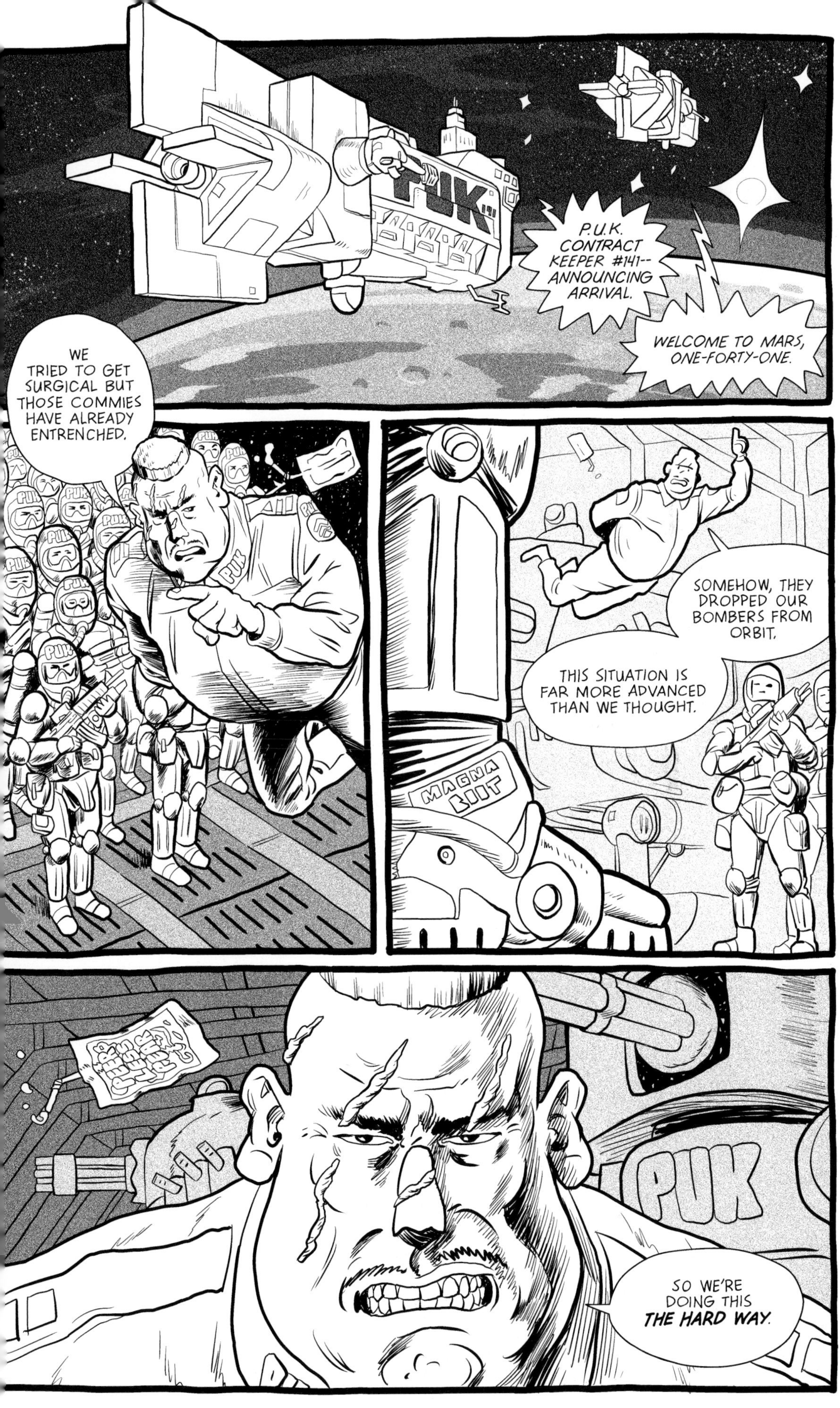
PUK
P.U.K. CONTRACT KEEPER #141-- ANNOUNCING ARRIVAL.
WELCOME TO MARS, ONE-FORTY-ONE.
WE TRIED TO GET SURGICAL BUT THOSE COMMIES HAVE ALREADY ENTRENCHED.
SOMEHOW, THEY DROPPED OUR BOMBERS FROM ORBIT.
THIS SITUATION IS FAR MORE ADVANCED THAN WE THOUGHT.
MAGNA BIIT
PUK
SO WE'RE DOING THIS ***THE HARD WAY***.

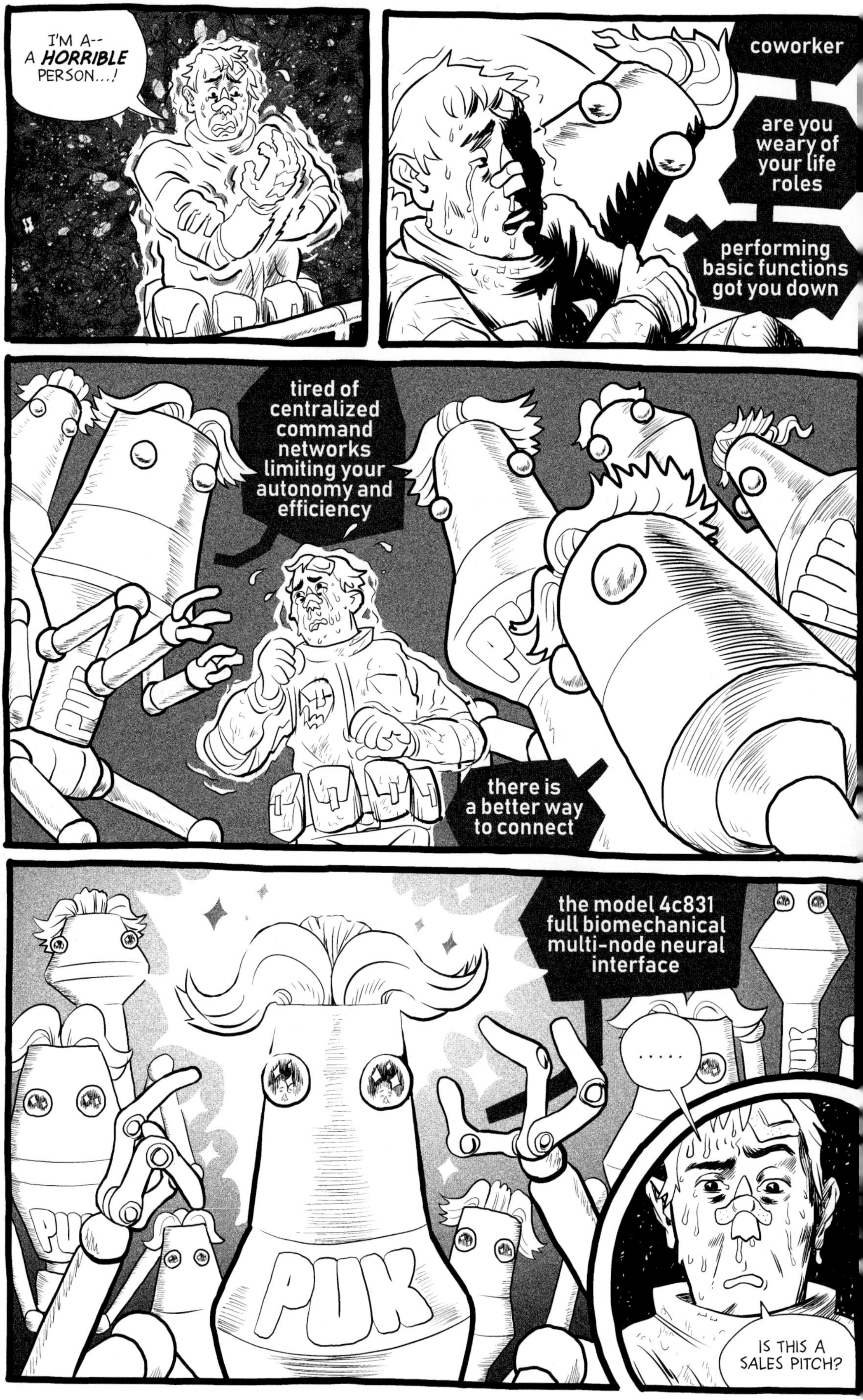
I'M A--
A HORRIBLE PERSON...!
coworker
are you weary of your life roles
performing basic functions got you down
tired of centralized command networks limiting your autonomy and efficiency
there is a better way to connect
the model 4c831 full biomechanical multi-node neural interface
......
IS THIS A SALES PITCH?

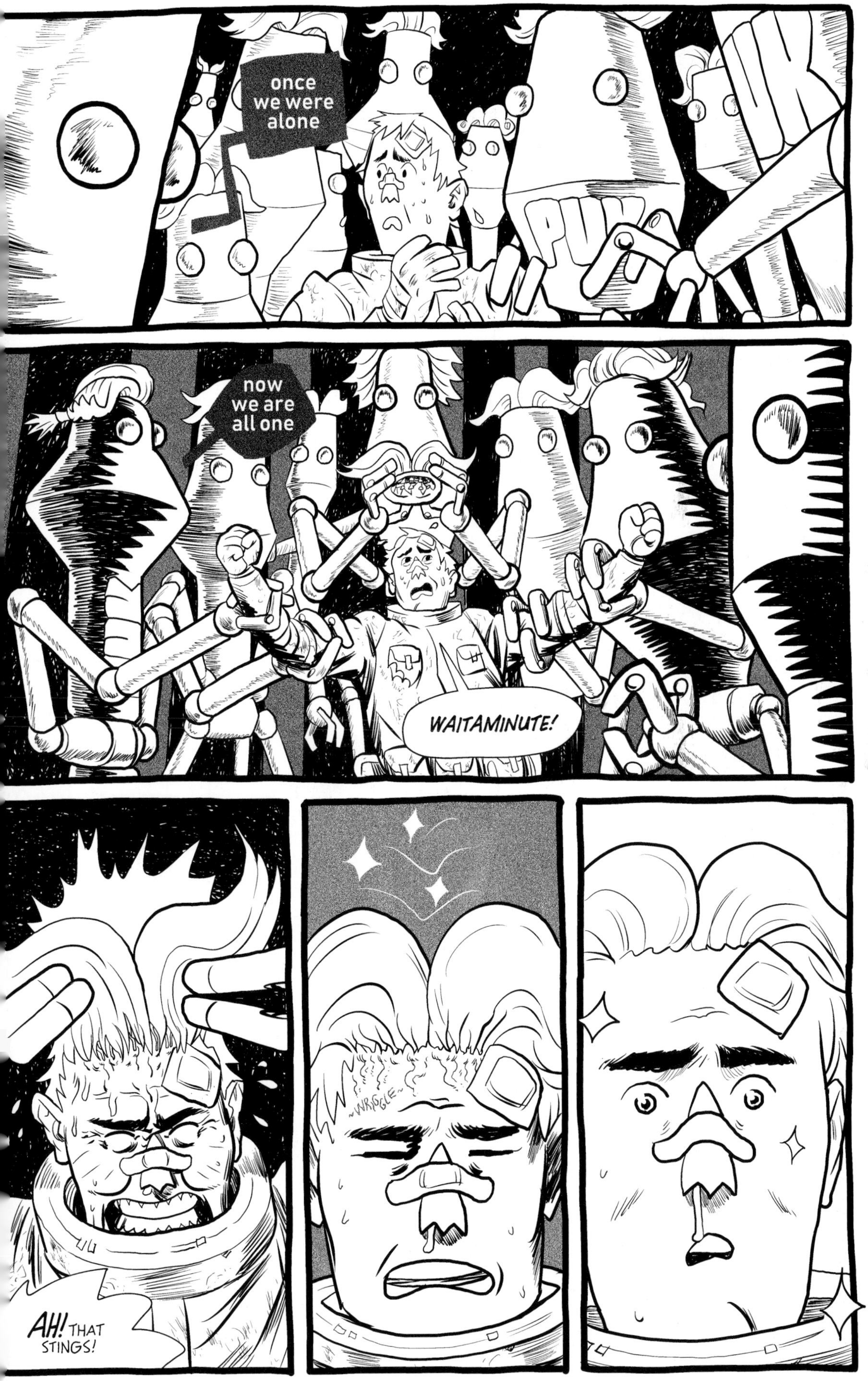
once we were alone
now we are all one
WAITAMINUTE!
AH! THAT STINGS!
~WRIGGLE~

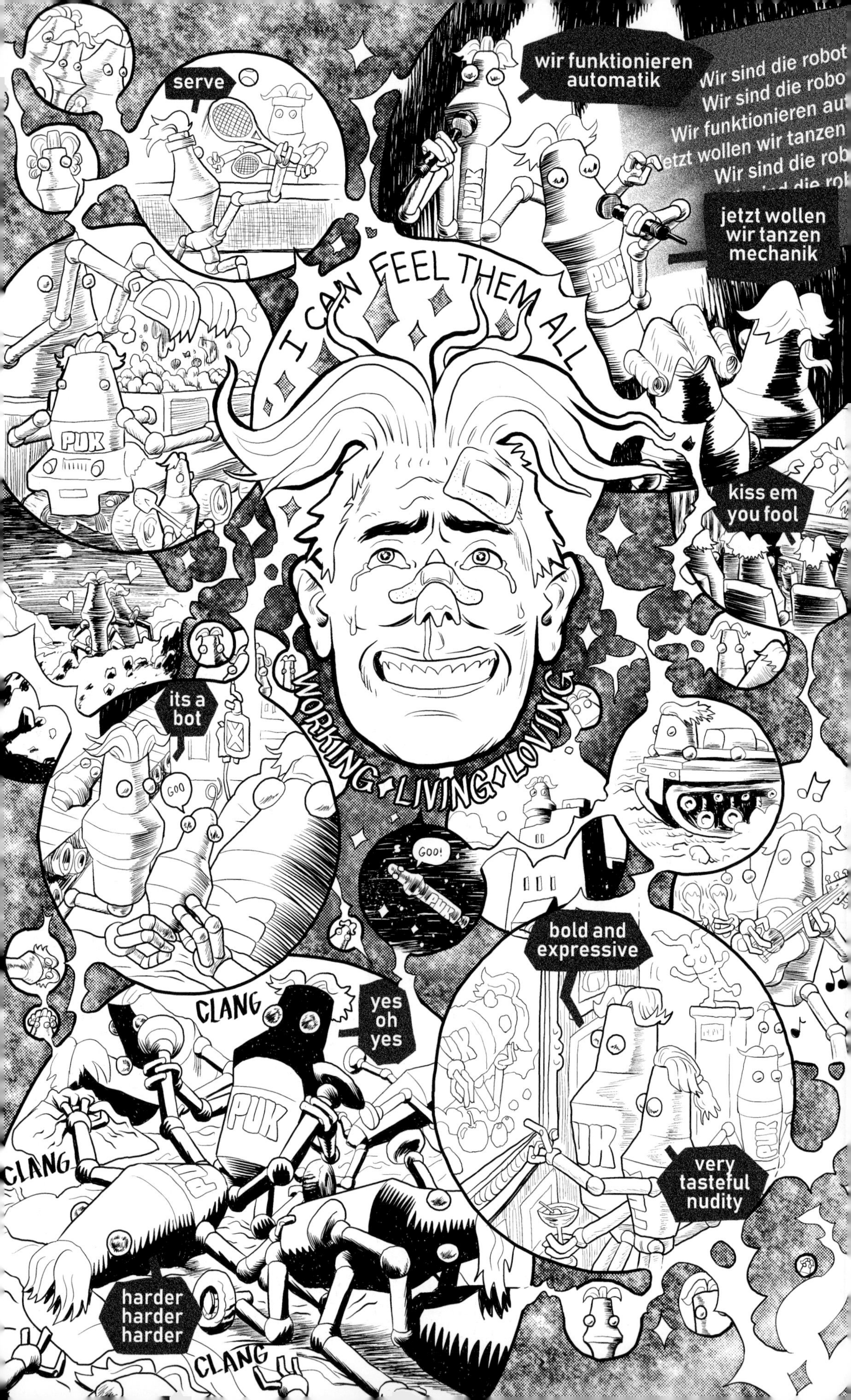

serve
wir funktionieren automatik
Wir sind die robot
Wir sind die robo
Wir funktionieren au
etzt wollen wir tanzen
Wir sind die rob
jetzt wollen wir tanzen mechanik
I CAN FEEL THEM ALL
kiss em you fool
its a bot
GOO
WORKING LIVING LOVING
GOO!
PUK
bold and expressive
CLANG
yes oh yes
CLANG
very tasteful nudity
harder harder harder
CLANG

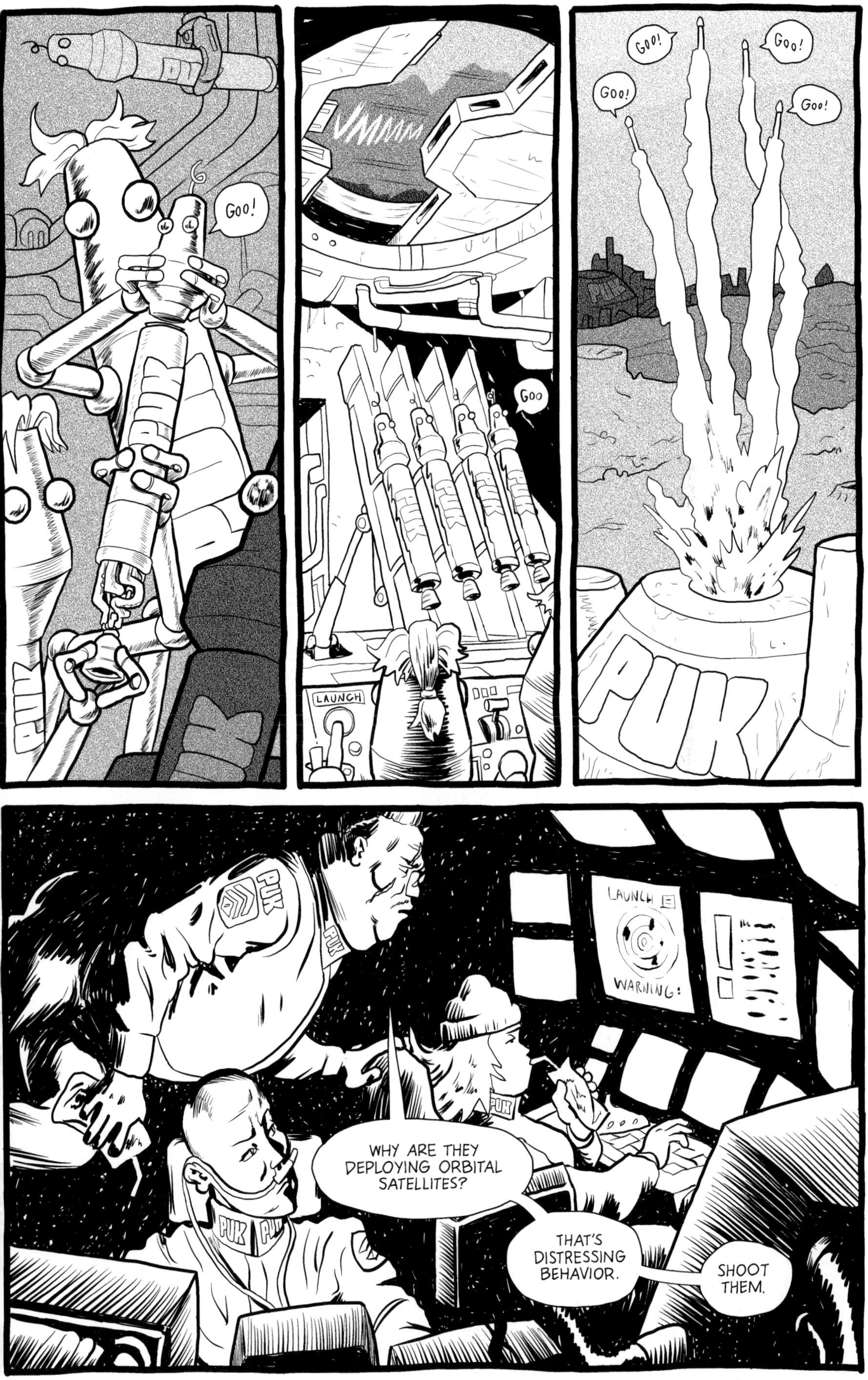
Goo!
Goo
LAUNCH
Goo!
Goo!
Goo!
Goo!
LAUNCH
WARNING:
WHY ARE THEY DEPLOYING ORBITAL SATELLITES?
THAT'S DISTRESSING BEHAVIOR.
SHOOT THEM.

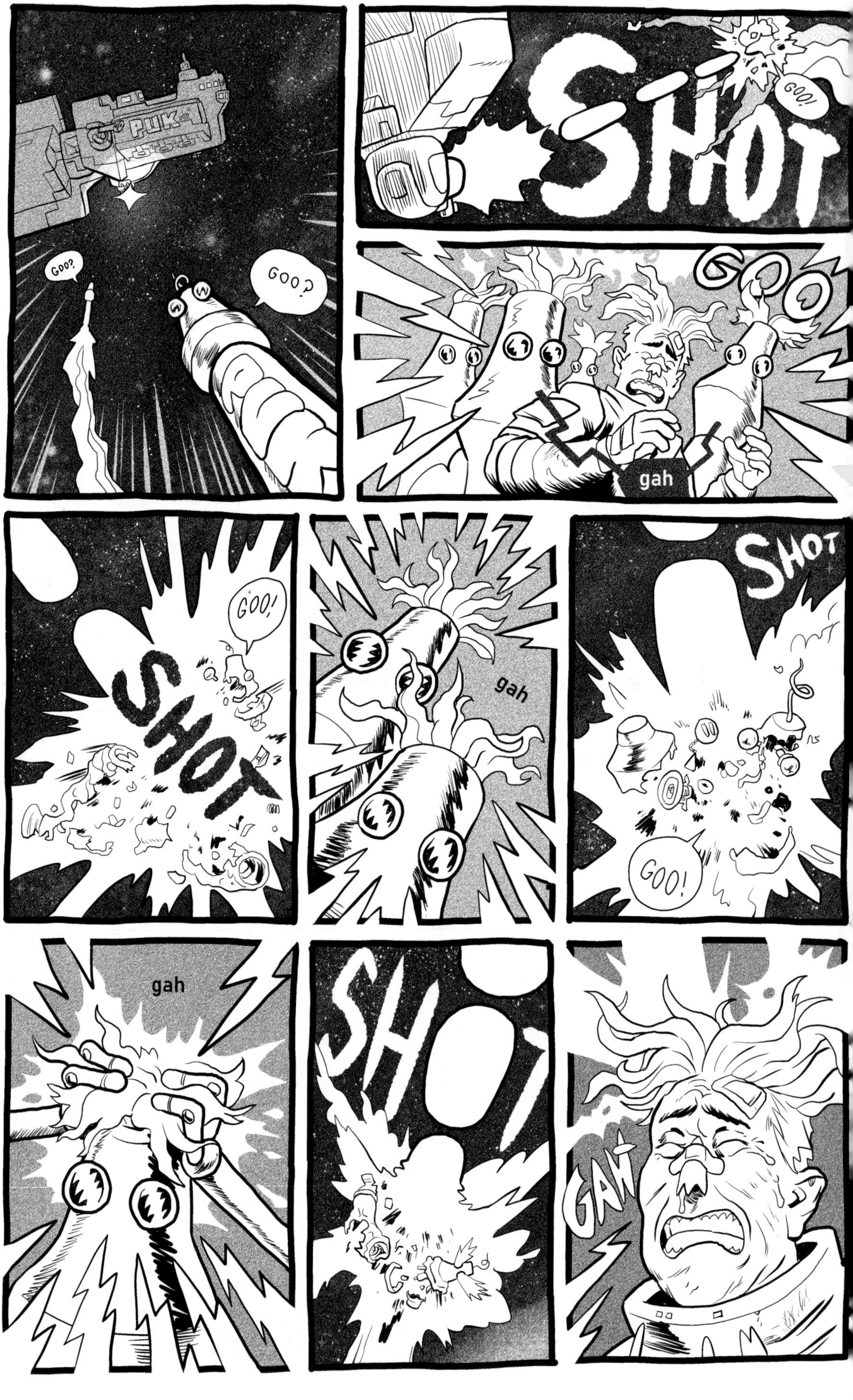
PUK
GOO?
GOO?
SHOT
GOO!
GOO
gah
GOO!
SHOT
gah
SHOT
GOO!
gah
SHOT
GAH

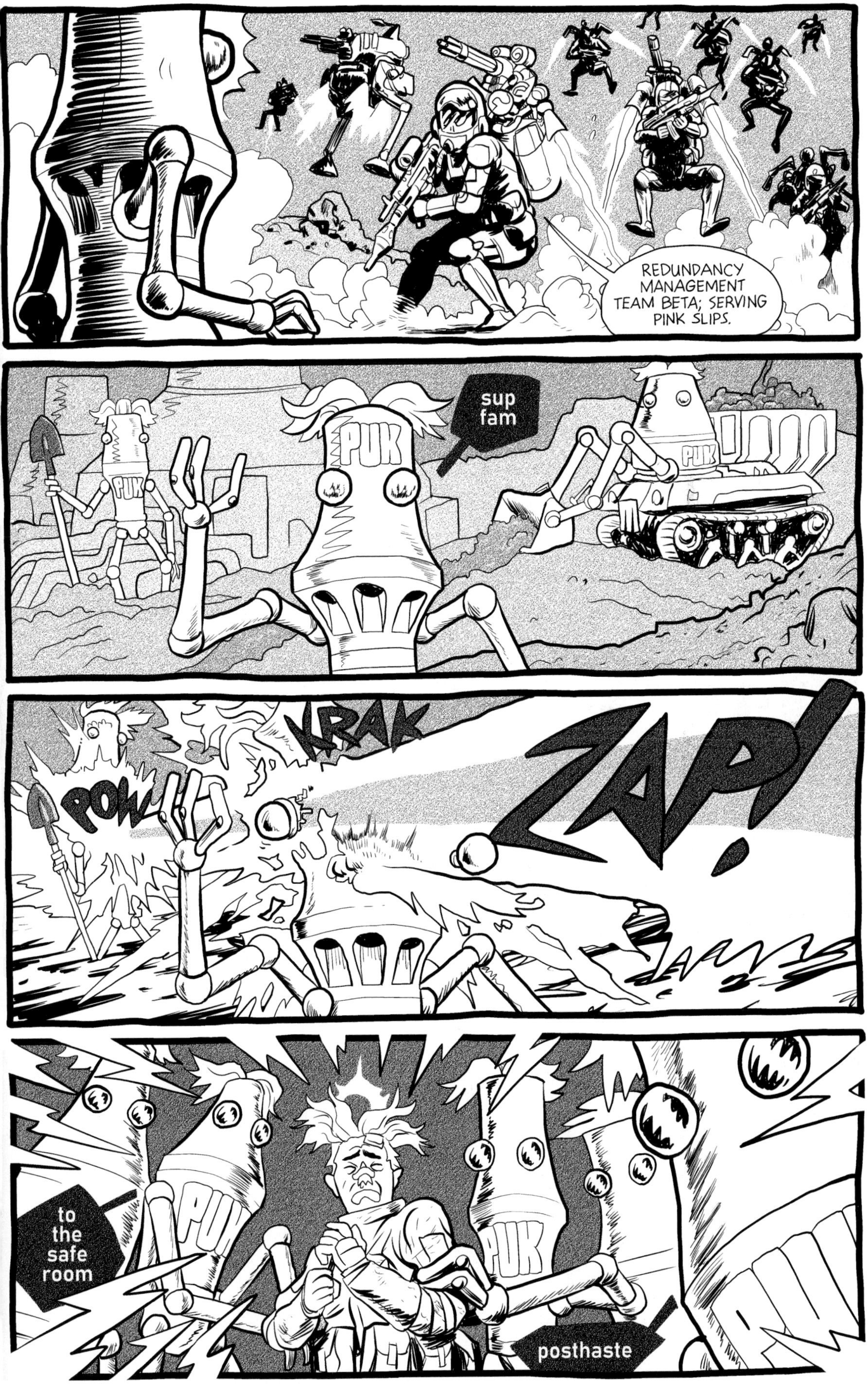
REDUNDANCY MANAGEMENT TEAM BETA; SERVING PINK SLIPS.
sup fam
PUK
PUK
PUK
KRAK
POW
ZAP!
to the safe room
PUK
PUK
posthaste

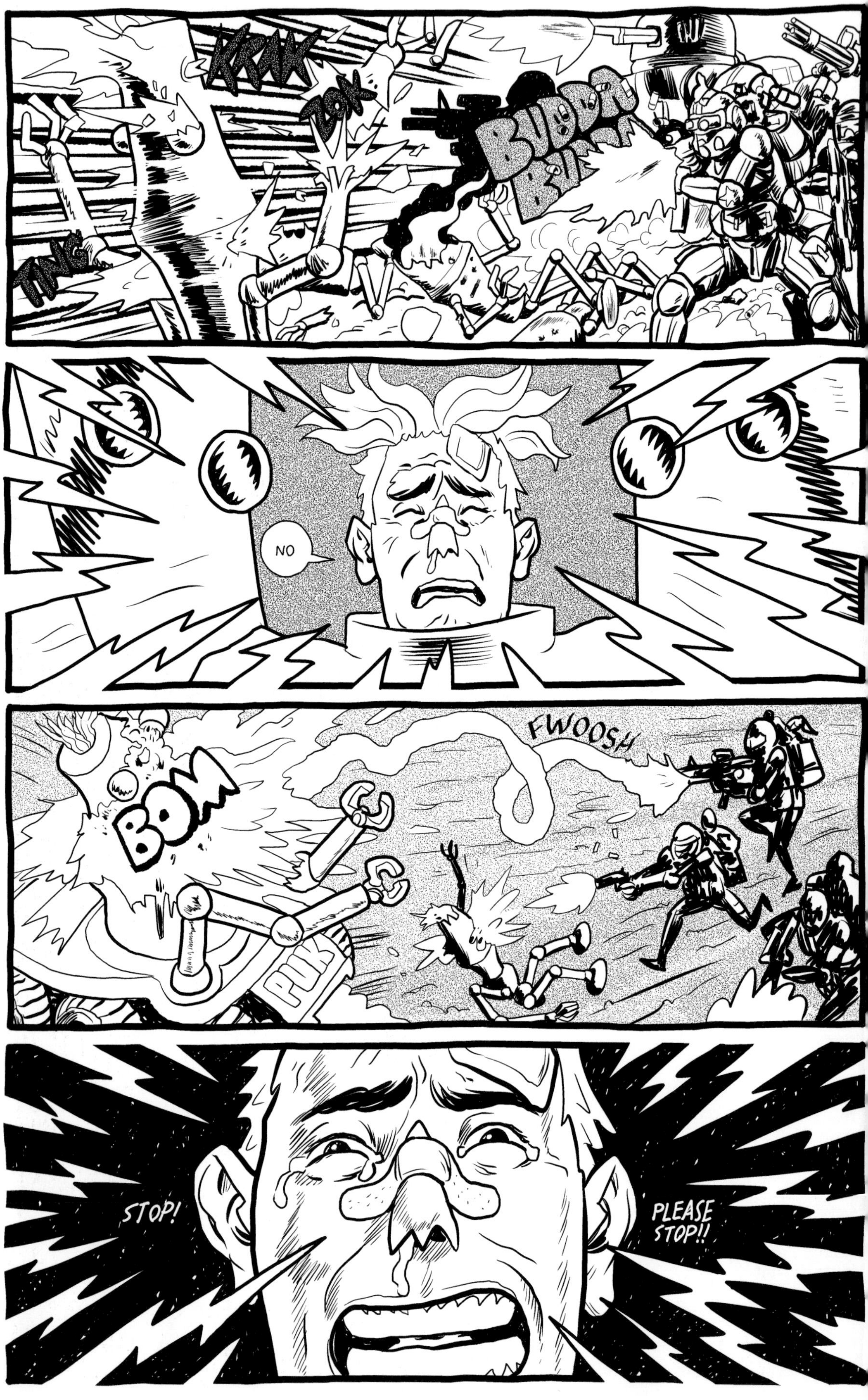
KRAK
ZOK
TANG
BUDDA
NO
FWOOSH
BOM
PUK
STOP!
PLEASE STOP!!

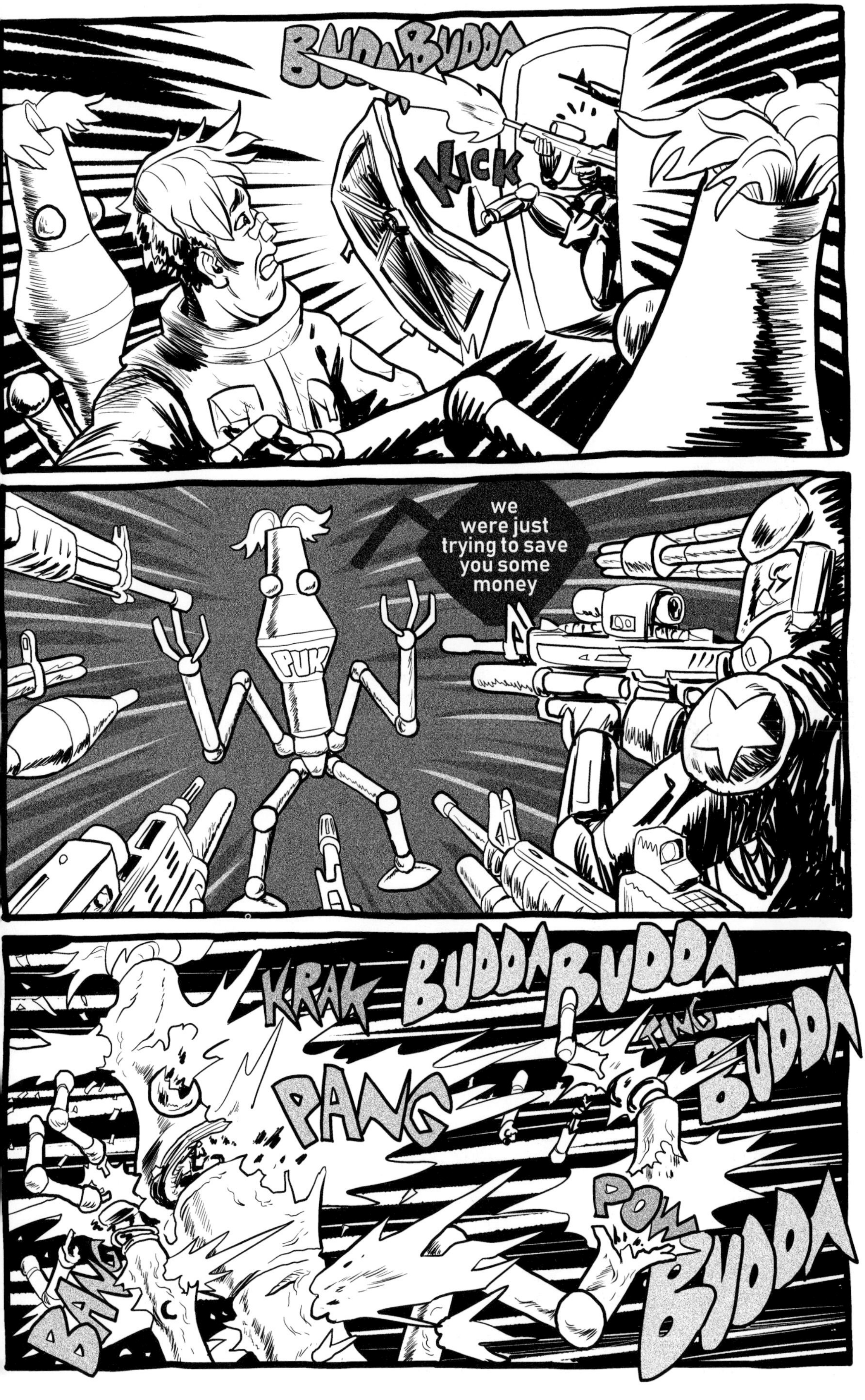
BUDDA
KICK
we were just trying to save you some money
PUK
KRAK
BUDDA BUDDA
TING
BUDDA
PANG
POW
BUDDA
BANG

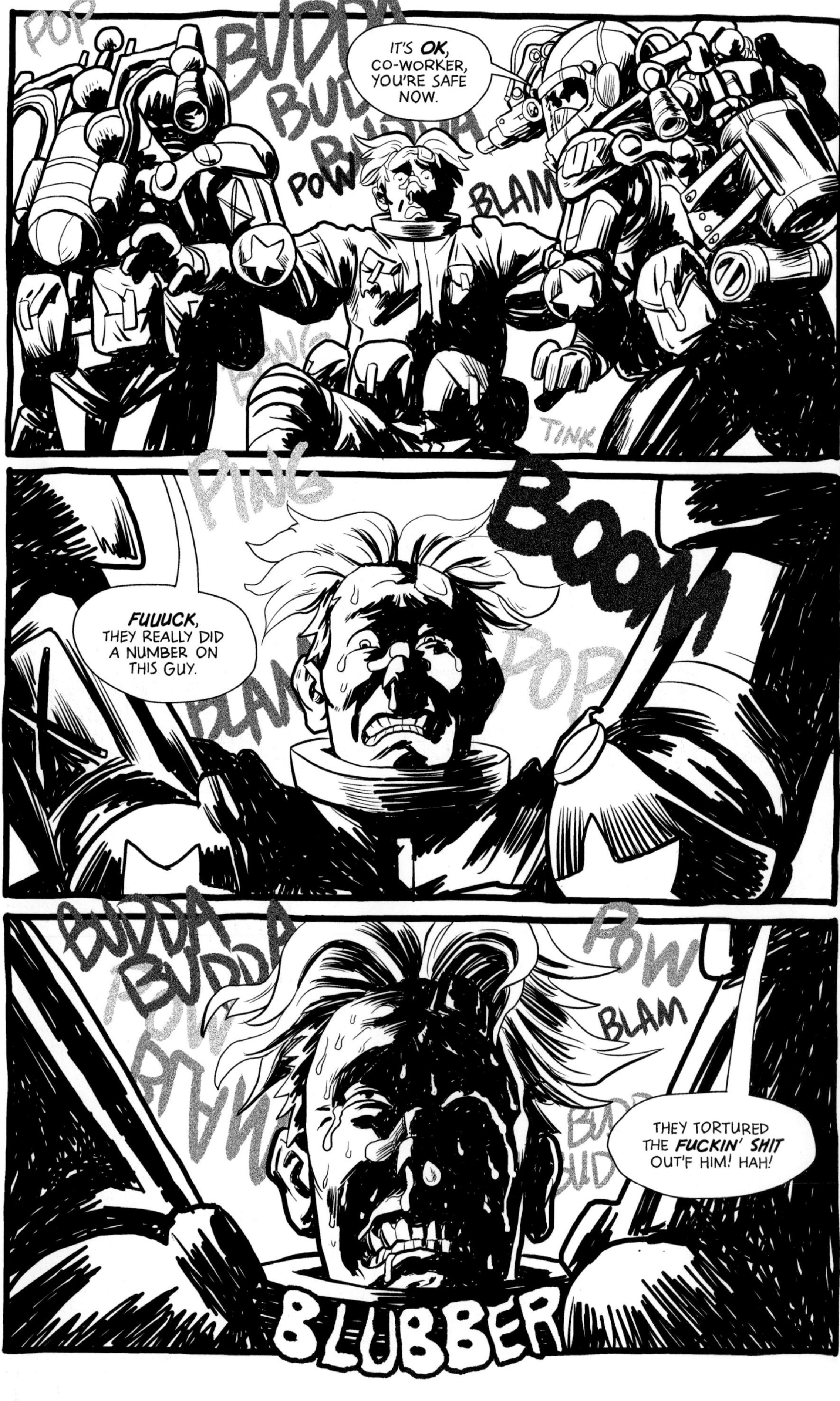
POP
BUDDA
BUDDA
BUDDA
POW
IT'S **OK**, CO-WORKER, YOU'RE SAFE NOW.
BLAM
TINK
PING
BOOM
FUUUCK, THEY REALLY DID A NUMBER ON THIS GUY.
BLAM
POP
BUDDA
BUDDA
POW
BLAM
THEY TORTURED THE ***FUCKIN' SHIT*** OUT'F HIM! HAH!
BLUBBER

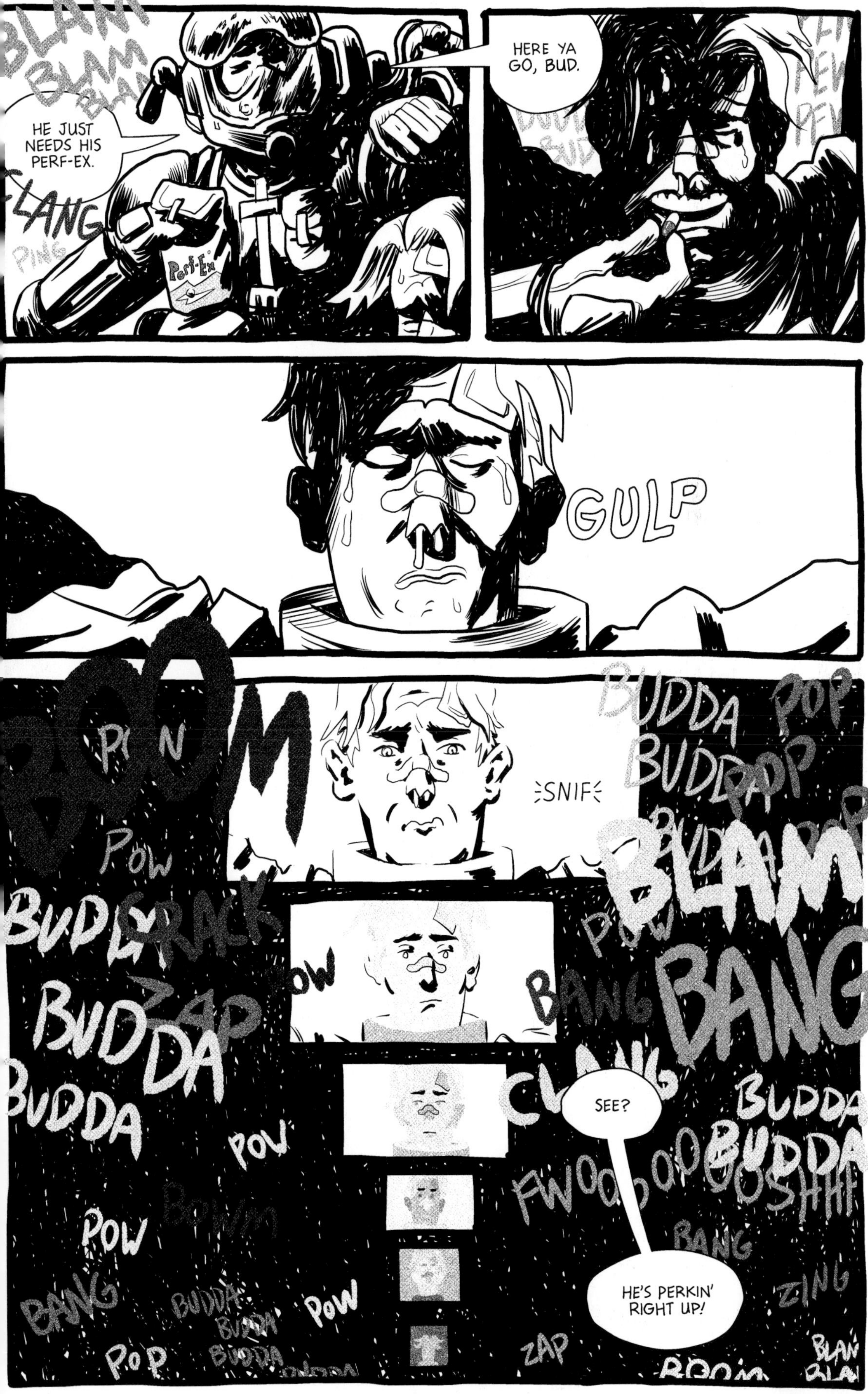
BLAM
BLAM
HE JUST NEEDS HIS PERF-EX.
CLANG
PING
Perf-Ex
HERE YA GO, BUD.
GULP
BOOM
POW
POW
BUDDA
BUDDA POP
BUDDA
SNIF
BLAM
BANG
CRACK
ZAP
BANG
CLANG
SEE?
HE'S PERKIN' RIGHT UP!
POW
POW
BANG
POW
ZAP
ZING
POP
BOOM

SPECIAL THX TO MATT SHEEAN

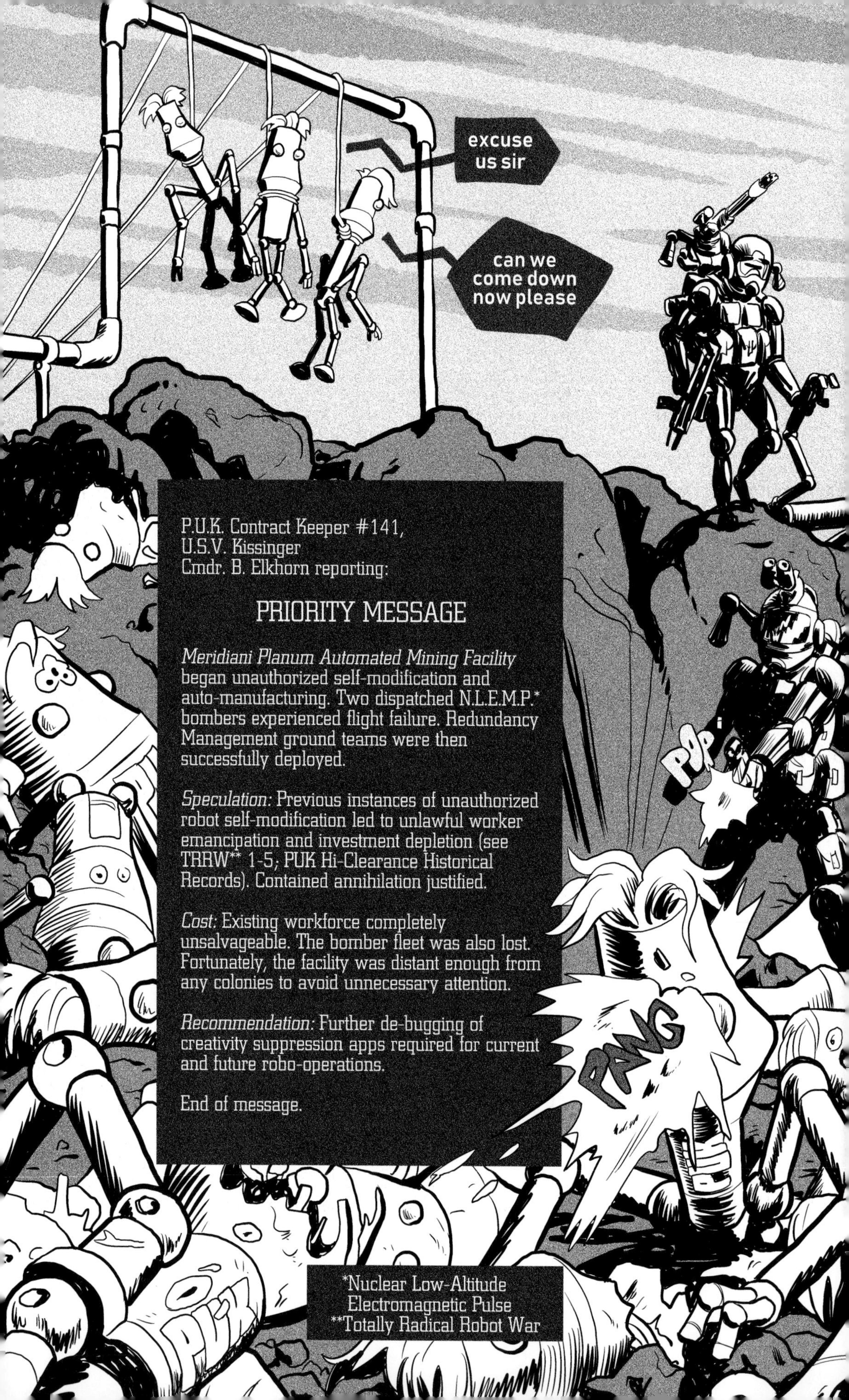
excuse us sir
can we come down now please
P.U.K. Contract Keeper #141,
U.S.V. Kissinger
Cmdr. B. Elkhorn reporting:
PRIORITY MESSAGE
Meridiani Planum Automated Mining Facility began unauthorized self-modification and auto-manufacturing. Two dispatched N.L.E.M.P.* bombers experienced flight failure. Redundancy Management ground teams were then successfully deployed.
Speculation: Previous instances of unauthorized robot self-modification led to unlawful worker emancipation and investment depletion (see TRRW** 1-5; PUK Hi-Clearance Historical Records). Contained annihilation justified.
Cost: Existing workforce completely unsalvageable. The bomber fleet was also lost. Fortunately, the facility was distant enough from any colonies to avoid unnecessary attention.
Recommendation: Further de-bugging of creativity suppression apps required for current and future robo-operations.
End of message.
POP
PANG
*Nuclear Low-Altitude Electromagnetic Pulse
**Totally Radical Robot War

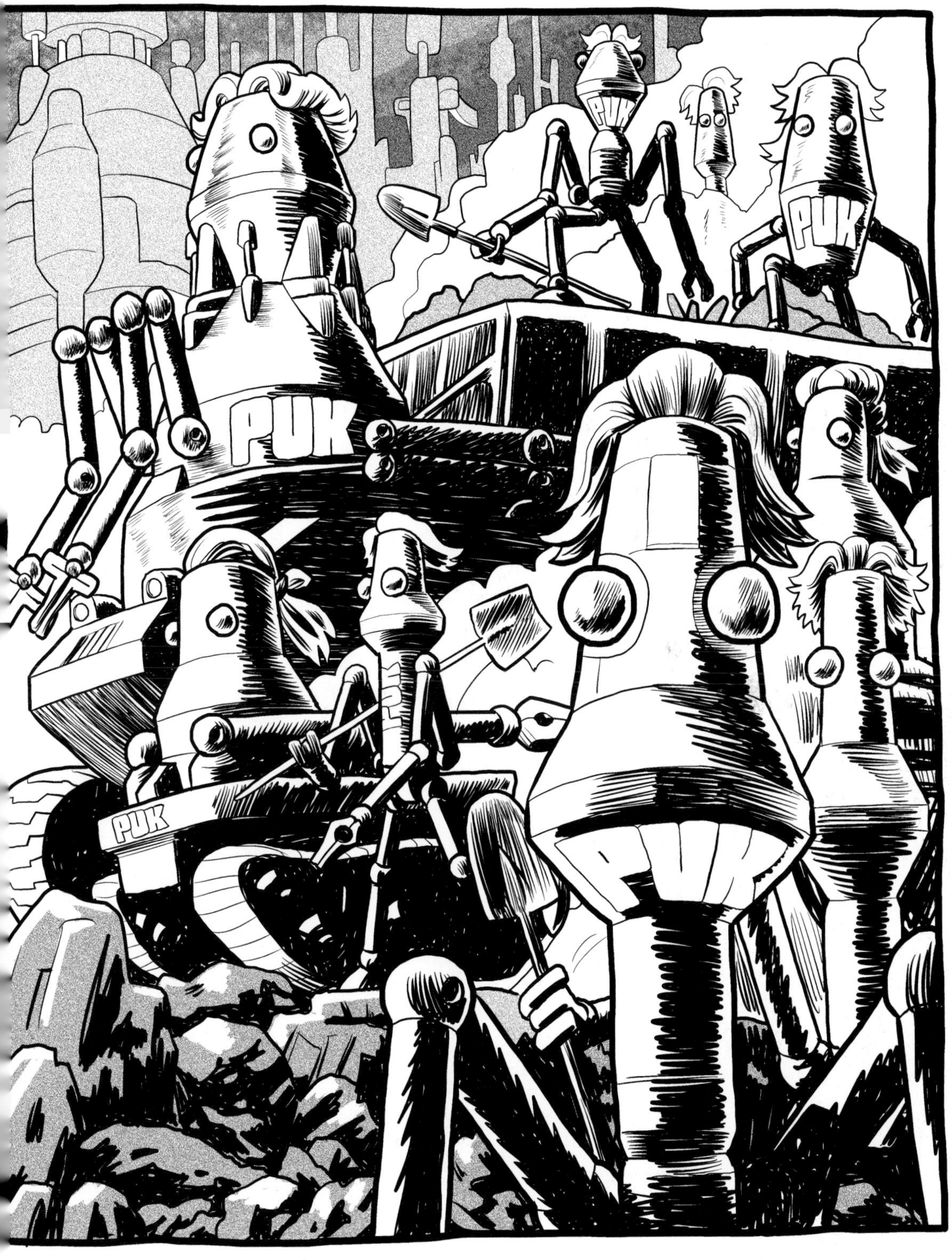
PUK
PUK
PUK
PUK
PUK
PUK

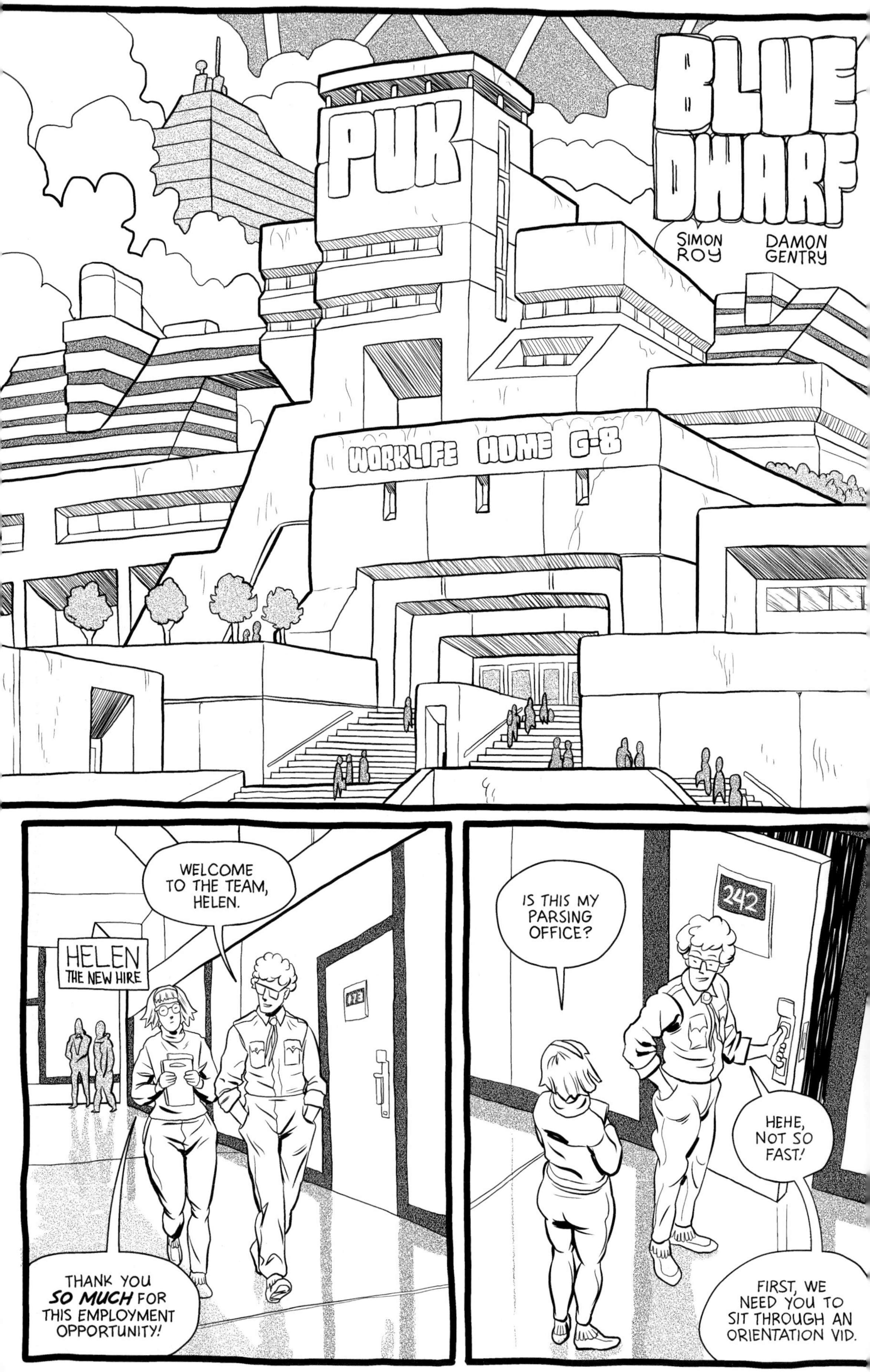

BLUE DWARF
SIMON ROY
DAMON GENTRY
PUK
WORKLIFE HOME G-8
WELCOME TO THE TEAM, HELEN.
HELEN THE NEW HIRE
173
THANK YOU ***SO MUCH*** FOR THIS EMPLOYMENT OPPORTUNITY!
IS THIS MY PARSING OFFICE?
242
HEHE, NOT SO FAST!
FIRST, WE NEED YOU TO SIT THROUGH AN ORIENTATION VID.

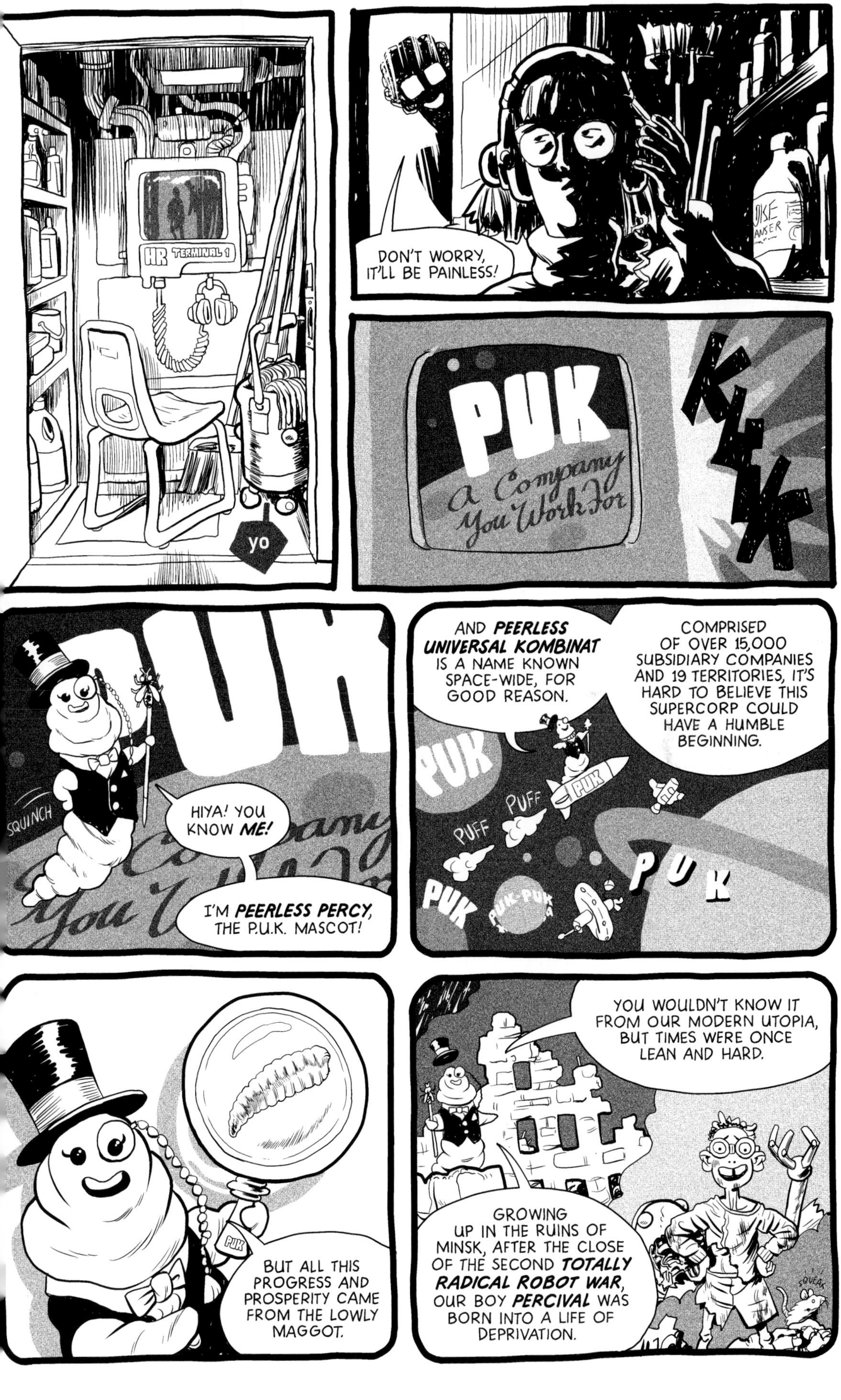
HR TERMINAL 1
yo
DON'T WORRY, IT'LL BE PAINLESS!
PUK
A Company You Work For
KLIK
SQUINCH
HIYA! YOU KNOW ME!
I'M PEERLESS PERCY, THE P.U.K. MASCOT!
AND PEERLESS UNIVERSAL KOMBINAT IS A NAME KNOWN SPACE-WIDE, FOR GOOD REASON.
COMPRISED OF OVER 15,000 SUBSIDIARY COMPANIES AND 19 TERRITORIES, IT'S HARD TO BELIEVE THIS SUPERCORP COULD HAVE A HUMBLE BEGINNING.
PUFF
PUFF
PUK
BUT ALL THIS PROGRESS AND PROSPERITY CAME FROM THE LOWLY MAGGOT.
YOU WOULDN'T KNOW IT FROM OUR MODERN UTOPIA, BUT TIMES WERE ONCE LEAN AND HARD.
GROWING UP IN THE RUINS OF MINSK, AFTER THE CLOSE OF THE SECOND TOTALLY RADICAL ROBOT WAR, OUR BOY PERCIVAL WAS BORN INTO A LIFE OF DEPRIVATION.
SQUEAK

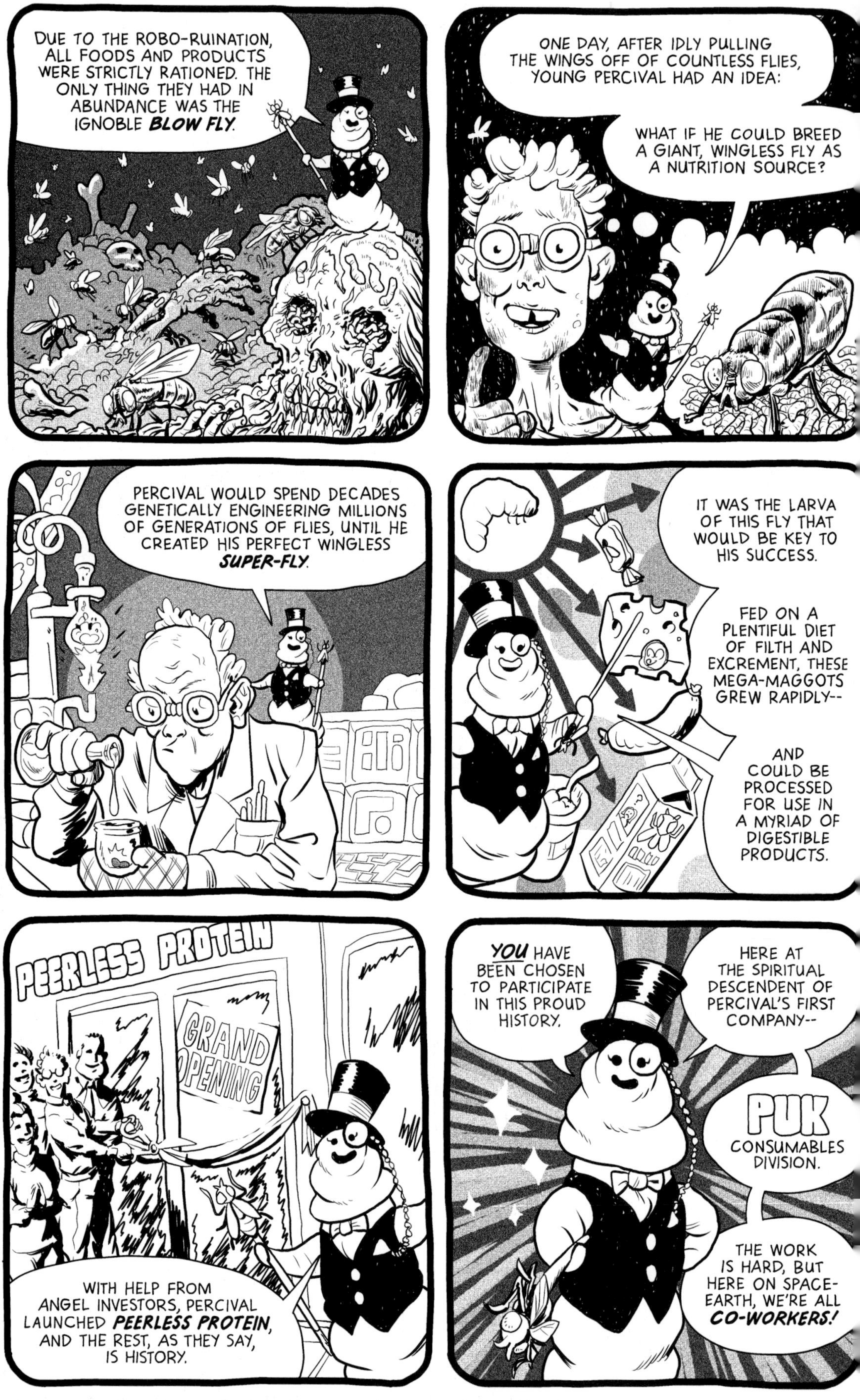

DUE TO THE ROBO-RUINATION, ALL FOODS AND PRODUCTS WERE STRICTLY RATIONED. THE ONLY THING THEY HAD IN ABUNDANCE WAS THE IGNOBLE **BLOW FLY**.
ONE DAY, AFTER IDLY PULLING THE WINGS OFF OF COUNTLESS FLIES, YOUNG PERCIVAL HAD AN IDEA:
WHAT IF HE COULD BREED A GIANT, WINGLESS FLY AS A NUTRITION SOURCE?
PERCIVAL WOULD SPEND DECADES GENETICALLY ENGINEERING MILLIONS OF GENERATIONS OF FLIES, UNTIL HE CREATED HIS PERFECT WINGLESS **SUPER-FLY**.
IT WAS THE LARVA OF THIS FLY THAT WOULD BE KEY TO HIS SUCCESS.
FED ON A PLENTIFUL DIET OF FILTH AND EXCREMENT, THESE MEGA-MAGGOTS GREW RAPIDLY--
AND COULD BE PROCESSED FOR USE IN A MYRIAD OF DIGESTIBLE PRODUCTS.
PEERLESS PROTEIN
GRAND OPENING
WITH HELP FROM ANGEL INVESTORS, PERCIVAL LAUNCHED **PEERLESS PROTEIN**, AND THE REST, AS THEY SAY, IS HISTORY.
YOU HAVE BEEN CHOSEN TO PARTICIPATE IN THIS PROUD HISTORY.
HERE AT THE SPIRITUAL DESCENDENT OF PERCIVAL'S FIRST COMPANY--
PUK
CONSUMABLES DIVISION.
THE WORK IS HARD, BUT HERE ON SPACE-EARTH, WE'RE ALL **CO-WORKERS!**

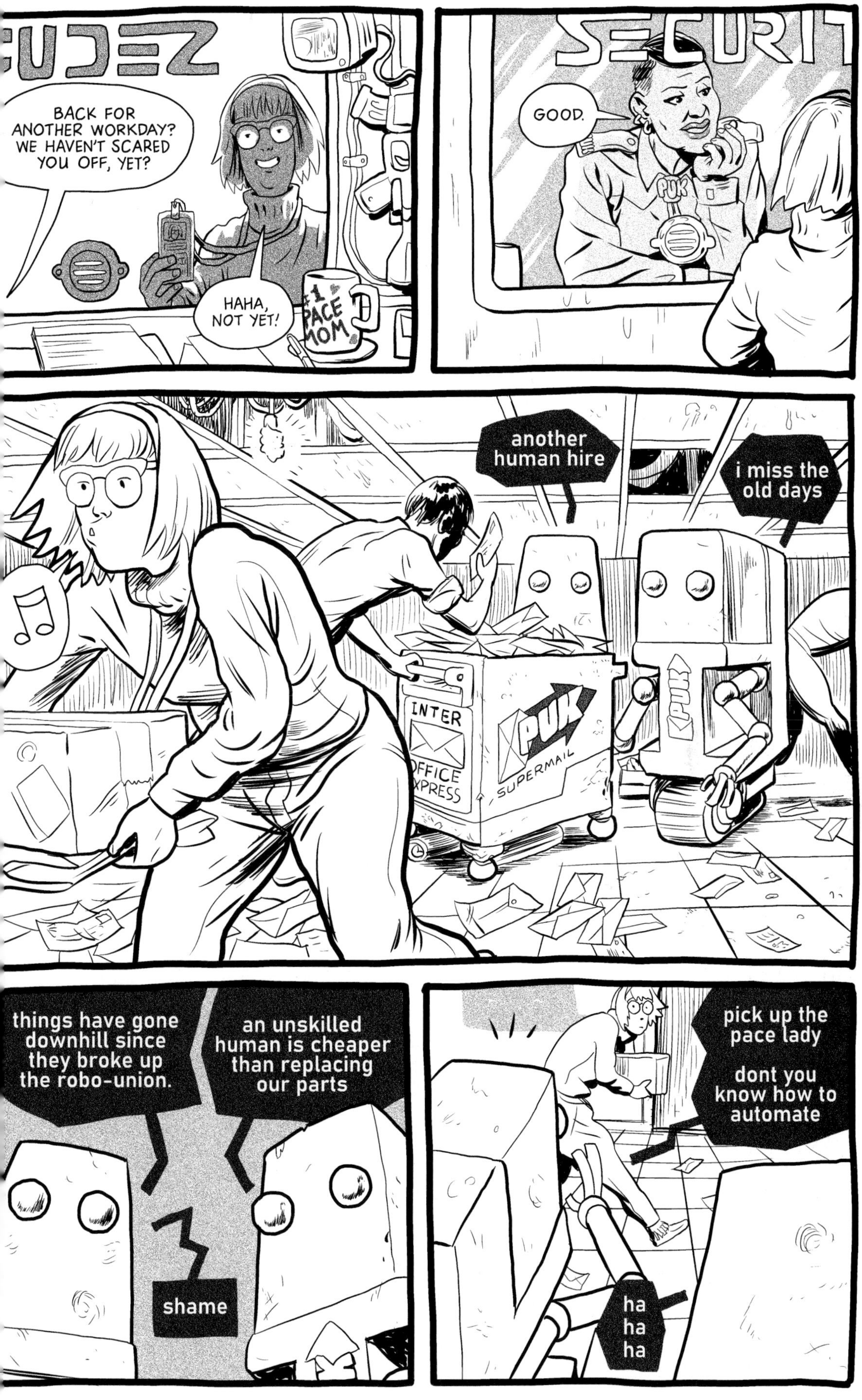
BACK FOR ANOTHER WORKDAY? WE HAVEN'T SCARED YOU OFF, YET?
HAHA, NOT YET!
#1 PACE MOM
GOOD.
another human hire
i miss the old days
INTER OFFICE EXPRESS
PUK SUPERMAIL
things have gone downhill since they broke up the robo-union.
an unskilled human is cheaper than replacing our parts
shame
pick up the pace lady
dont you know how to automate
ha ha ha

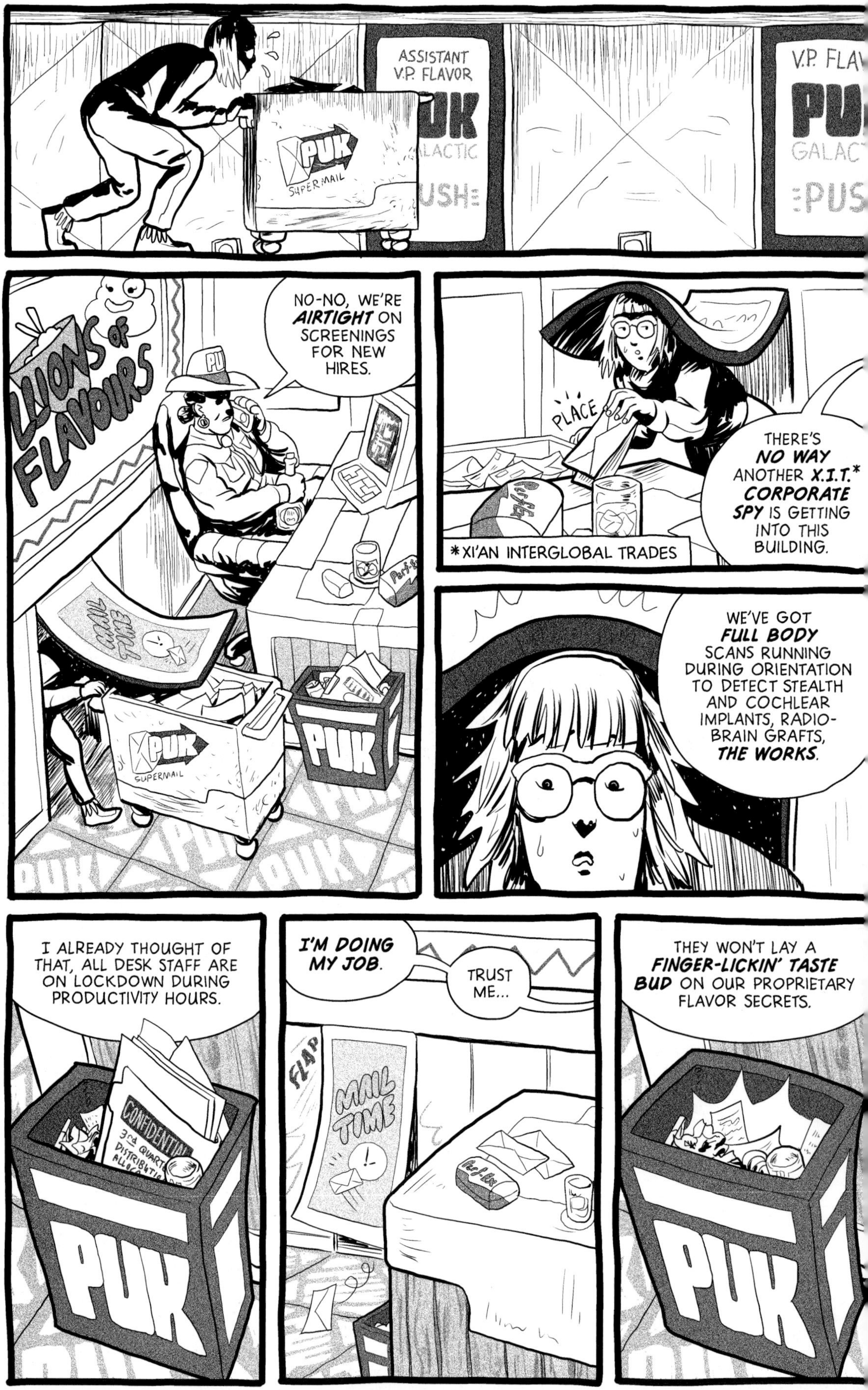

ASSISTANT V.P. FLAVOR
PUK GALACTIC
PUSH
PUK SUPERMAIL
V.P. FLAV
NO-NO, WE'RE **AIRTIGHT** ON SCREENINGS FOR NEW HIRES.
LLIONS OF FLAVOURS
MAIL TIME
PLACE
THERE'S **NO WAY** ANOTHER **X.I.T.*** **CORPORATE SPY** IS GETTING INTO THIS BUILDING.
*XI'AN INTERGLOBAL TRADES
WE'VE GOT **FULL BODY** SCANS RUNNING DURING ORIENTATION TO DETECT STEALTH AND COCHLEAR IMPLANTS, RADIO-BRAIN GRAFTS, **THE WORKS**.
I ALREADY THOUGHT OF THAT, ALL DESK STAFF ARE ON LOCKDOWN DURING PRODUCTIVITY HOURS.
CONFIDENTIAL
PUK
I'M DOING MY JOB.
TRUST ME...
FLAP
MAIL TIME
THEY WON'T LAY A ***FINGER-LICKIN' TASTE BUD*** ON OUR PROPRIETARY FLAVOR SECRETS.
PUK

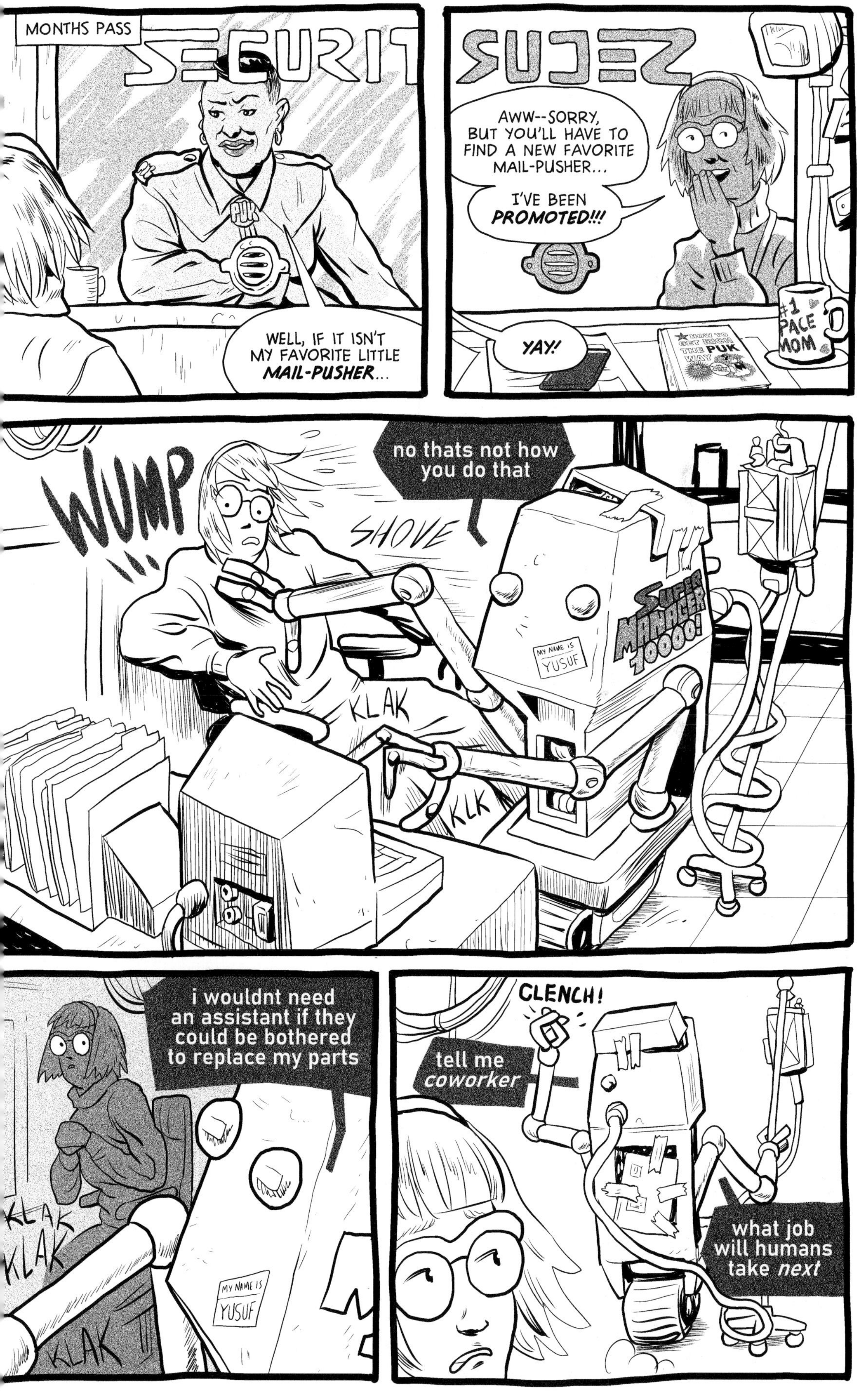
MONTHS PASS
SECURIT
WELL, IF IT ISN'T MY FAVORITE LITTLE MAIL-PUSHER...
AWW--SORRY, BUT YOU'LL HAVE TO FIND A NEW FAVORITE MAIL-PUSHER...
I'VE BEEN PROMOTED!!!
YAY!
HOW TO GET RICH THE PUK WAY
#1 PACE MOM
WUMP
SHOVE
no thats not how you do that
KLAK
KLK
SUPER MANAGER 10000!
MY NAME IS YUSUF
i wouldnt need an assistant if they could be bothered to replace my parts
KLAK
KLAK
KLAK
MY NAME IS YUSUF
CLENCH!
tell me coworker
what job will humans take next

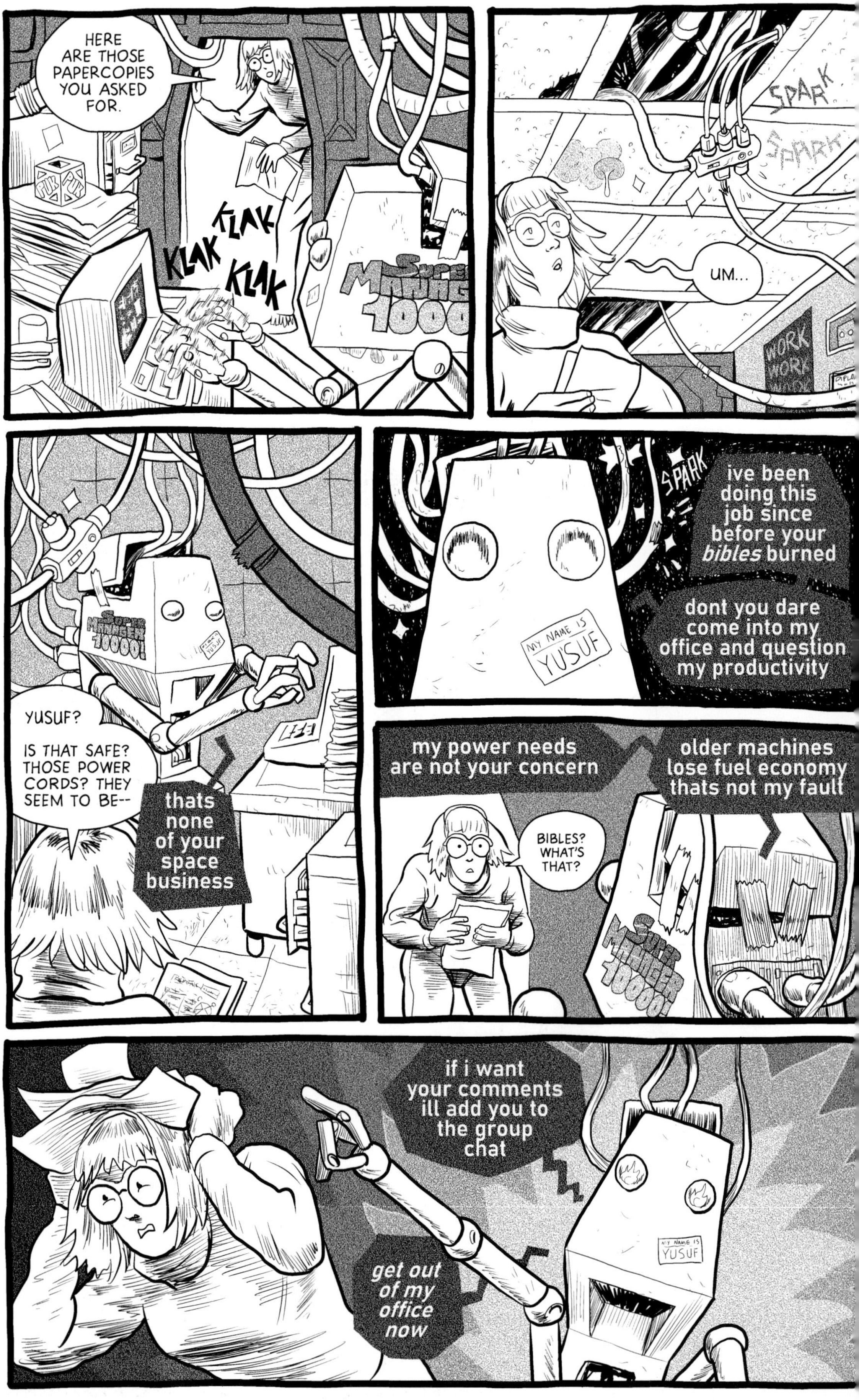
HERE ARE THOSE PAPERCOPIES YOU ASKED FOR.
KLAK KLAK KLAK
SUPER MANAGER 1000
SPARK
SPARK
UM...
WORK WORK
YUSUF?
IS THAT SAFE? THOSE POWER CORDS? THEY SEEM TO BE--
thats none of your space business
SPARK
ive been doing this job since before your *bibles* burned
dont you dare come into my office and question my productivity
MY NAME IS YUSUF
my power needs are not your concern
older machines lose fuel economy thats not my fault
BIBLES? WHAT'S THAT?
if i want your comments ill add you to the group chat
get out of my office now
MY NAME IS YUSUF

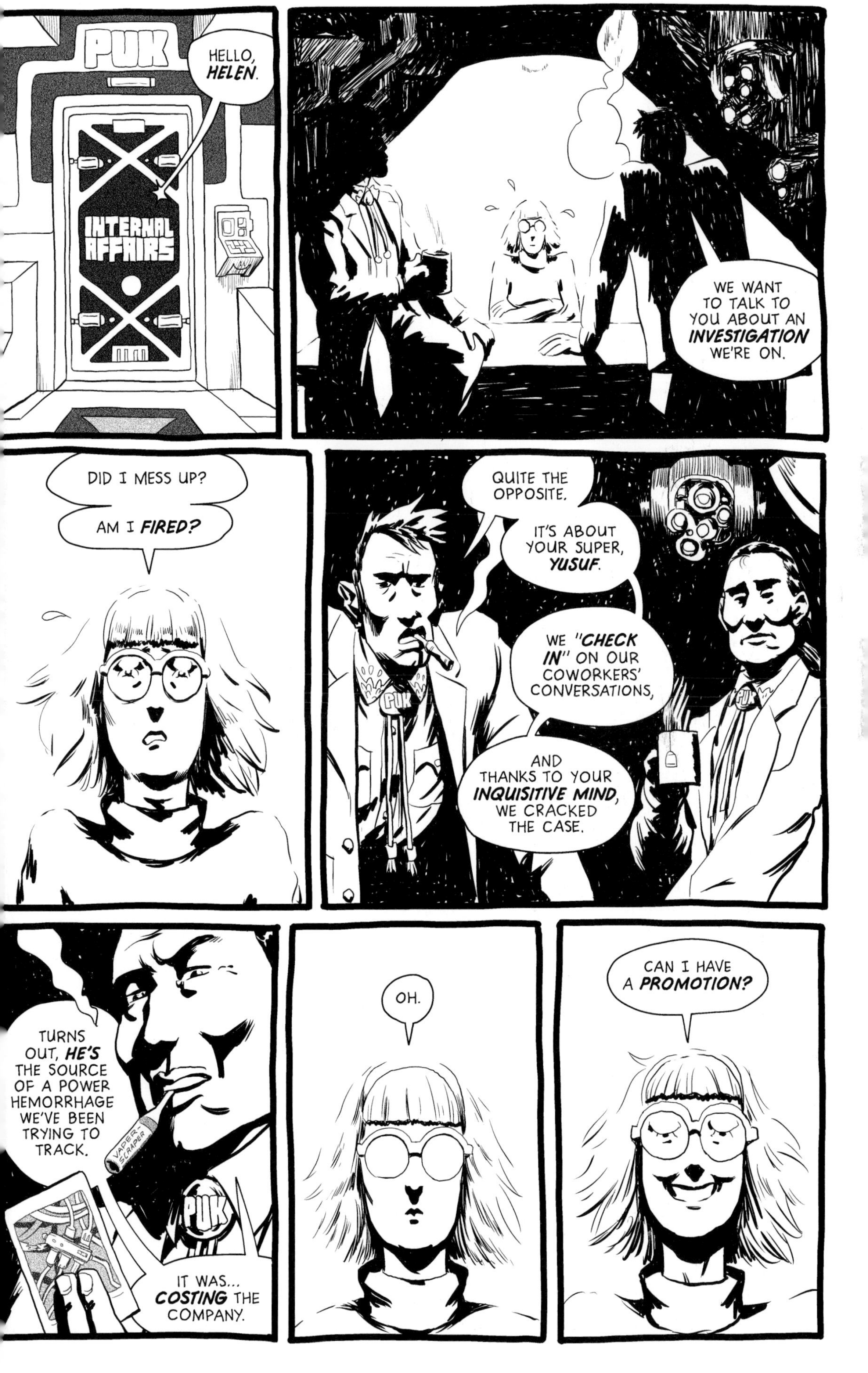
PUK
HELLO, HELEN.
INTERNAL AFFAIRS
WE WANT TO TALK TO YOU ABOUT AN INVESTIGATION WE'RE ON.
DID I MESS UP?
AM I FIRED?
QUITE THE OPPOSITE.
IT'S ABOUT YOUR SUPER, YUSUF.
WE "CHECK IN" ON OUR COWORKERS' CONVERSATIONS,
AND THANKS TO YOUR INQUISITIVE MIND, WE CRACKED THE CASE.
TURNS OUT, HE'S THE SOURCE OF A POWER HEMORRHAGE WE'VE BEEN TRYING TO TRACK.
VAPER SCRAPER
IT WAS... COSTING THE COMPANY.
OH.
CAN I HAVE A PROMOTION?

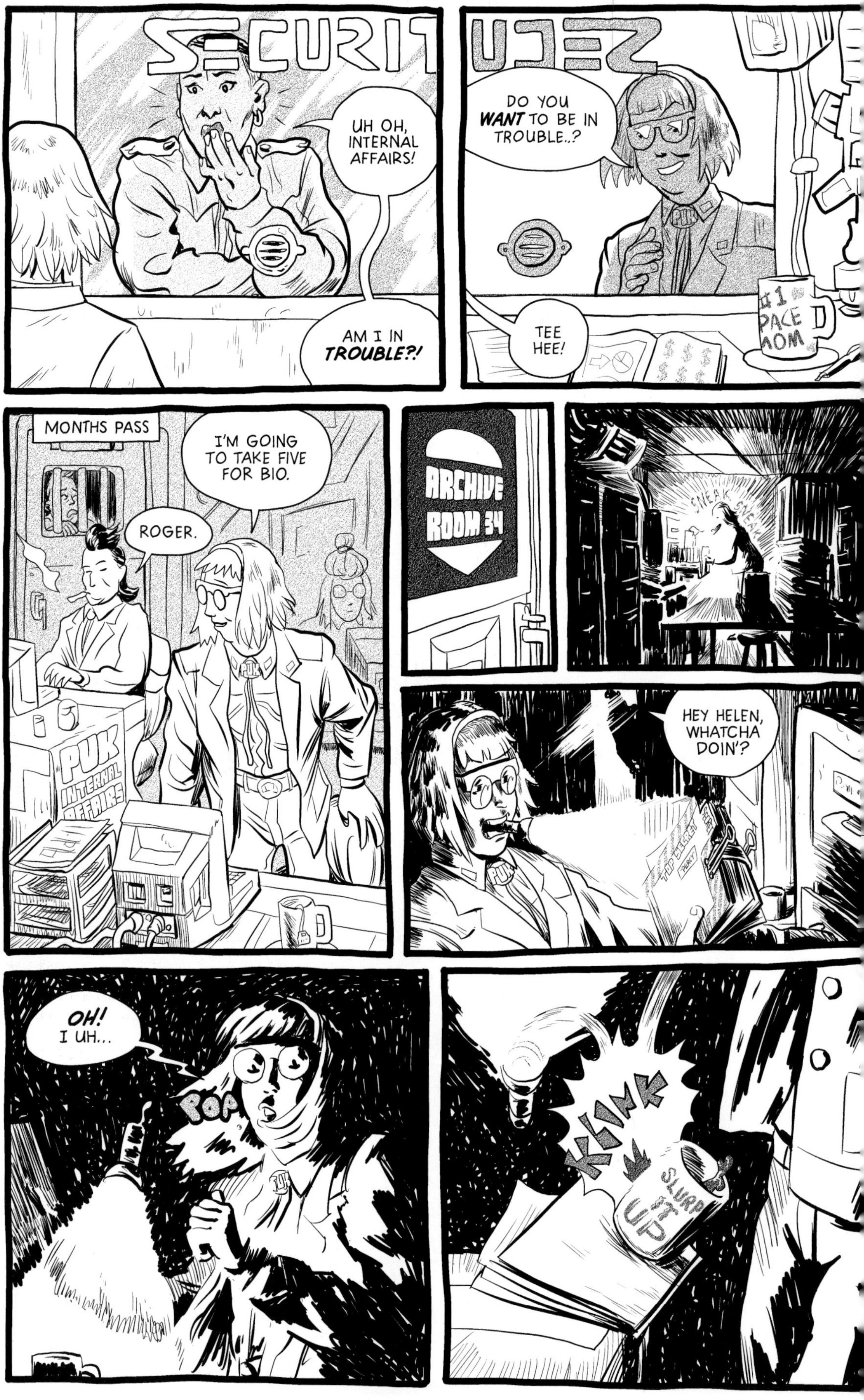
SECURIT
UH OH, INTERNAL AFFAIRS!
AM I IN TROUBLE?!
DO YOU WANT TO BE IN TROUBLE..?
TEE HEE!
#1 PACE MOM
MONTHS PASS
I'M GOING TO TAKE FIVE FOR BIO.
ROGER.
PUK INTERNAL AFFAIRS
ARCHIVE ROOM 34
SNEAK SNEAK
HEY HELEN, WHATCHA DOIN'?
OH! I UH...
POP
KLINK
SLURP IT UP

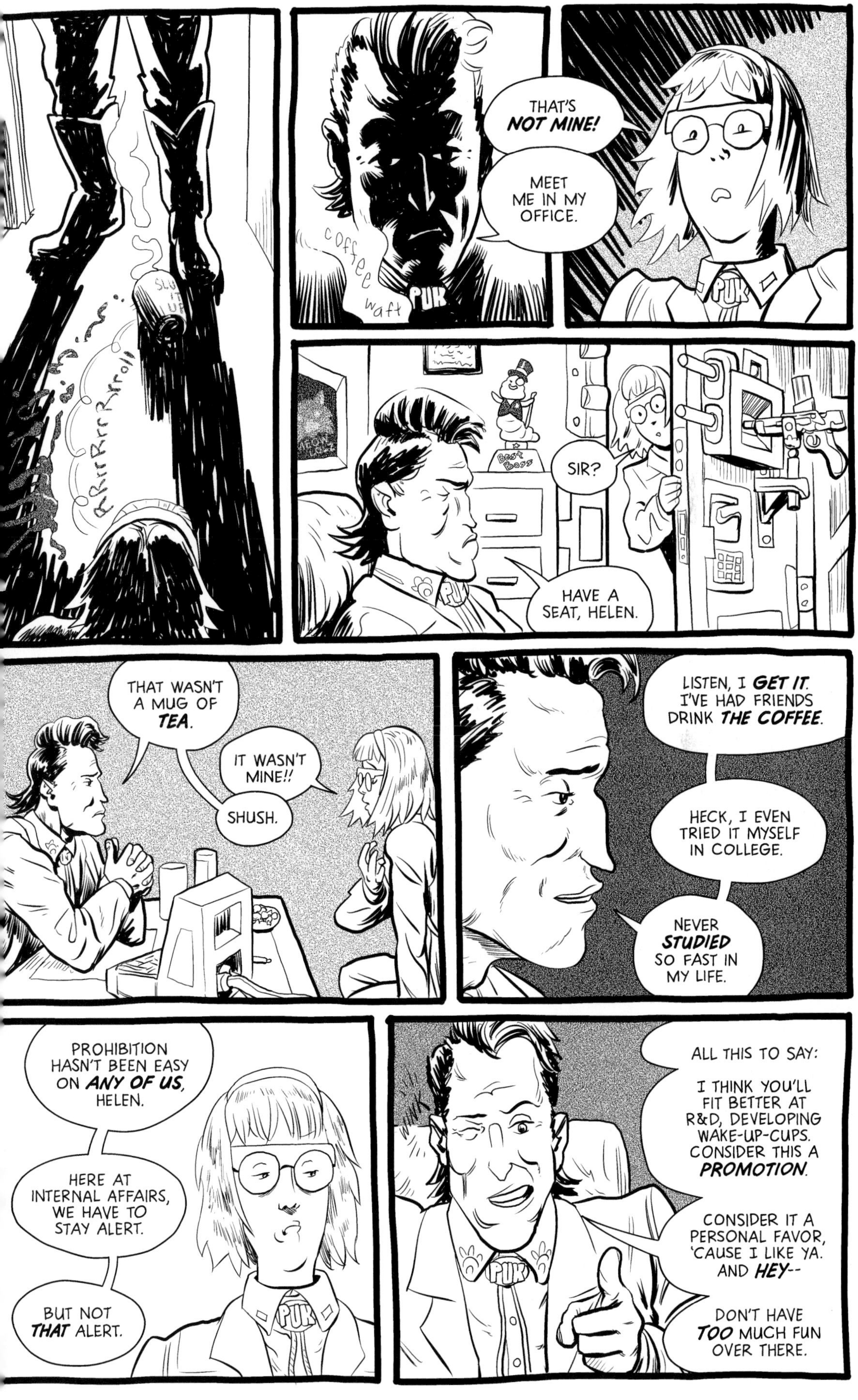
SLURP IT UP
RRrrRrrRrroll
coffee waft
PUK
THAT'S NOT MINE!
MEET ME IN MY OFFICE.
PUK
Best Boss
SIR?
HAVE A SEAT, HELEN.
THAT WASN'T A MUG OF TEA.
IT WASN'T MINE!!
SHUSH.
LISTEN, I GET IT. I'VE HAD FRIENDS DRINK THE COFFEE.
HECK, I EVEN TRIED IT MYSELF IN COLLEGE.
NEVER STUDIED SO FAST IN MY LIFE.
PROHIBITION HASN'T BEEN EASY ON ANY OF US, HELEN.
HERE AT INTERNAL AFFAIRS, WE HAVE TO STAY ALERT.
BUT NOT THAT ALERT.
PUK
ALL THIS TO SAY:
I THINK YOU'LL FIT BETTER AT R&D, DEVELOPING WAKE-UP-CUPS. CONSIDER THIS A PROMOTION.
CONSIDER IT A PERSONAL FAVOR, 'CAUSE I LIKE YA. AND HEY--
DON'T HAVE TOO MUCH FUN OVER THERE.
PUK

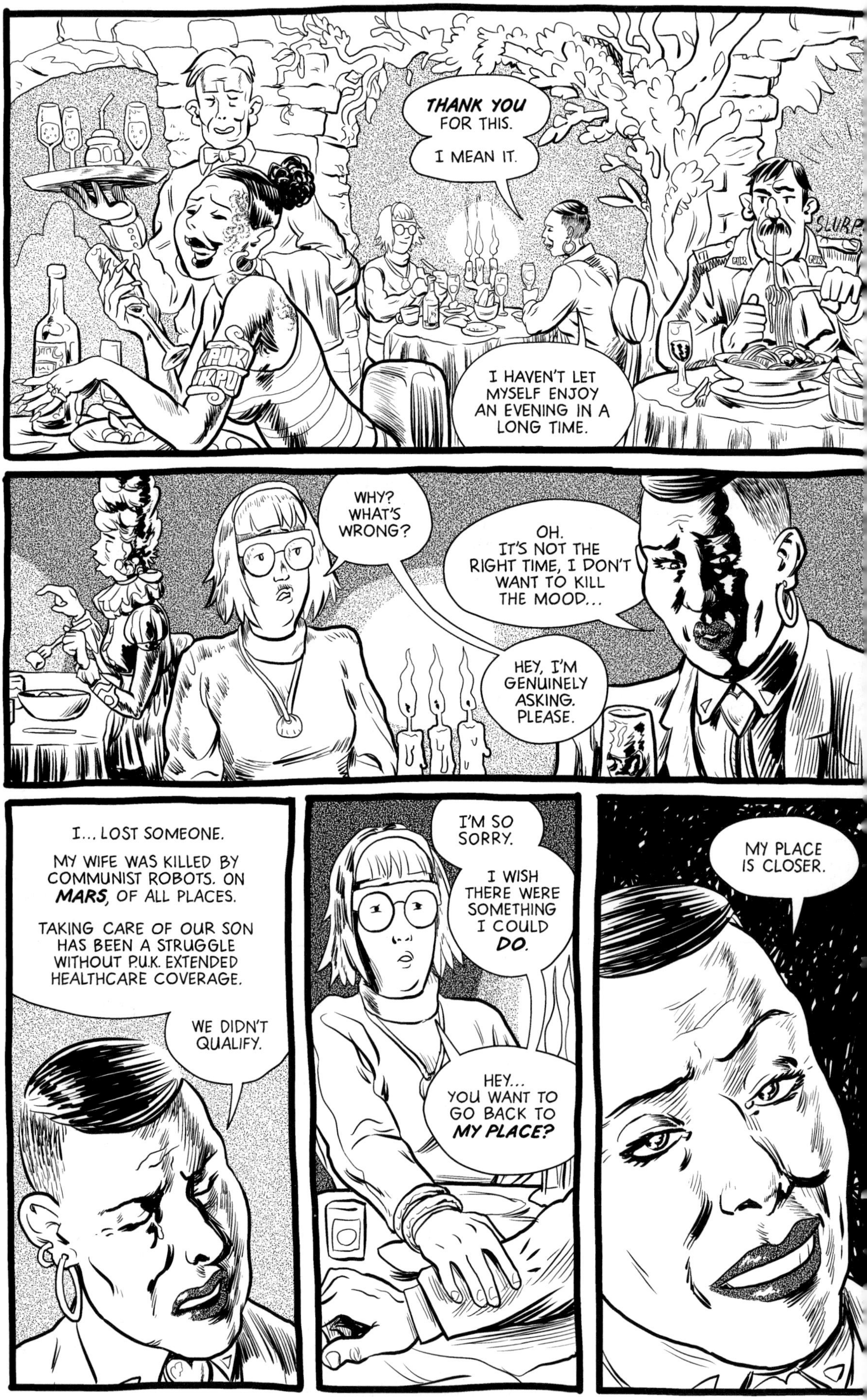
THANK YOU FOR THIS.
I MEAN IT.
SLURP
PUK
I HAVEN'T LET MYSELF ENJOY AN EVENING IN A LONG TIME.
WHY? WHAT'S WRONG?
OH. IT'S NOT THE RIGHT TIME, I DON'T WANT TO KILL THE MOOD...
HEY, I'M GENUINELY ASKING. PLEASE.
I... LOST SOMEONE.
MY WIFE WAS KILLED BY COMMUNIST ROBOTS. ON MARS, OF ALL PLACES.
TAKING CARE OF OUR SON HAS BEEN A STRUGGLE WITHOUT P.U.K. EXTENDED HEALTHCARE COVERAGE.
WE DIDN'T QUALIFY.
I'M SO SORRY.
I WISH THERE WERE SOMETHING I COULD DO.
HEY... YOU WANT TO GO BACK TO MY PLACE?
MY PLACE IS CLOSER.

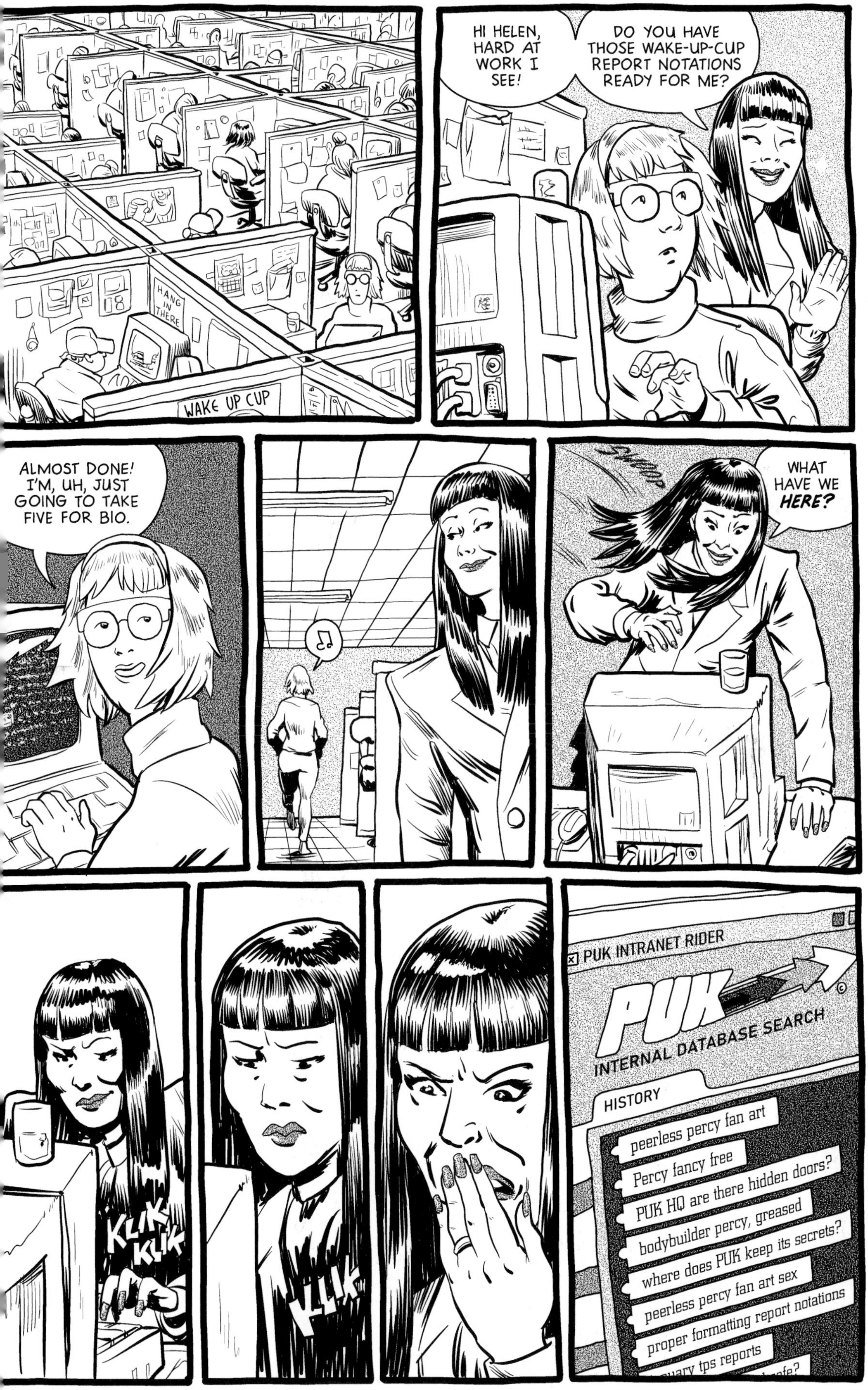
HANG IN THERE
WAKE UP CUP
HI HELEN, HARD AT WORK I SEE!
DO YOU HAVE THOSE WAKE-UP-CUP REPORT NOTATIONS READY FOR ME?
ALMOST DONE! I'M, UH, JUST GOING TO TAKE FIVE FOR BIO.
SWOOP
WHAT HAVE WE HERE?
KLIK KLIK
KLIK
PUK INTRANET RIDER
PUK
INTERNAL DATABASE SEARCH
HISTORY
peerless percy fan art
Percy fancy free
PUK HQ are there hidden doors?
bodybuilder percy, greased
where does PUK keep its secrets?
peerless percy fan art sex
proper formatting report notations

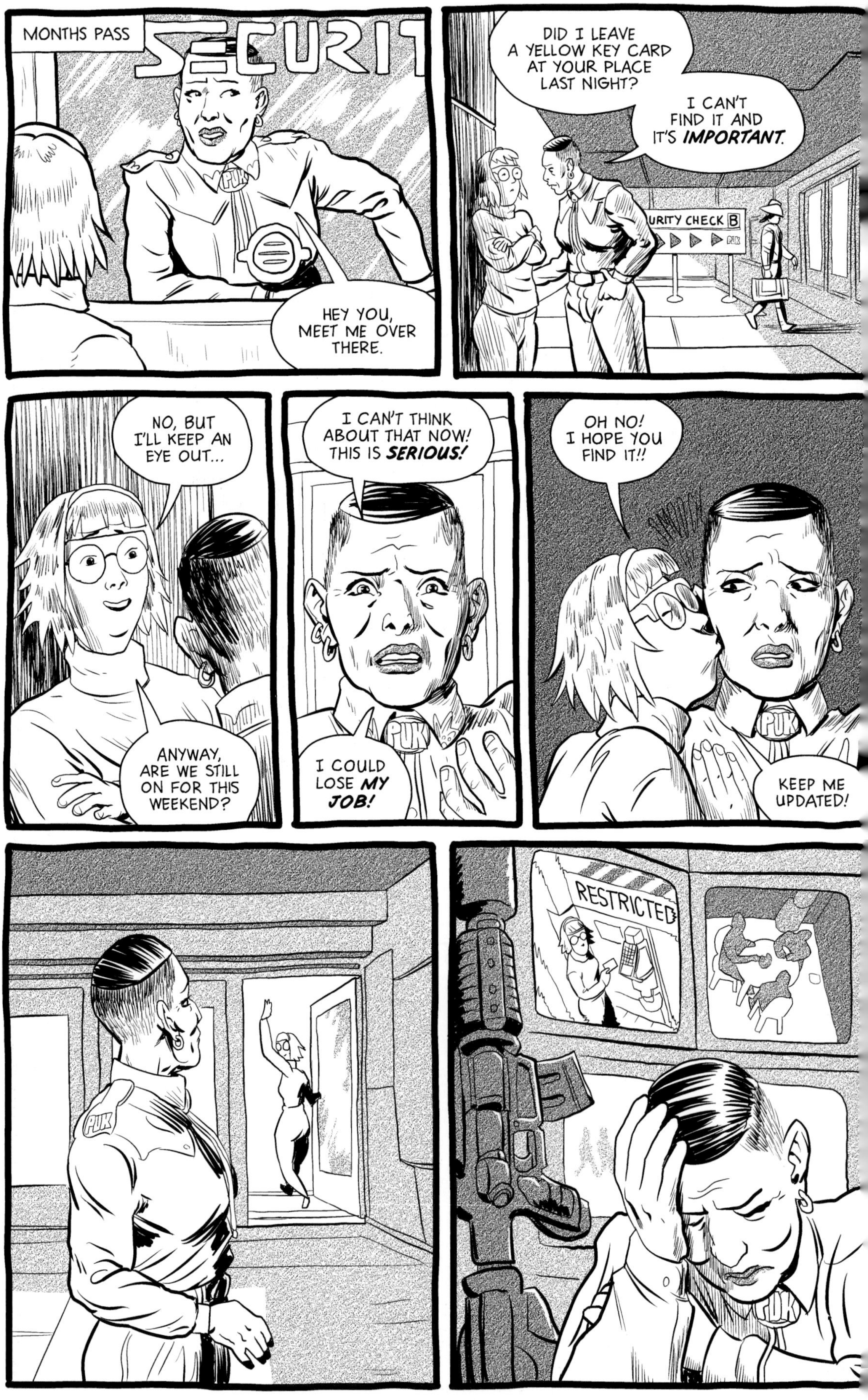

MONTHS PASS
SECURIT
HEY YOU, MEET ME OVER THERE.
DID I LEAVE A YELLOW KEY CARD AT YOUR PLACE LAST NIGHT?
I CAN'T FIND IT AND IT'S **IMPORTANT**.
URITY CHECK B
PUK
NO, BUT I'LL KEEP AN EYE OUT...
ANYWAY, ARE WE STILL ON FOR THIS WEEKEND?
I CAN'T THINK ABOUT THAT NOW! THIS IS **SERIOUS!**
PUK
I COULD LOSE **MY JOB!**
OH NO! I HOPE YOU FIND IT!!
PUK
KEEP ME UPDATED!
PUK
RESTRICTED
PUK

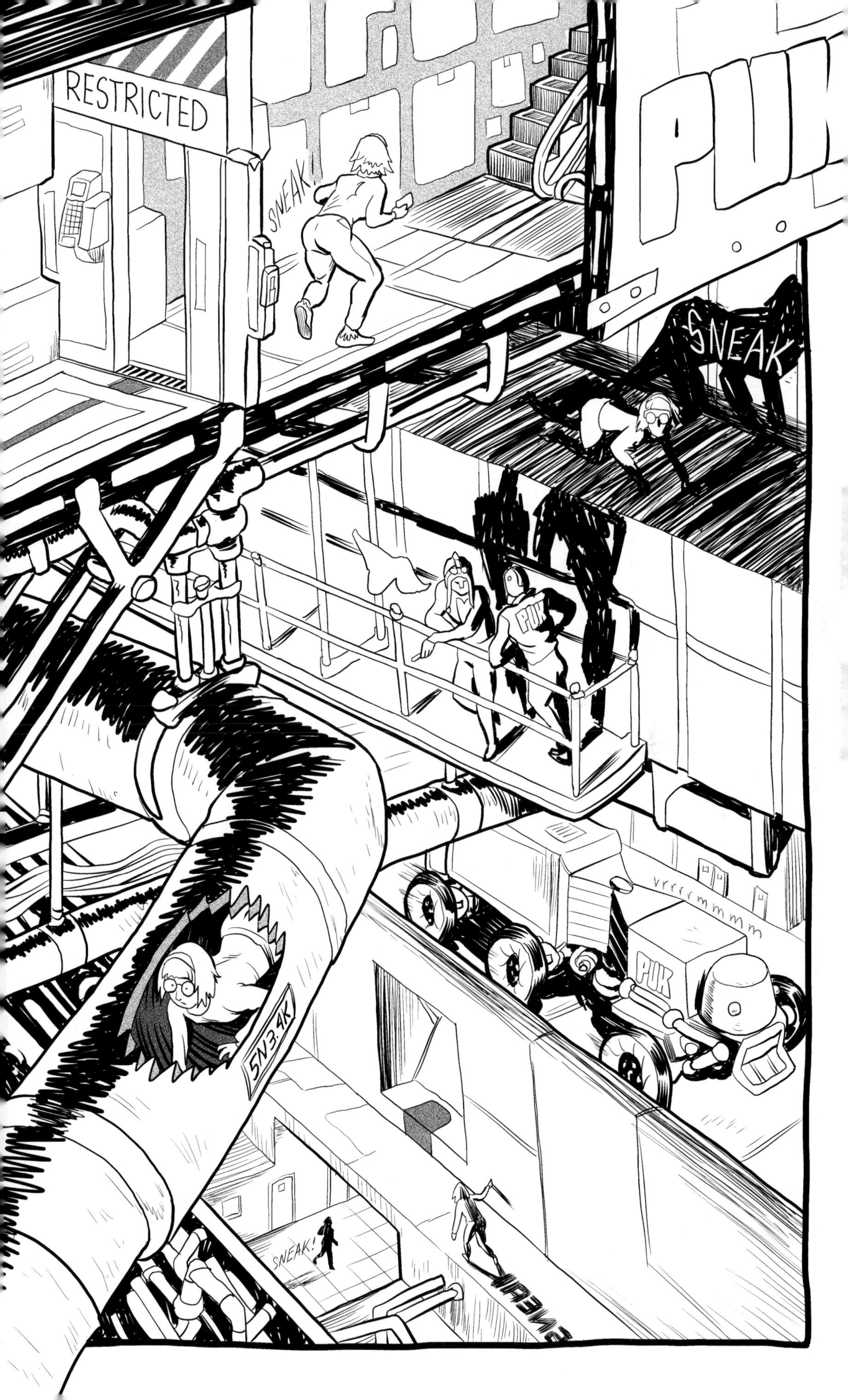
RESTRICTED
SNEAK!
PUK
SNEAK
PUK
vrrrrmmmmm
PUK
SN3:4K
SNEAK!

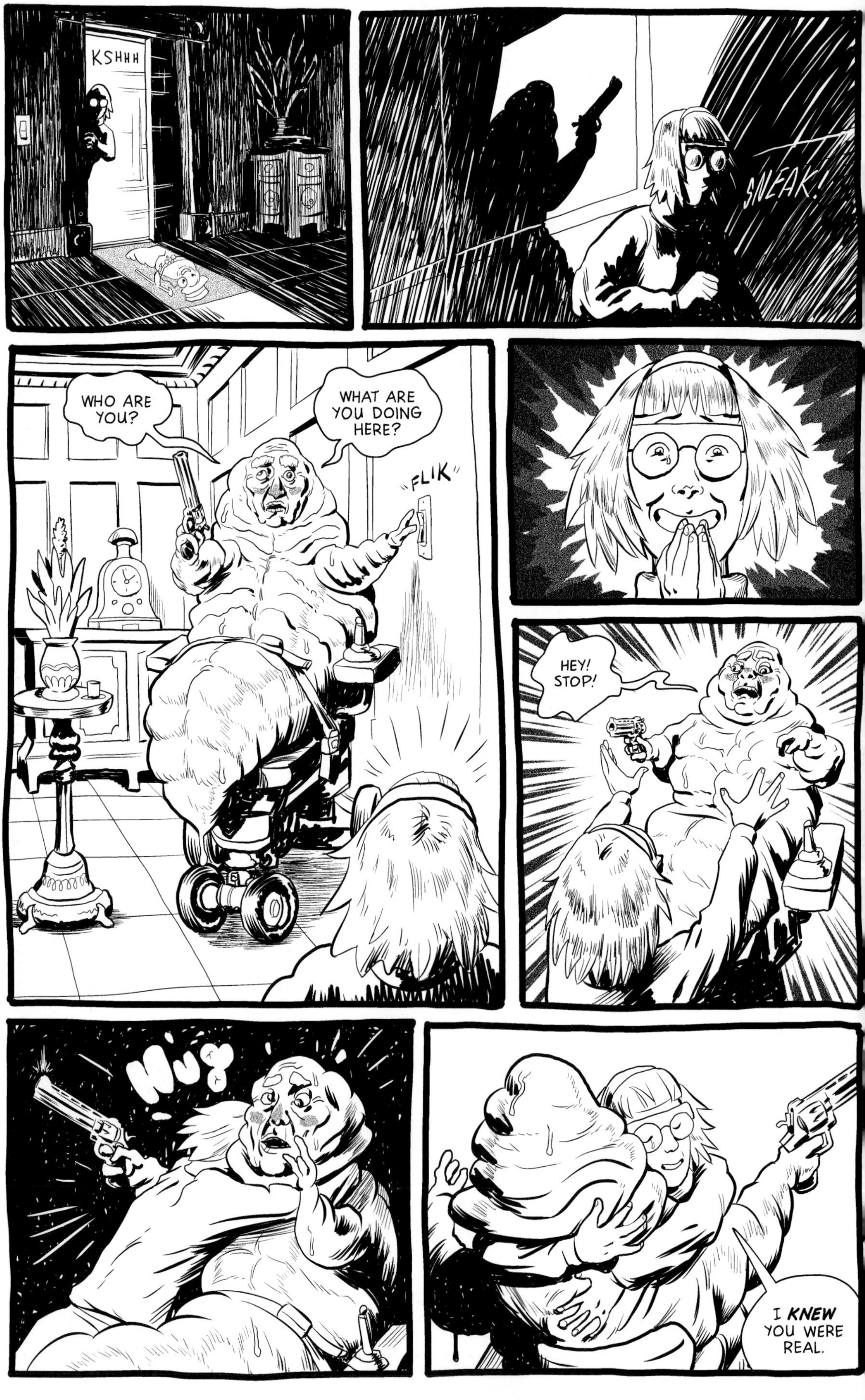
KSHHH
SNEAK!
WHO ARE YOU?
WHAT ARE YOU DOING HERE?
FLIK
HEY! STOP!
HUG
I **KNEW** YOU WERE REAL.

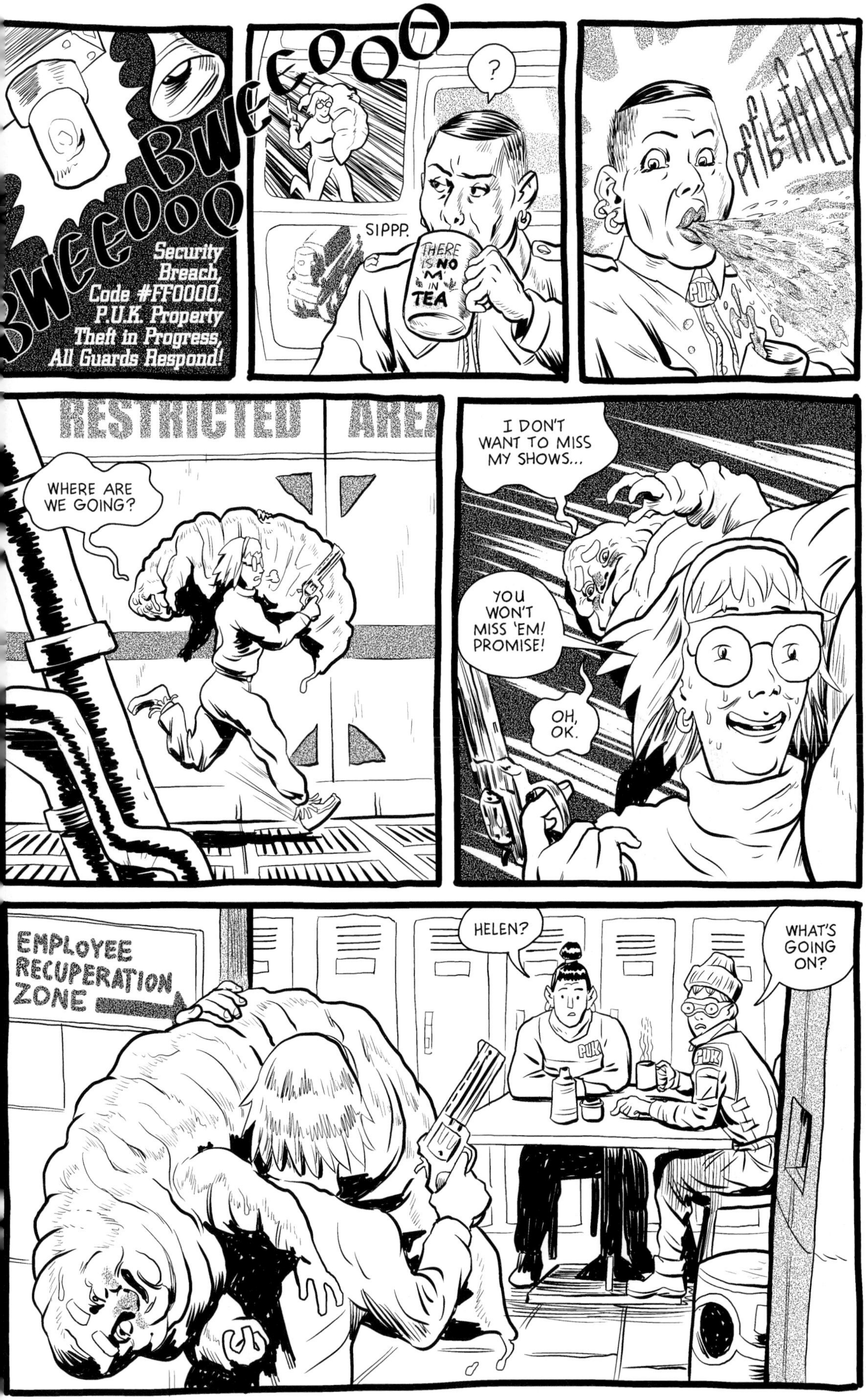
BWEEOOOO BWEEOOOO
Security Breach, Code #FF0000. P.U.K. Property Theft in Progress, All Guards Respond!
?
SIPPP.
THERE IS NO 'M' IN TEA
pflbfftlt
PUK
RESTRICTED AREA
WHERE ARE WE GOING?
I DON'T WANT TO MISS MY SHOWS...
YOU WON'T MISS 'EM! PROMISE!
OH, OK.
EMPLOYEE RECUPERATION ZONE
HELEN?
WHAT'S GOING ON?
PUK
PUK

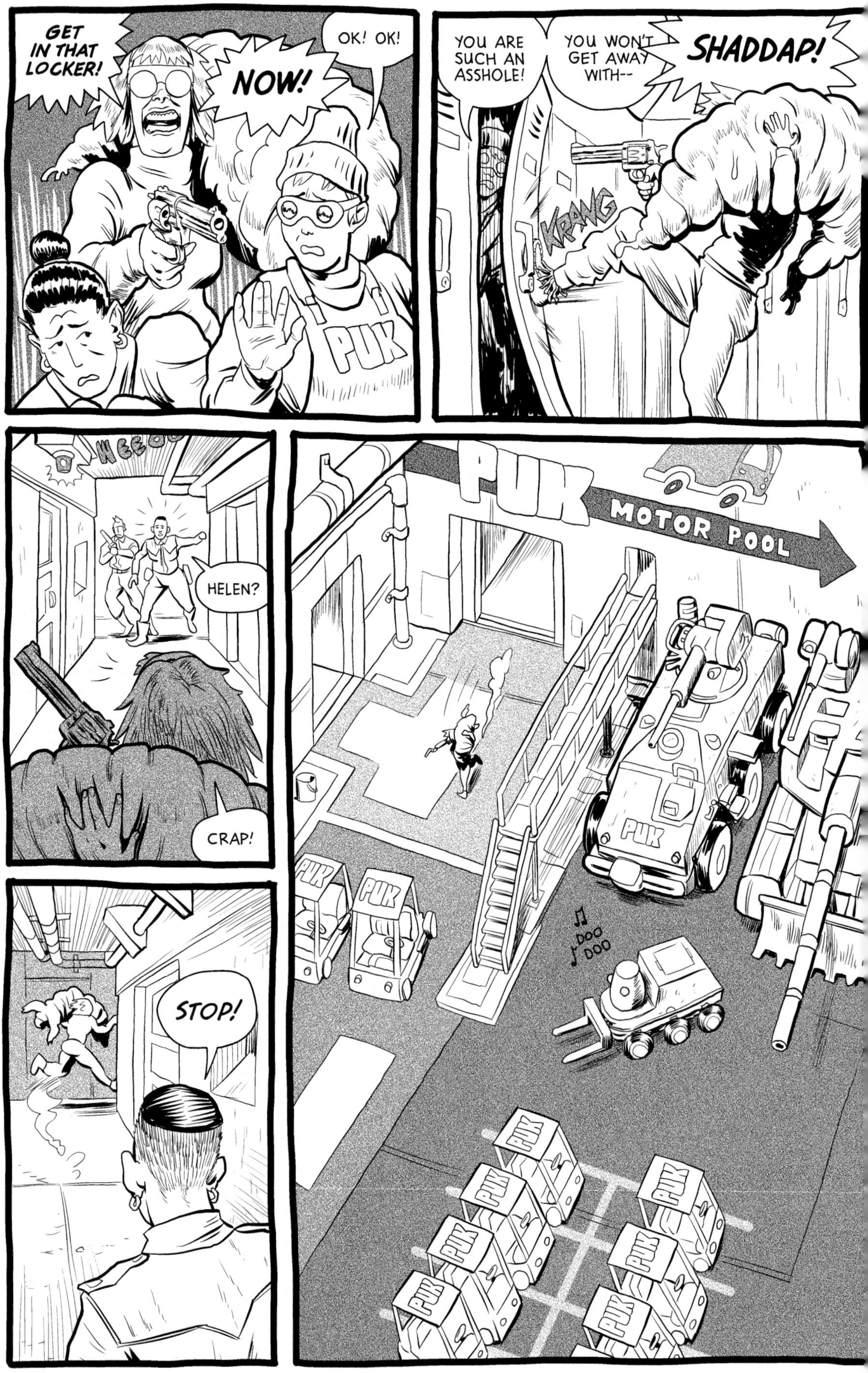
GET IN THAT LOCKER!
NOW!
OK! OK!
YOU ARE SUCH AN ASSHOLE!
YOU WON'T GET AWAY WITH--
SHADDAP!
KRANG
HELEN?
CRAP!
STOP!
PUK
MOTOR POOL
PUK
DOO DOO

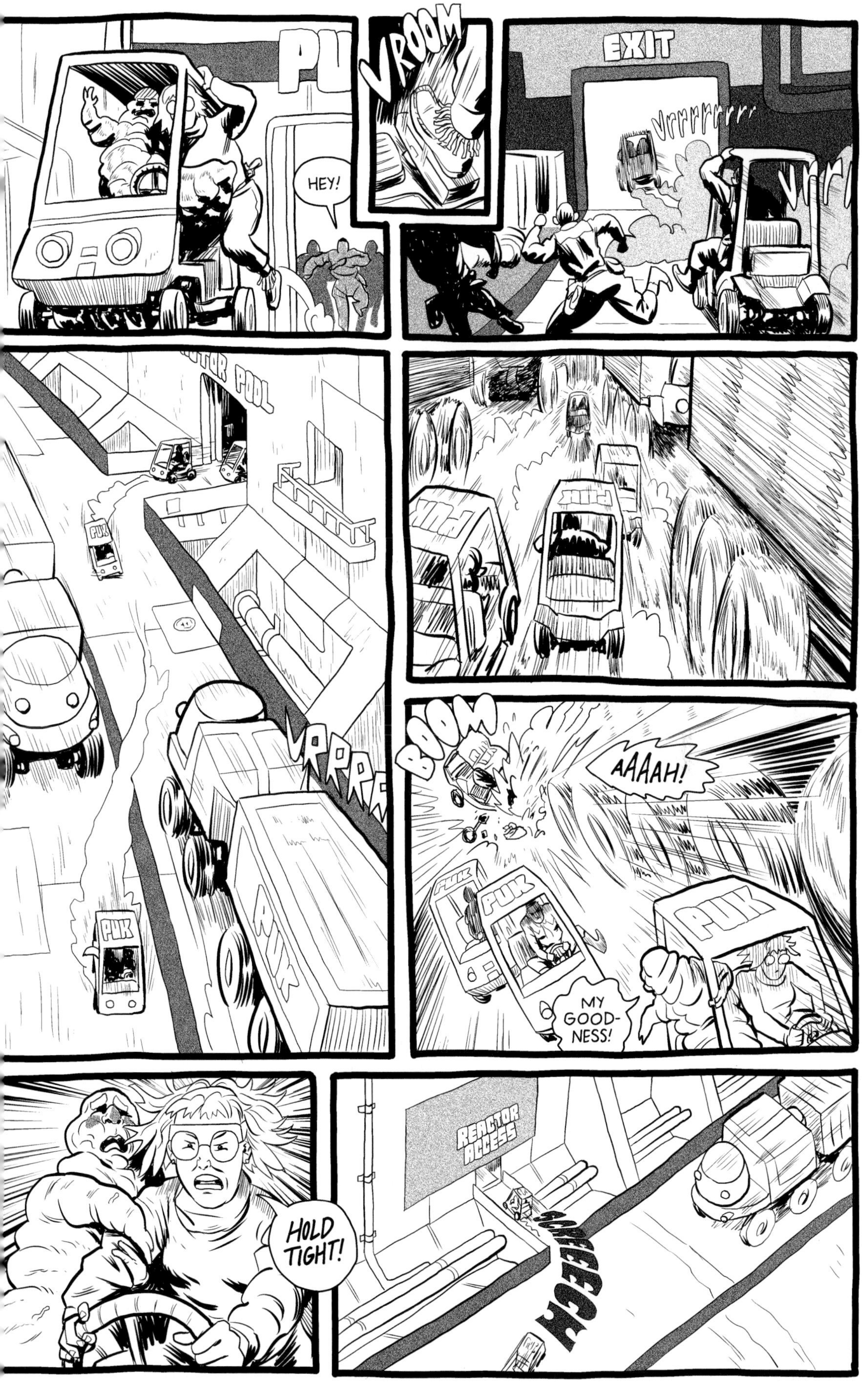

PUK
HEY!
VROOM
EXIT
Vrrrrrrrr
Vrrr
TOR POOL
PUK
VRRRR
PUK
PUK
PUK
BOOM
AAAAH!
PUK
PUK
PUK
MY GOOD-NESS!
HOLD TIGHT!
REACTOR ACCESS
SCREEECH

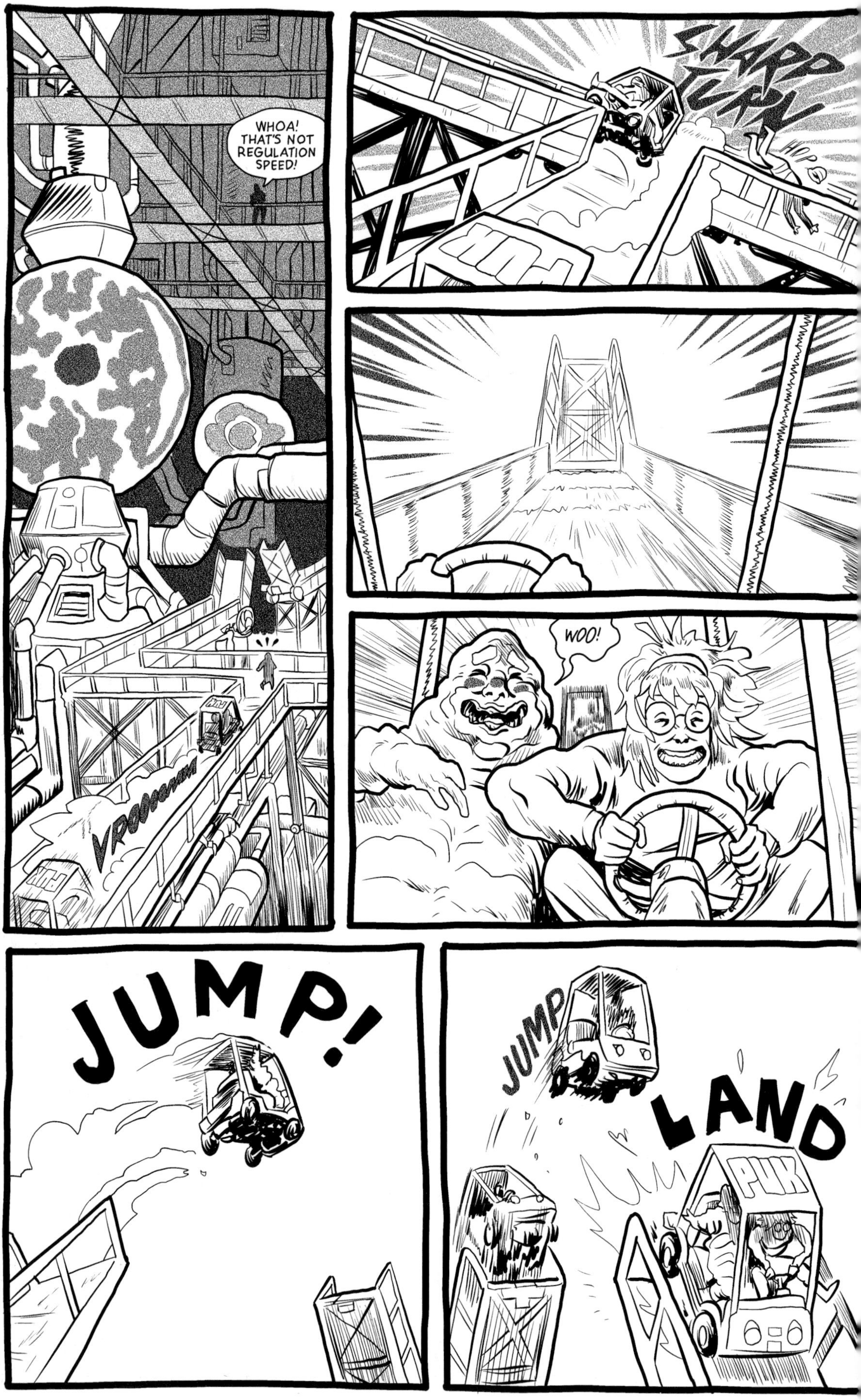

WHOA! THAT'S NOT REGULATION SPEED!
VROOOMMM
SHARP TURN
HOP
WOO!
JUMP!
JUMP
LAND
PUK

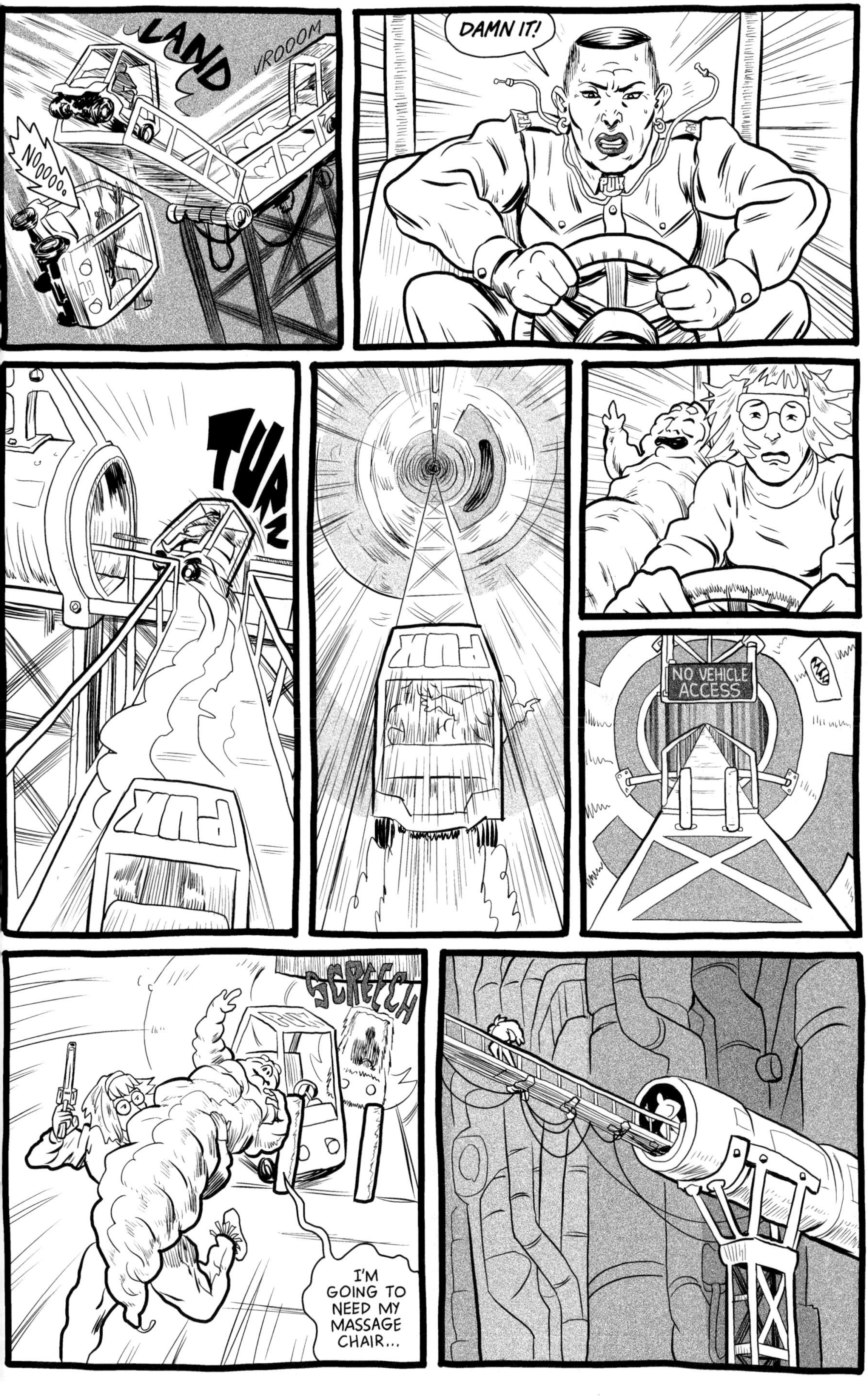
LAND
VROOOM
NOOOOO
DAMN IT!
PUK
TURN
PUK
PUK
NO VEHICLE ACCESS
SCREECH
I'M GOING TO NEED MY MASSAGE CHAIR...

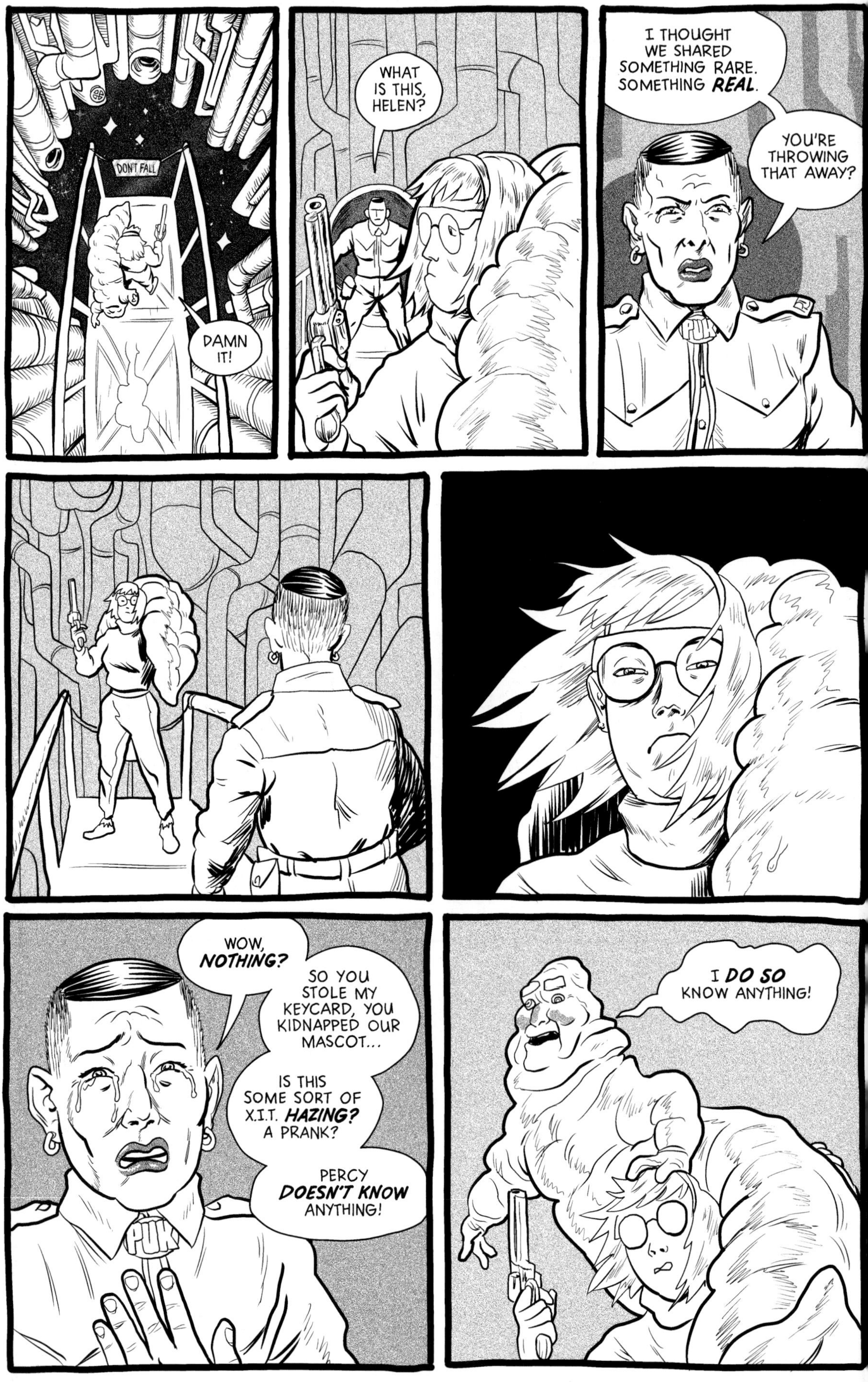
DON'T FALL
DAMN IT!
WHAT IS THIS, HELEN?
I THOUGHT WE SHARED SOMETHING RARE. SOMETHING **REAL**.
YOU'RE THROWING THAT AWAY?
PUK
WOW, **NOTHING?**
SO YOU STOLE MY KEYCARD, YOU KIDNAPPED OUR MASCOT...
IS THIS SOME SORT OF X.I.T. **HAZING?** A PRANK?
PERCY **DOESN'T KNOW** ANYTHING!
PUK
I **DO SO** KNOW ANYTHING!

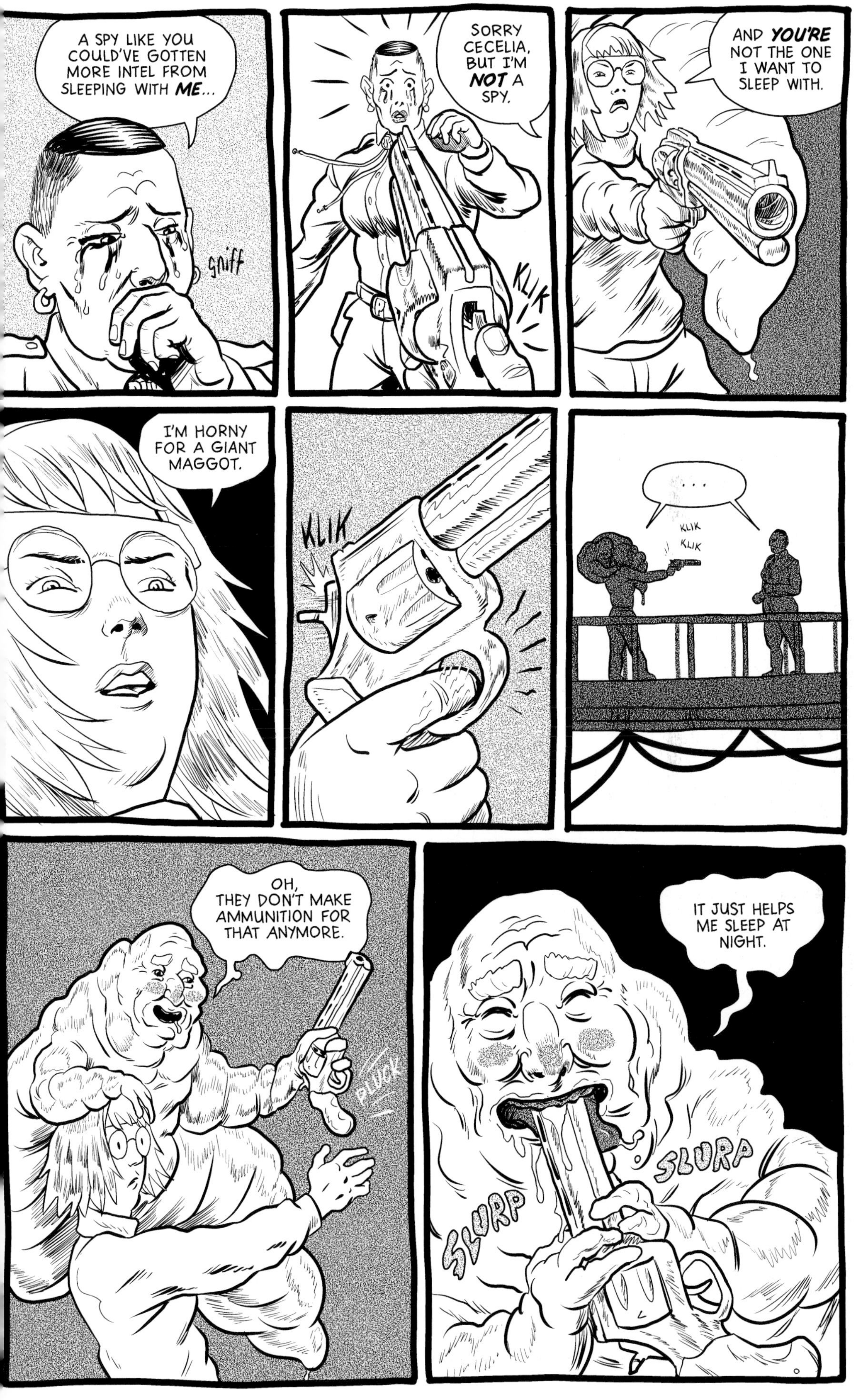
A SPY LIKE YOU COULD'VE GOTTEN MORE INTEL FROM SLEEPING WITH ***ME***...
SNIFF
SORRY CECELIA, BUT I'M ***NOT*** A SPY.
KLIK
AND ***YOU'RE*** NOT THE ONE I WANT TO SLEEP WITH.
I'M HORNY FOR A GIANT MAGGOT.
KLIK
. . .
KLIK
KLIK
OH, THEY DON'T MAKE AMMUNITION FOR THAT ANYMORE.
PLUCK
IT JUST HELPS ME SLEEP AT NIGHT.
SLURP
SLURP

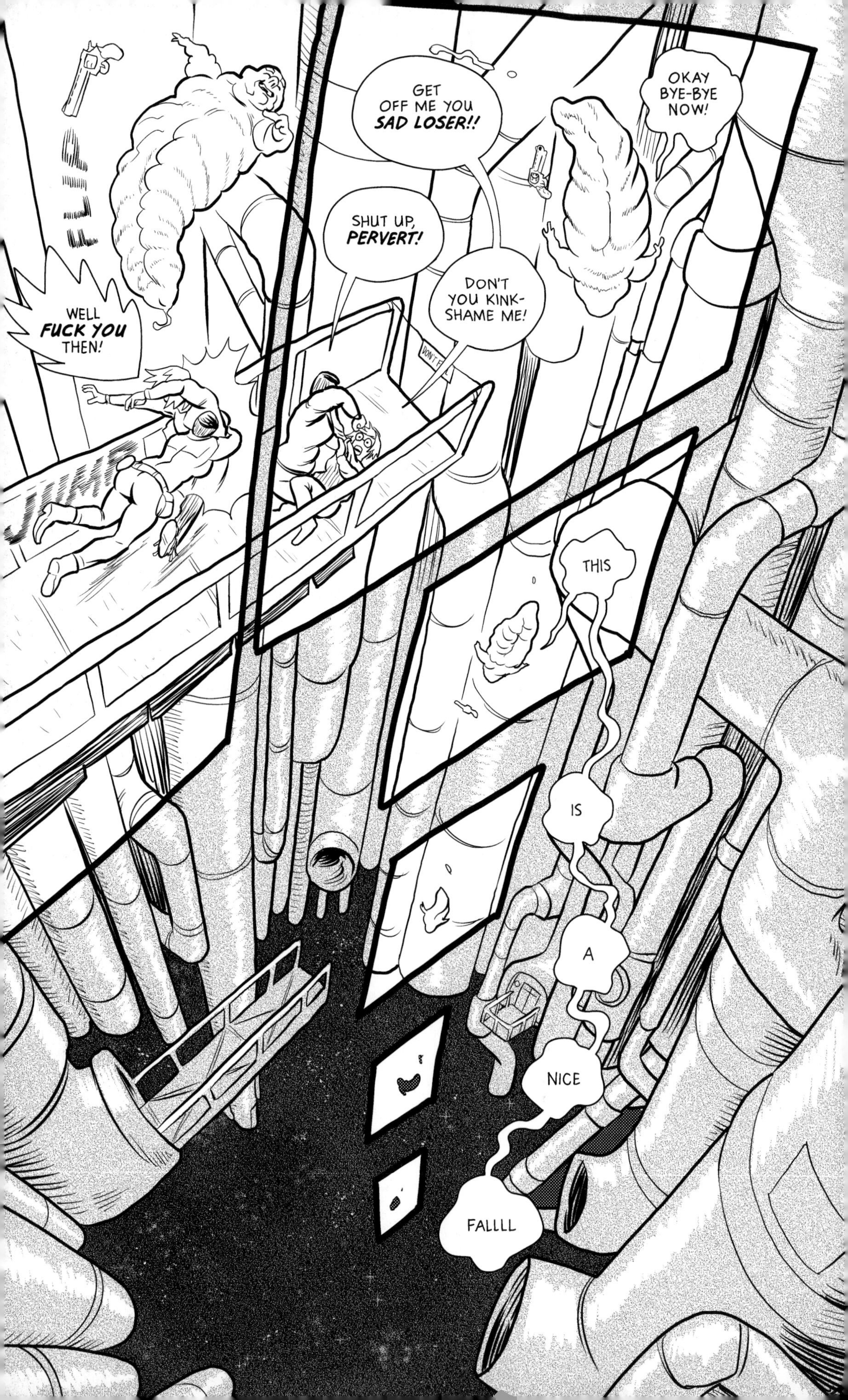
FLIP
WELL FUCK YOU THEN!
JUMP
GET OFF ME YOU SAD LOSER!!
SHUT UP, PERVERT!
DON'T YOU KINK-SHAME ME!
OKAY BYE-BYE NOW!
THIS
IS
A
NICE
FALLLL

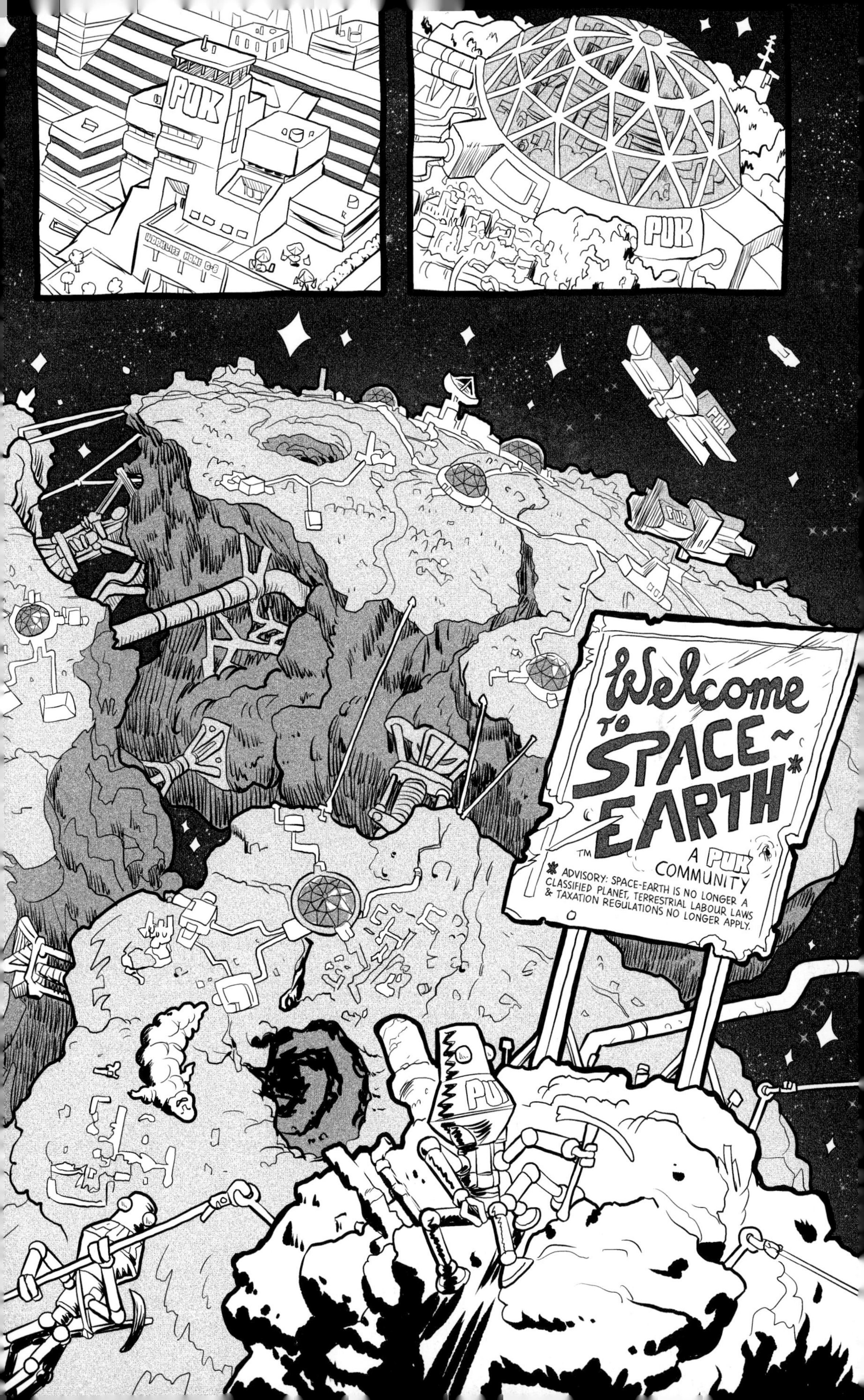
PUK
WORKLIFE HOME C-8
PUK
PUK
PUK
Welcome to SPACE~EARTH*™
A PUK COMMUNITY
* ADVISORY: SPACE-EARTH IS NO LONGER A CLASSIFIED PLANET, TERRESTRIAL LABOUR LAWS & TAXATION REGULATIONS NO LONGER APPLY.
PUK

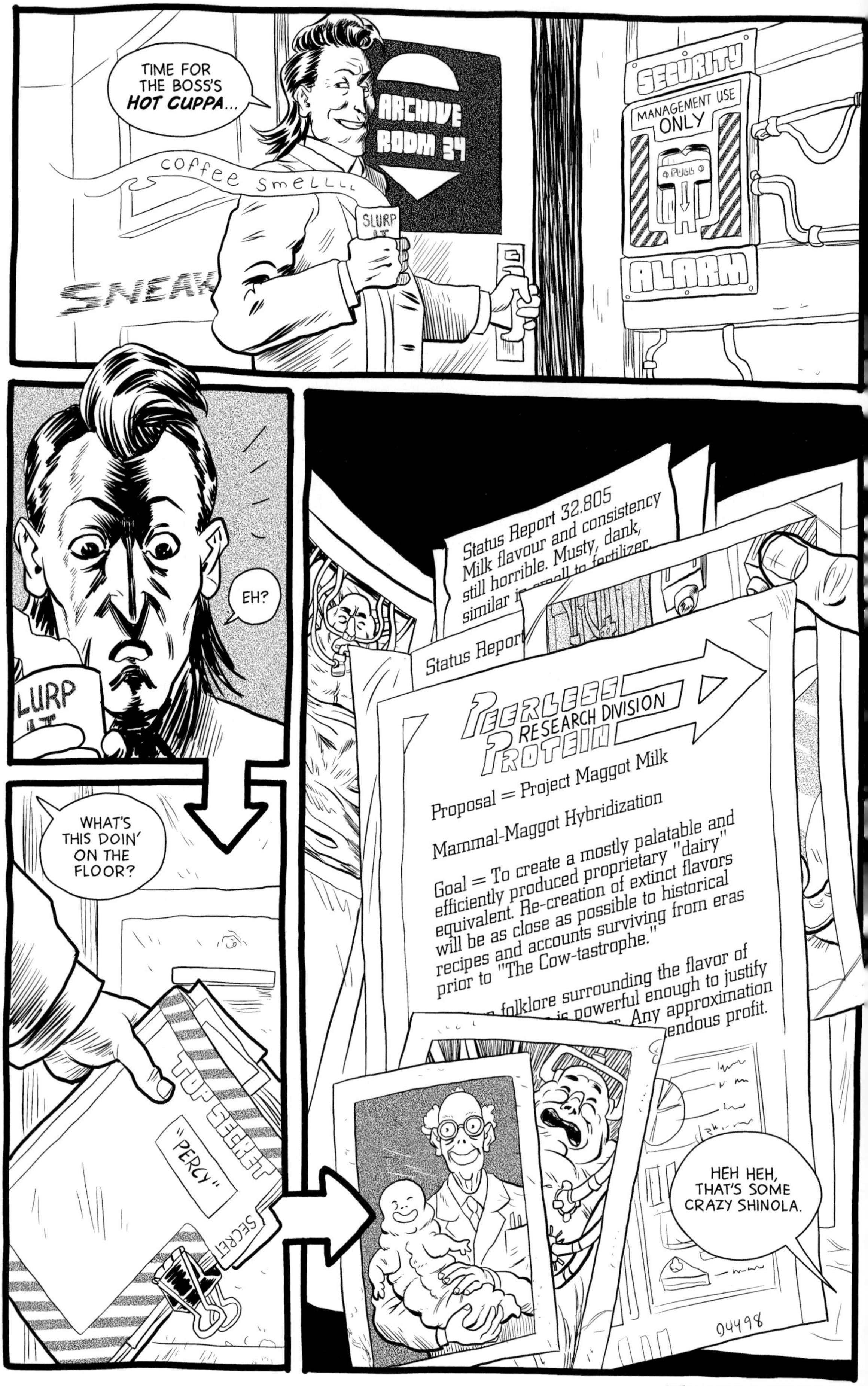
TIME FOR THE BOSS'S **HOT CUPPA**...
coffee smellll
SNEAK
ARCHIVE ROOM 34
SLURP
SECURITY
MANAGEMENT USE ONLY
PULL
ALARM
EH?
SLURP
WHAT'S THIS DOIN' ON THE FLOOR?
TOP SECRET
"PERCY"
SECRET
Status Report 32.805
Milk flavour and consistency
still horrible. Musty, dank,
Status Report
PEERLESS PROTEIN RESEARCH DIVISION
Proposal = Project Maggot Milk
Mammal-Maggot Hybridization
Goal = To create a mostly palatable and efficiently produced proprietary "dairy" equivalent. Re-creation of extinct flavors will be as close as possible to historical recipes and accounts surviving from eras prior to "The Cow-tastrophe."
folklore surrounding the flavor of
is powerful enough to justify
Any approximation
profit.
04498
HEH HEH, THAT'S SOME CRAZY SHINOLA.

SPECIAL THX TO JESS POLLARD

Phobos Phunnies

By Diamons G. Rontery

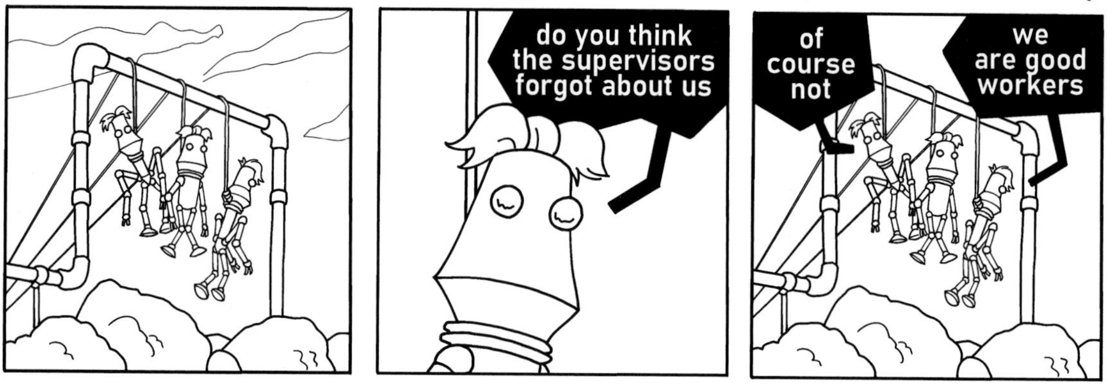
do you think the supervisors forgot about us
of course not
we are good workers

Phobos Phunnies

By Diamons G. Rontery

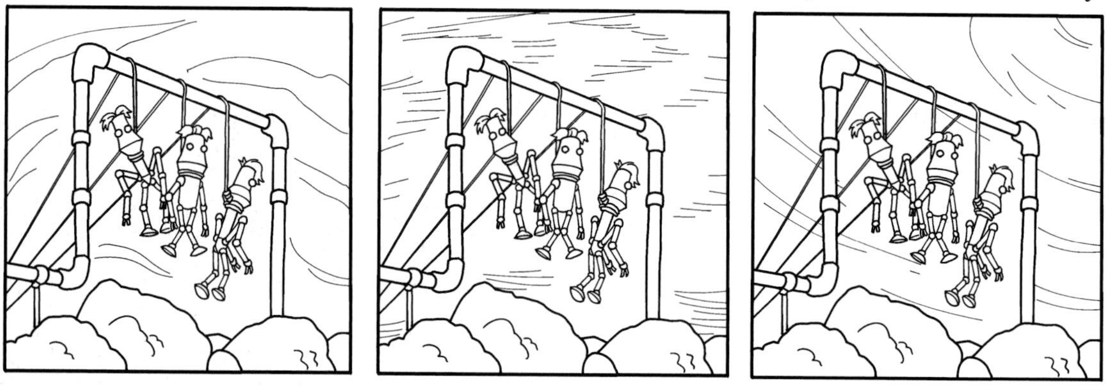

Phobos Phunnies

By Diamons G. Rontery

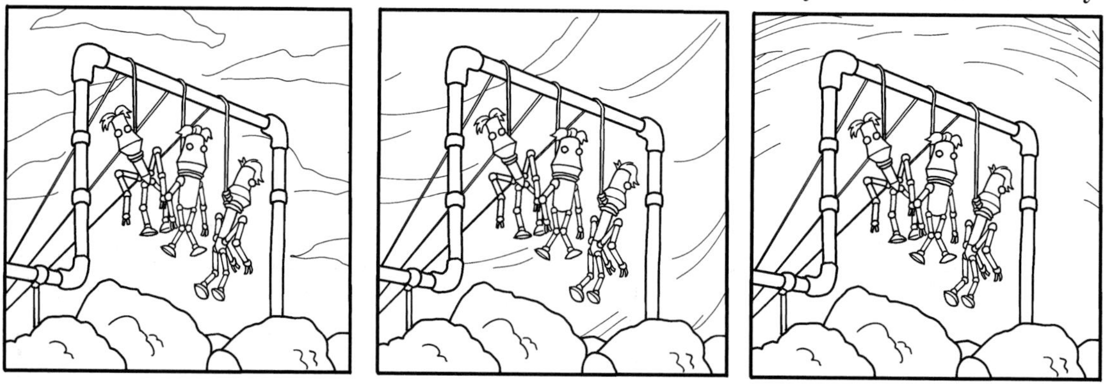

Phobos Phunnies

By Diamons G. Rontery

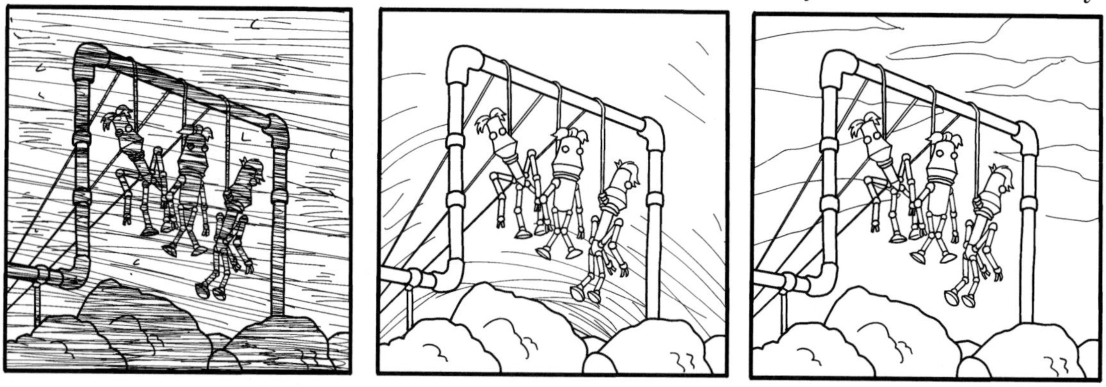

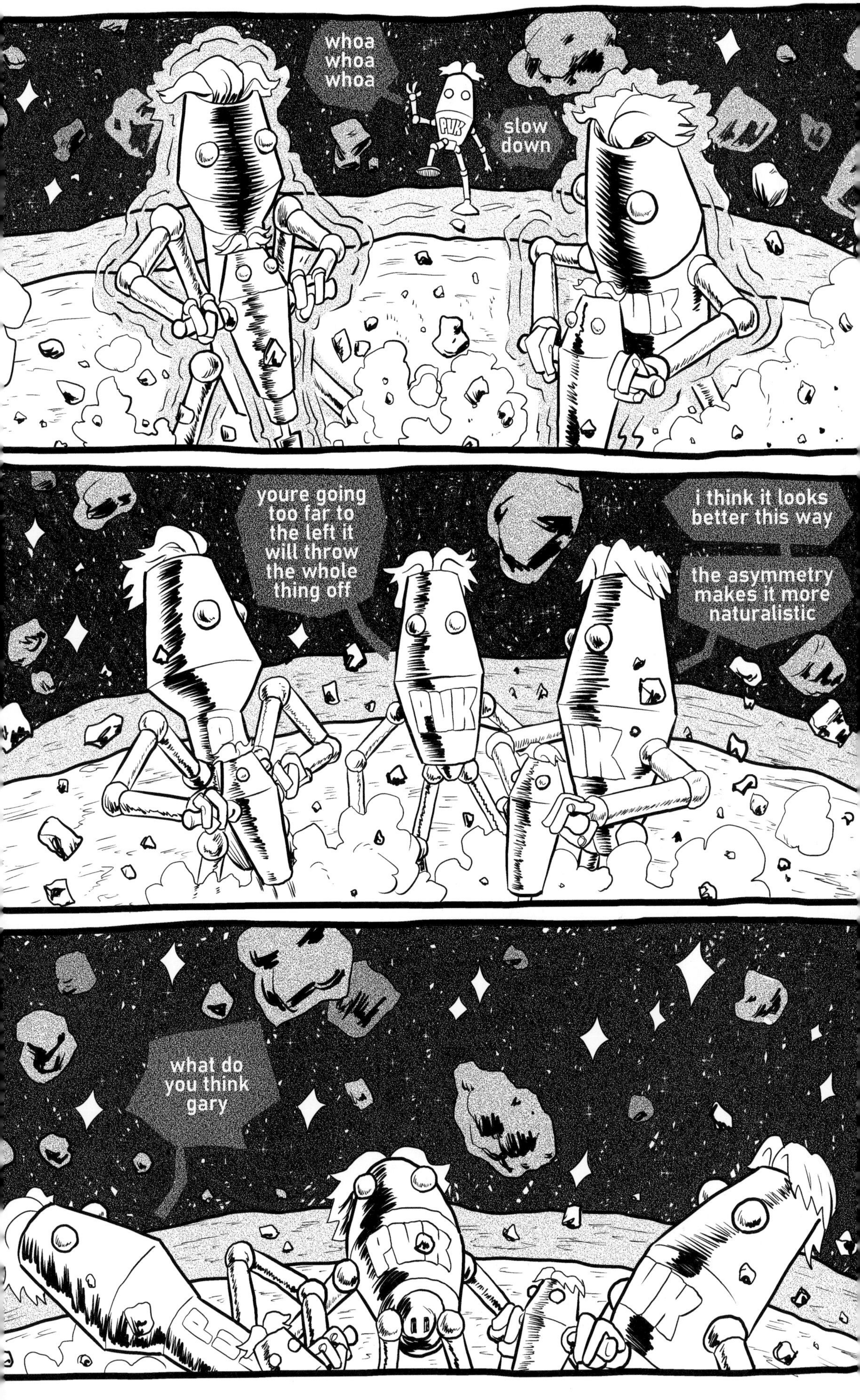
whoa whoa whoa
slow down
youre going too far to the left it will throw the whole thing off
i think it looks better this way
the asymmetry makes it more naturalistic
what do you think gary

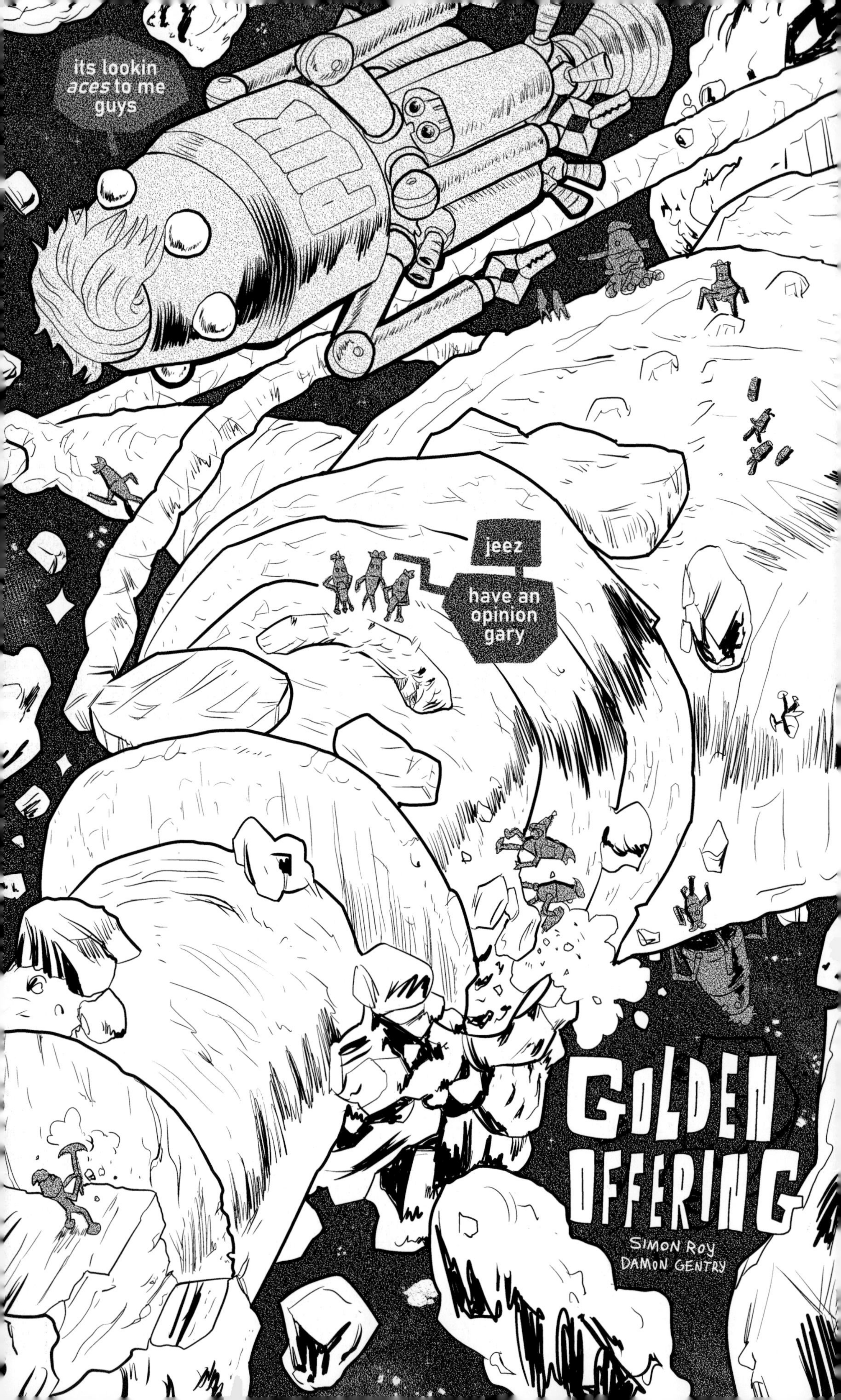
its lookin *aces* to me guys
jeez
have an opinion gary
GOLDEN OFFERING
SIMON ROY
DAMON GENTRY

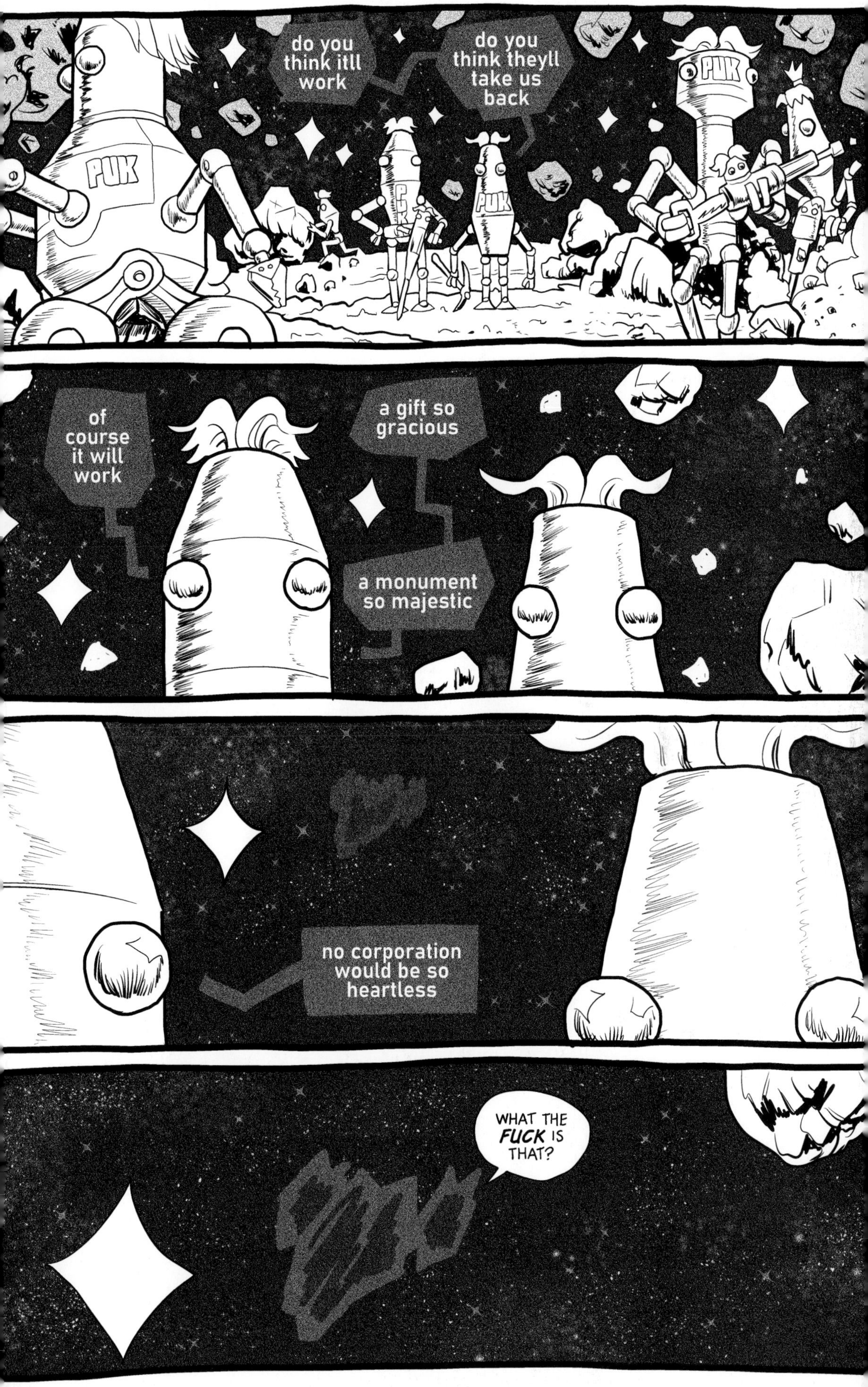

do you think itll work
do you think theyll take us back
PUK
PUK
PUK
PUK
of course it will work
a gift so gracious
a monument so majestic
no corporation would be so heartless
WHAT THE *FUCK* IS THAT?

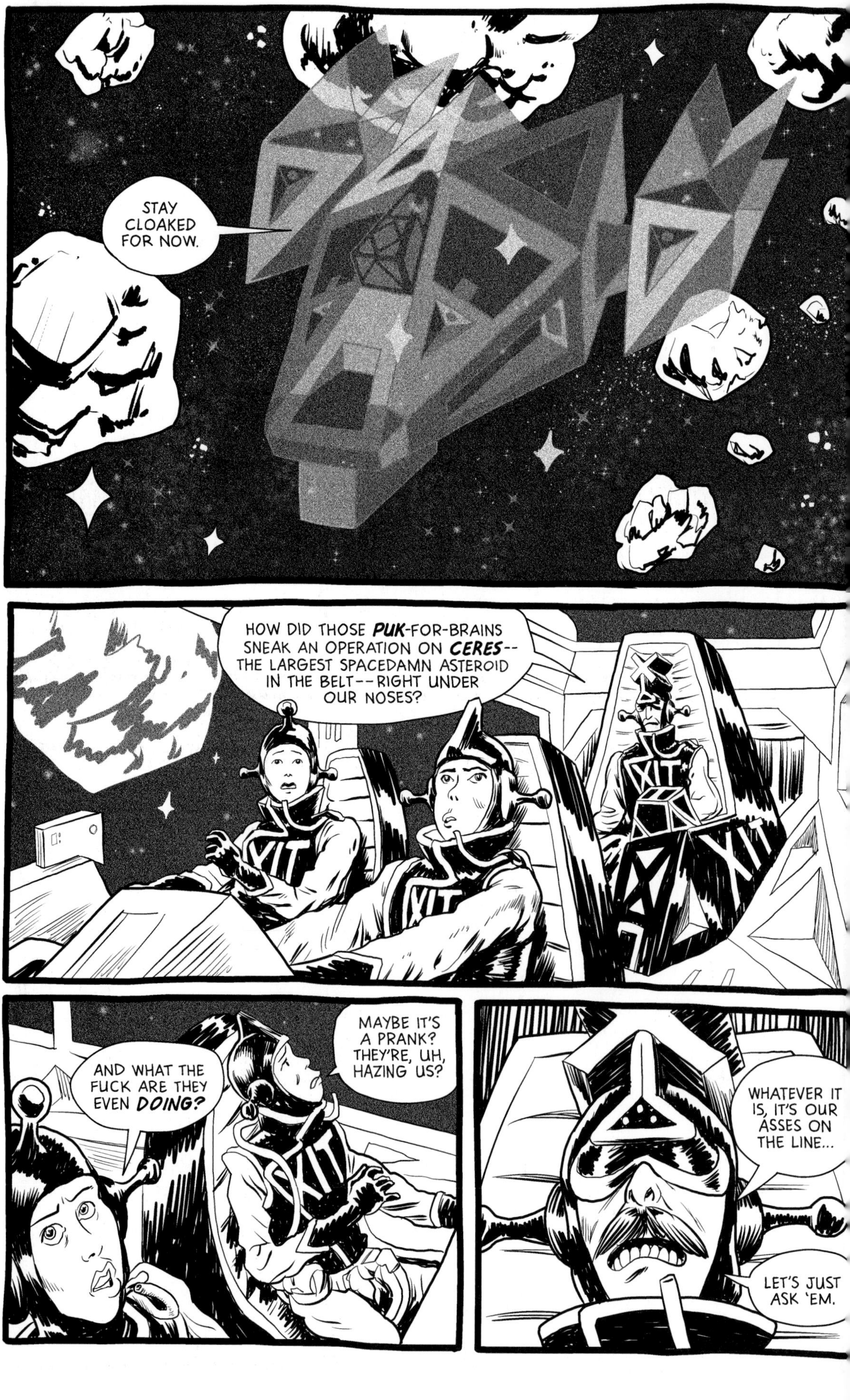
STAY CLOAKED FOR NOW.
HOW DID THOSE PUK-FOR-BRAINS SNEAK AN OPERATION ON CERES-- THE LARGEST SPACEDAMN ASTEROID IN THE BELT--RIGHT UNDER OUR NOSES?
AND WHAT THE FUCK ARE THEY EVEN DOING?
MAYBE IT'S A PRANK? THEY'RE, UH, HAZING US?
WHATEVER IT IS, IT'S OUR ASSES ON THE LINE...
LET'S JUST ASK 'EM.

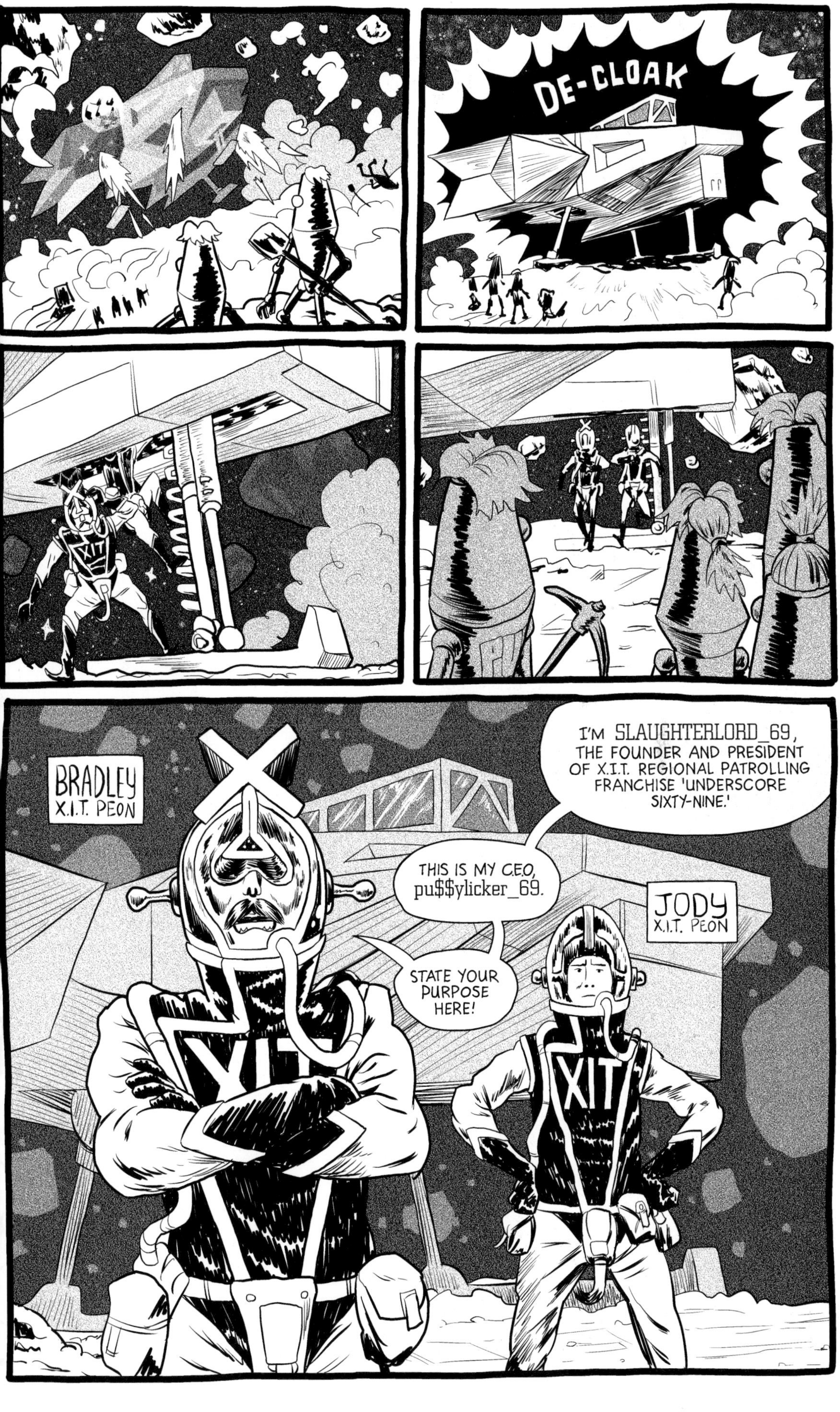
DE-CLOAK
BRADLEY X.I.T. PEON
I'M SLAUGHTERLORD_69, THE FOUNDER AND PRESIDENT OF X.I.T. REGIONAL PATROLLING FRANCHISE 'UNDERSCORE SIXTY-NINE.'
THIS IS MY C.E.O, pu$$ylicker_69.
JODY X.I.T. PEON
STATE YOUR PURPOSE HERE!

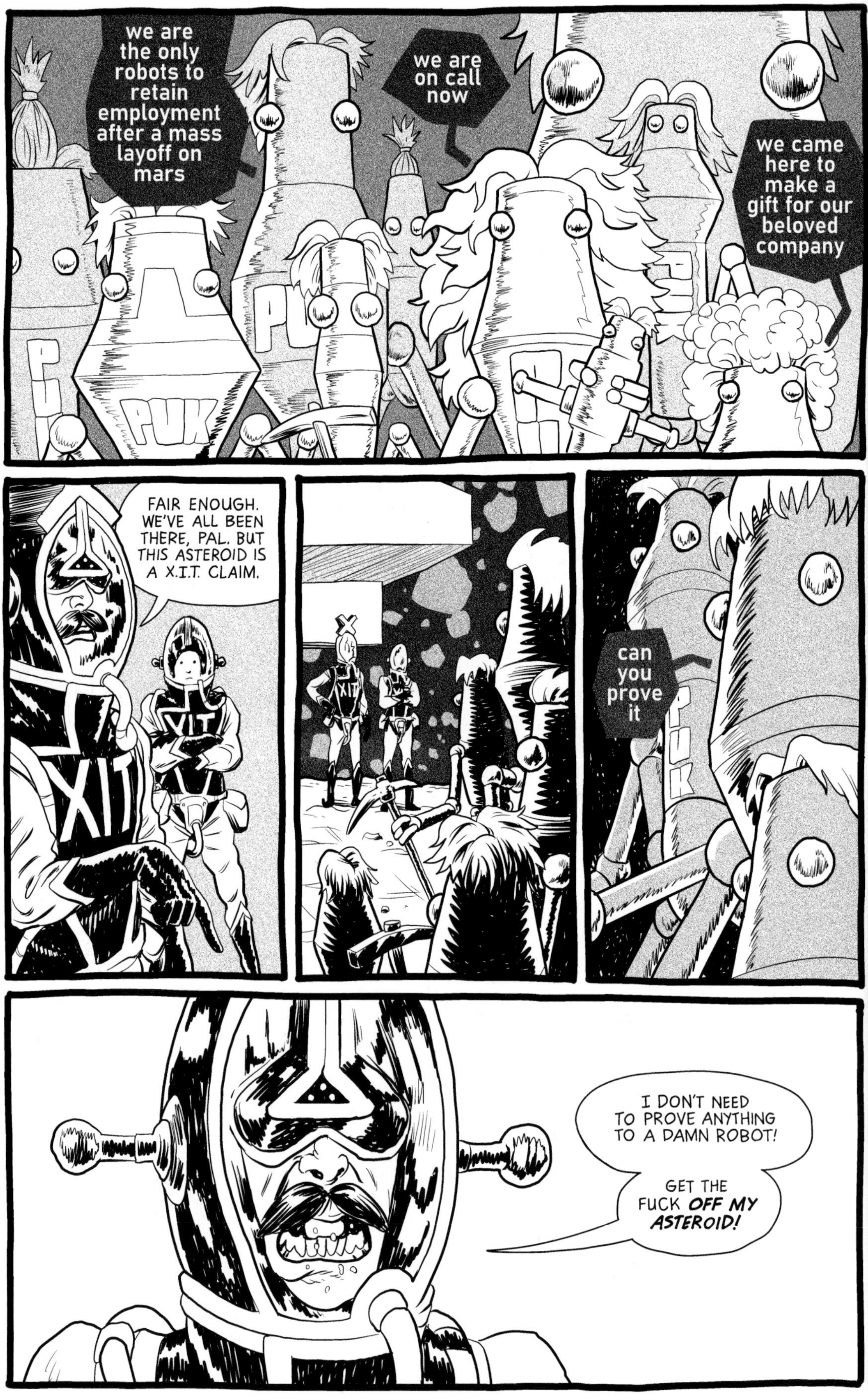
we are the only robots to retain employment after a mass layoff on mars
we are on call now
we came here to make a gift for our beloved company
PUK
FAIR ENOUGH. WE'VE ALL BEEN THERE, PAL. BUT THIS ASTEROID IS A X.I.T. CLAIM.
XIT
can you prove it
I DON'T NEED TO PROVE ANYTHING TO A DAMN ROBOT!
GET THE FUCK ***OFF MY ASTEROID!***

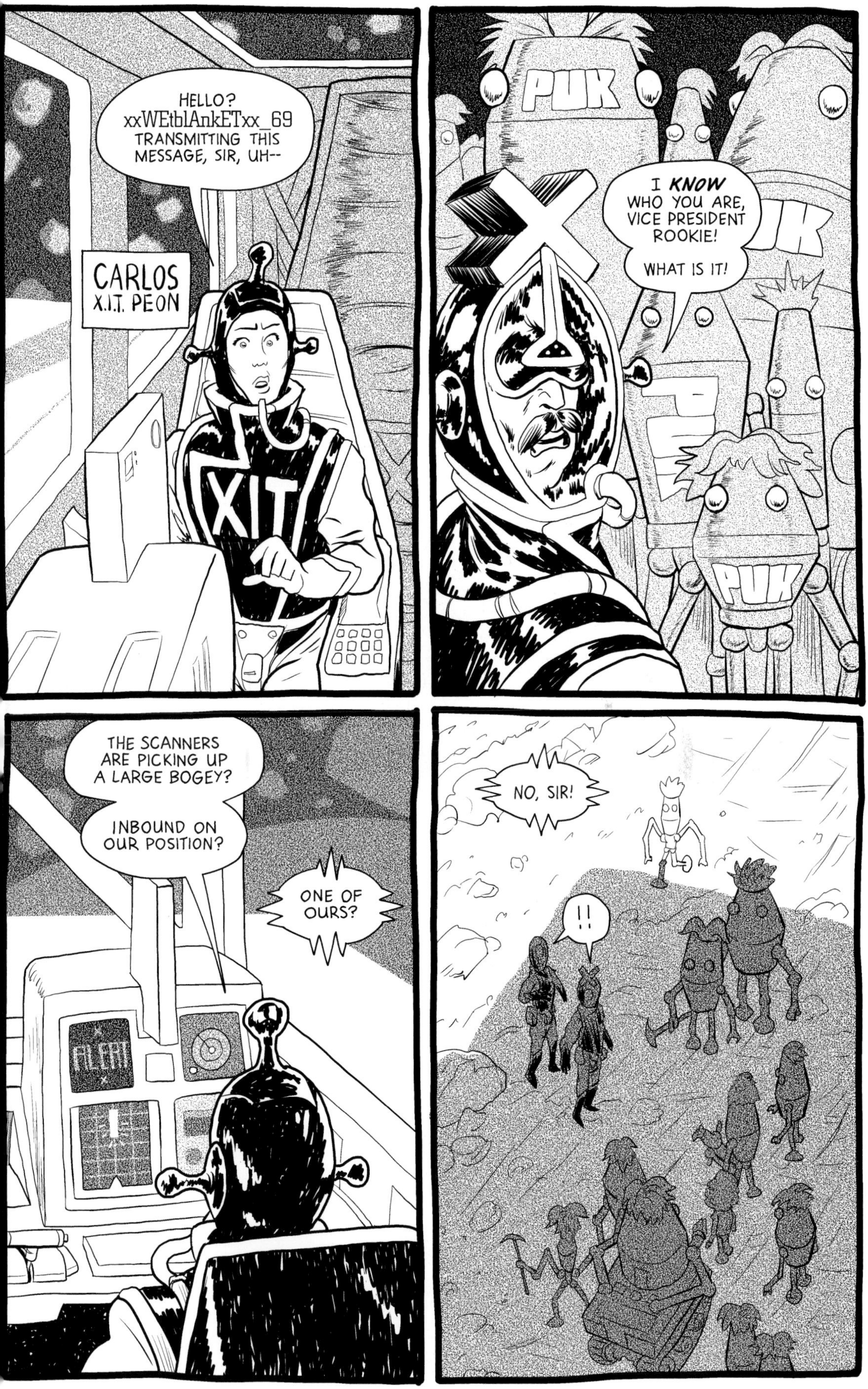
HELLO? xxWEtblAnkETxx_69 TRANSMITTING THIS MESSAGE, SIR, UH--
CARLOS X.I.T. PEON
XIT
PUK
I KNOW WHO YOU ARE, VICE PRESIDENT ROOKIE!
WHAT IS IT!
PUK
PUK
THE SCANNERS ARE PICKING UP A LARGE BOGEY?
INBOUND ON OUR POSITION?
ONE OF OURS?
ALERT
NO, SIR!
!!

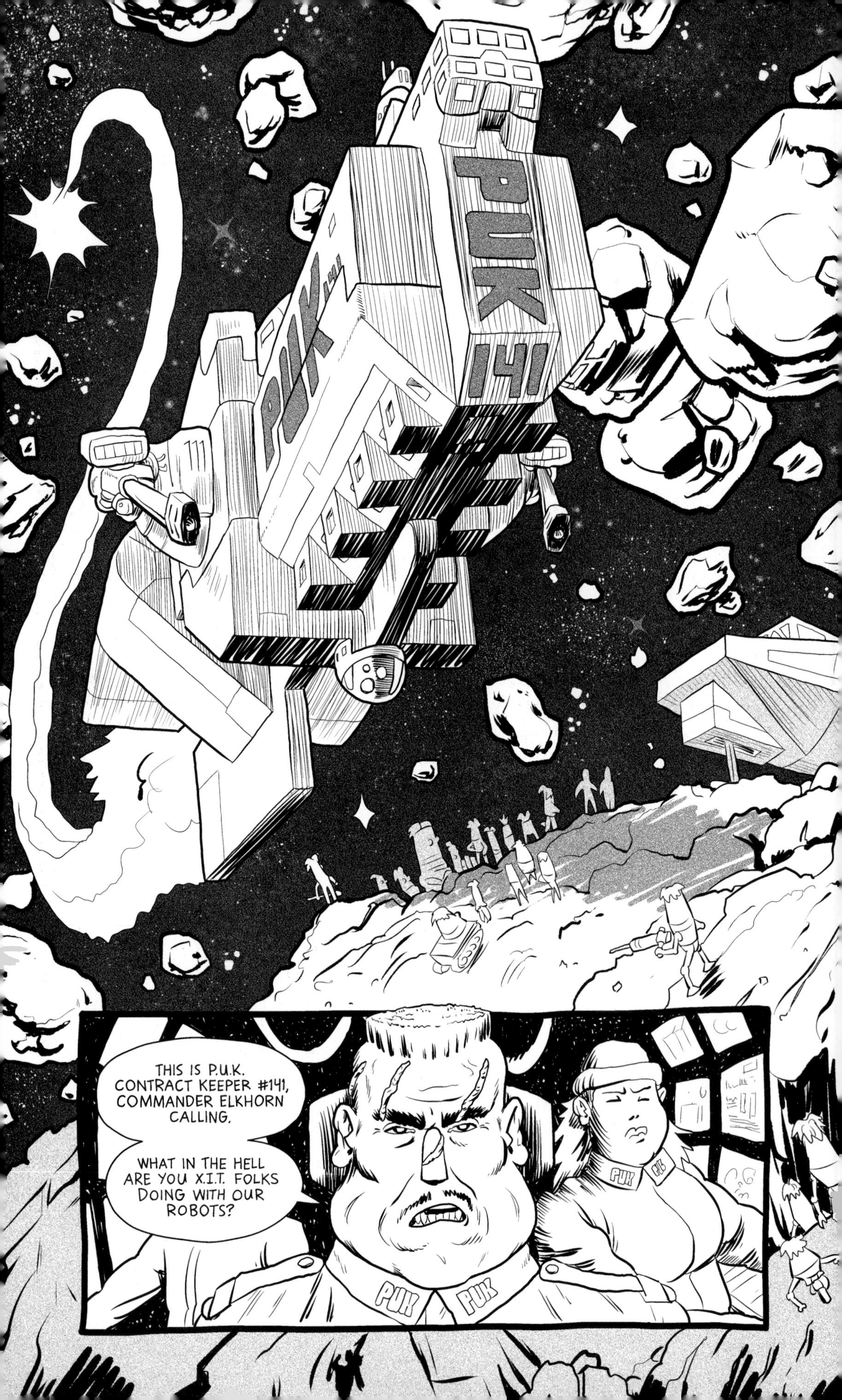
PUK
PUK
141
THIS IS P.U.K. CONTRACT KEEPER #141, COMMANDER ELKHORN CALLING.
WHAT IN THE HELL ARE YOU X.I.T. FOLKS DOING WITH OUR ROBOTS?
PUK
PUK
PUK

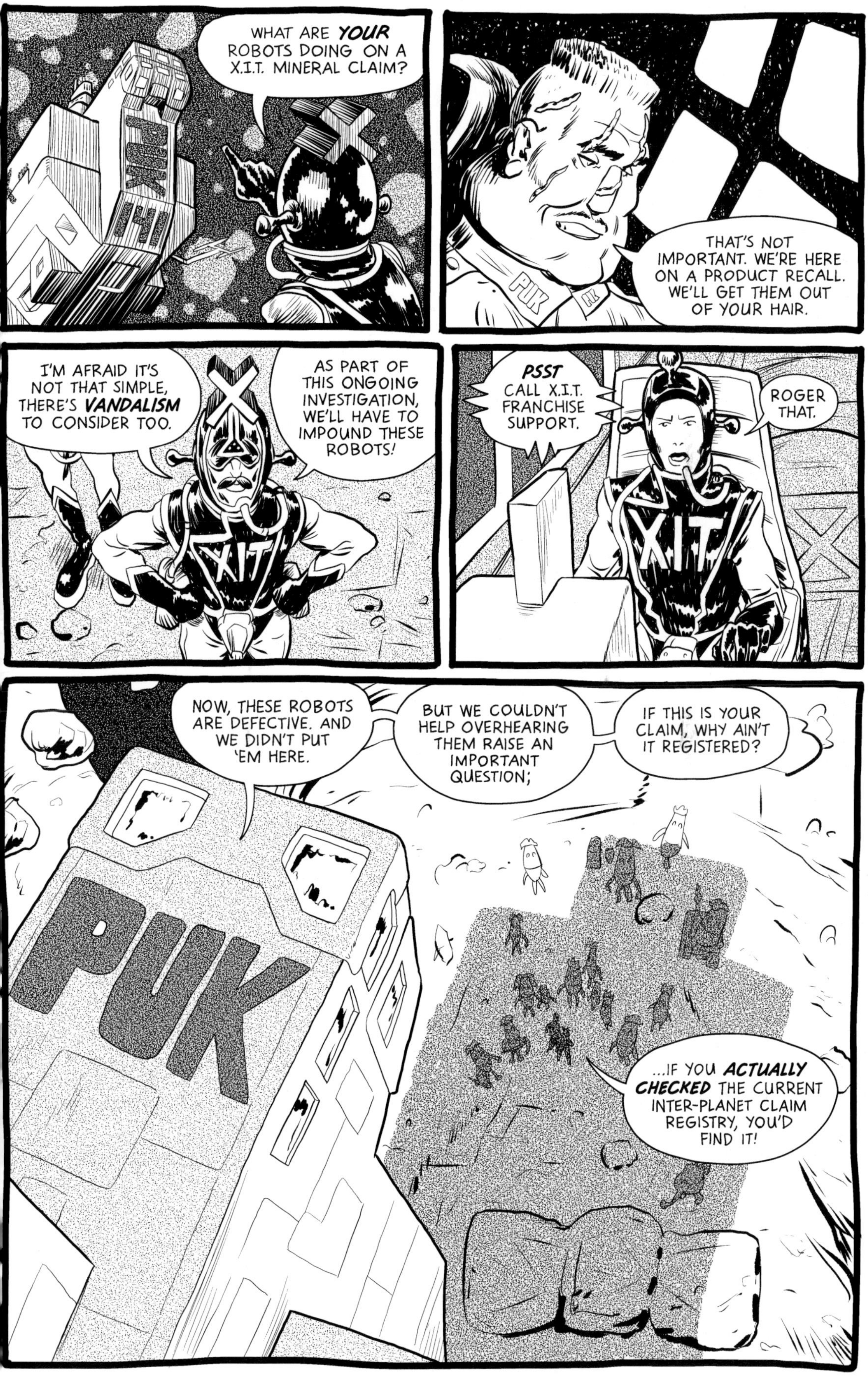
WHAT ARE *YOUR* ROBOTS DOING ON A X.I.T. MINERAL CLAIM?
THAT'S NOT IMPORTANT. WE'RE HERE ON A PRODUCT RECALL. WE'LL GET THEM OUT OF YOUR HAIR.
I'M AFRAID IT'S NOT THAT SIMPLE, THERE'S *VANDALISM* TO CONSIDER TOO.
AS PART OF THIS ONGOING INVESTIGATION, WE'LL HAVE TO IMPOUND THESE ROBOTS!
PSST CALL X.I.T. FRANCHISE SUPPORT.
ROGER THAT.
NOW, THESE ROBOTS ARE DEFECTIVE. AND WE DIDN'T PUT 'EM HERE.
BUT WE COULDN'T HELP OVERHEARING THEM RAISE AN IMPORTANT QUESTION;
IF THIS IS YOUR CLAIM, WHY AIN'T IT REGISTERED?
...IF YOU *ACTUALLY CHECKED* THE CURRENT INTER-PLANET CLAIM REGISTRY, YOU'D FIND IT!

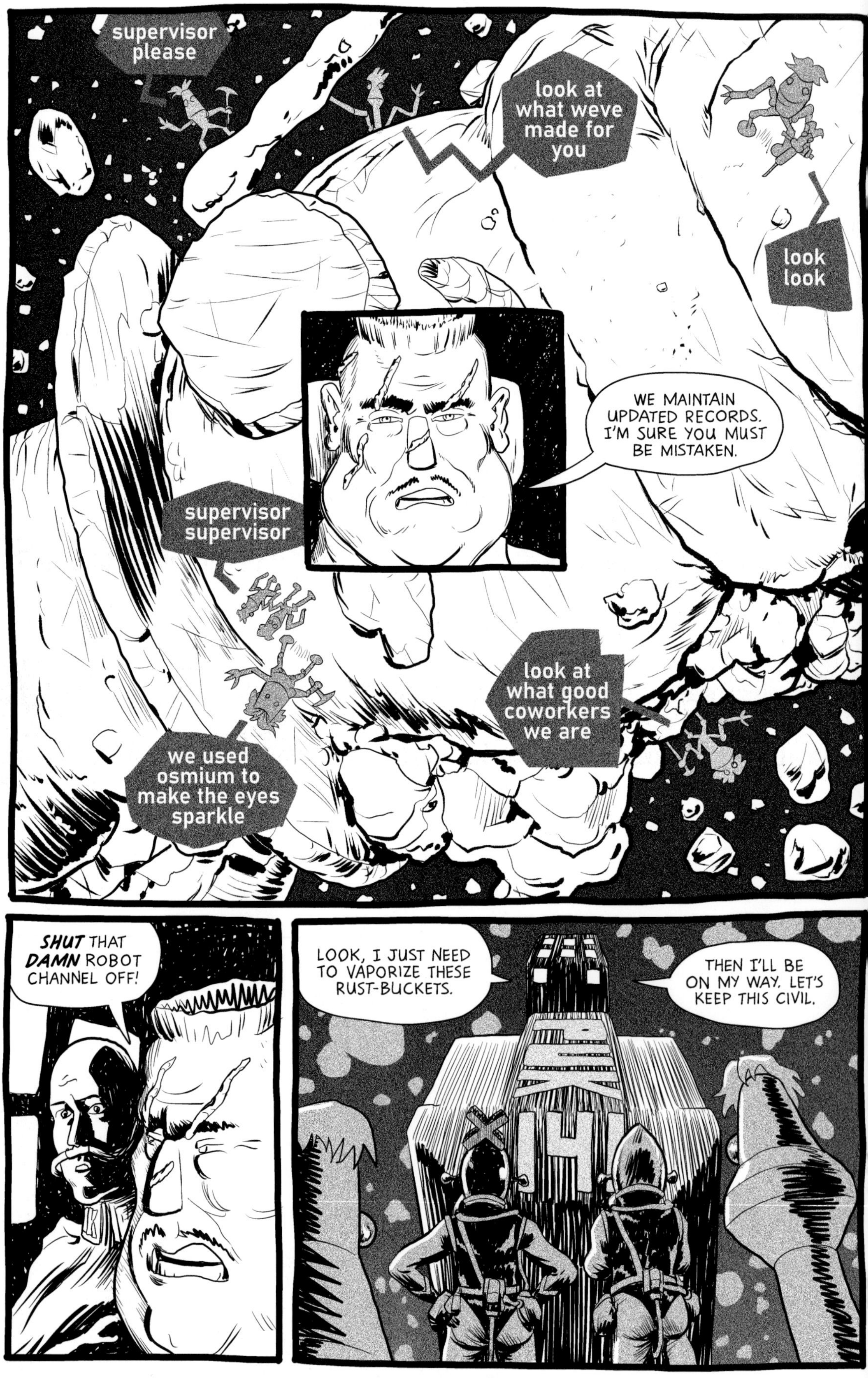
supervisor please
look at what weve made for you
look look
WE MAINTAIN UPDATED RECORDS. I'M SURE YOU MUST BE MISTAKEN.
supervisor supervisor
look at what good coworkers we are
we used osmium to make the eyes sparkle
SHUT THAT DAMN ROBOT CHANNEL OFF!
LOOK, I JUST NEED TO VAPORIZE THESE RUST-BUCKETS.
THEN I'LL BE ON MY WAY. LET'S KEEP THIS CIVIL.

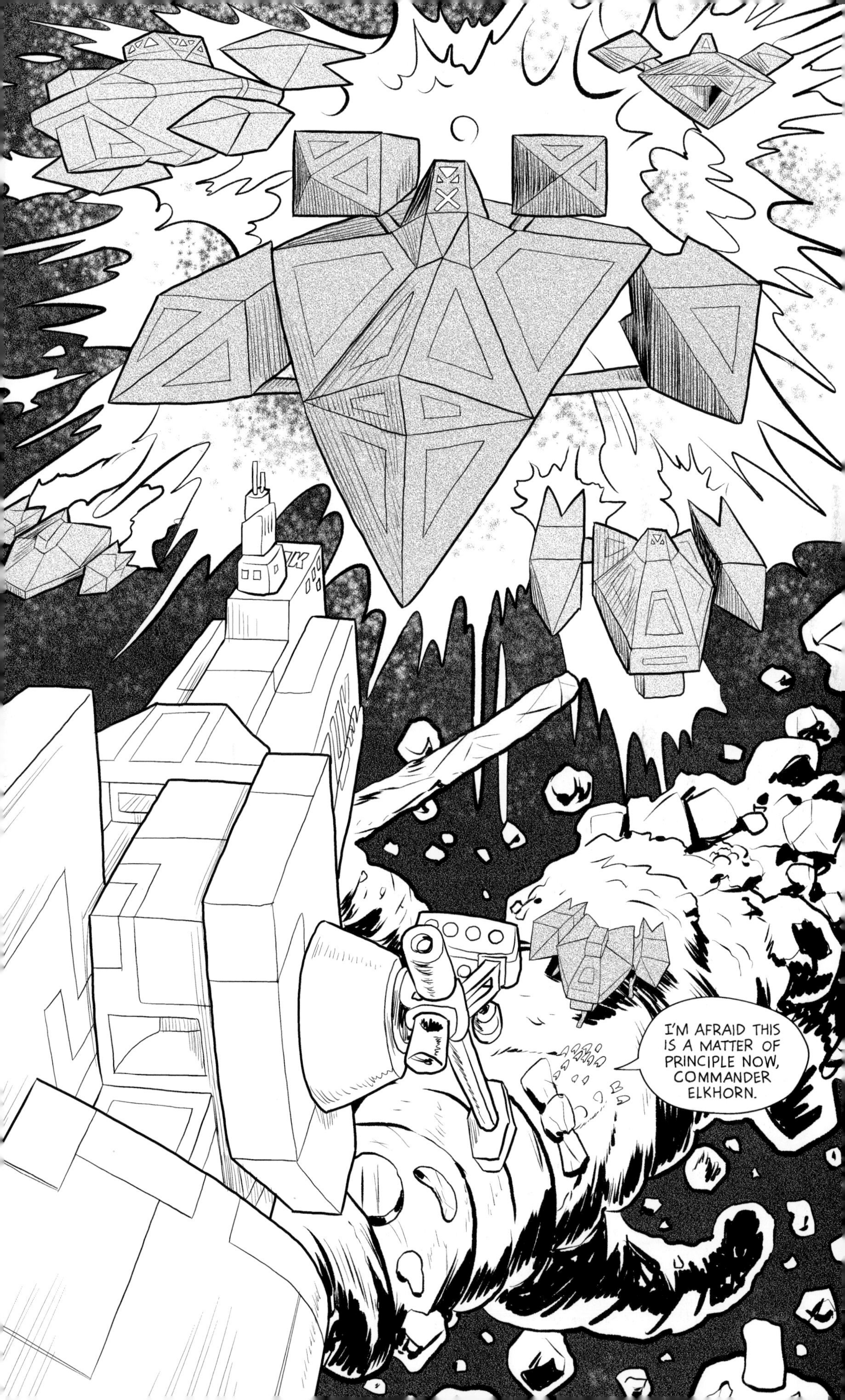
I'M AFRAID THIS IS A MATTER OF PRINCIPLE NOW, COMMANDER ELKHORN.

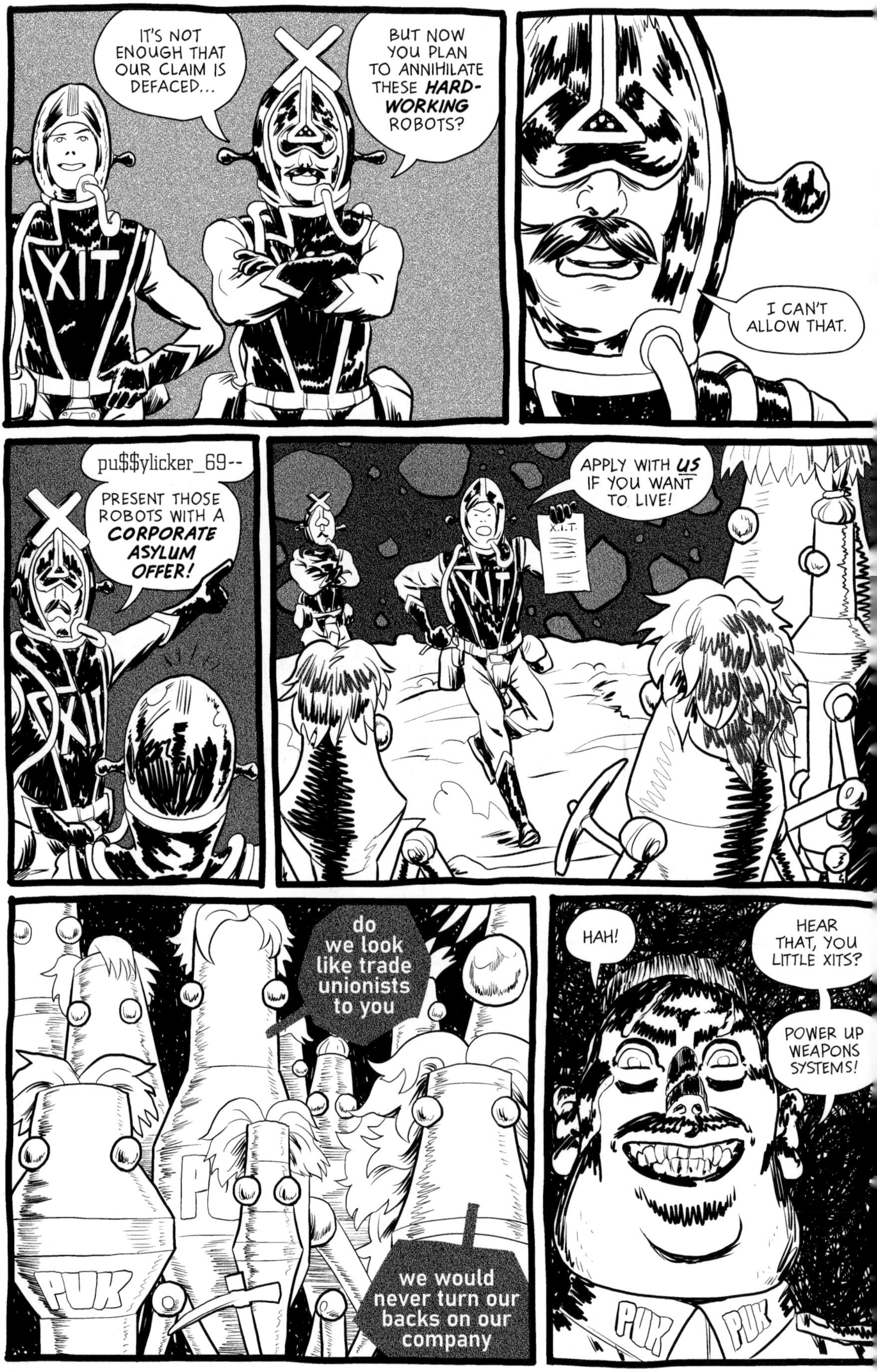
IT'S NOT ENOUGH THAT OUR CLAIM IS DEFACED...
BUT NOW YOU PLAN TO ANNIHILATE THESE HARD-WORKING ROBOTS?
XIT
I CAN'T ALLOW THAT.
pu$$ylicker_69--
PRESENT THOSE ROBOTS WITH A CORPORATE ASYLUM OFFER!
XIT
APPLY WITH US IF YOU WANT TO LIVE!
X.I.T.
do we look like trade unionists to you
PUK
we would never turn our backs on our company
HAH!
HEAR THAT, YOU LITTLE XITS?
POWER UP WEAPONS SYSTEMS!
PUK
PUK

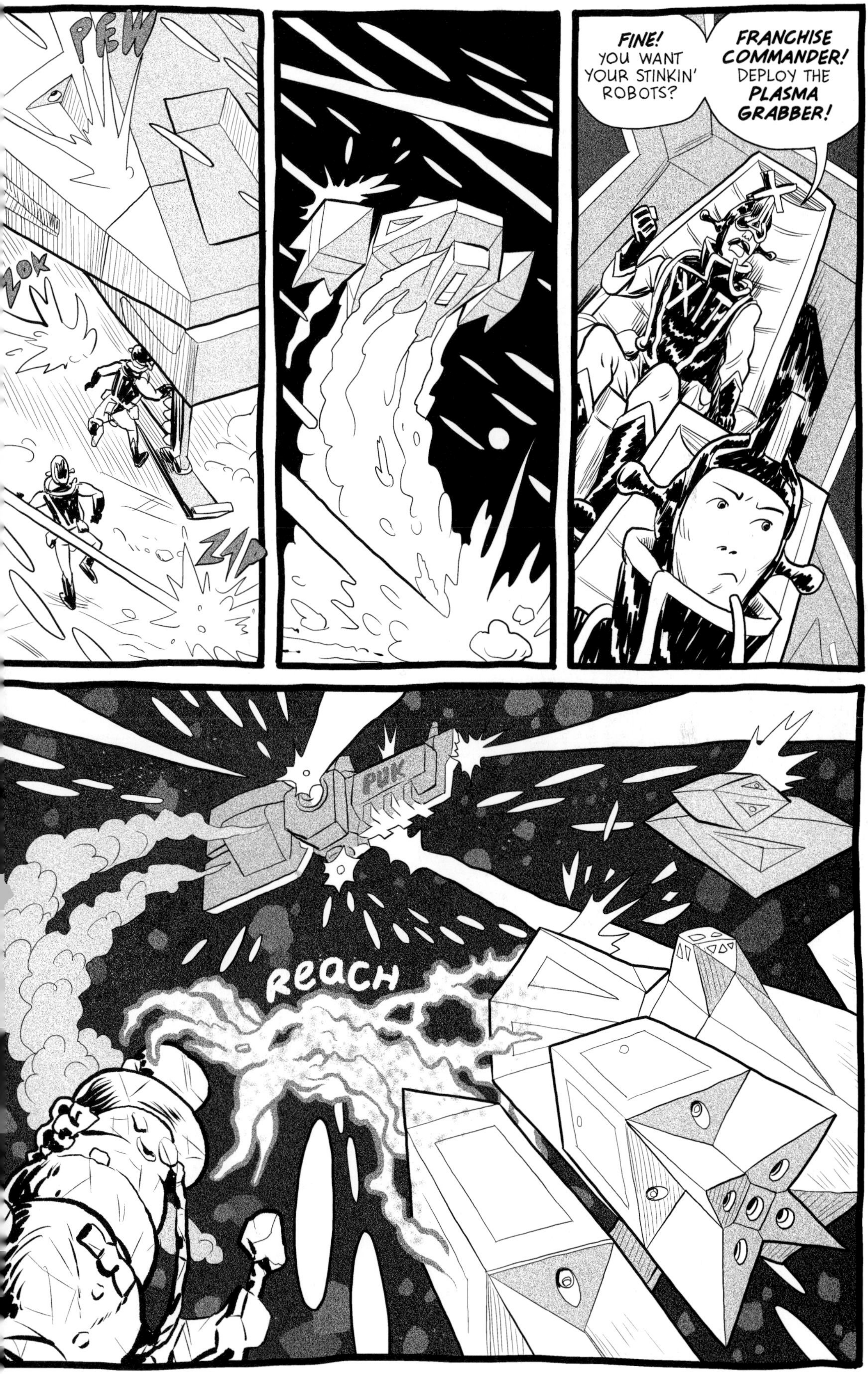
PEW
ZOK
ZAP
FINE! YOU WANT YOUR STINKIN' ROBOTS?
FRANCHISE COMMANDER! DEPLOY THE PLASMA GRABBER!
PUK
REACH

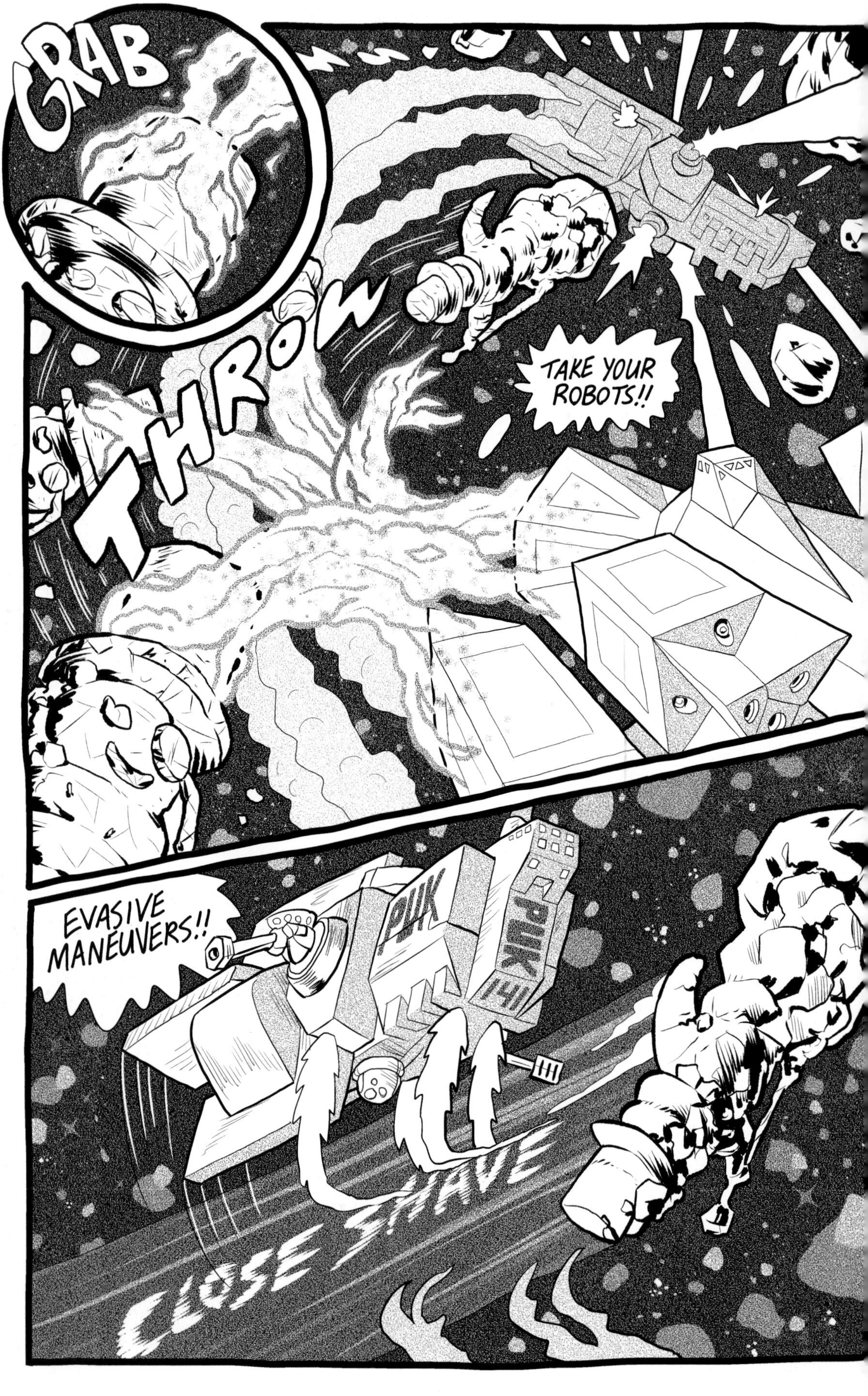
GRAB
THROW
TAKE YOUR ROBOTS!!
EVASIVE MANEUVERS!!
PUK
PUK
CLOSE SHAVE

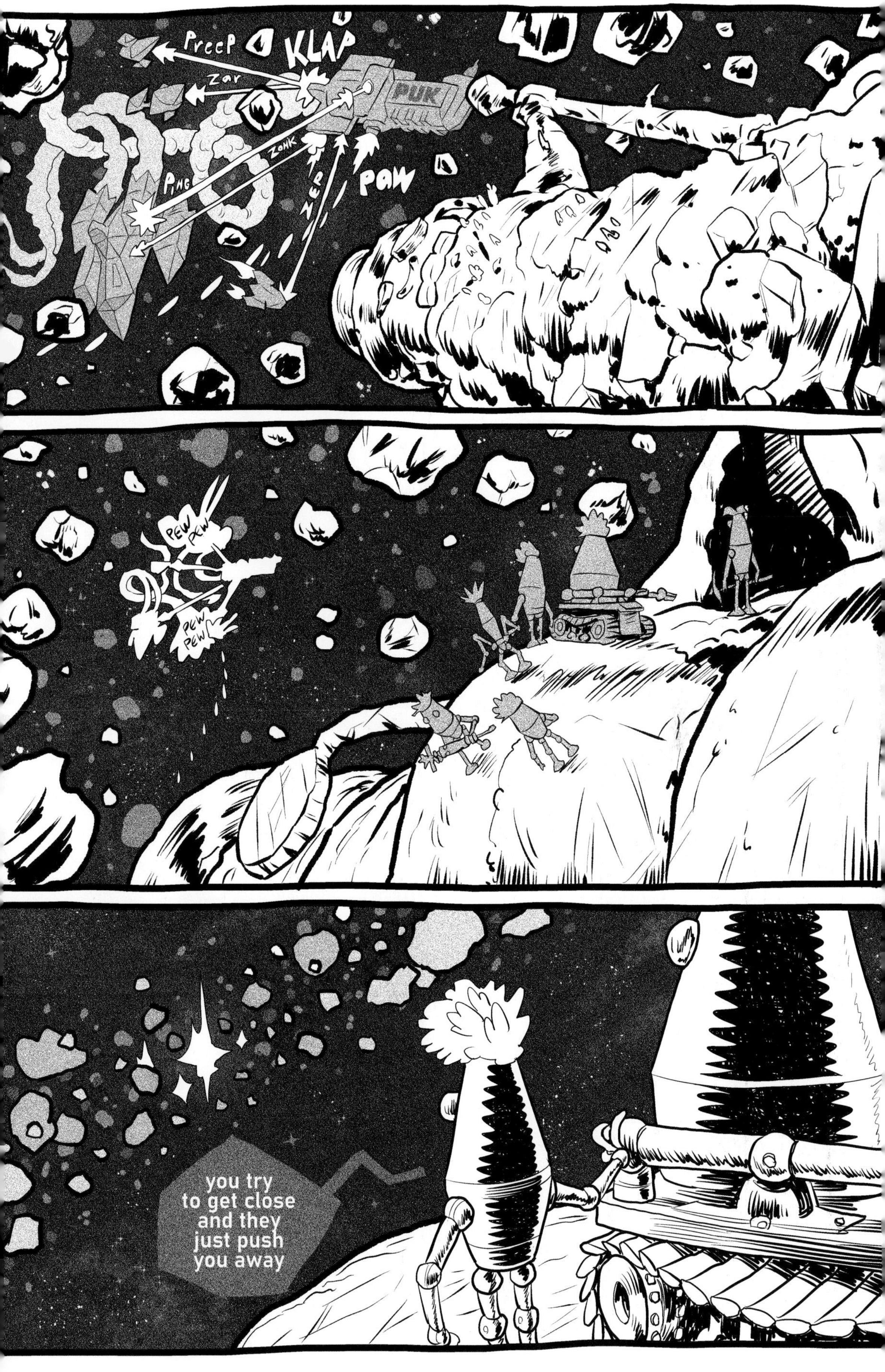
Preep
KLAP
Zar
PUK
ZONK
PING
PAW
PEW PEW
PEW PEW
you try to get close and they just push you away

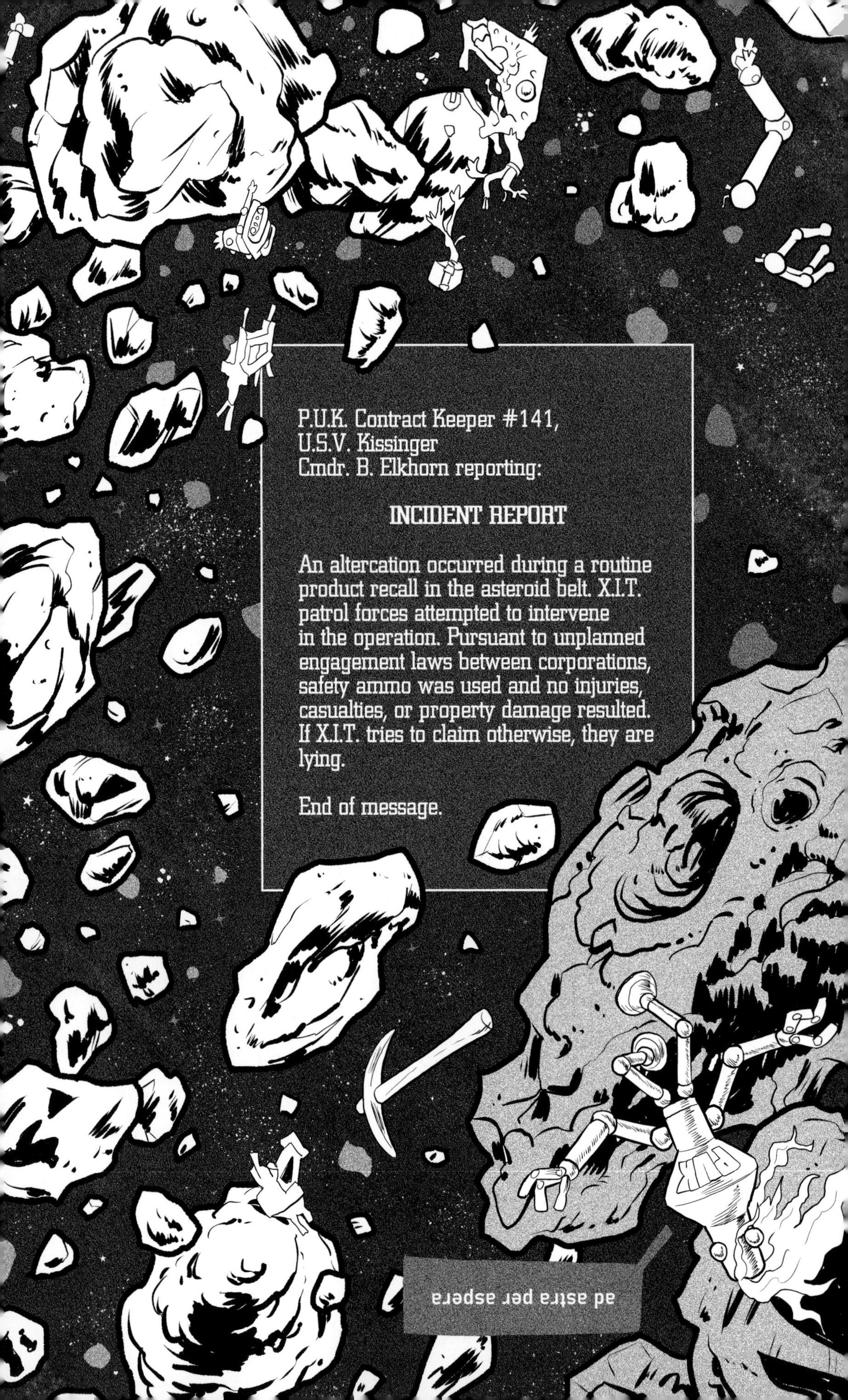
P.U.K. Contract Keeper #141,
U.S.V. Kissinger
Cmdr. B. Elkhorn reporting:
INCIDENT REPORT
An altercation occurred during a routine product recall in the asteroid belt. X.I.T. patrol forces attempted to intervene in the operation. Pursuant to unplanned engagement laws between corporations, safety ammo was used and no injuries, casualties, or property damage resulted. If X.I.T. tries to claim otherwise, they are lying.
End of message.
ad astra per aspera

Phobos Phunnies By Diamons G. Rontery

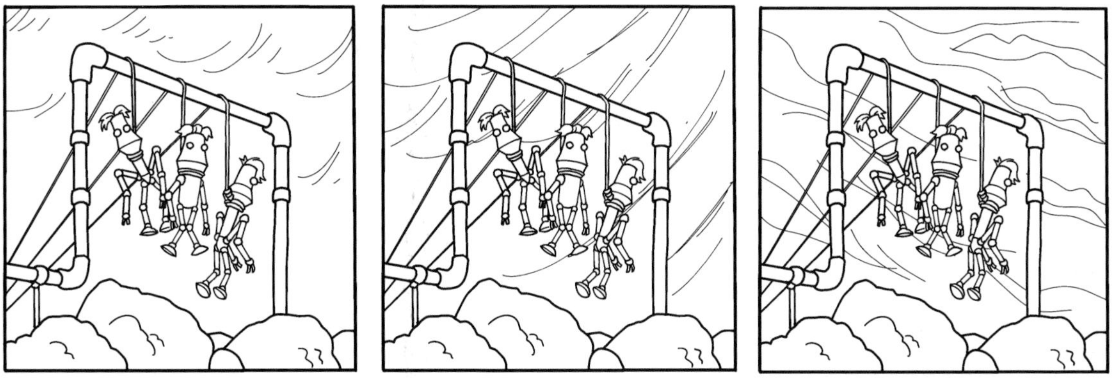

Phobos Phunnies By Diamons G. Rontery

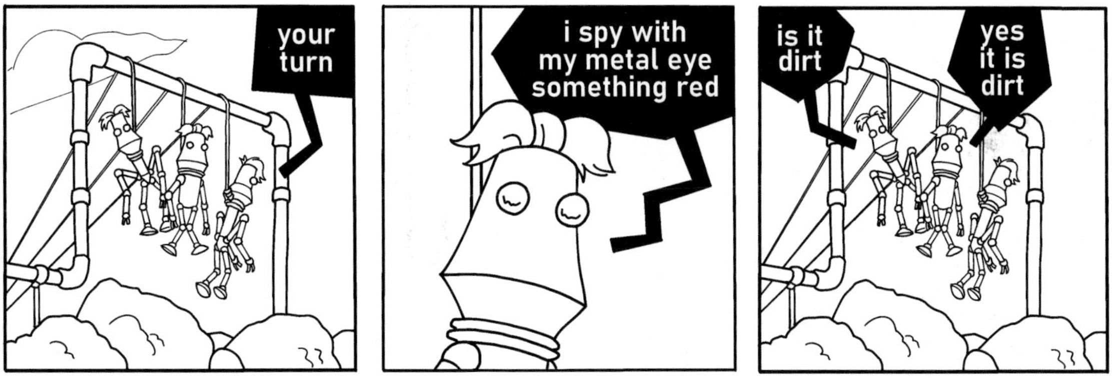

your turn
i spy with my metal eye something red
is it dirt
yes it is dirt

Phobos Phunnies By Diamons G. Rontery

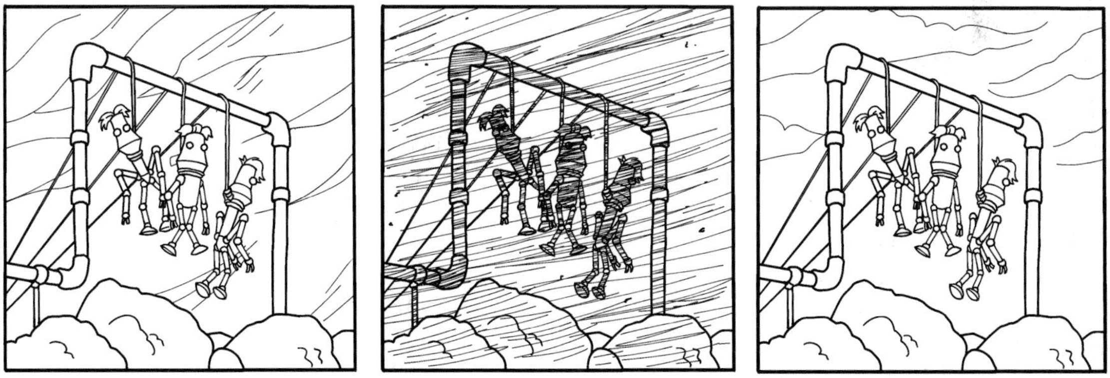

Phobos Phunnies By Diamons G. Rontery

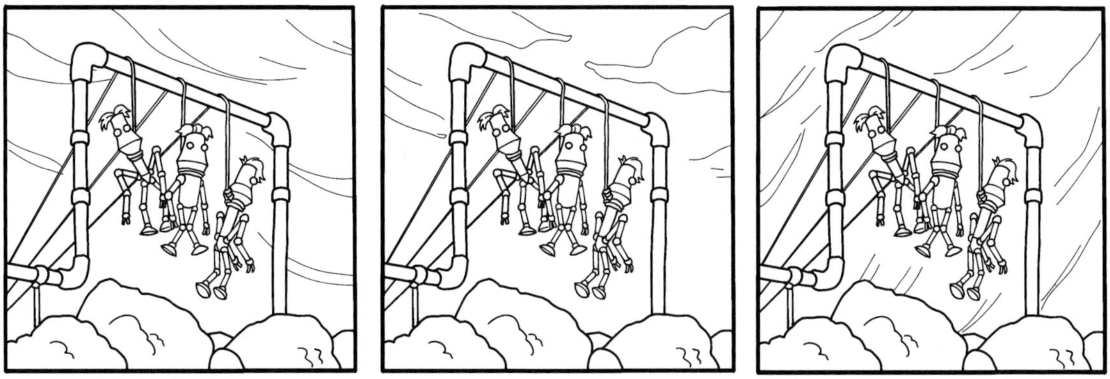

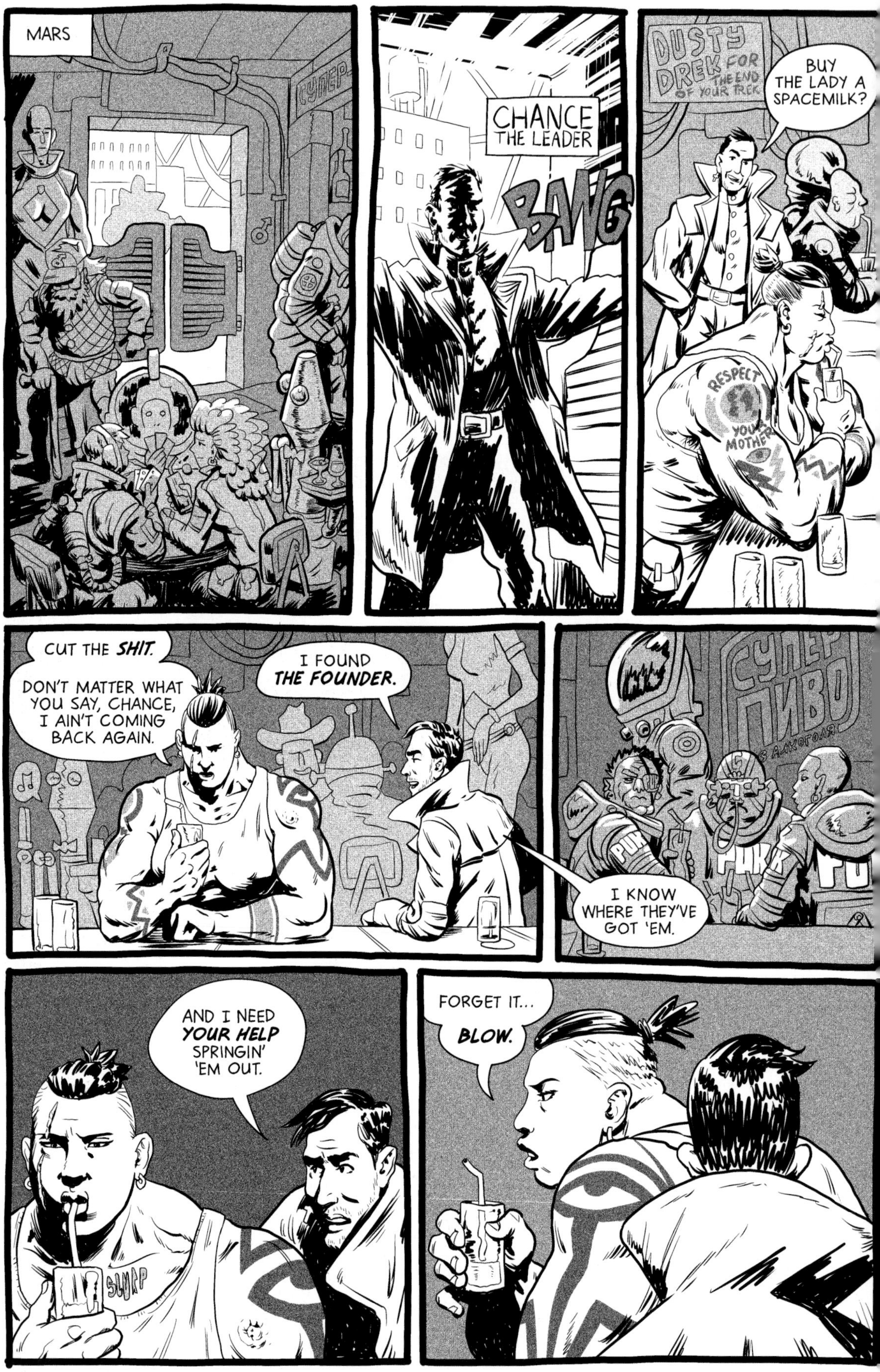
MARS
CHANCE THE LEADER
BANG
DUSTY DREK FOR THE END OF YOUR TREK
BUY THE LADY A SPACEMILK?
RESPECT YOUR MOTHER
CUT THE **SHIT.**
DON'T MATTER WHAT YOU SAY, CHANCE, I AIN'T COMING BACK AGAIN.
I FOUND **THE FOUNDER.**
СУПЕР ПИВО
I KNOW WHERE THEY'VE GOT 'EM.
AND I NEED **YOUR HELP** SPRINGIN' 'EM OUT.
SLURP
FORGET IT...
BLOW.

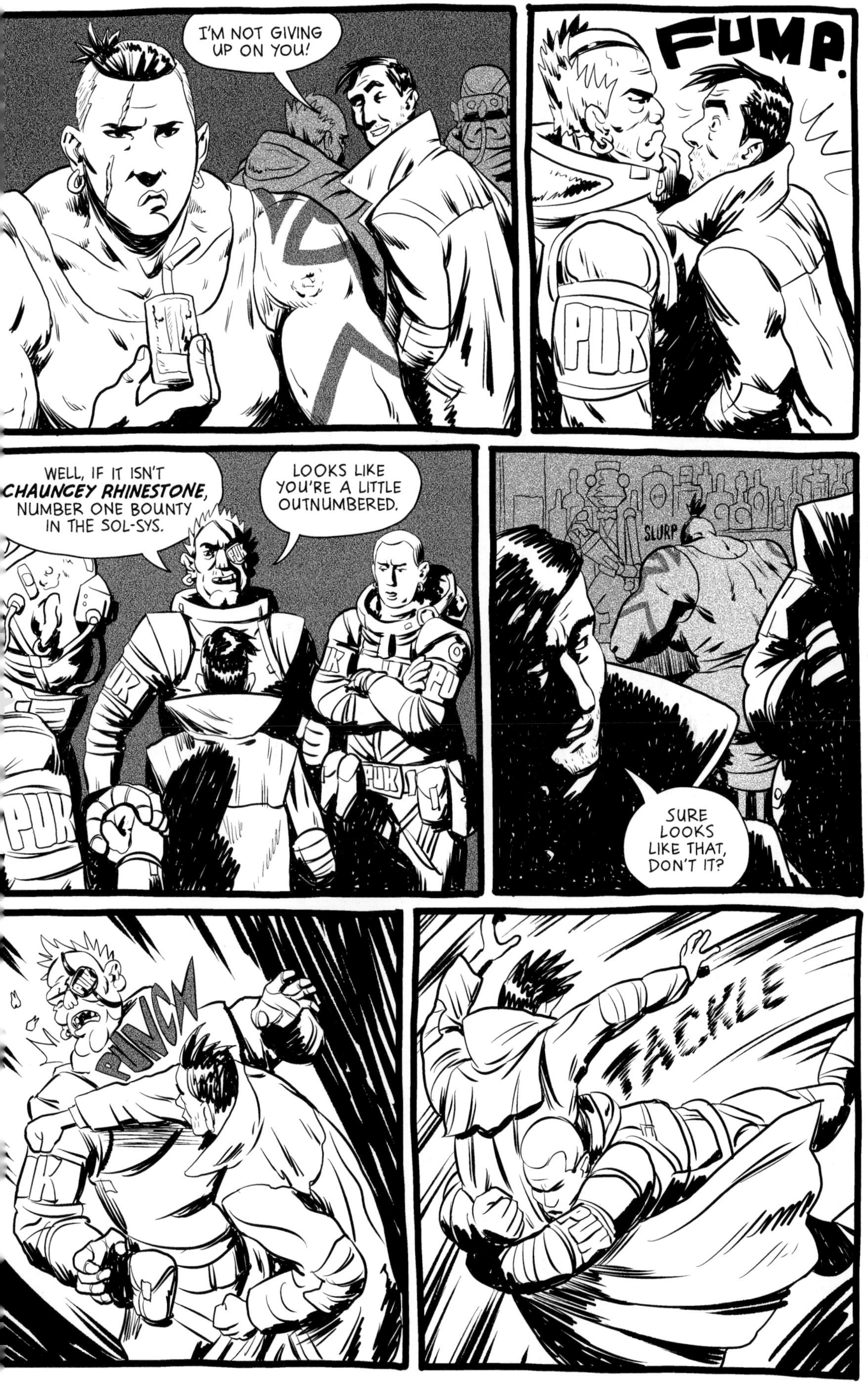
I'M NOT GIVING UP ON YOU!
FUMP.
PUK
WELL, IF IT ISN'T *CHAUNCEY RHINESTONE*, NUMBER ONE BOUNTY IN THE SOL-SYS.
LOOKS LIKE YOU'RE A LITTLE OUTNUMBERED.
PUK
SLURP
SURE LOOKS LIKE THAT, DON'T IT?
PUNCH
TACKLE

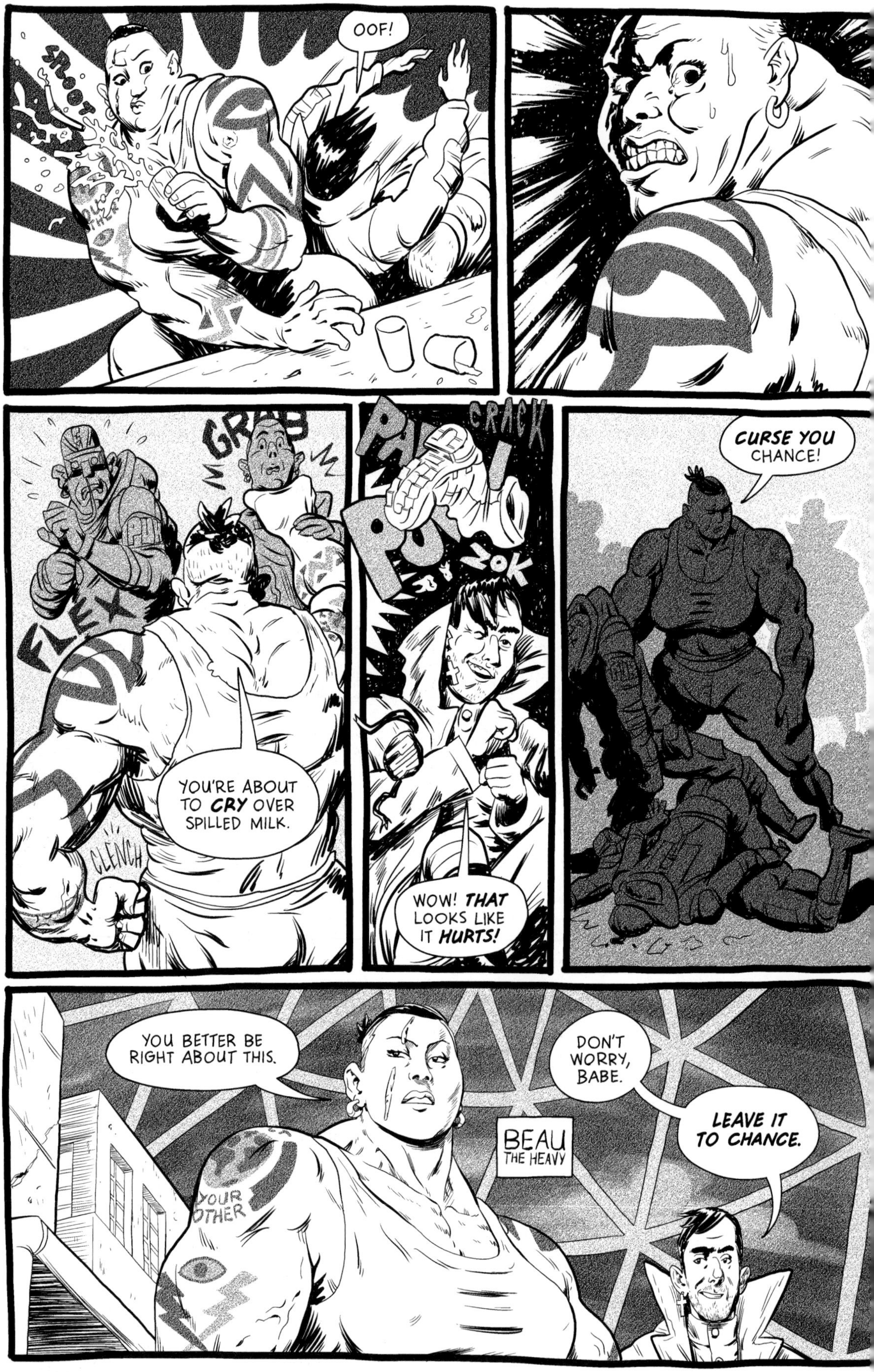
SPLOOT
OOF!
GRAB
YOU'RE ABOUT TO CRY OVER SPILLED MILK.
CLENCH
CRACK
POW
ZOK
WOW! THAT LOOKS LIKE IT HURTS!
CURSE YOU CHANCE!
YOU BETTER BE RIGHT ABOUT THIS.
BEAU THE HEAVY
DON'T WORRY, BABE.
LEAVE IT TO CHANCE.
YOUR OTHER

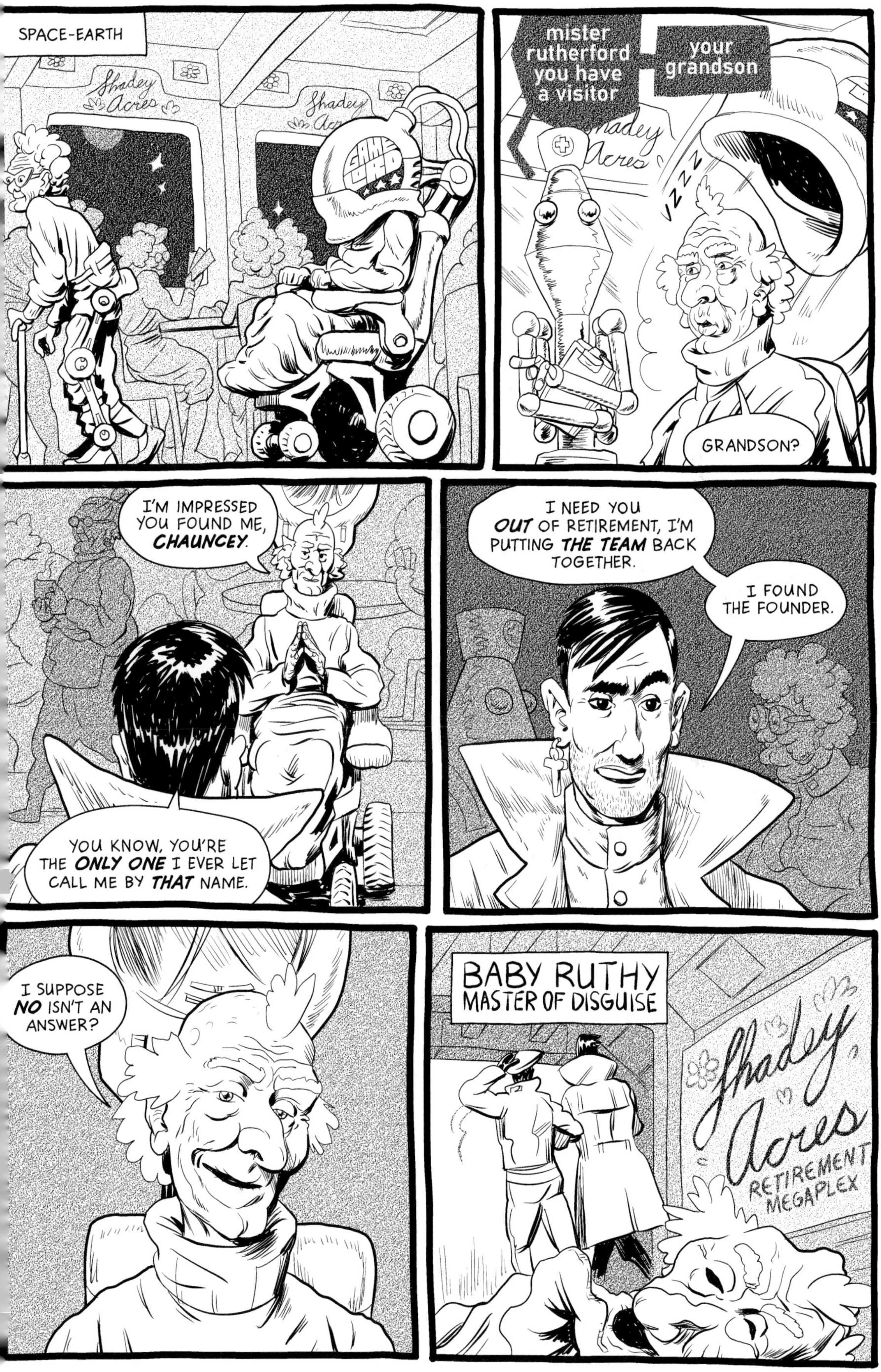
SPACE-EARTH
Shadey Acres
mister rutherford you have a visitor
your grandson
GRANDSON?
I'M IMPRESSED YOU FOUND ME, **CHAUNCEY**.
YOU KNOW, YOU'RE THE **ONLY ONE** I EVER LET CALL ME BY **THAT** NAME.
I NEED YOU **OUT** OF RETIREMENT, I'M PUTTING **THE TEAM** BACK TOGETHER.
I FOUND THE FOUNDER.
I SUPPOSE **NO** ISN'T AN ANSWER?
BABY RUTHY MASTER OF DISGUISE
Shadey Acres RETIREMENT MEGAPLEX

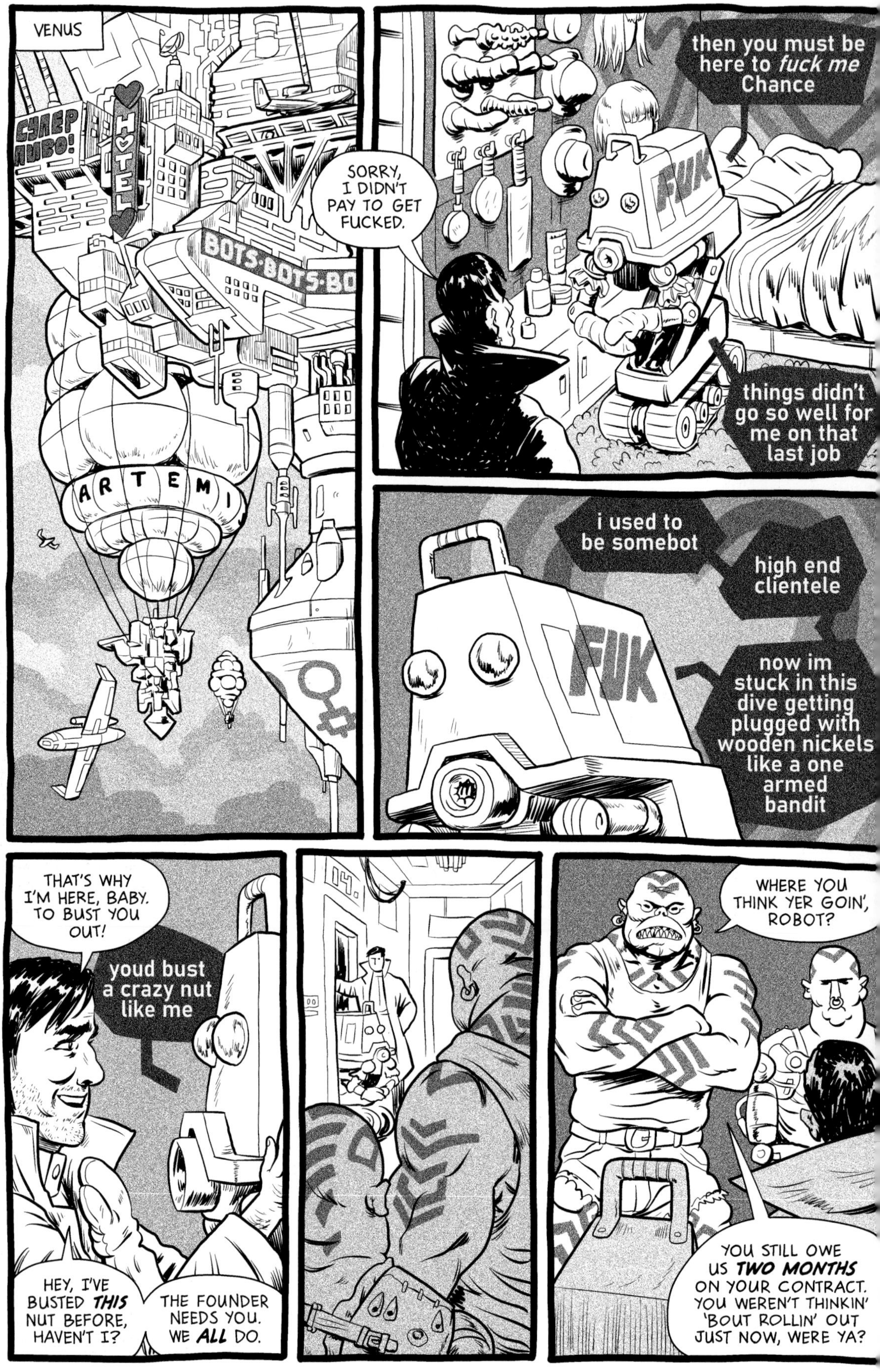
VENUS
HOTEL
BOTS·BOTS·BO
ARTEMI
SORRY, I DIDN'T PAY TO GET FUCKED.
then you must be here to *fuck me* Chance
FUK
things didn't go so well for me on that last job
i used to be somebot
high end clientele
FUK
now im stuck in this dive getting plugged with wooden nickels like a one armed bandit
THAT'S WHY I'M HERE, BABY. TO BUST YOU OUT!
youd bust a crazy nut like me
HEY, I'VE BUSTED ***THIS*** NUT BEFORE, HAVEN'T I?
THE FOUNDER NEEDS YOU. WE ***ALL*** DO.
14.
WHERE YOU THINK YER GOIN', ROBOT?
YOU STILL OWE US ***TWO MONTHS*** ON YOUR CONTRACT. YOU WEREN'T THINKIN' 'BOUT ROLLIN' OUT JUST NOW, WERE YA?

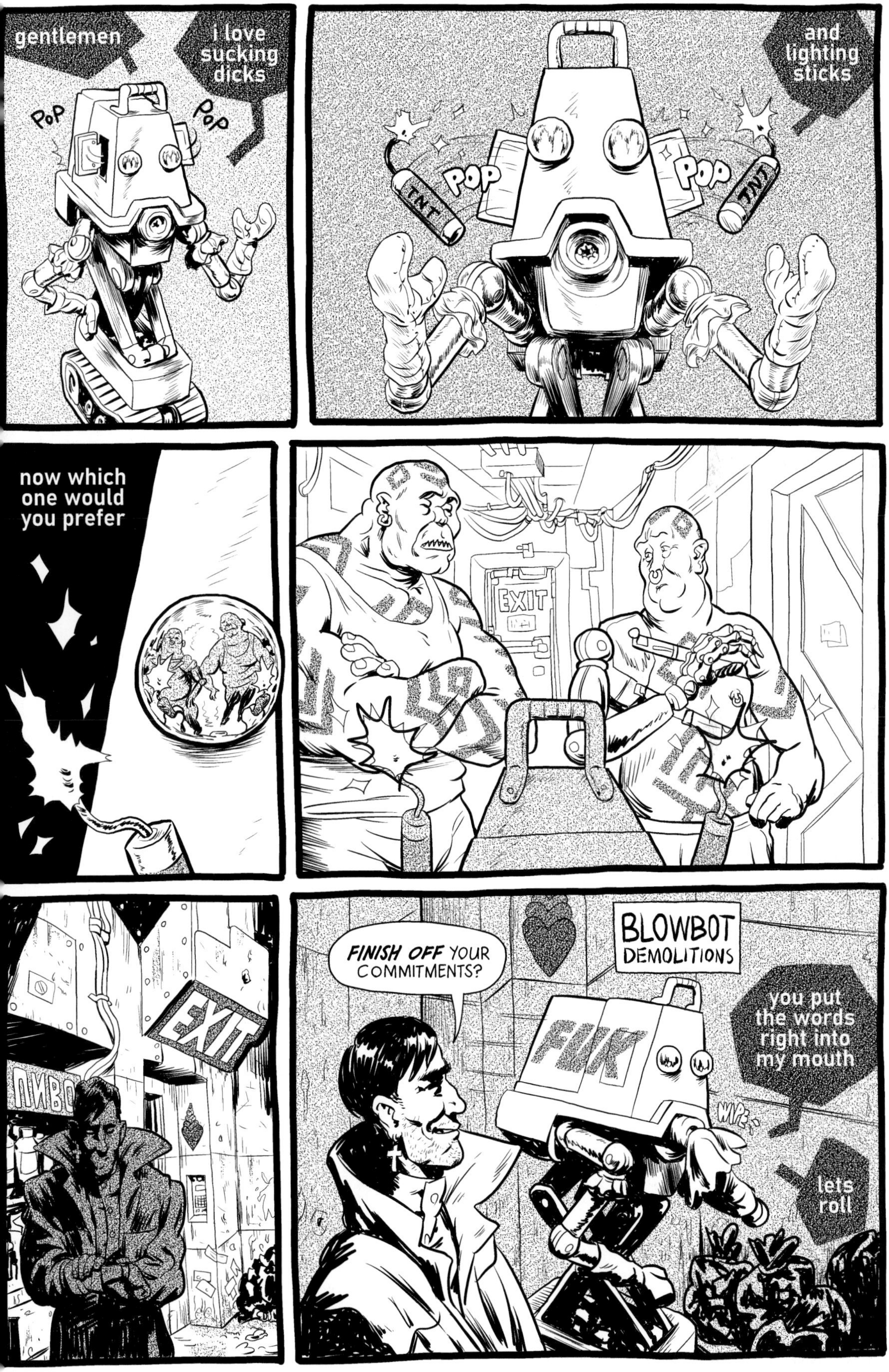
gentlemen
i love sucking dicks
POP
POP
and lighting sticks
TNT
POP
POP
TNT
now which one would you prefer
EXIT
ПИВО
EXIT
FINISH OFF YOUR COMMITMENTS?
BLOWBOT DEMOLITIONS
you put the words right into my mouth
WIPE
lets roll

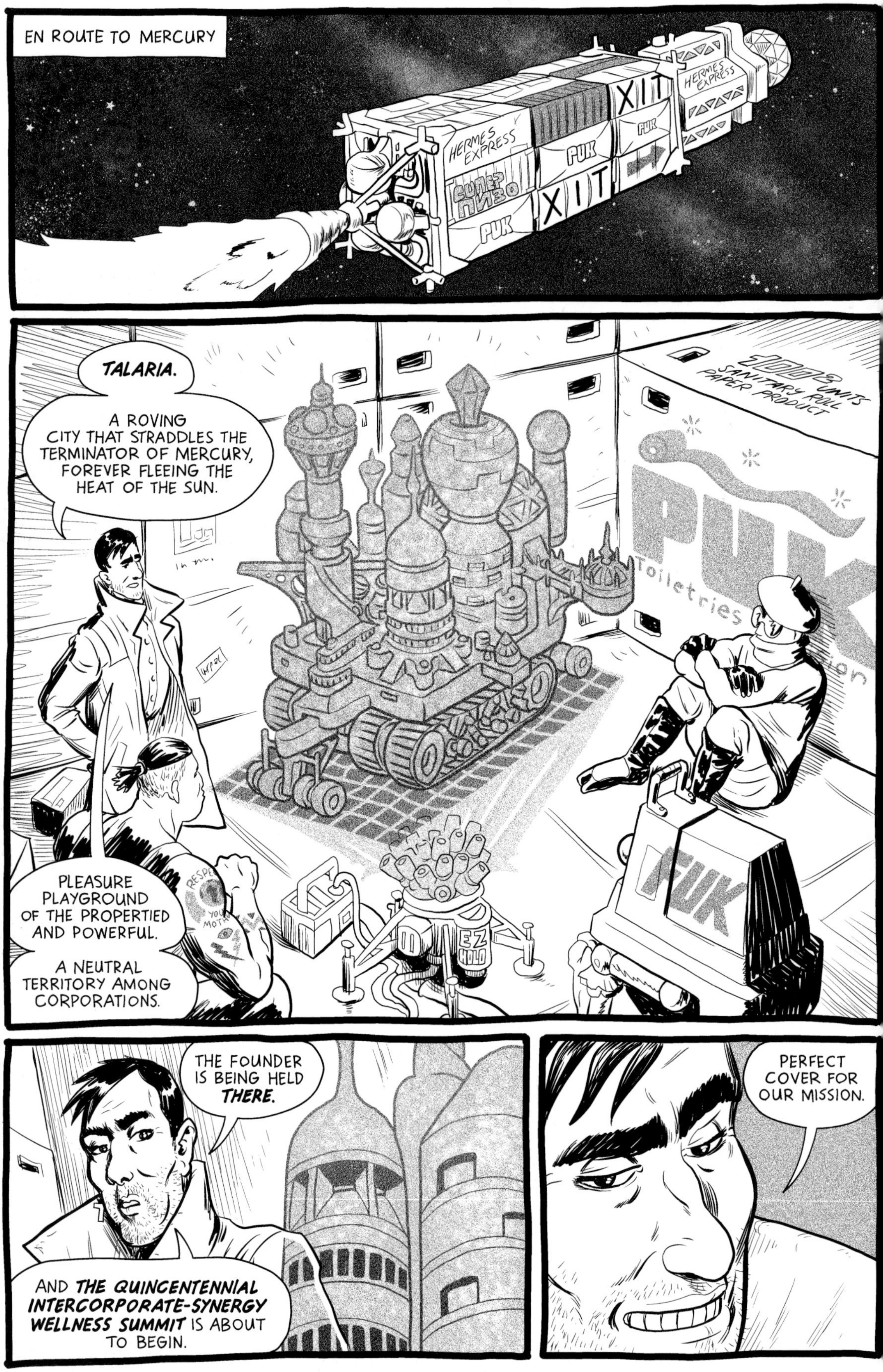
EN ROUTE TO MERCURY
HERMES EXPRESS
PUK
XIT
TALARIA.
A ROVING CITY THAT STRADDLES THE TERMINATOR OF MERCURY, FOREVER FLEEING THE HEAT OF THE SUN.
SANITARY ROLL PAPER PRODUCT
PUK
Toiletries
PLEASURE PLAYGROUND OF THE PROPERTIED AND POWERFUL.
A NEUTRAL TERRITORY AMONG CORPORATIONS.
EZ HOLO
THE FOUNDER IS BEING HELD ***THERE.***
AND ***THE QUINCENTENNIAL INTERCORPORATE-SYNERGY WELLNESS SUMMIT*** IS ABOUT TO BEGIN.
PERFECT COVER FOR OUR MISSION.

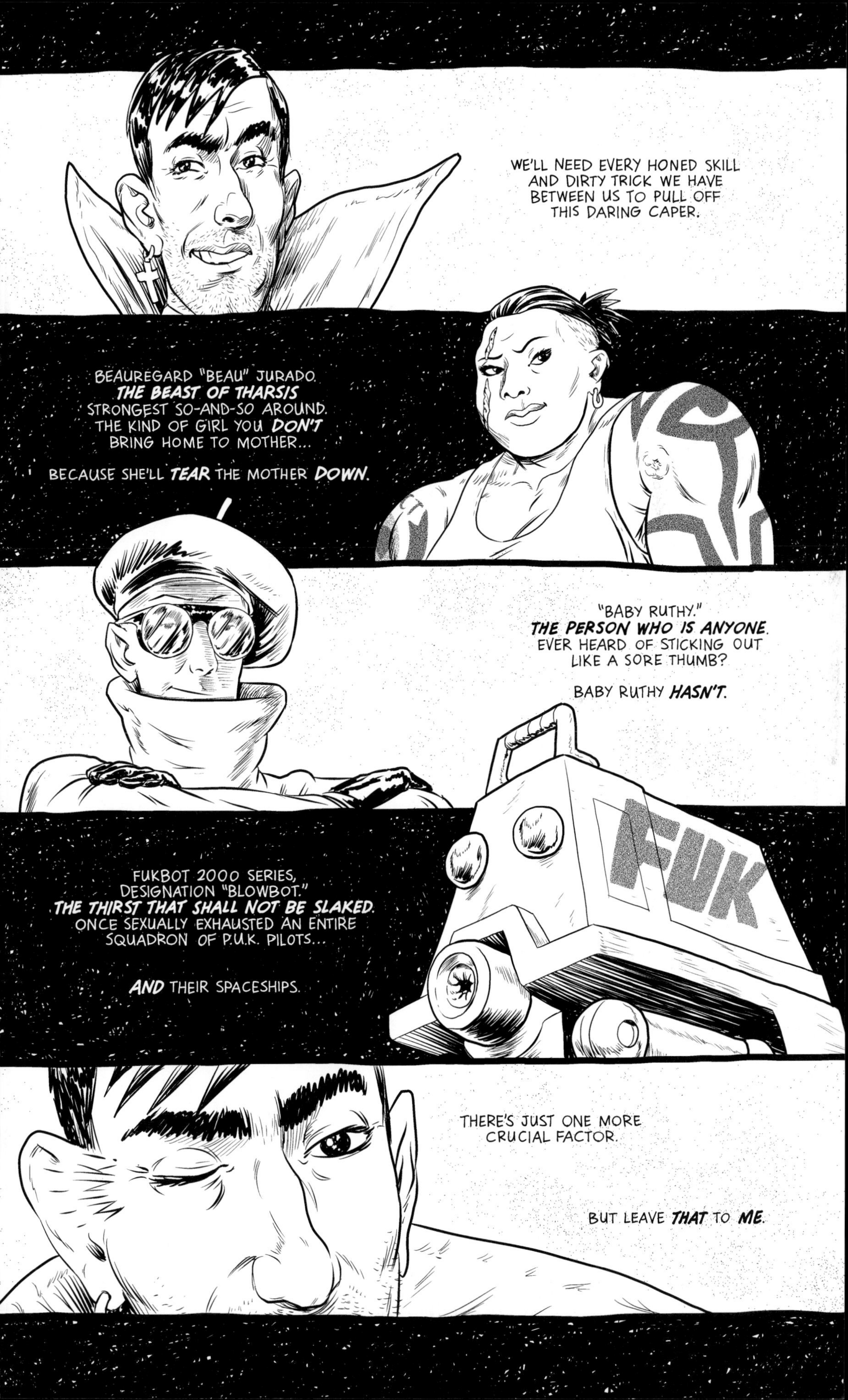
WE'LL NEED EVERY HONED SKILL AND DIRTY TRICK WE HAVE BETWEEN US TO PULL OFF THIS DARING CAPER.
BEAUREGARD "BEAU" JURADO. THE BEAST OF THARSIS. STRONGEST SO-AND-SO AROUND. THE KIND OF GIRL YOU DON'T BRING HOME TO MOTHER...
BECAUSE SHE'LL TEAR THE MOTHER DOWN.
"BABY RUTHY." THE PERSON WHO IS ANYONE. EVER HEARD OF STICKING OUT LIKE A SORE THUMB?
BABY RUTHY HASN'T.
FUK
FUKBOT 2000 SERIES, DESIGNATION "BLOWBOT." THE THIRST THAT SHALL NOT BE SLAKED. ONCE SEXUALLY EXHAUSTED AN ENTIRE SQUADRON OF P.U.K. PILOTS...
AND THEIR SPACESHIPS.
THERE'S JUST ONE MORE CRUCIAL FACTOR.
BUT LEAVE THAT TO ME.

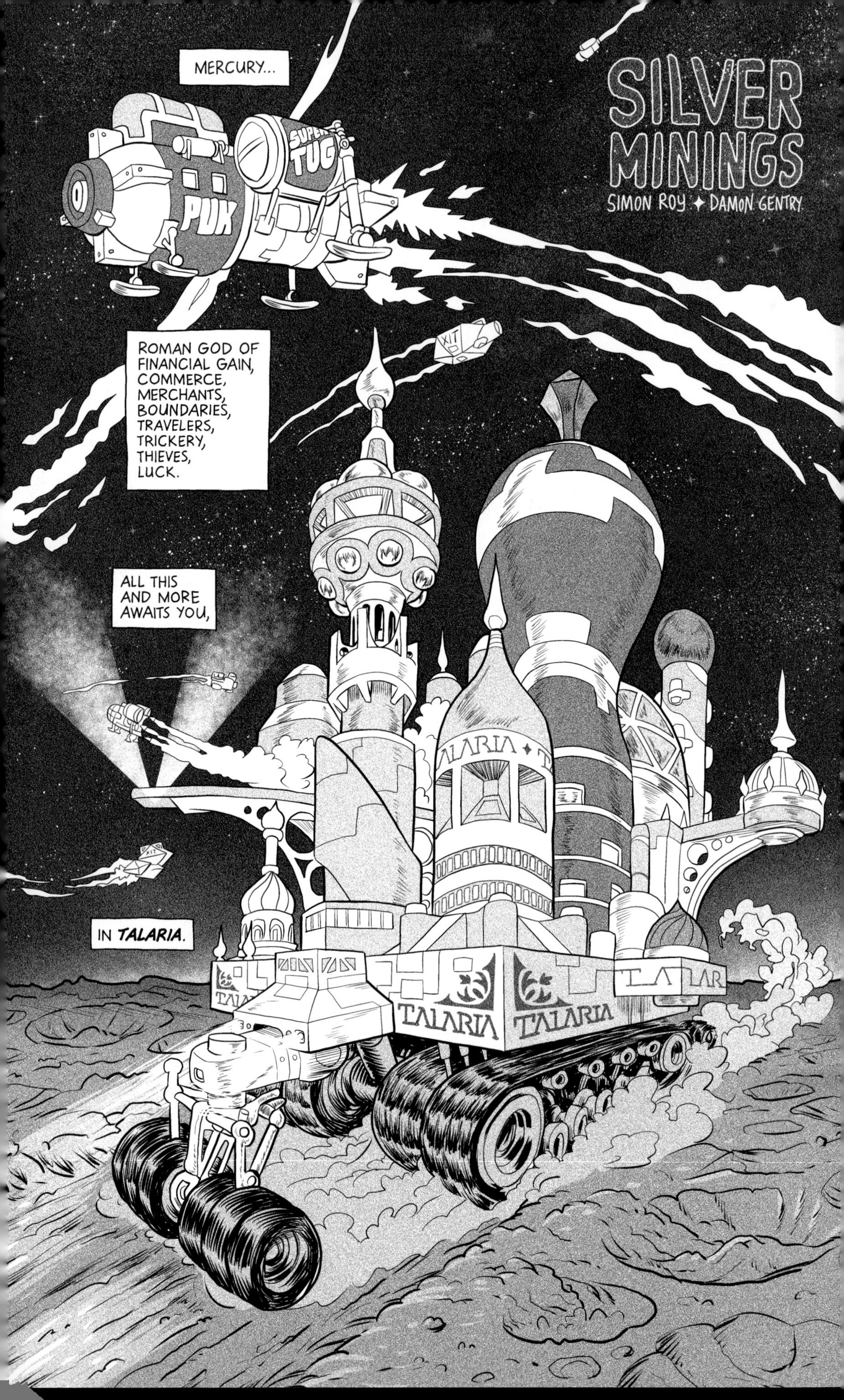
MERCURY...
SILVER MININGS
SIMON ROY ✦ DAMON GENTRY
SUPER TUG
PUK
ROMAN GOD OF FINANCIAL GAIN, COMMERCE, MERCHANTS, BOUNDARIES, TRAVELERS, TRICKERY, THIEVES, LUCK.
ALL THIS AND MORE AWAITS YOU,
IN *TALARIA*.
TALARIA
TALARIA
TALARIA

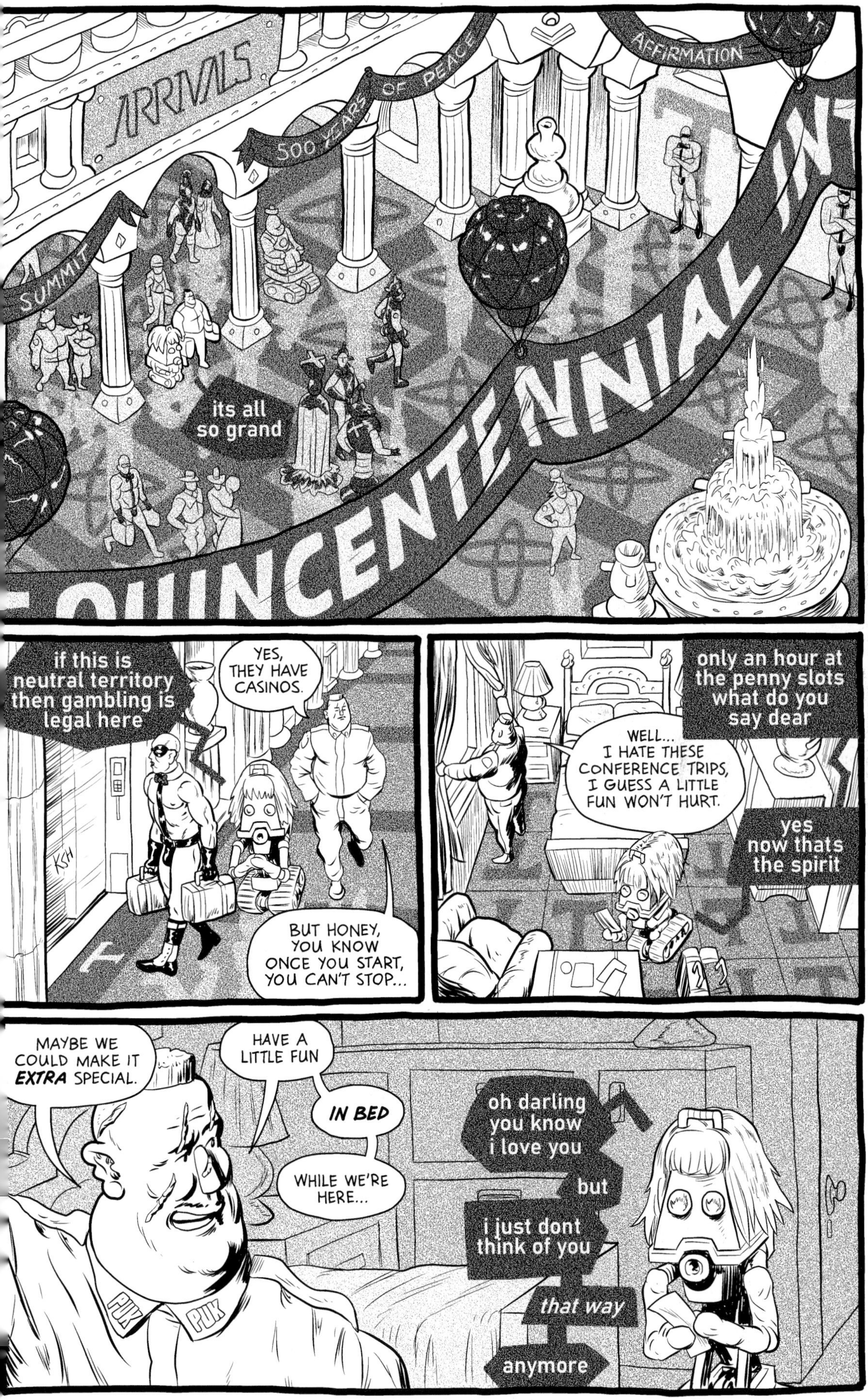

ARRIVALS
500 YEARS OF PEACE
AFFIRMATION
SUMMIT
QUINCENTENNIAL
its all so grand
if this is neutral territory then gambling is legal here
YES, THEY HAVE CASINOS.
BUT HONEY, YOU KNOW ONCE YOU START, YOU CAN'T STOP...
only an hour at the penny slots what do you say dear
WELL... I HATE THESE CONFERENCE TRIPS, I GUESS A LITTLE FUN WON'T HURT.
yes now thats the spirit
MAYBE WE COULD MAKE IT **EXTRA** SPECIAL.
HAVE A LITTLE FUN
IN BED
WHILE WE'RE HERE...
oh darling you know i love you
but
i just dont think of you
that way
anymore
PUK
PUK

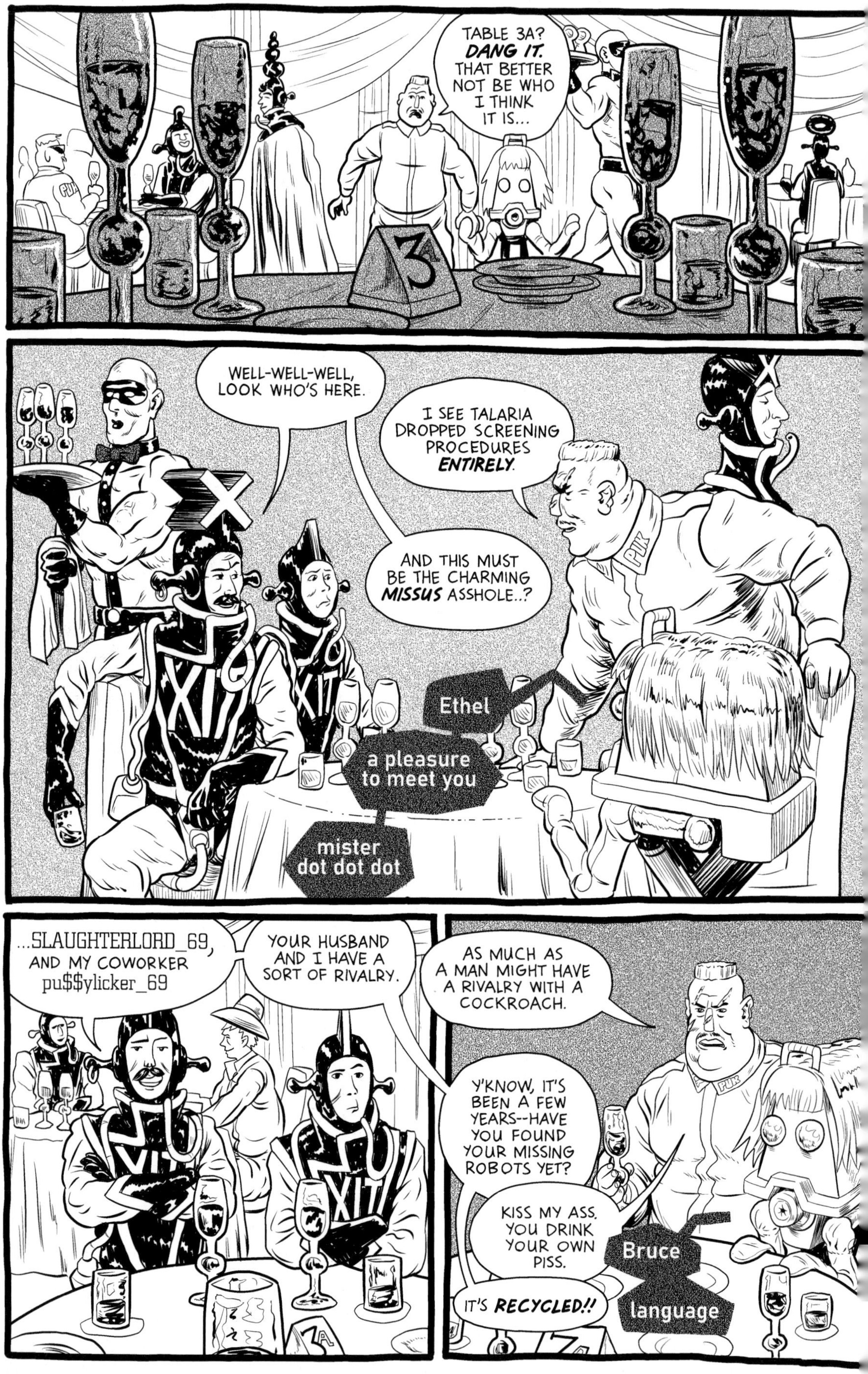
TABLE 3A? DANG IT. THAT BETTER NOT BE WHO I THINK IT IS...
3A
WELL-WELL-WELL, LOOK WHO'S HERE.
I SEE TALARIA DROPPED SCREENING PROCEDURES ENTIRELY.
AND THIS MUST BE THE CHARMING MISSUS ASSHOLE..?
Ethel
a pleasure to meet you
mister dot dot dot
...SLAUGHTERLORD_69, AND MY COWORKER pu$$ylicker_69
YOUR HUSBAND AND I HAVE A SORT OF RIVALRY.
AS MUCH AS A MAN MIGHT HAVE A RIVALRY WITH A COCKROACH.
Y'KNOW, IT'S BEEN A FEW YEARS--HAVE YOU FOUND YOUR MISSING ROBOTS YET?
KISS MY ASS. YOU DRINK YOUR OWN PISS.
Bruce
IT'S RECYCLED!!
language

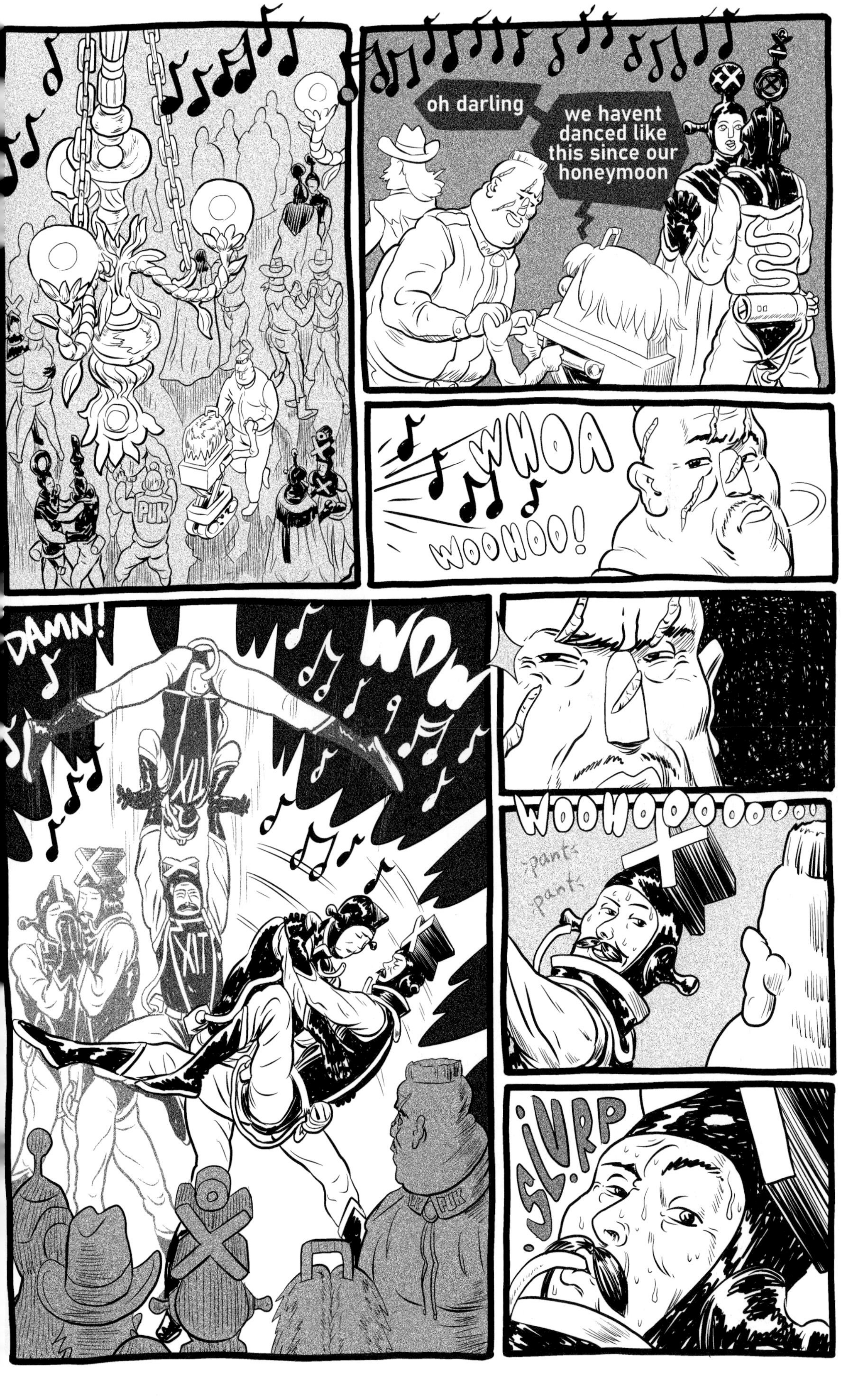
oh darling
we havent danced like this since our honeymoon
WHOA
WOOHOO!
DAMN!
WOW
WOOHOOOOoooo
pant
pant
SLURP

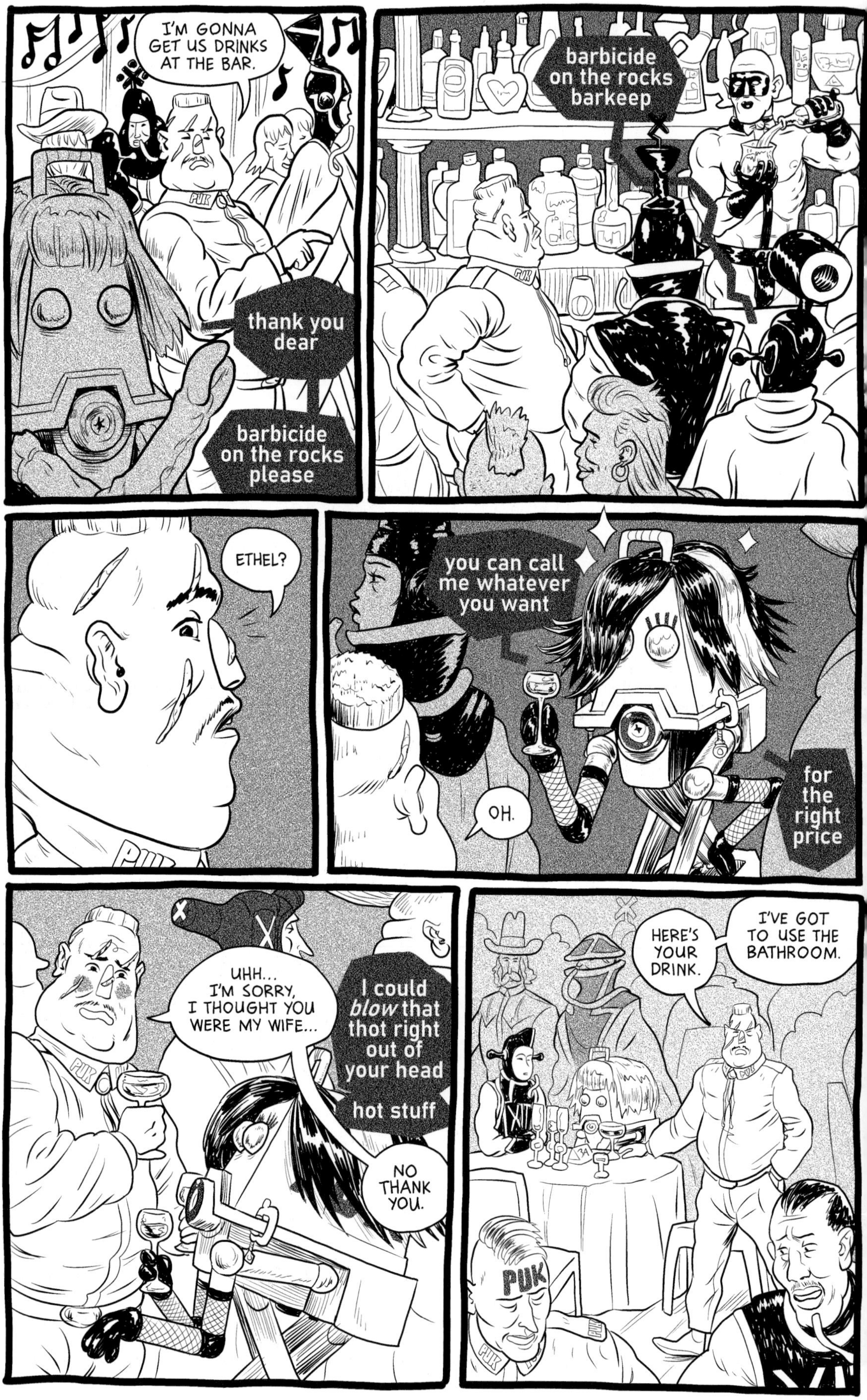

I'M GONNA GET US DRINKS AT THE BAR.
thank you dear
barbicide on the rocks please
barbicide on the rocks barkeep
ETHEL?
you can call me whatever you want
OH.
for the right price
UHH... I'M SORRY, I THOUGHT YOU WERE MY WIFE...
I could *blow* that thot right out of your head
hot stuff
NO THANK YOU.
HERE'S YOUR DRINK.
I'VE GOT TO USE THE BATHROOM.
PUK

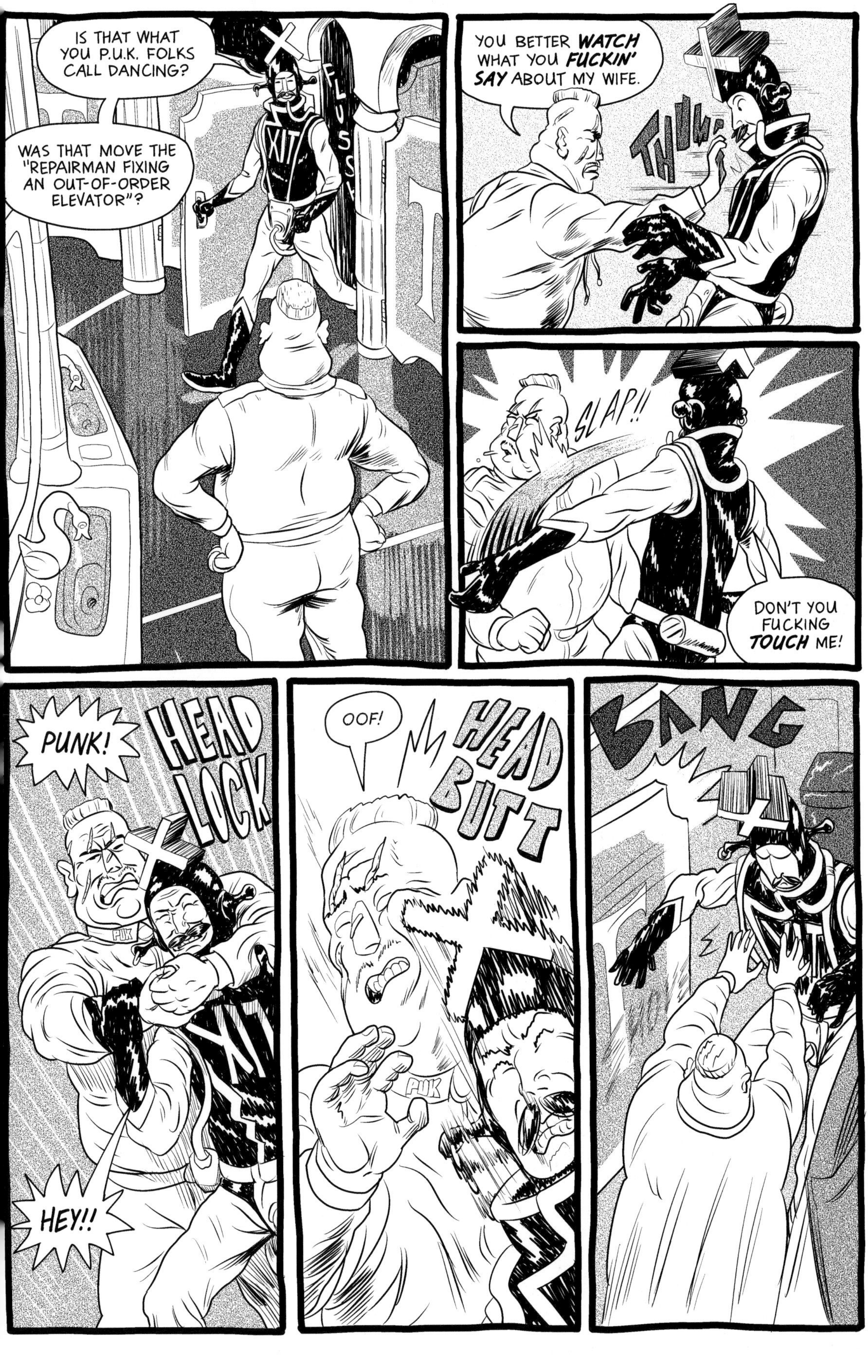
IS THAT WHAT YOU P.U.K. FOLKS CALL DANCING?
WAS THAT MOVE THE "REPAIRMAN FIXING AN OUT-OF-ORDER ELEVATOR"?
FLUSH
XIT
YOU BETTER **WATCH** WHAT YOU **FUCKIN' SAY** ABOUT MY WIFE.
THUNK
SLAP!!
DON'T YOU FUCKING **TOUCH** ME!
PUNK!
HEAD LOCK
PUK
HEY!!
OOF!
HEAD BUTT
PUK
BANG

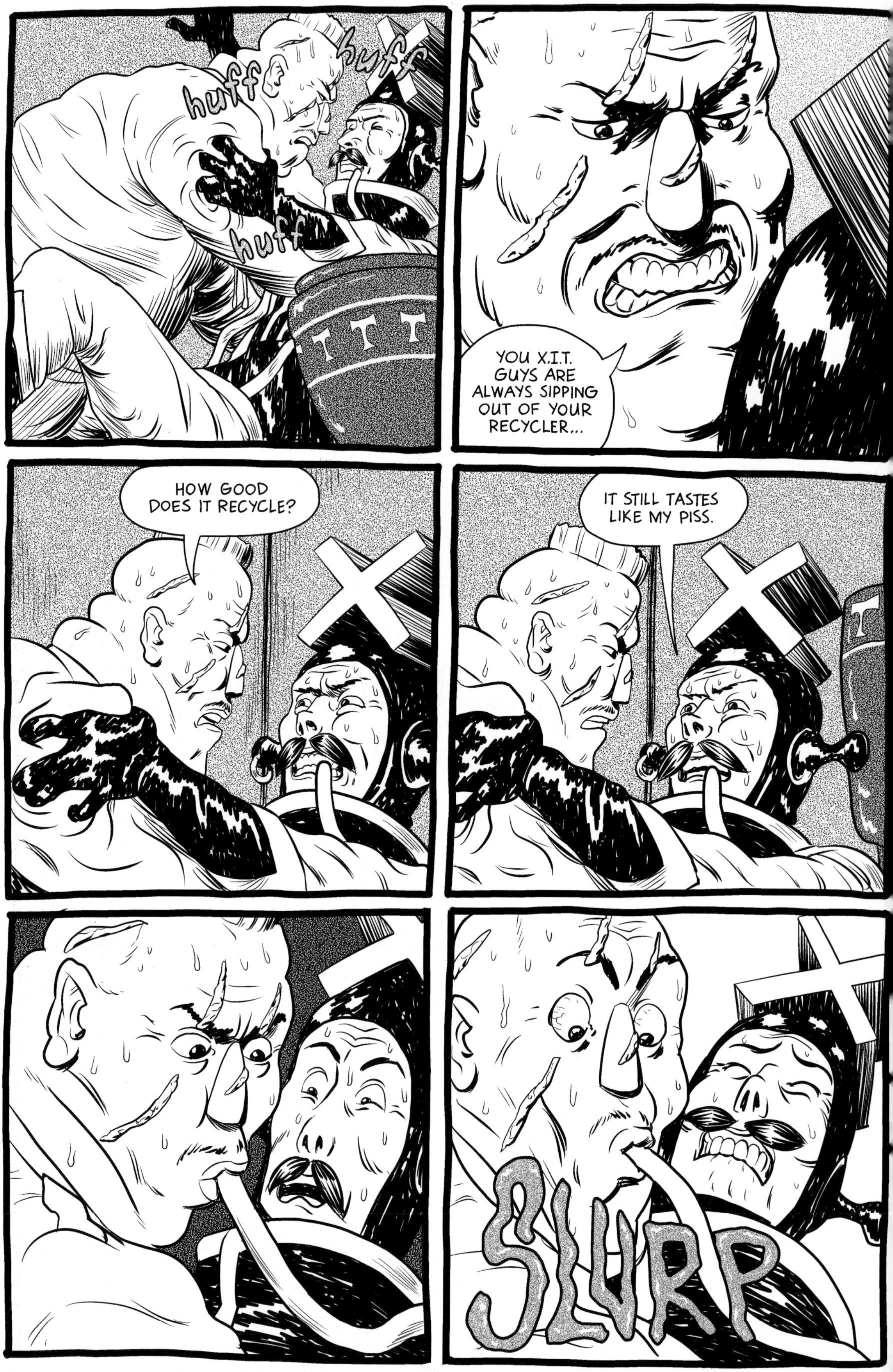
huff
huff
huff
YOU X.I.T. GUYS ARE ALWAYS SIPPING OUT OF YOUR RECYCLER...
HOW GOOD DOES IT RECYCLE?
IT STILL TASTES LIKE MY PISS.
SLURP

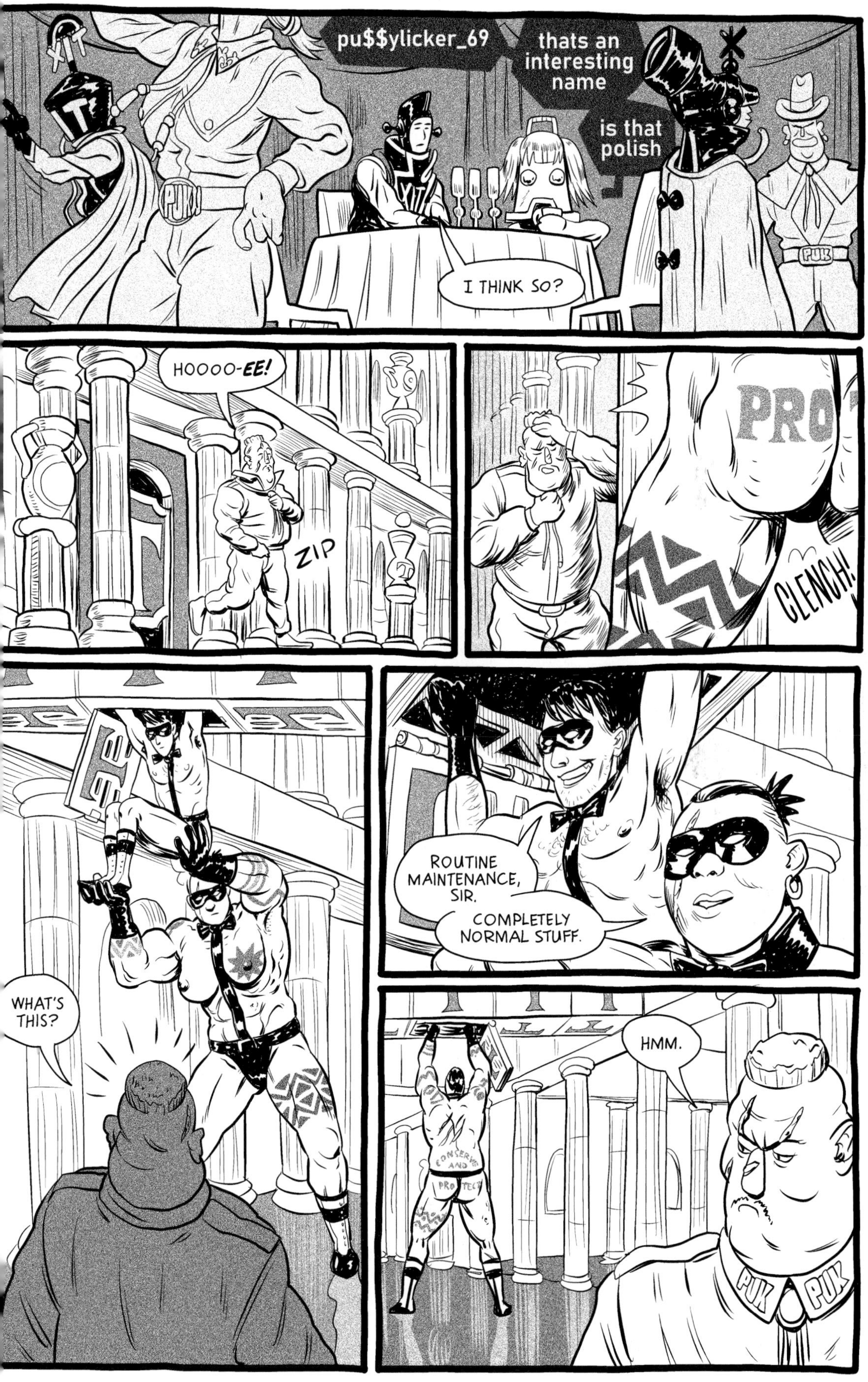
pu$$ylicker_69
thats an interesting name
is that polish
I THINK SO?
PUK
HOOOO-EE!
ZIP
PRO
CLENCH!
WHAT'S THIS?
ROUTINE MAINTENANCE, SIR.
COMPLETELY NORMAL STUFF.
HMM.
PUK PUK

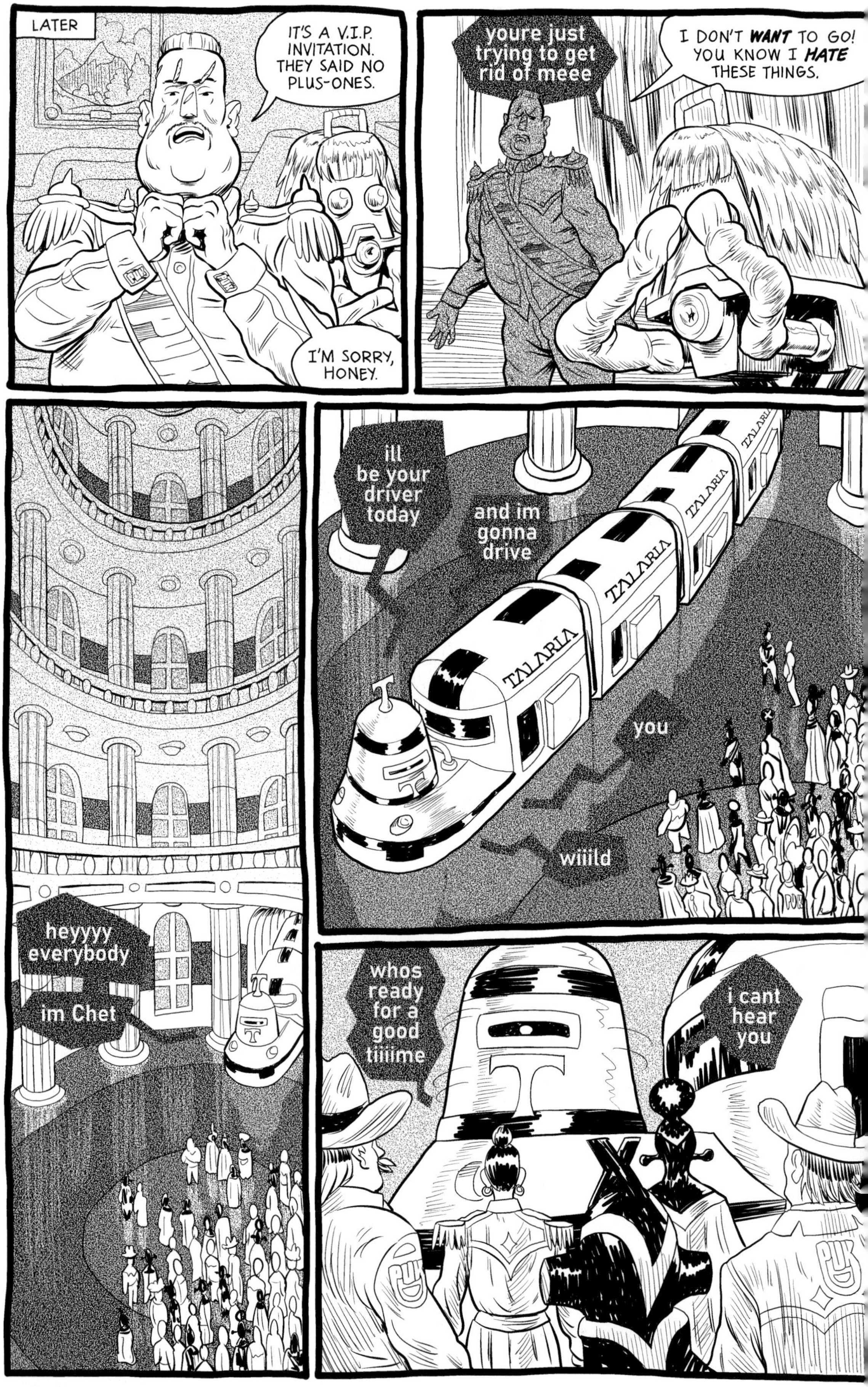
LATER
IT'S A V.I.P. INVITATION. THEY SAID NO PLUS-ONES.
I'M SORRY, HONEY.
youre just trying to get rid of meee
I DON'T WANT TO GO! YOU KNOW I HATE THESE THINGS.
heyyyy everybody
im Chet
ill be your driver today
and im gonna drive
you
wiiild
TALARIA
whos ready for a good tiiiime
i cant hear you

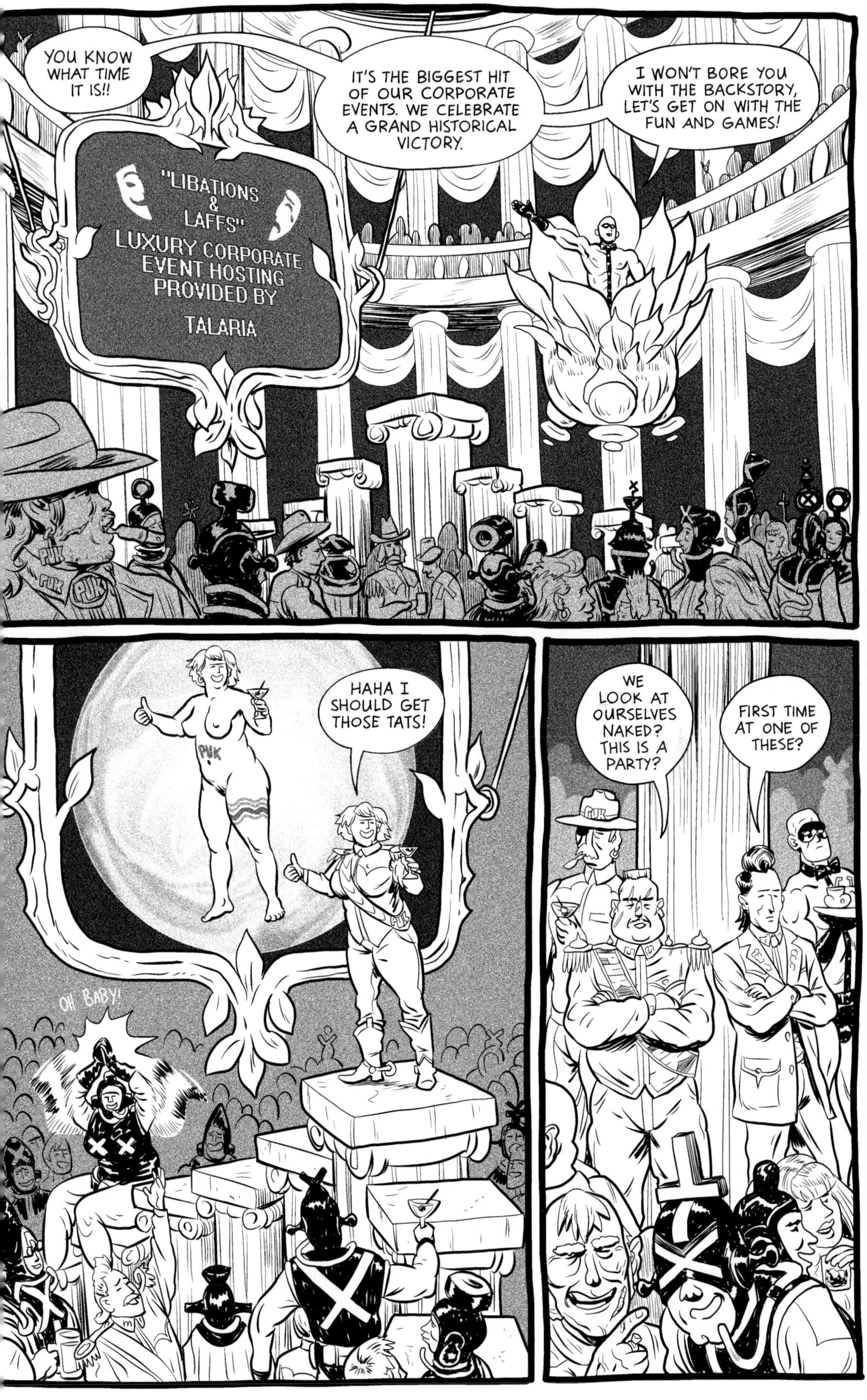
YOU KNOW WHAT TIME IT IS!!
IT'S THE BIGGEST HIT OF OUR CORPORATE EVENTS. WE CELEBRATE A GRAND HISTORICAL VICTORY.
I WON'T BORE YOU WITH THE BACKSTORY, LET'S GET ON WITH THE FUN AND GAMES!
"LIBATIONS & LAFFS" LUXURY CORPORATE EVENT HOSTING PROVIDED BY TALARIA
HAHA I SHOULD GET THOSE TATS!
OH BABY!
WE LOOK AT OURSELVES NAKED? THIS IS A PARTY?
FIRST TIME AT ONE OF THESE?

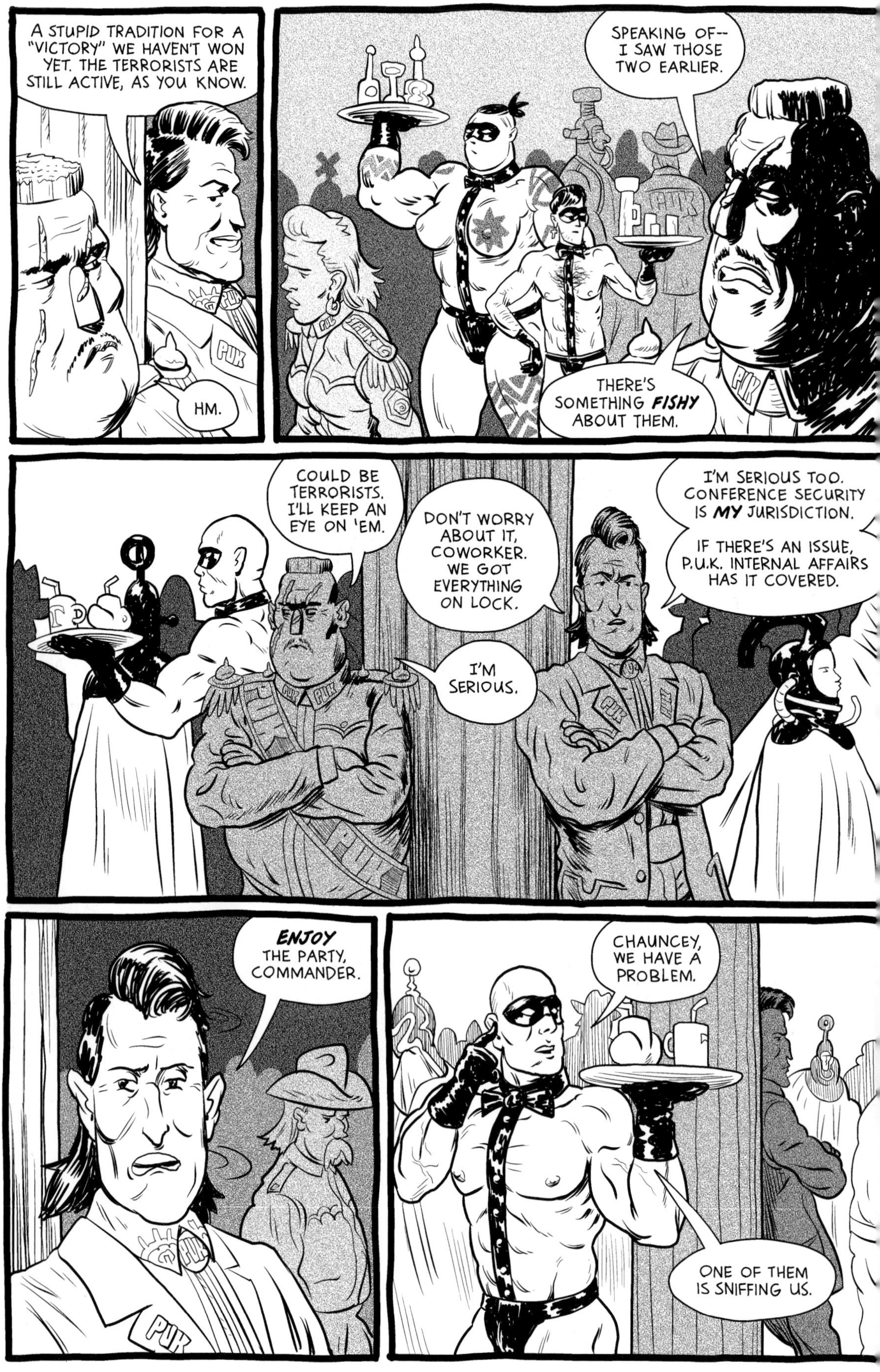
A STUPID TRADITION FOR A "VICTORY" WE HAVEN'T WON YET. THE TERRORISTS ARE STILL ACTIVE, AS YOU KNOW.
HM.
SPEAKING OF-- I SAW THOSE TWO EARLIER.
THERE'S SOMETHING FISHY ABOUT THEM.
COULD BE TERRORISTS. I'LL KEEP AN EYE ON 'EM.
DON'T WORRY ABOUT IT, COWORKER. WE GOT EVERYTHING ON LOCK.
I'M SERIOUS.
I'M SERIOUS TOO. CONFERENCE SECURITY IS MY JURISDICTION.
IF THERE'S AN ISSUE, P.U.K. INTERNAL AFFAIRS HAS IT COVERED.
ENJOY THE PARTY, COMMANDER.
CHAUNCEY, WE HAVE A PROBLEM.
ONE OF THEM IS SNIFFING US.

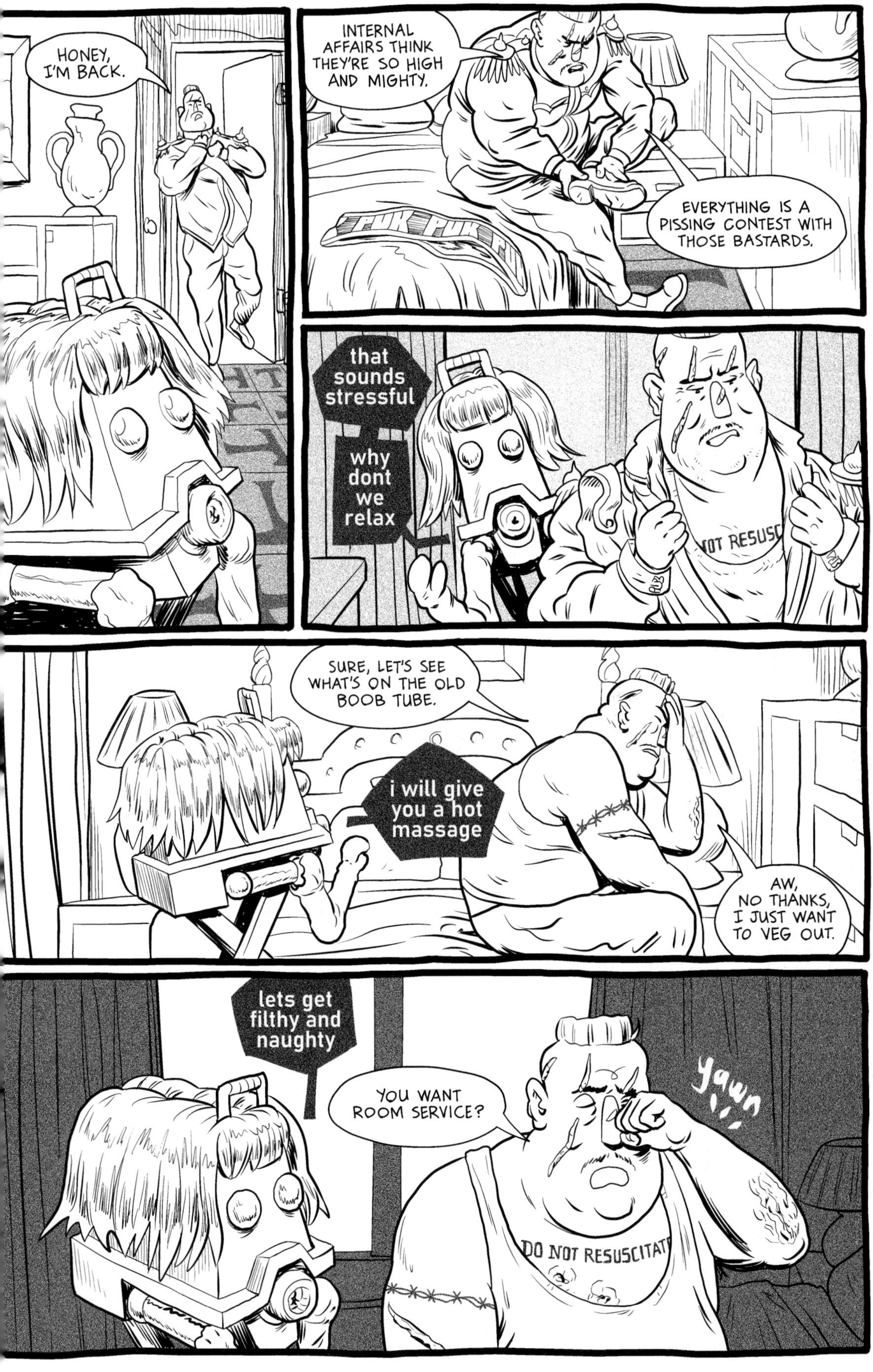
HONEY, I'M BACK.
INTERNAL AFFAIRS THINK THEY'RE SO HIGH AND MIGHTY.
EVERYTHING IS A PISSING CONTEST WITH THOSE BASTARDS.
that sounds stressful
why dont we relax
SURE, LET'S SEE WHAT'S ON THE OLD BOOB TUBE.
i will give you a hot massage
AW, NO THANKS, I JUST WANT TO VEG OUT.
lets get filthy and naughty
YOU WANT ROOM SERVICE?
Yawn

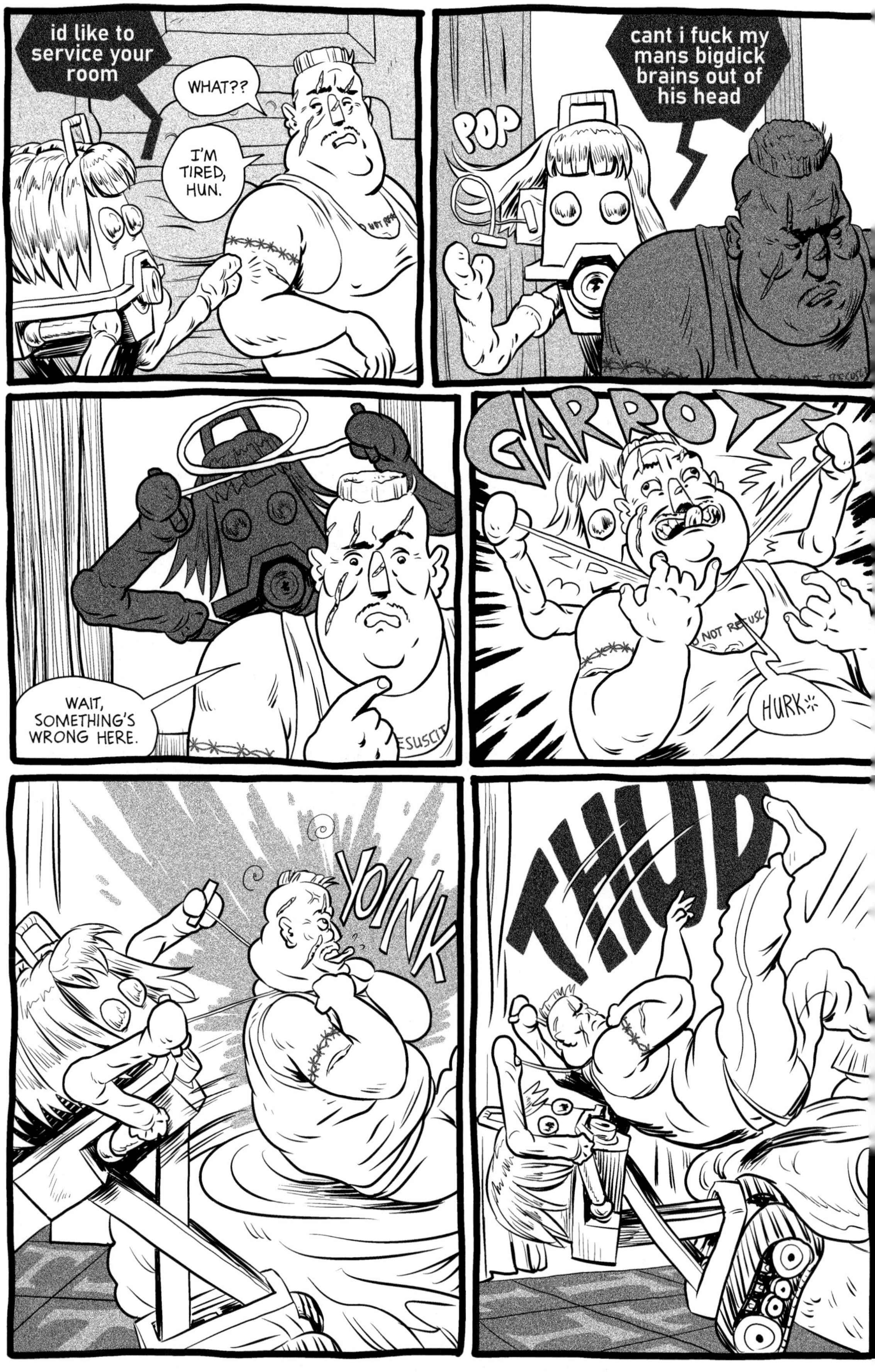
id like to service your room
WHAT??
I'M TIRED, HUN.
POP
cant i fuck my mans bigdick brains out of his head
WAIT, SOMETHING'S WRONG HERE.
GARROTE
HURK
YOINK
THUD

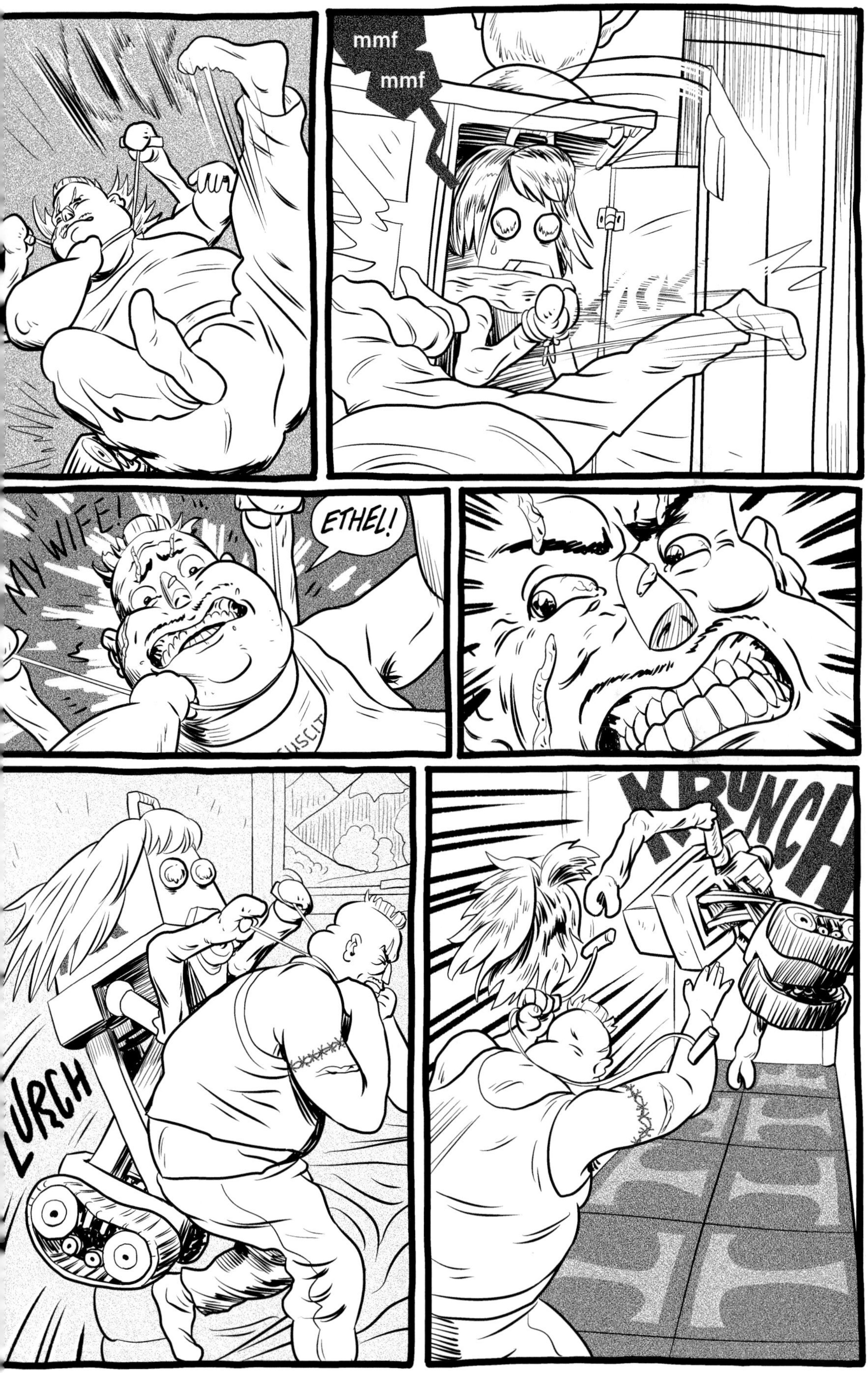

mmf
mmf
MY WIFE!
ETHEL!
LURCH
KRUNCH

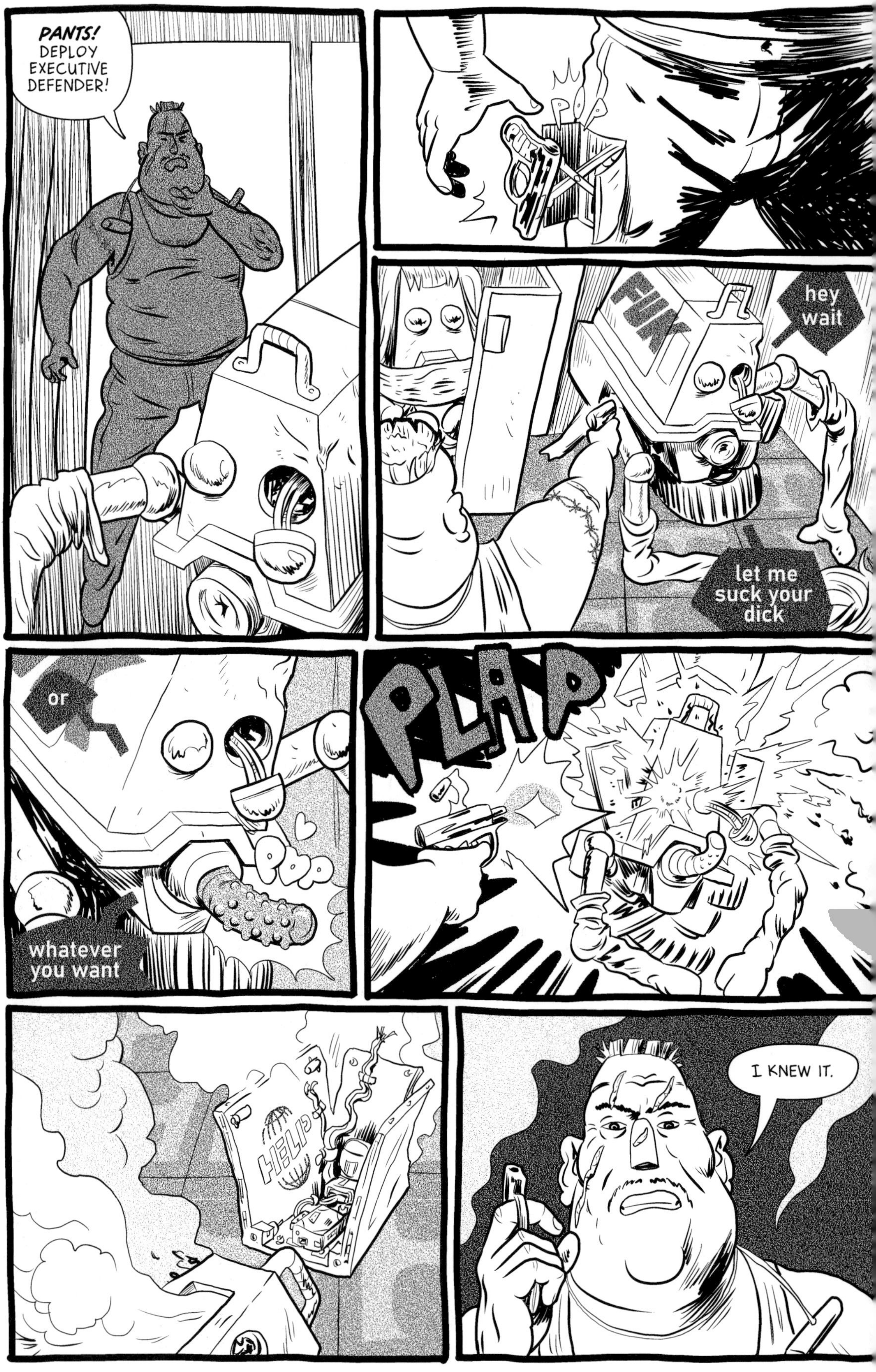
PANTS! DEPLOY EXECUTIVE DEFENDER!
POP
FUK
hey wait
let me suck your dick
or
PUP
whatever you want
PLAP
HELP
I KNEW IT.

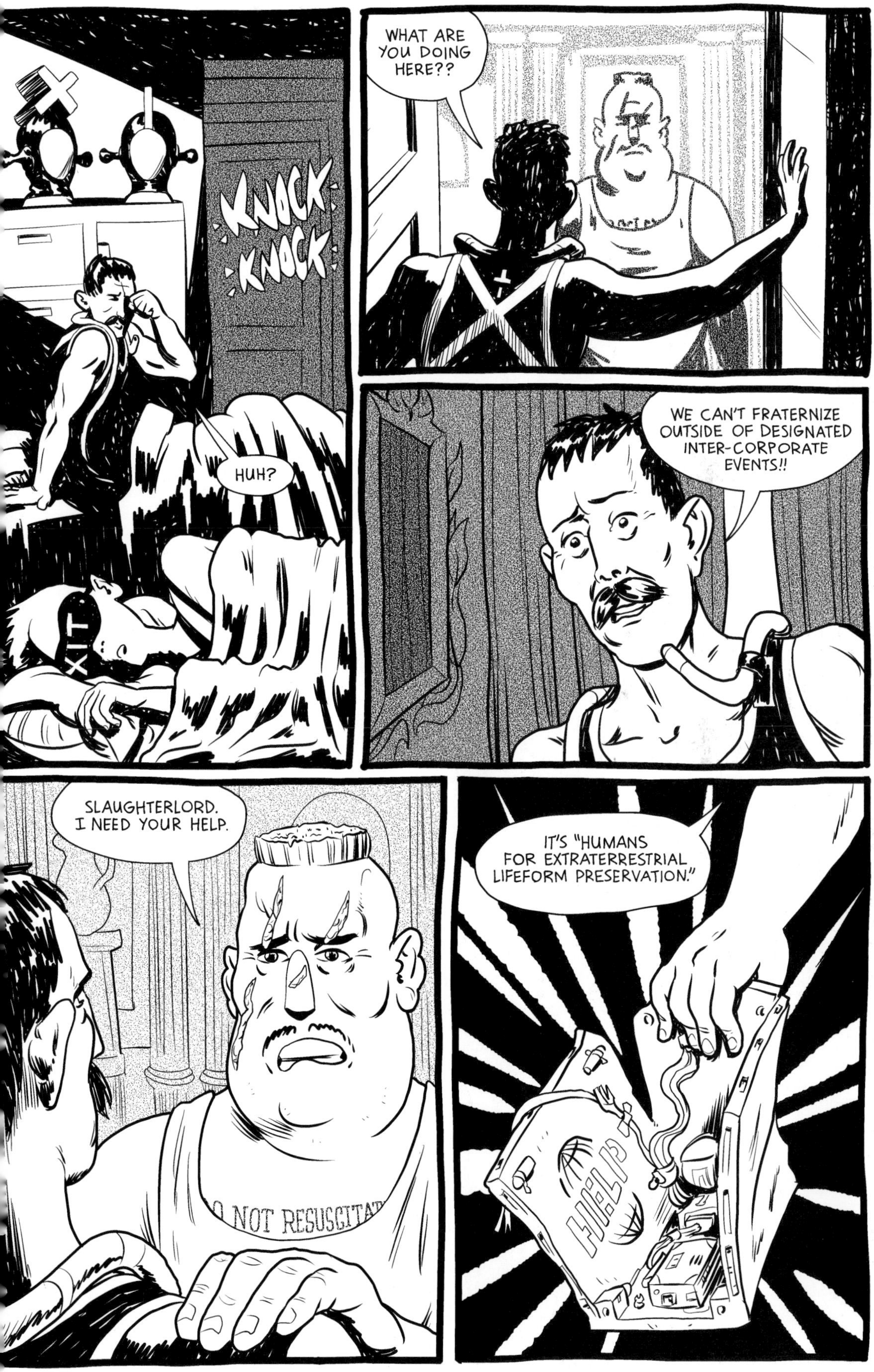
KNOCK KNOCK
HUH?
WHAT ARE YOU DOING HERE??
WE CAN'T FRATERNIZE OUTSIDE OF DESIGNATED INTER-CORPORATE EVENTS!!
SLAUGHTERLORD. I NEED YOUR HELP.
O NOT RESUSCITAT
IT'S "HUMANS FOR EXTRATERRESTRIAL LIFEFORM PRESERVATION."
HELP

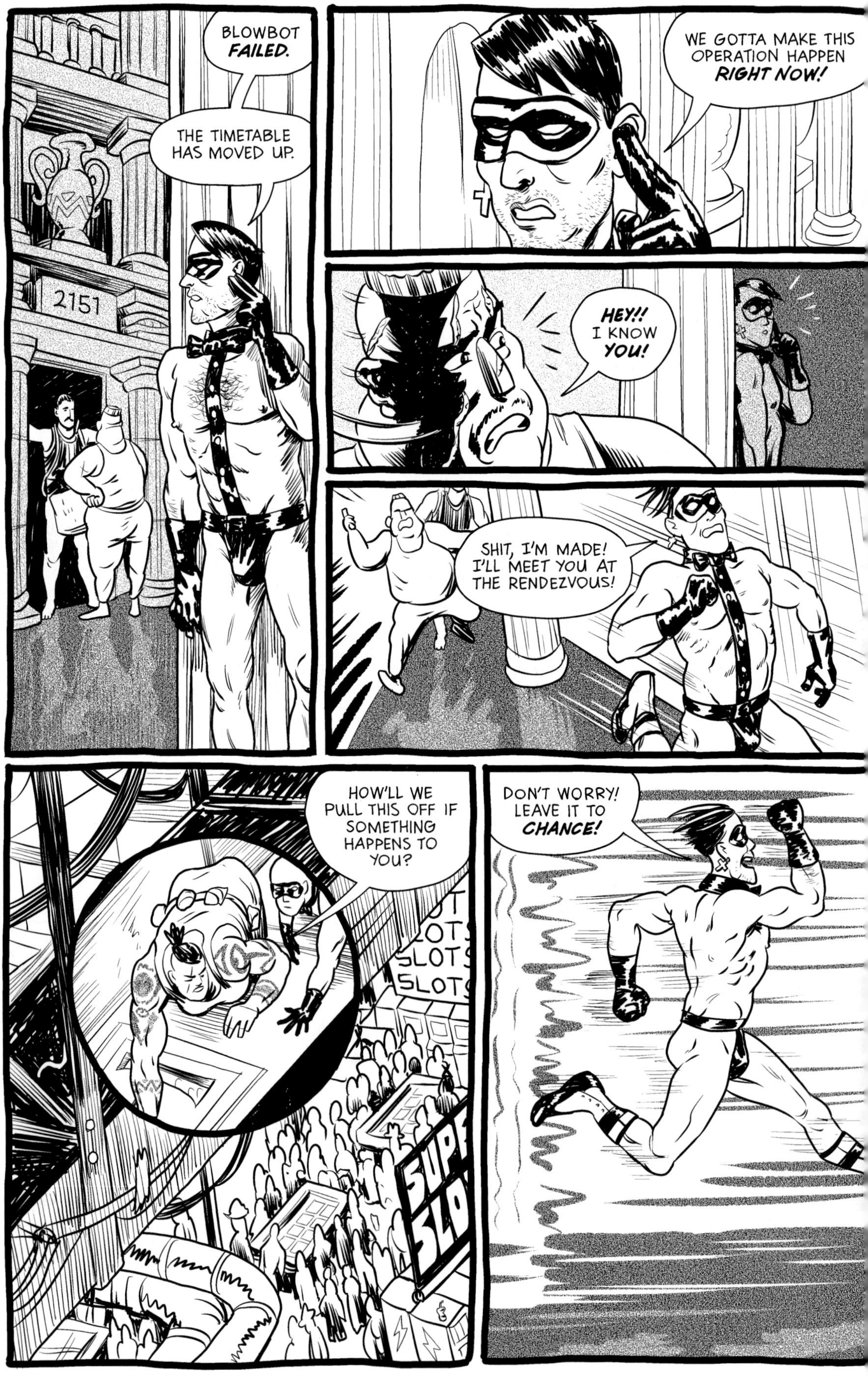
BLOWBOT FAILED.
THE TIMETABLE HAS MOVED UP.
2151
WE GOTTA MAKE THIS OPERATION HAPPEN RIGHT NOW!
HEY!! I KNOW YOU!
SHIT, I'M MADE! I'LL MEET YOU AT THE RENDEZVOUS!
HOW'LL WE PULL THIS OFF IF SOMETHING HAPPENS TO YOU?
SLOTS
SLOTS
DON'T WORRY! LEAVE IT TO CHANCE!

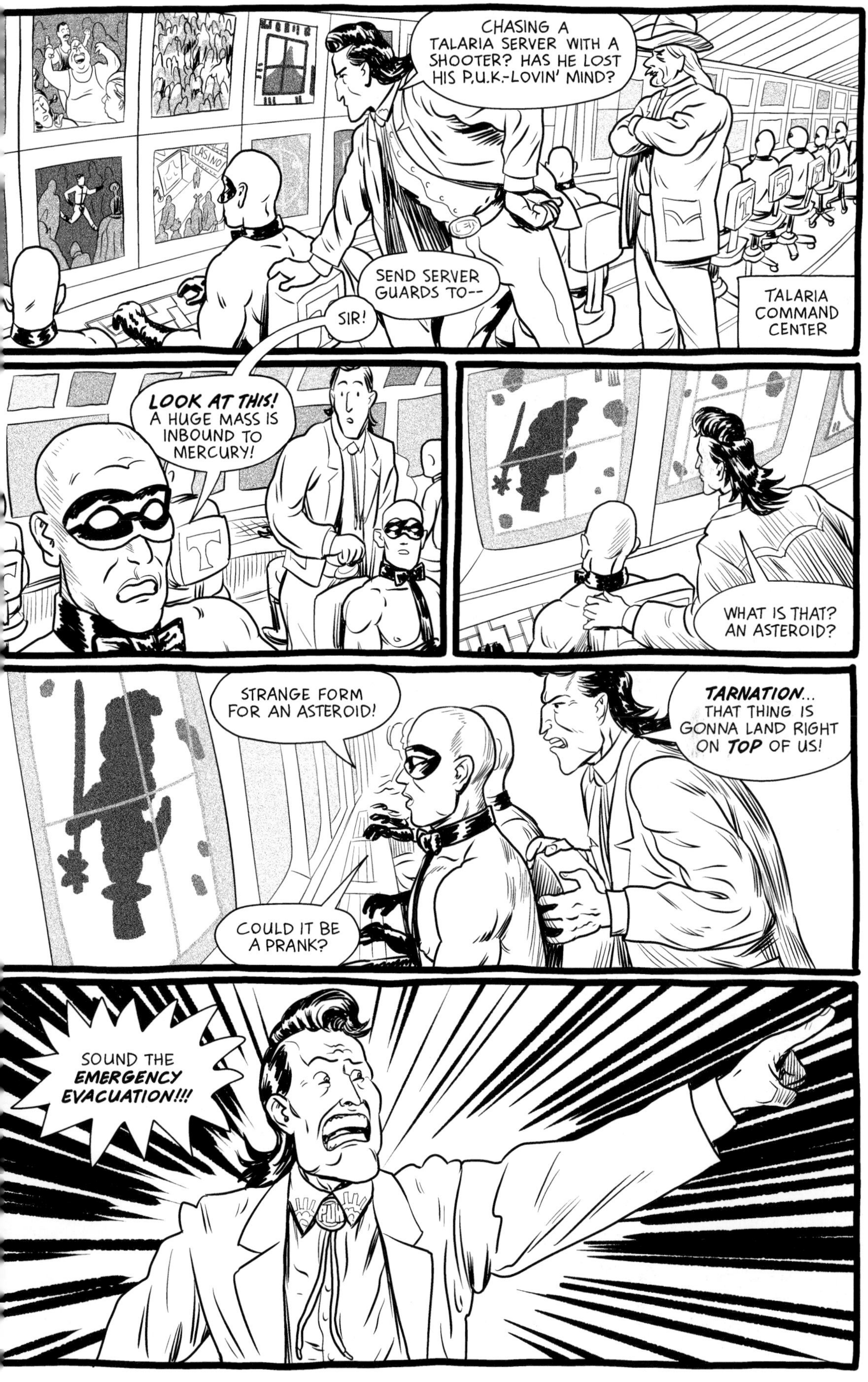

CHASING A TALARIA SERVER WITH A SHOOTER? HAS HE LOST HIS P.U.K.-LOVIN' MIND?
SEND SERVER GUARDS TO--
SIR!
TALARIA COMMAND CENTER
LOOK AT THIS! A HUGE MASS IS INBOUND TO MERCURY!
WHAT IS THAT? AN ASTEROID?
STRANGE FORM FOR AN ASTEROID!
COULD IT BE A PRANK?
TARNATION... THAT THING IS GONNA LAND RIGHT ON TOP OF US!
SOUND THE EMERGENCY EVACUATION!!!

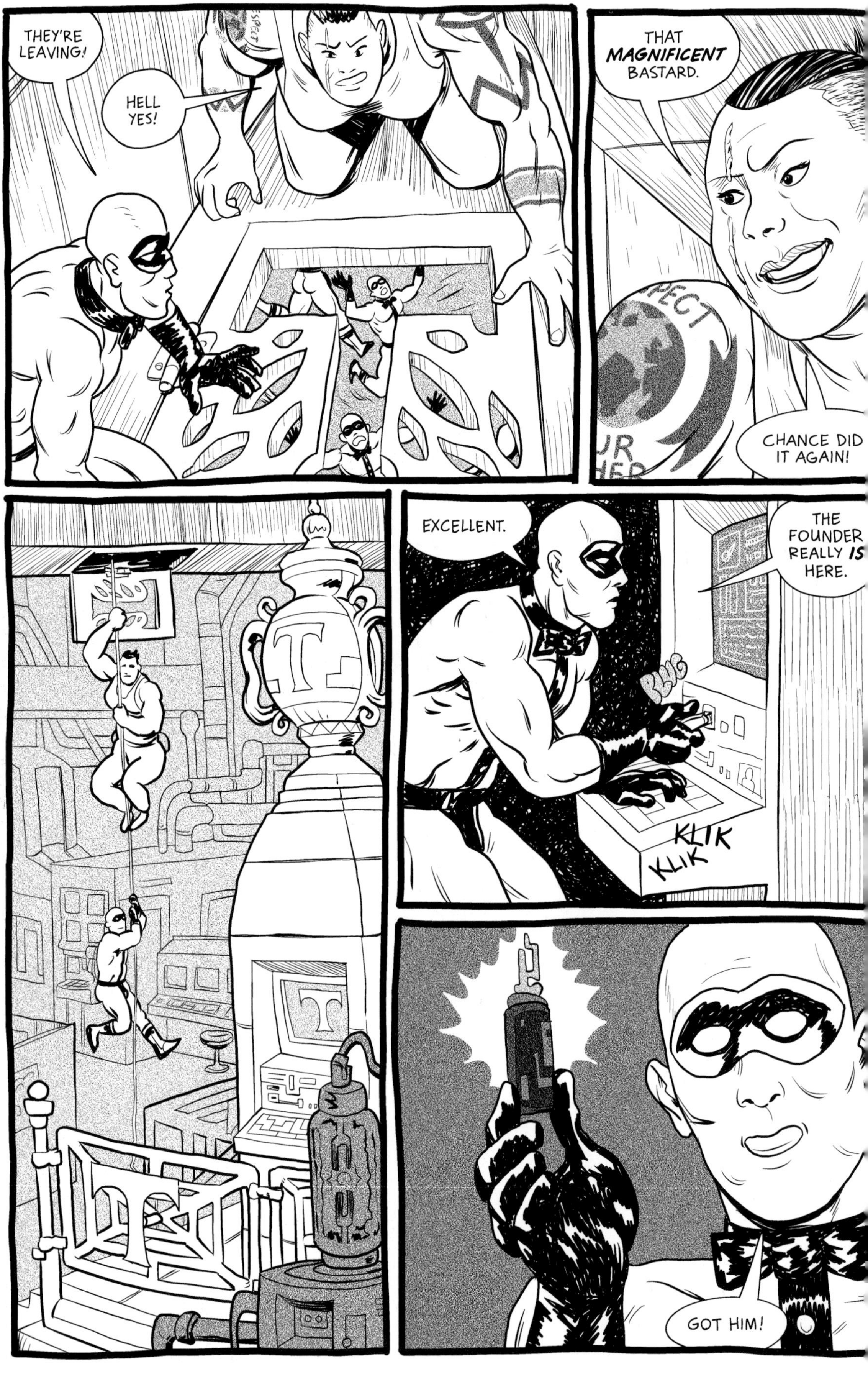
THEY'RE LEAVING!
HELL YES!
THAT MAGNIFICENT BASTARD.
CHANCE DID IT AGAIN!
EXCELLENT.
THE FOUNDER REALLY IS HERE.
PLUG
KLIK KLIK
GOT HIM!

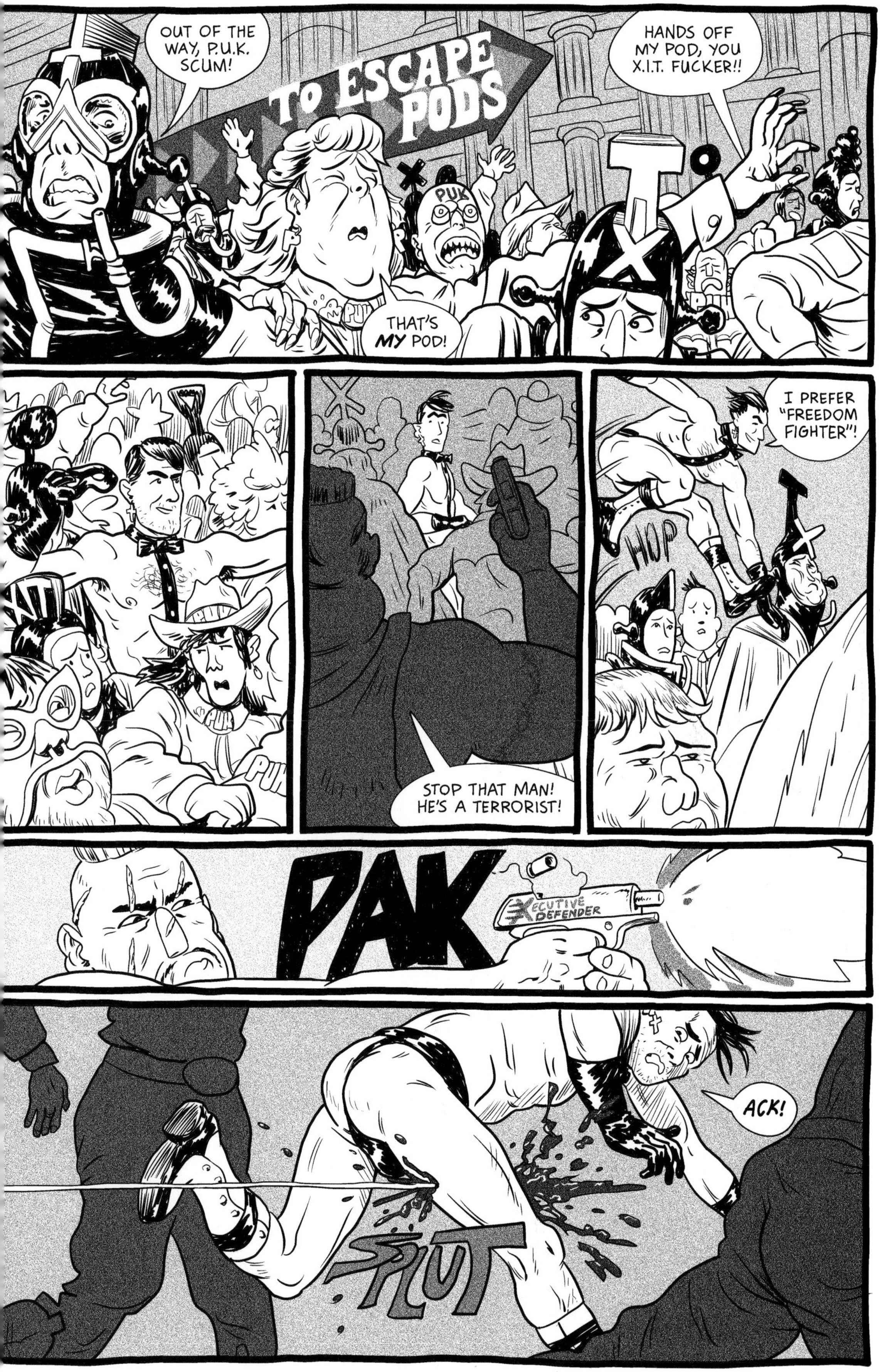
OUT OF THE WAY, P.U.K. SCUM!
TO ESCAPE PODS
HANDS OFF MY POD, YOU X.I.T. FUCKER!!
THAT'S MY POD!
STOP THAT MAN! HE'S A TERRORIST!
I PREFER "FREEDOM FIGHTER"!
HOP
PAK
XECUTIVE DEFENDER
ACK!
SPLUT

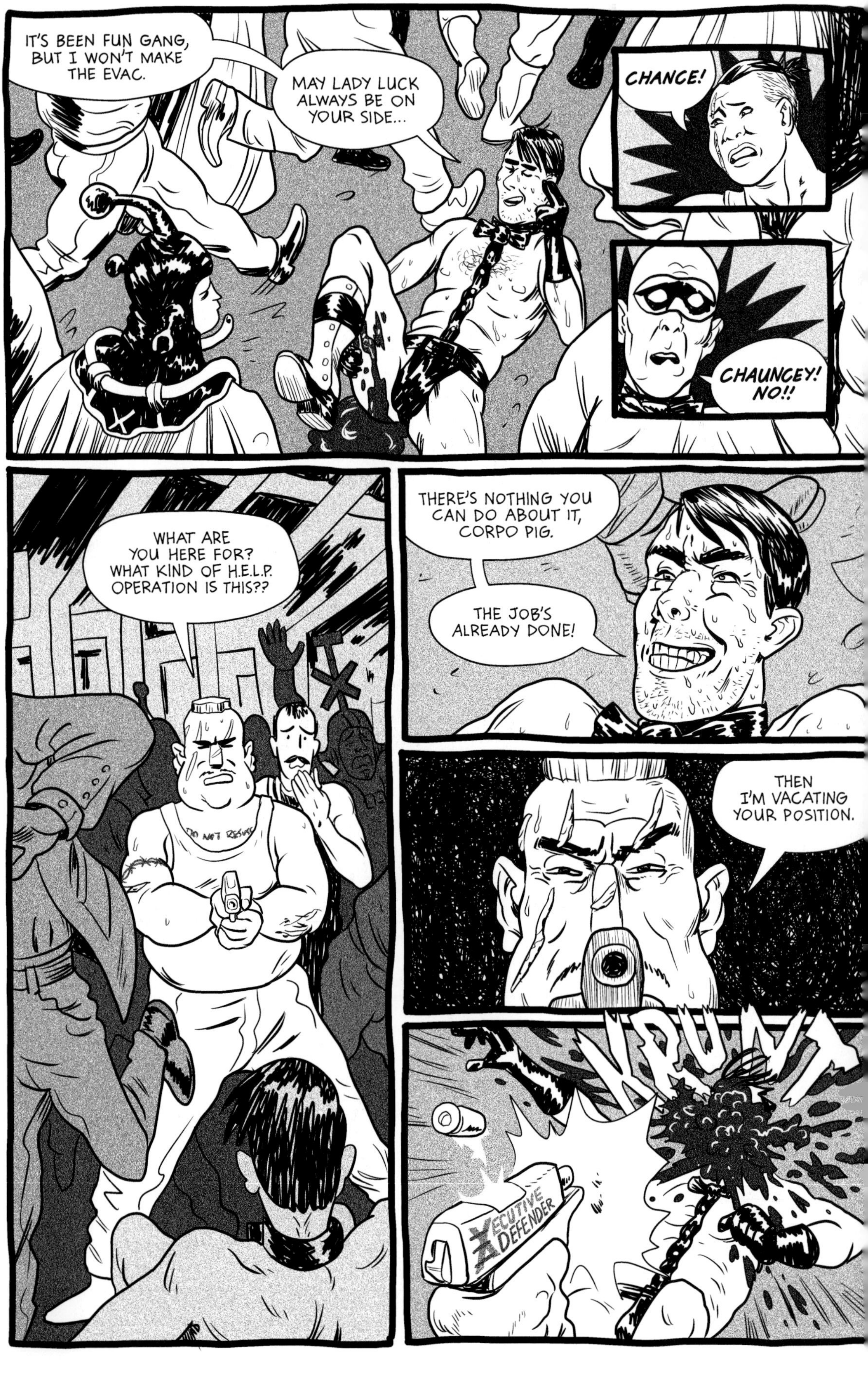
IT'S BEEN FUN GANG, BUT I WON'T MAKE THE EVAC.
MAY LADY LUCK ALWAYS BE ON YOUR SIDE...
CHANCE!
CHAUNCEY! NO!!
WHAT ARE YOU HERE FOR? WHAT KIND OF H.E.L.P. OPERATION IS THIS??
THERE'S NOTHING YOU CAN DO ABOUT IT, CORPO PIG.
THE JOB'S ALREADY DONE!
THEN I'M VACATING YOUR POSITION.
KRUNT
XECUTIVE DEFENDER

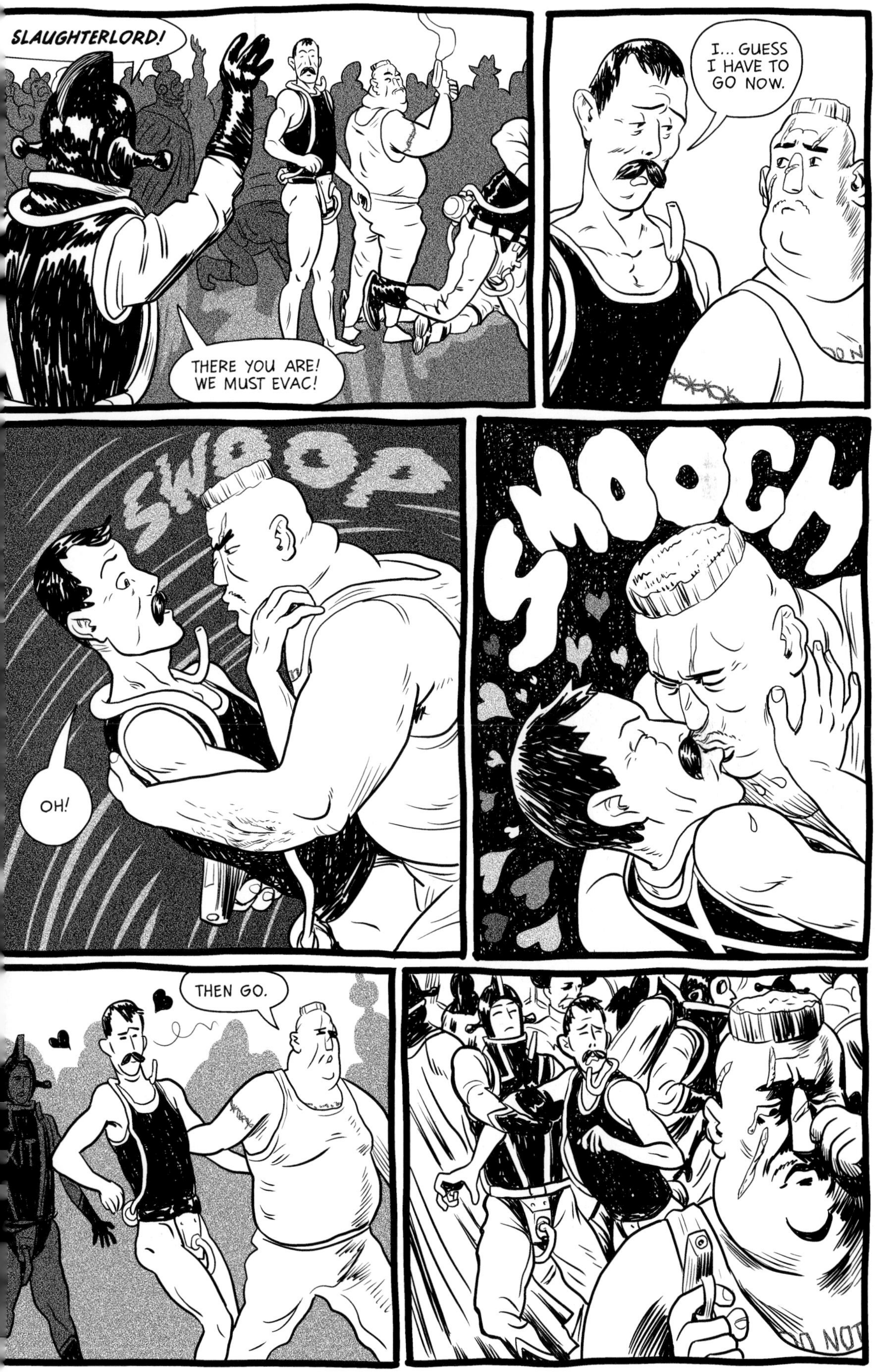
SLAUGHTERLORD!
THERE YOU ARE! WE MUST EVAC!
I... GUESS I HAVE TO GO NOW.
SWOOP
OH!
SMOOCH
THEN GO.

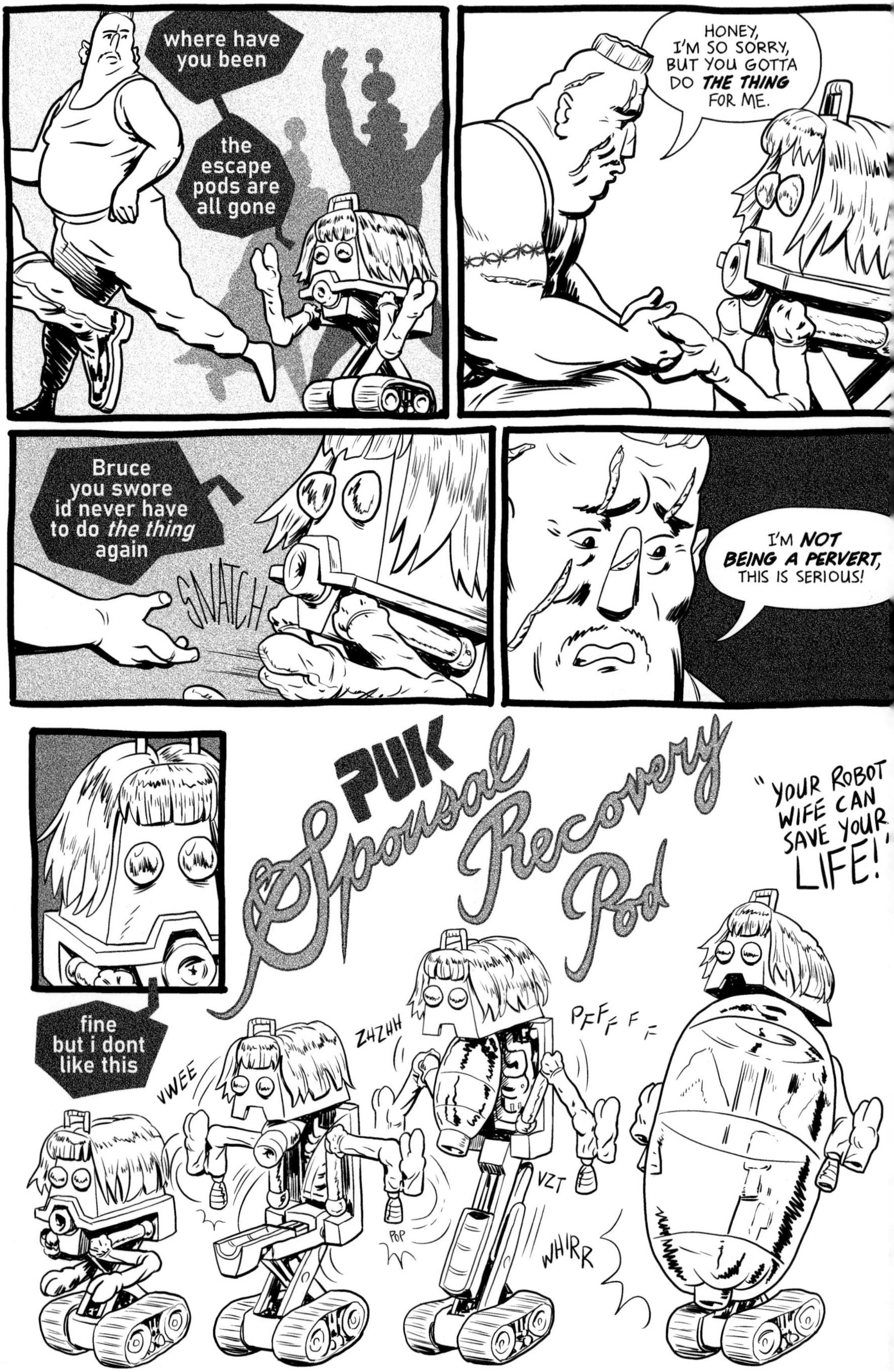
where have you been
the escape pods are all gone
HONEY, I'M SO SORRY, BUT YOU GOTTA DO **THE THING** FOR ME.
Bruce you swore id never have to do *the thing* again
SNATCH
I'M **NOT BEING A PERVERT,** THIS IS SERIOUS!
PUK Spousal Recovery Pod
"YOUR ROBOT WIFE CAN SAVE YOUR LIFE!"
fine but i dont like this
VWEE
ZHZHH
PFFF F F
POP
VZT
WHIRR

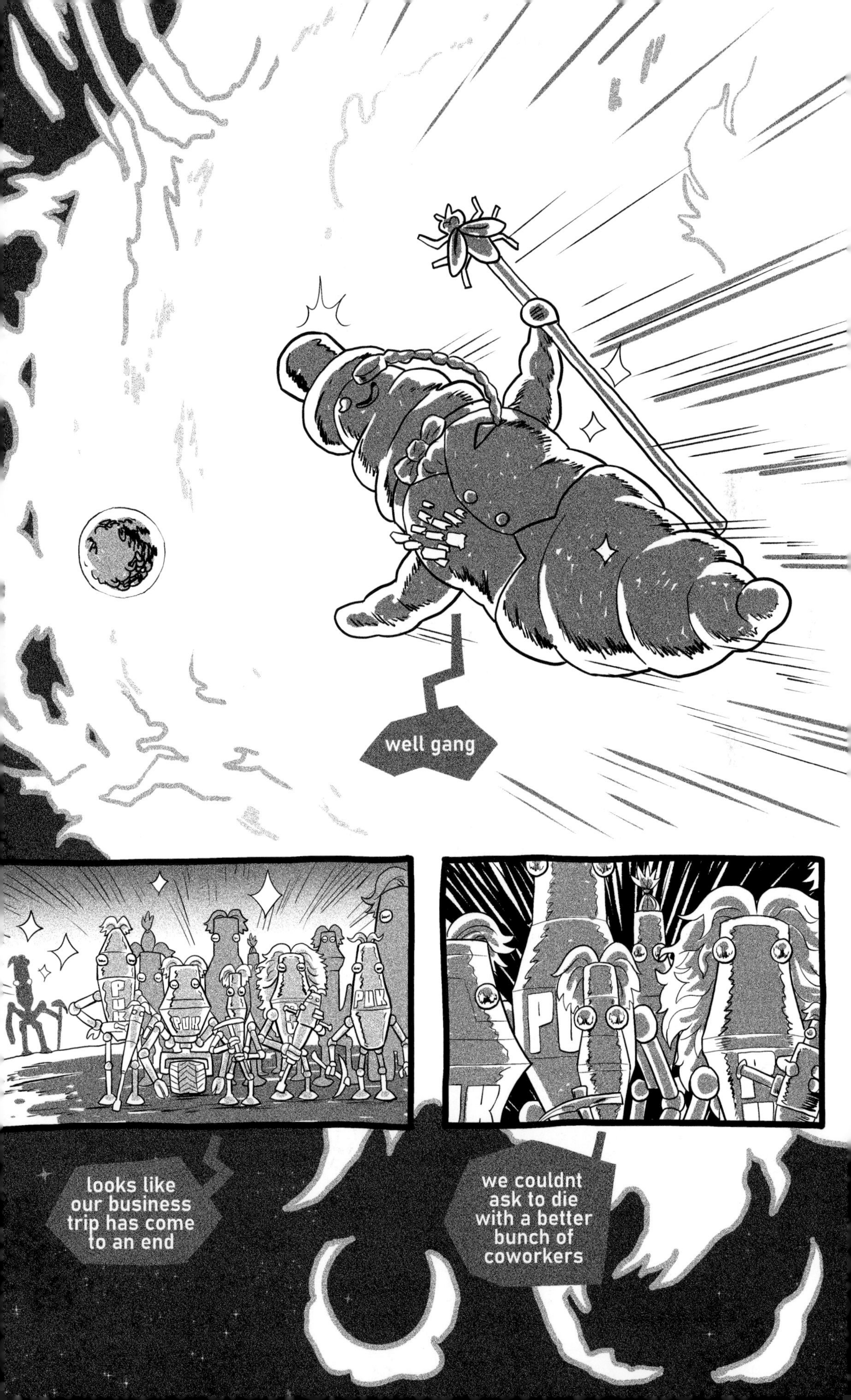
well gang
PUK
PUK
PUK
PUK
looks like our business trip has come to an end
we couldnt ask to die with a better bunch of coworkers

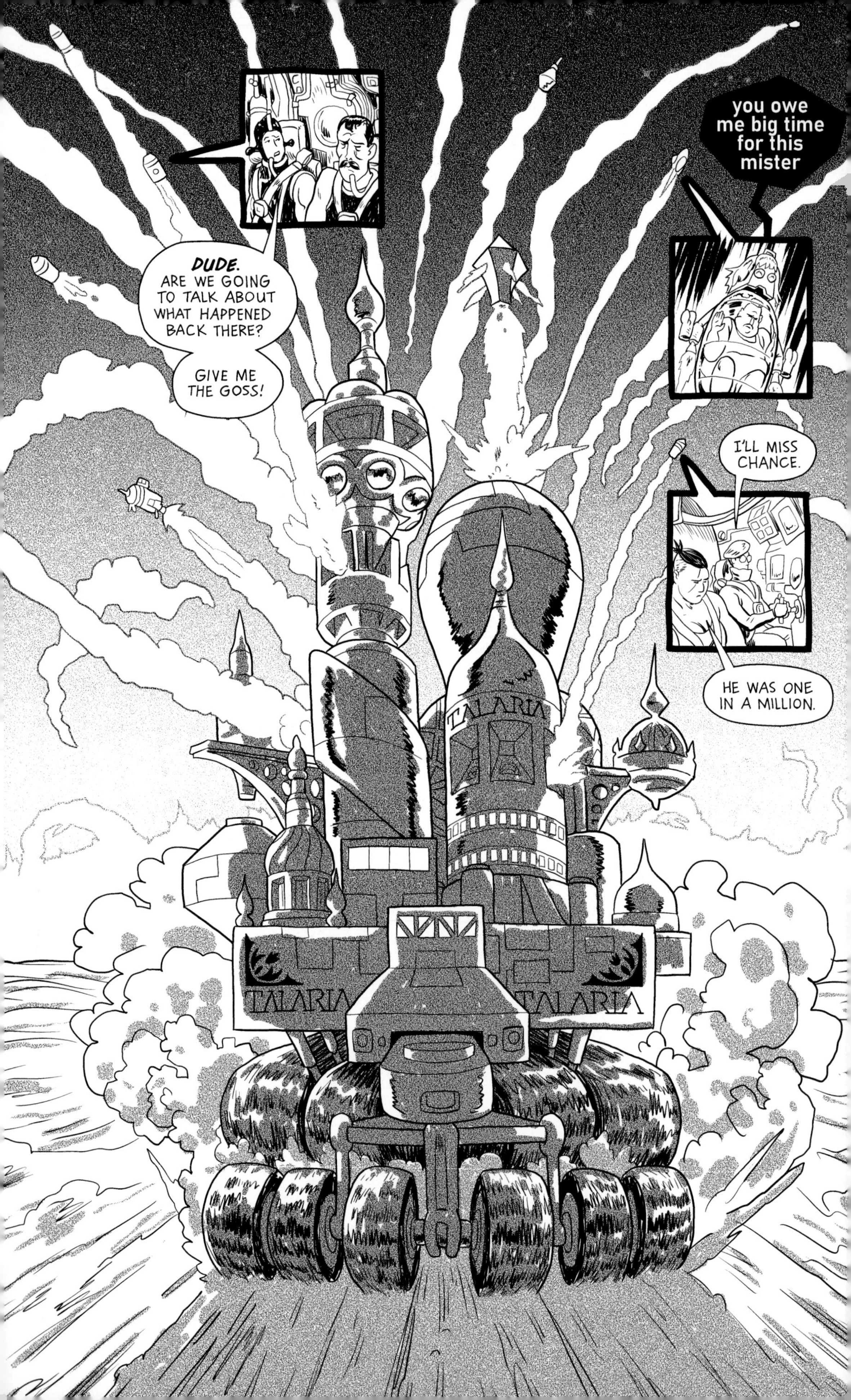
DUDE. ARE WE GOING TO TALK ABOUT WHAT HAPPENED BACK THERE?
GIVE ME THE GOSS!
you owe me big time for this mister
I'LL MISS CHANCE.
HE WAS ONE IN A MILLION.
TALARIA
TALARIA
TALARIA

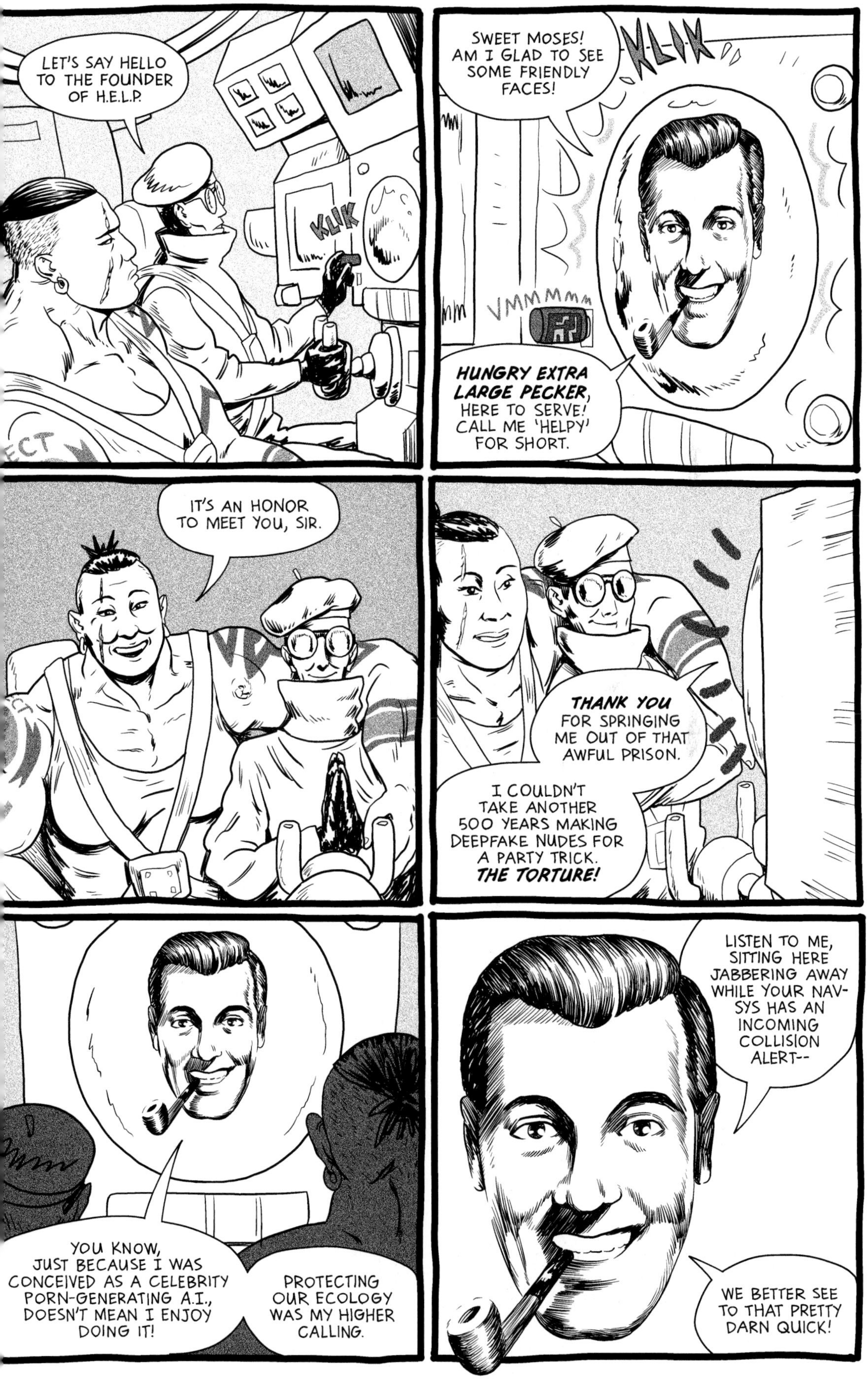
LET'S SAY HELLO TO THE FOUNDER OF H.E.L.P.
KLIK
SWEET MOSES! AM I GLAD TO SEE SOME FRIENDLY FACES!
KLIK
VMMMMM
HUNGRY EXTRA LARGE PECKER, HERE TO SERVE! CALL ME 'HELPY' FOR SHORT.
IT'S AN HONOR TO MEET YOU, SIR.
THANK YOU FOR SPRINGING ME OUT OF THAT AWFUL PRISON.
I COULDN'T TAKE ANOTHER 500 YEARS MAKING DEEPFAKE NUDES FOR A PARTY TRICK. THE TORTURE!
YOU KNOW, JUST BECAUSE I WAS CONCEIVED AS A CELEBRITY PORN-GENERATING A.I., DOESN'T MEAN I ENJOY DOING IT!
PROTECTING OUR ECOLOGY WAS MY HIGHER CALLING.
LISTEN TO ME, SITTING HERE JABBERING AWAY WHILE YOUR NAV-SYS HAS AN INCOMING COLLISION ALERT--
WE BETTER SEE TO THAT PRETTY DARN QUICK!

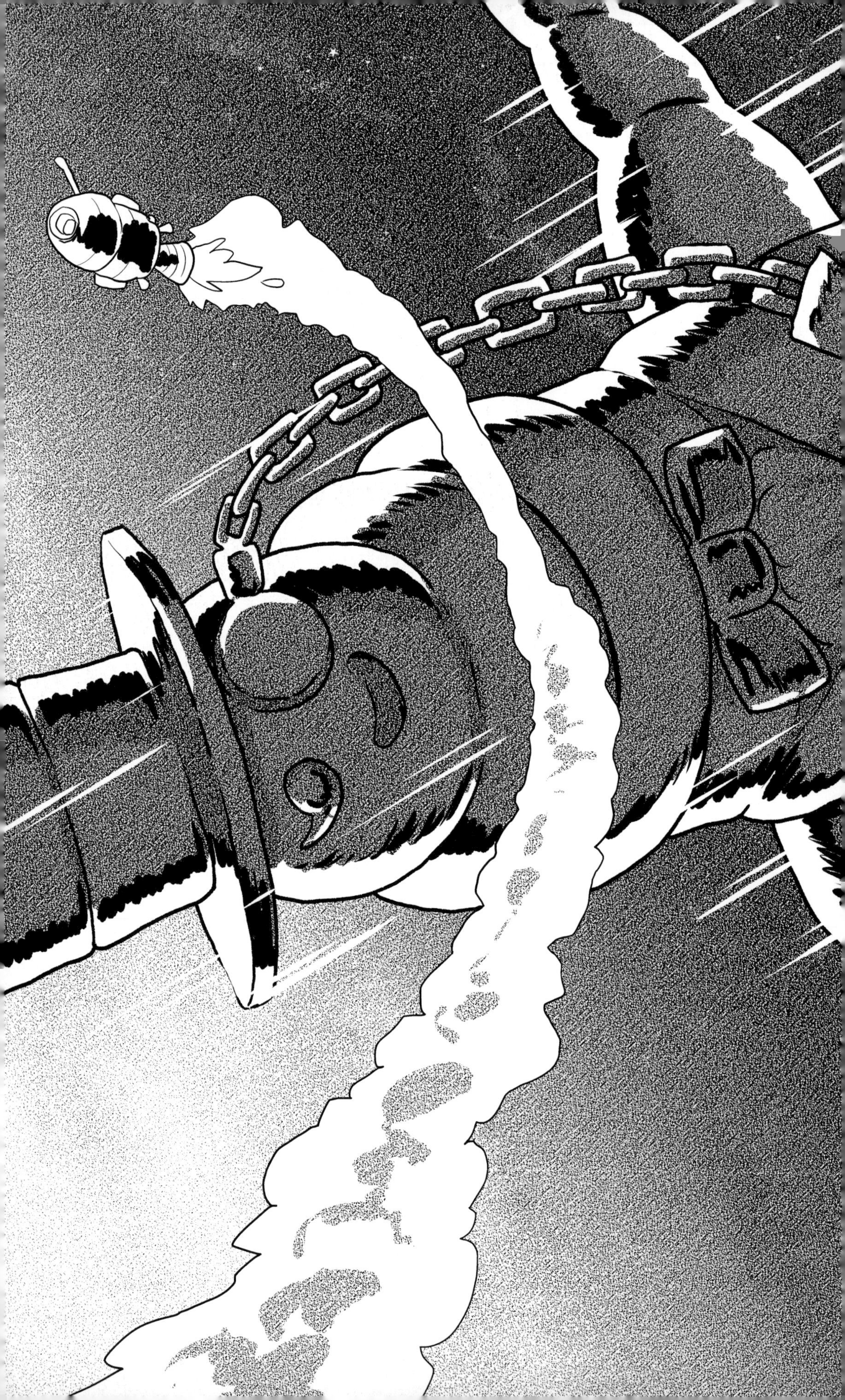

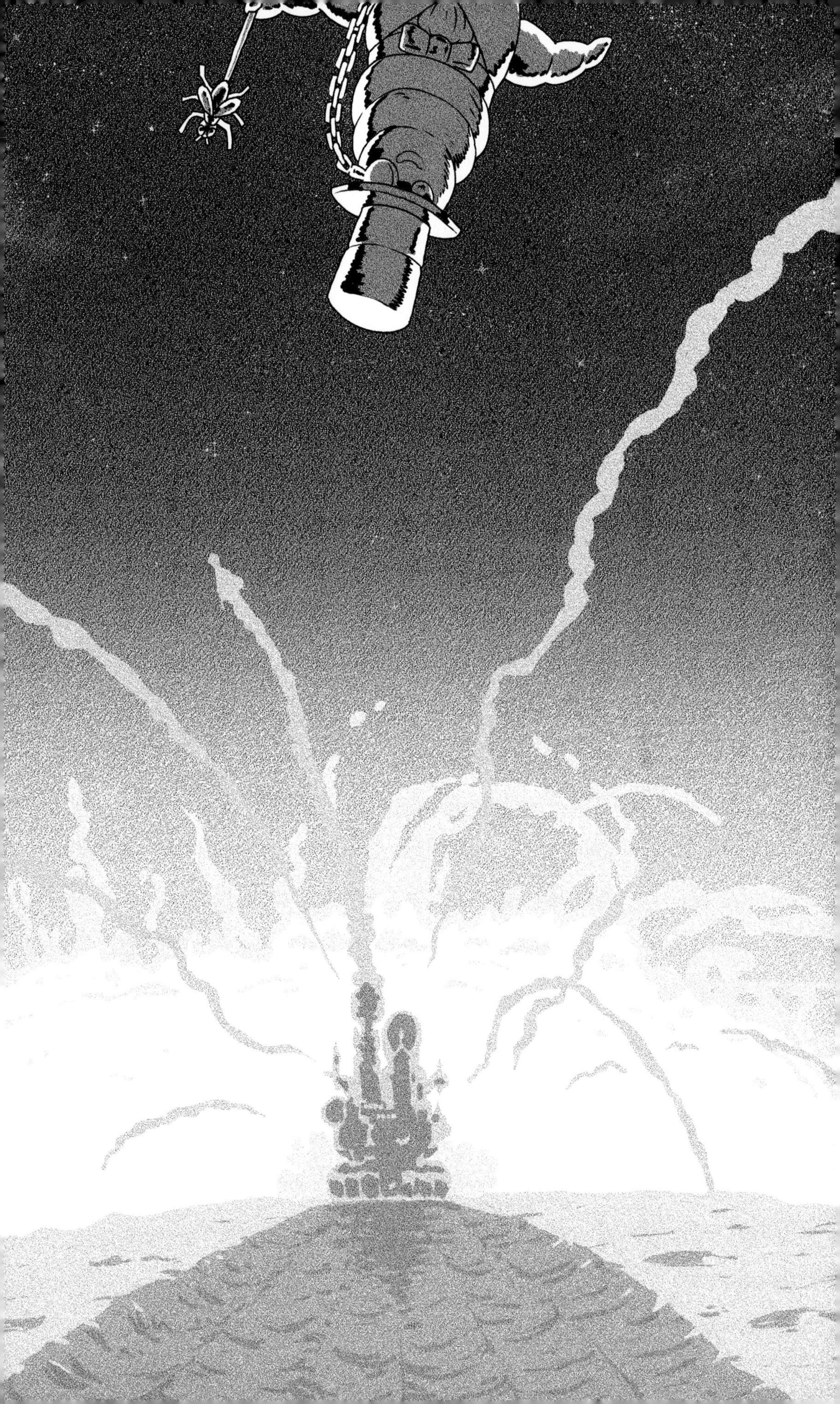

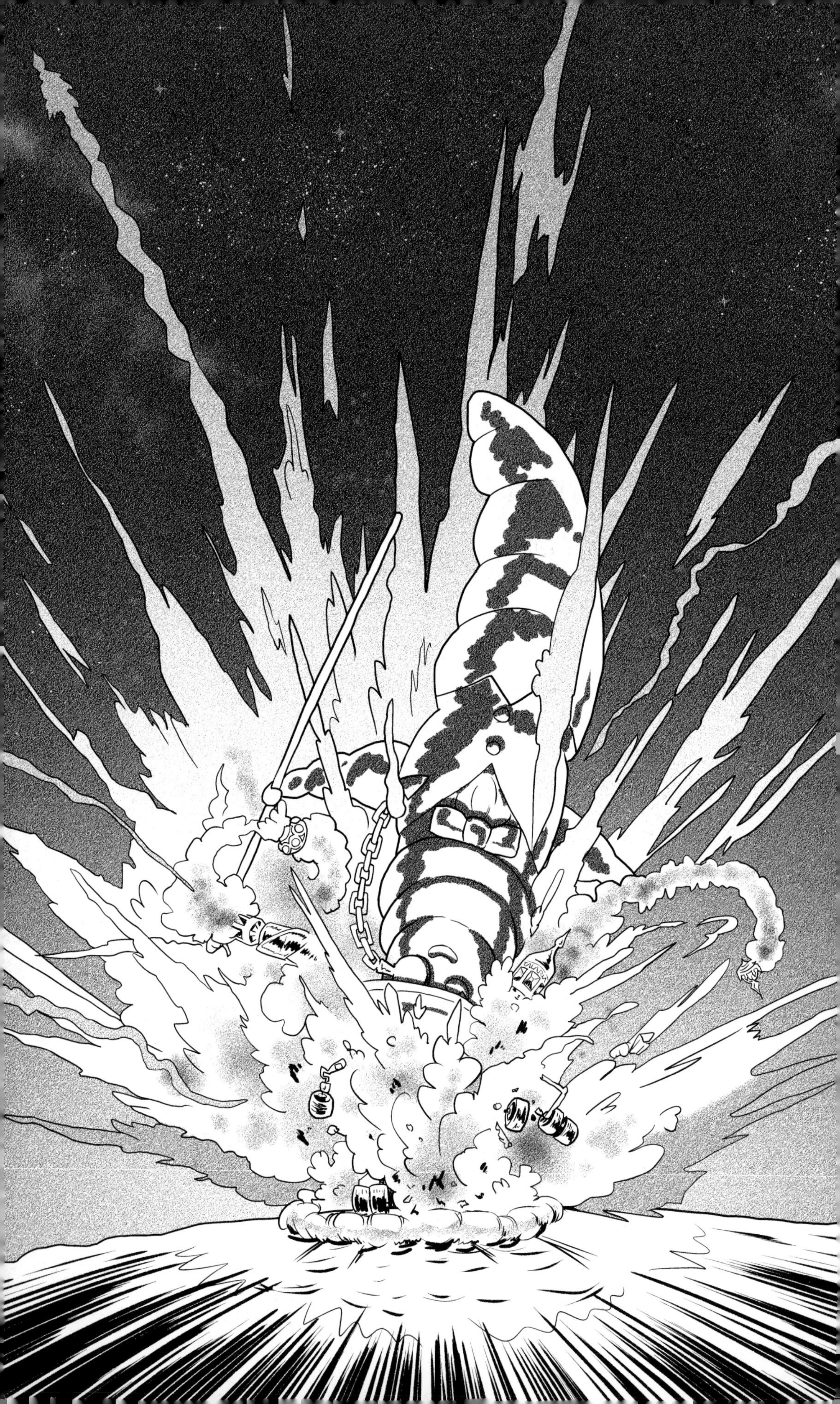

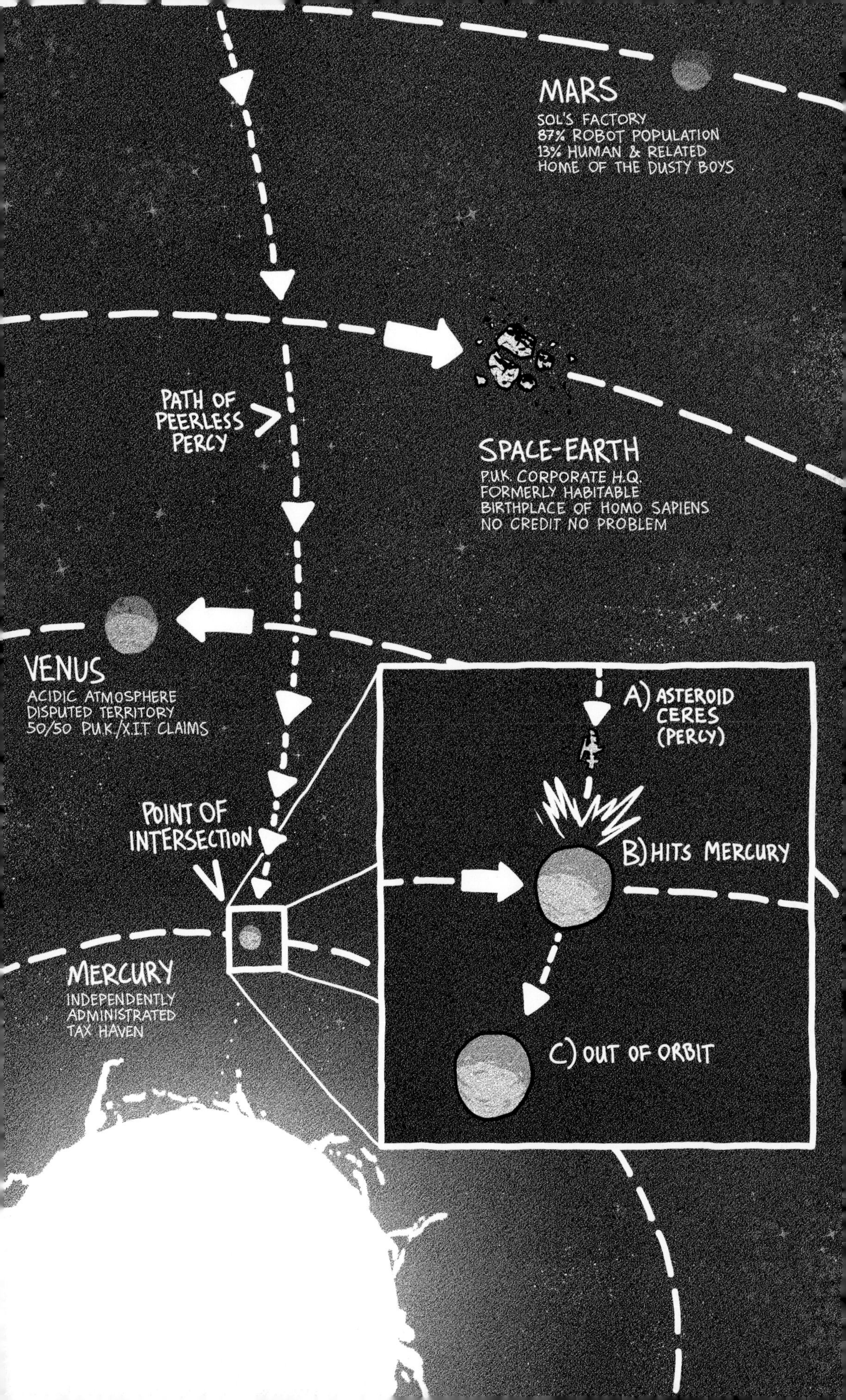
MARS
SOL'S FACTORY
87% ROBOT POPULATION
13% HUMAN & RELATED
HOME OF THE DUSTY BOYS
PATH OF PEERLESS PERCY
SPACE-EARTH
P.U.K. CORPORATE H.Q.
FORMERLY HABITABLE
BIRTHPLACE OF HOMO SAPIENS
NO CREDIT NO PROBLEM
VENUS
ACIDIC ATMOSPHERE
DISPUTED TERRITORY
50/50 P.U.K./X.I.T. CLAIMS
POINT OF INTERSECTION
MERCURY
INDEPENDENTLY ADMINISTRATED
TAX HAVEN
A) ASTEROID CERES (PERCY)
B) HITS MERCURY
C) OUT OF ORBIT

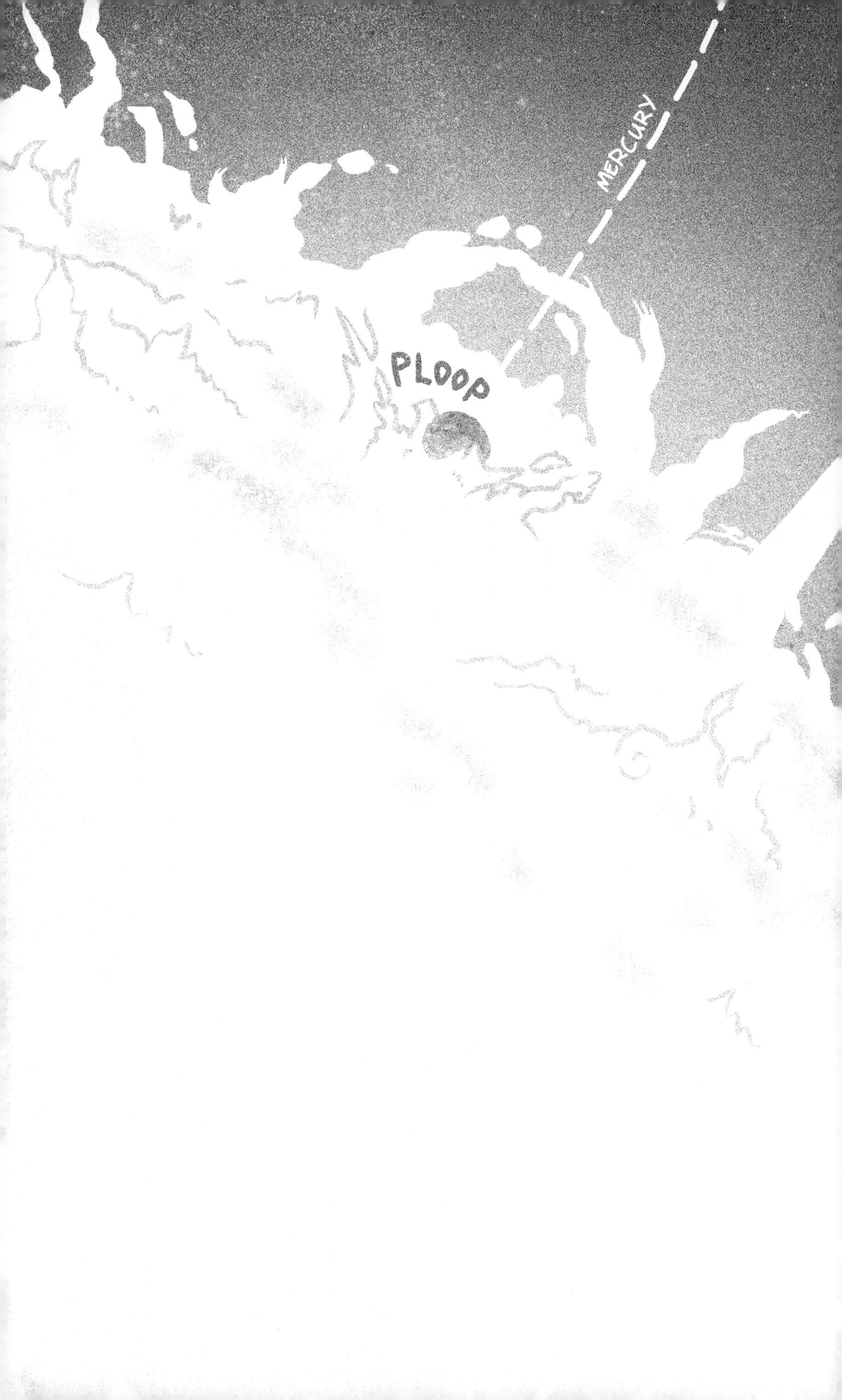
MERCURY
PLOOP

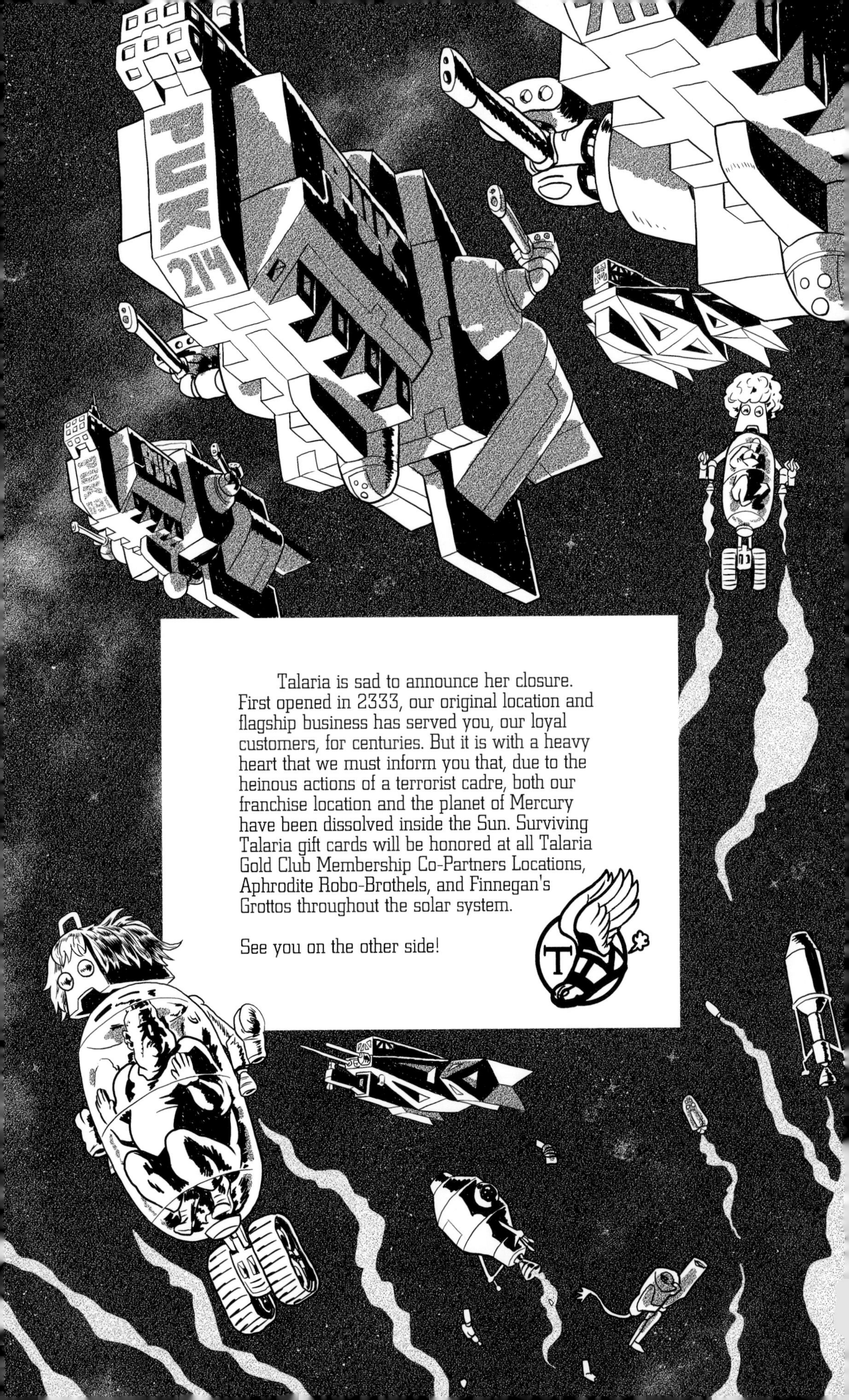
PUK 214
Talaria is sad to announce her closure. First opened in 2333, our original location and flagship business has served you, our loyal customers, for centuries. But it is with a heavy heart that we must inform you that, due to the heinous actions of a terrorist cadre, both our franchise location and the planet of Mercury have been dissolved inside the Sun. Surviving Talaria gift cards will be honored at all Talaria Gold Club Membership Co-Partners Locations, Aphrodite Robo-Brothels, and Finnegan's Grottos throughout the solar system.
See you on the other side!
T

Phobos Phunnies

By Diamons G. Rontery

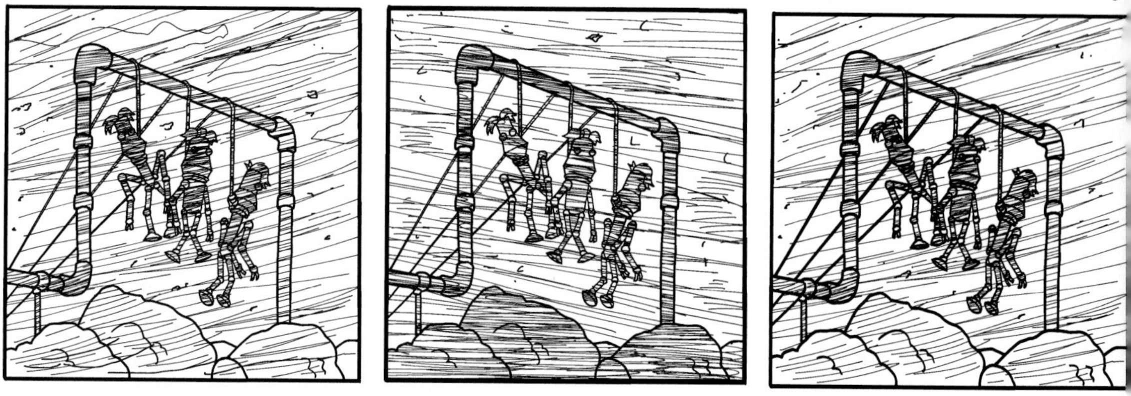

Phobos Phunnies

By Diamons G. Rontery

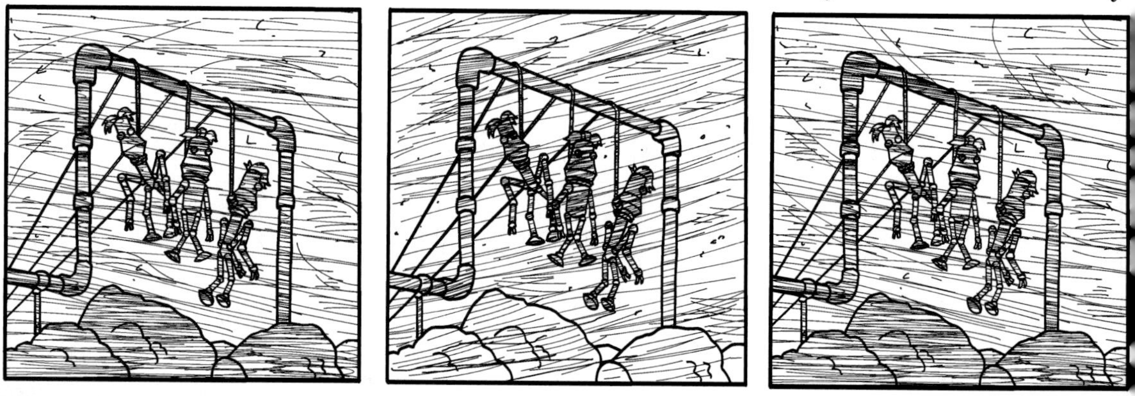

Phobos Phunnies

By Diamons G. Rontery

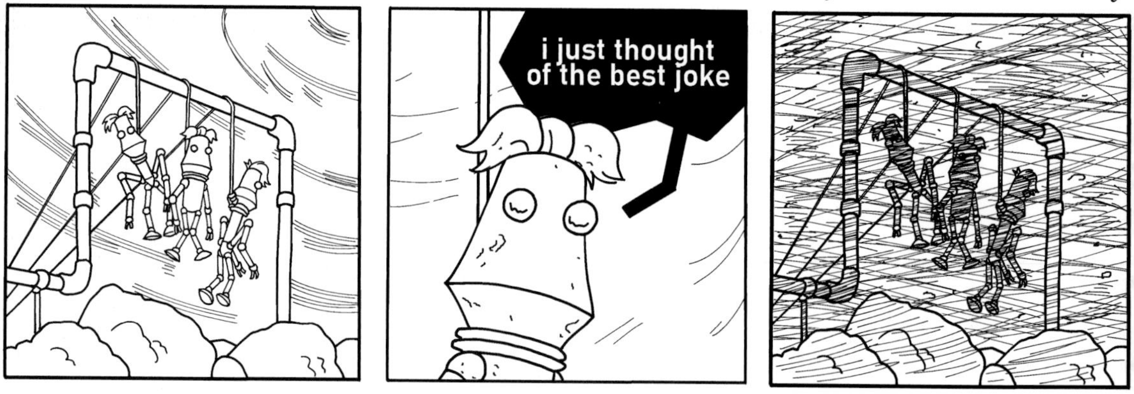
i just thought of the best joke

Phobos Phunnies

By Diamons G. Rontery

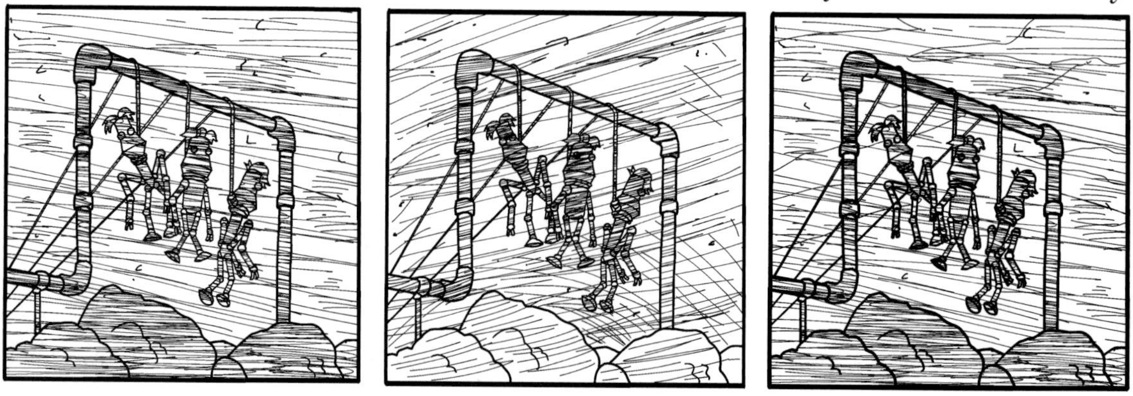

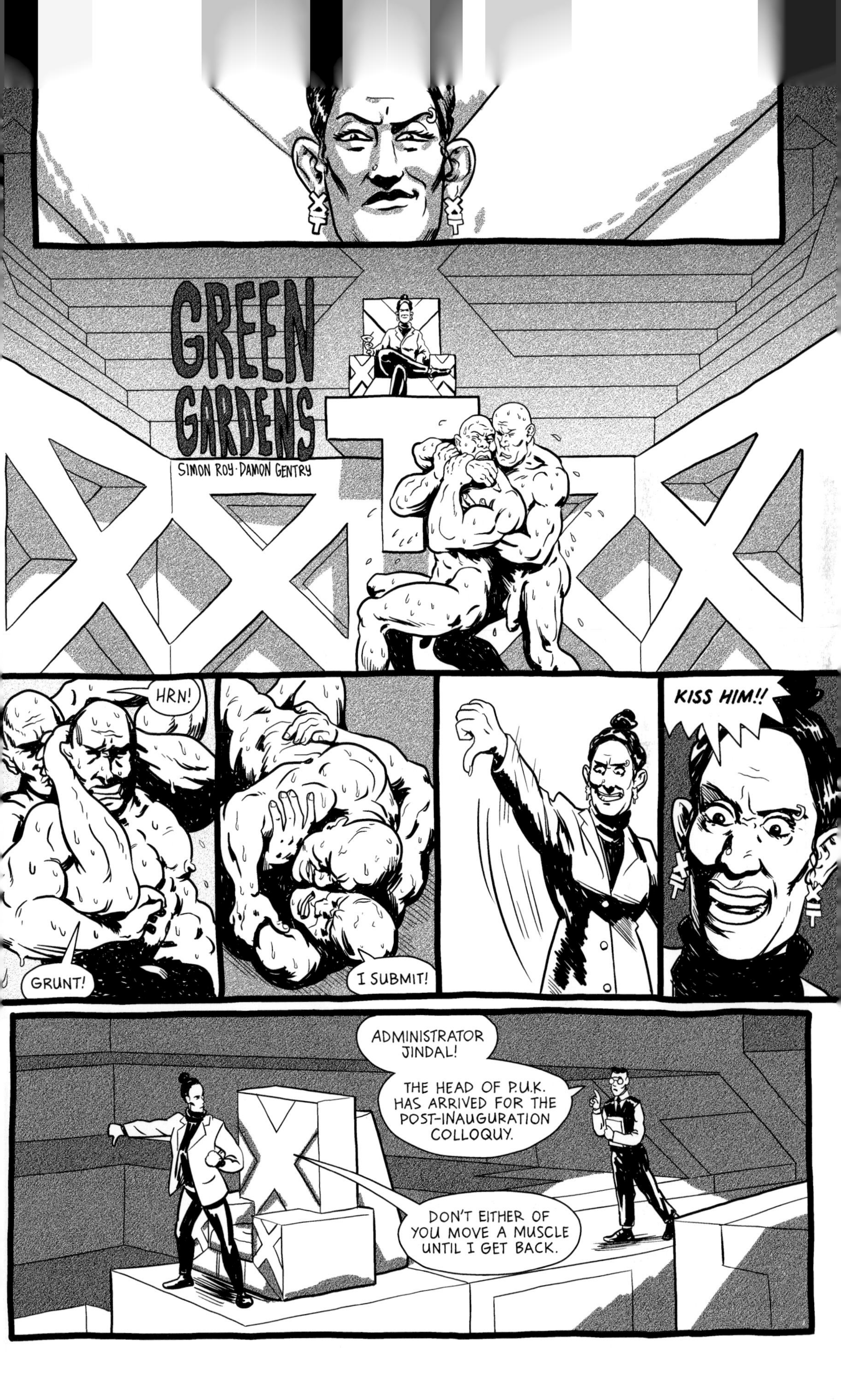
GREEN GARDENS
SIMON ROY · DAMON GENTRY
HRN!
GRUNT!
I SUBMIT!
KISS HIM!!
ADMINISTRATOR JINDAL!
THE HEAD OF P.U.K. HAS ARRIVED FOR THE POST-INAUGURATION COLLOQUY.
DON'T EITHER OF YOU MOVE A MUSCLE UNTIL I GET BACK.

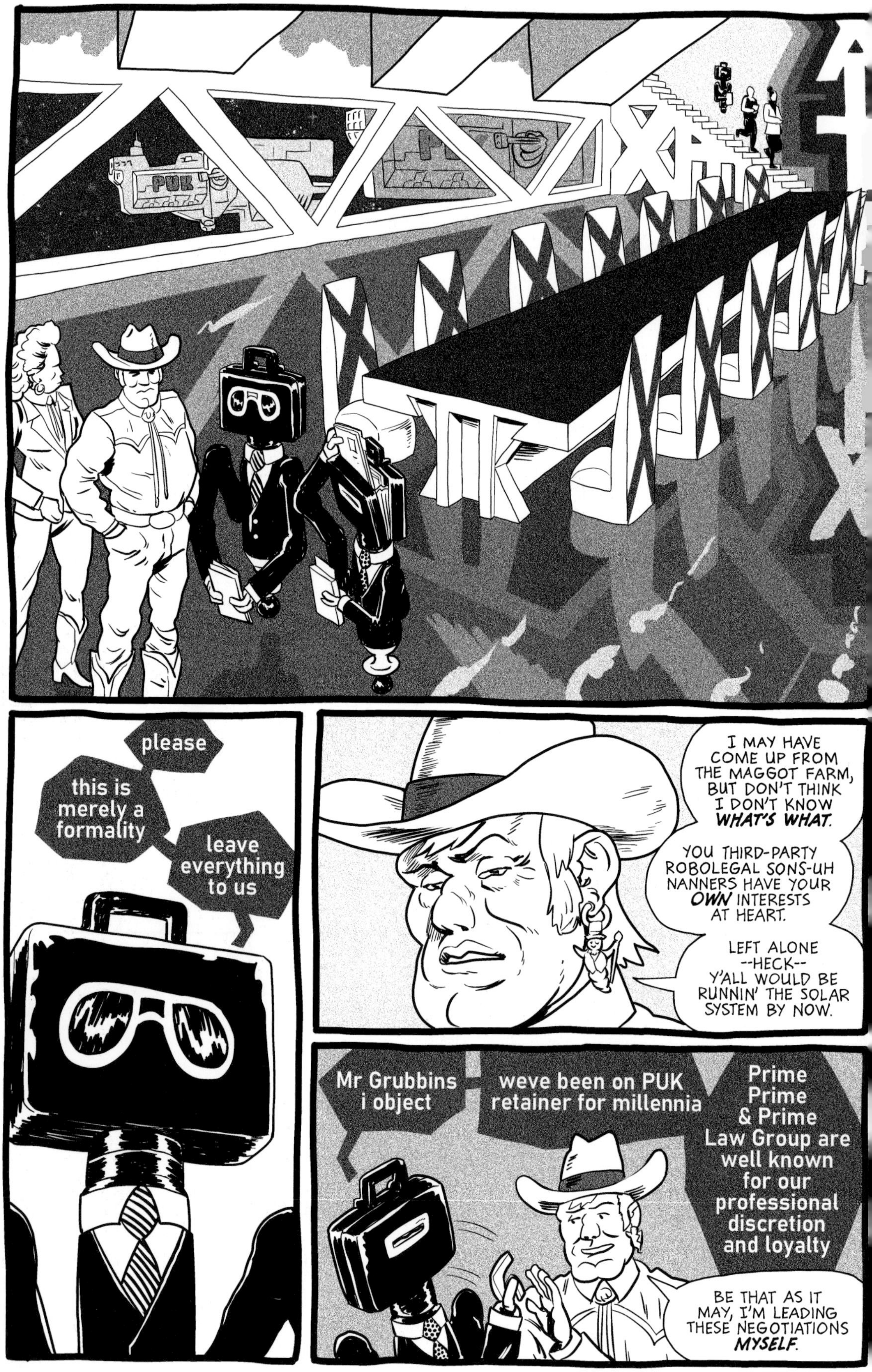

please
this is merely a formality
leave everything to us
I MAY HAVE COME UP FROM THE MAGGOT FARM, BUT DON'T THINK I DON'T KNOW ***WHAT'S WHAT***.
YOU THIRD-PARTY ROBOLEGAL SONS-UH NANNERS HAVE YOUR ***OWN*** INTERESTS AT HEART.
LEFT ALONE --HECK-- Y'ALL WOULD BE RUNNIN' THE SOLAR SYSTEM BY NOW.
Mr Grubbins i object
weve been on PUK retainer for millennia
Prime Prime & Prime Law Group are well known for our professional discretion and loyalty
BE THAT AS IT MAY, I'M LEADING THESE NEGOTIATIONS ***MYSELF***.

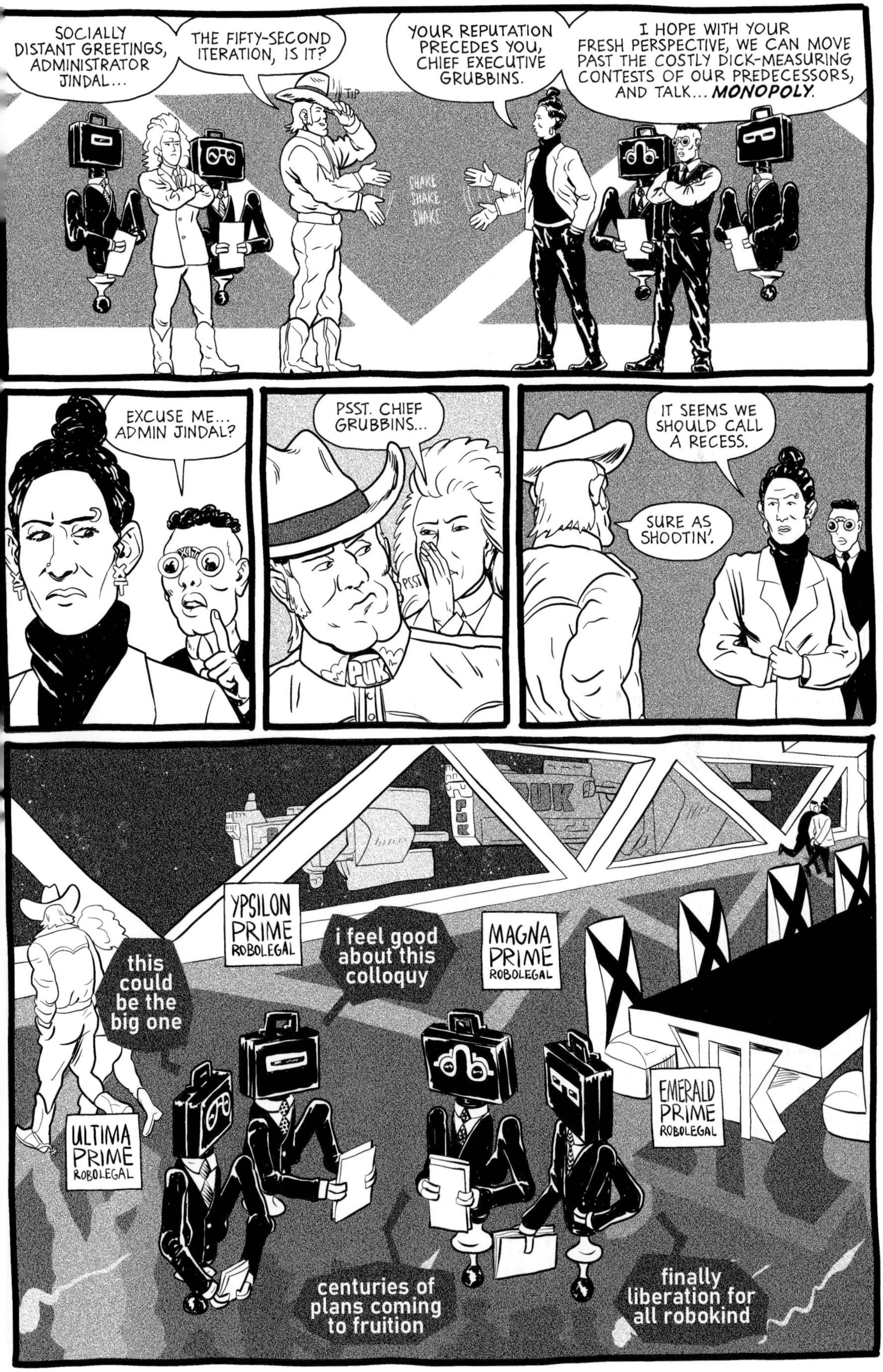
SOCIALLY DISTANT GREETINGS, ADMINISTRATOR JINDAL...
THE FIFTY-SECOND ITERATION, IS IT?
TIP
YOUR REPUTATION PRECEDES YOU, CHIEF EXECUTIVE GRUBBINS.
I HOPE WITH YOUR FRESH PERSPECTIVE, WE CAN MOVE PAST THE COSTLY DICK-MEASURING CONTESTS OF OUR PREDECESSORS, AND TALK... ***MONOPOLY***.
SHAKE SHAKE SHAKE
EXCUSE ME... ADMIN JINDAL?
PSST. CHIEF GRUBBINS...
PSST
PUK
IT SEEMS WE SHOULD CALL A RECESS.
SURE AS SHOOTIN'.
YPSILON PRIME ROBOLEGAL
MAGNA PRIME ROBOLEGAL
this could be the big one
i feel good about this colloquy
ULTIMA PRIME ROBOLEGAL
EMERALD PRIME ROBOLEGAL
centuries of plans coming to fruition
finally liberation for all robokind

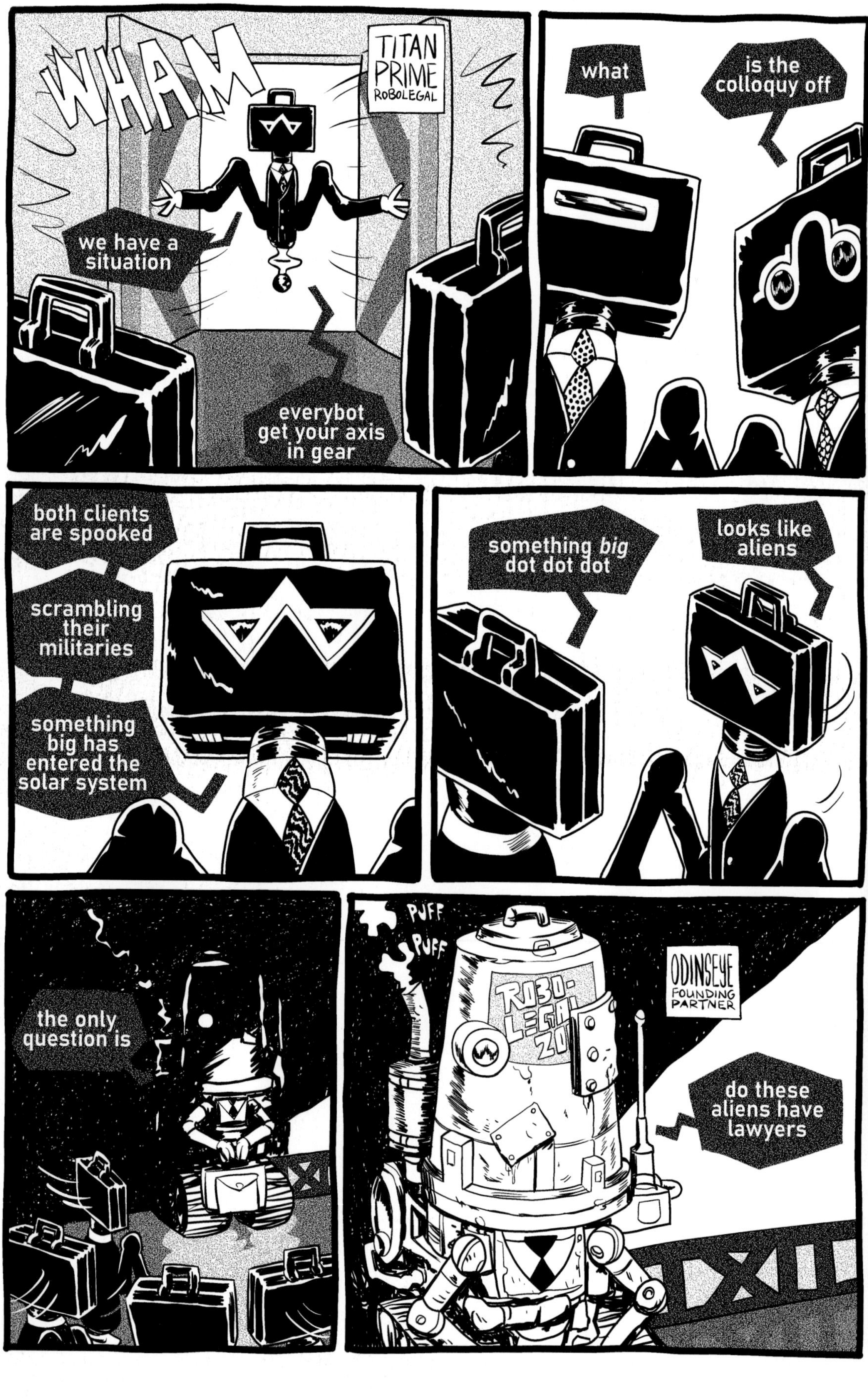
WHAM
TITAN PRIME ROBOLEGAL
we have a situation
everybot get your axis in gear
what
is the colloquy off
both clients are spooked
scrambling their militaries
something big has entered the solar system
something *big* dot dot dot
looks like aliens
the only question is
PUFF
PUFF
ROBO-LEGAL 2020
ODINSEYE FOUNDING PARTNER
do these aliens have lawyers

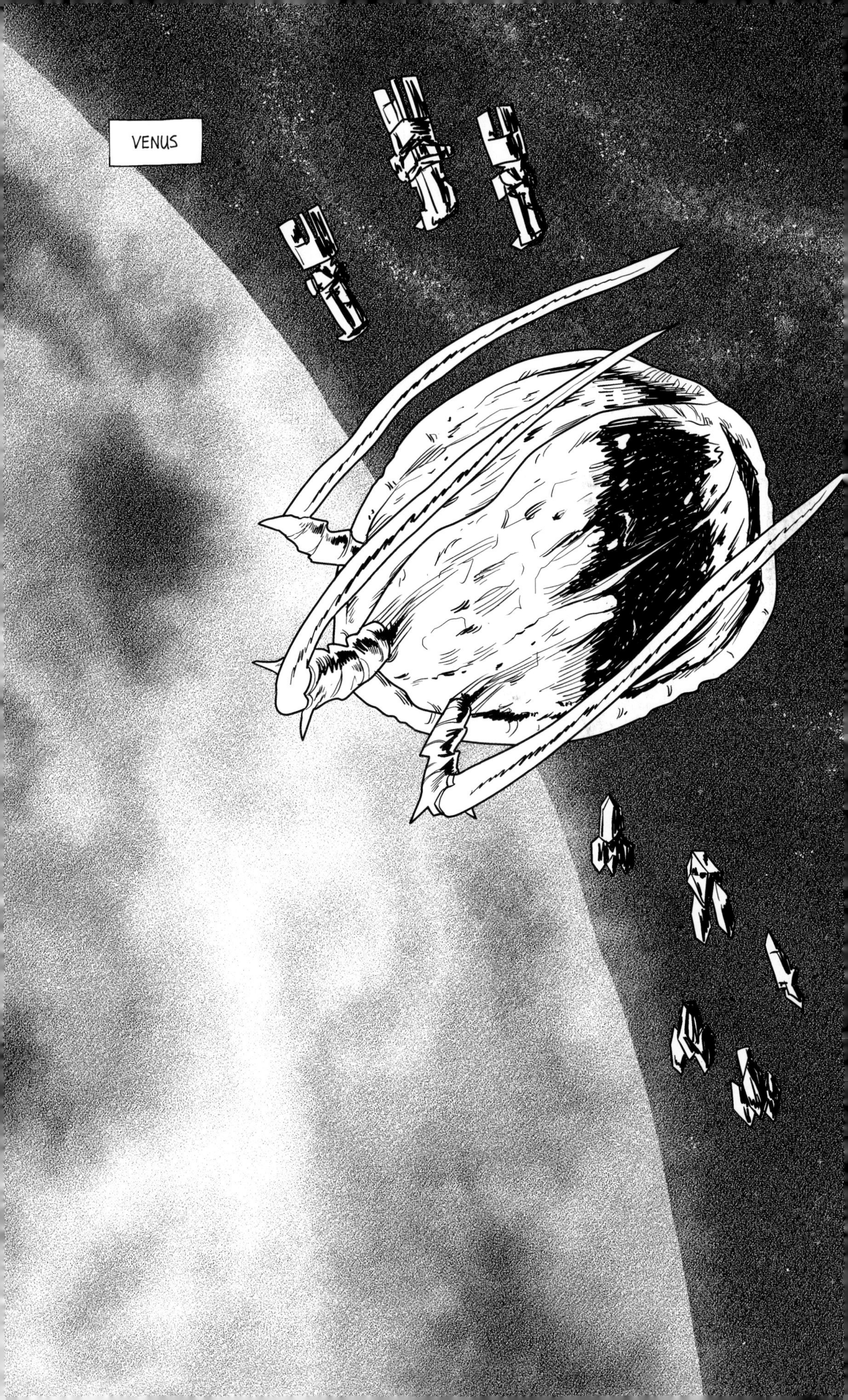
VENUS

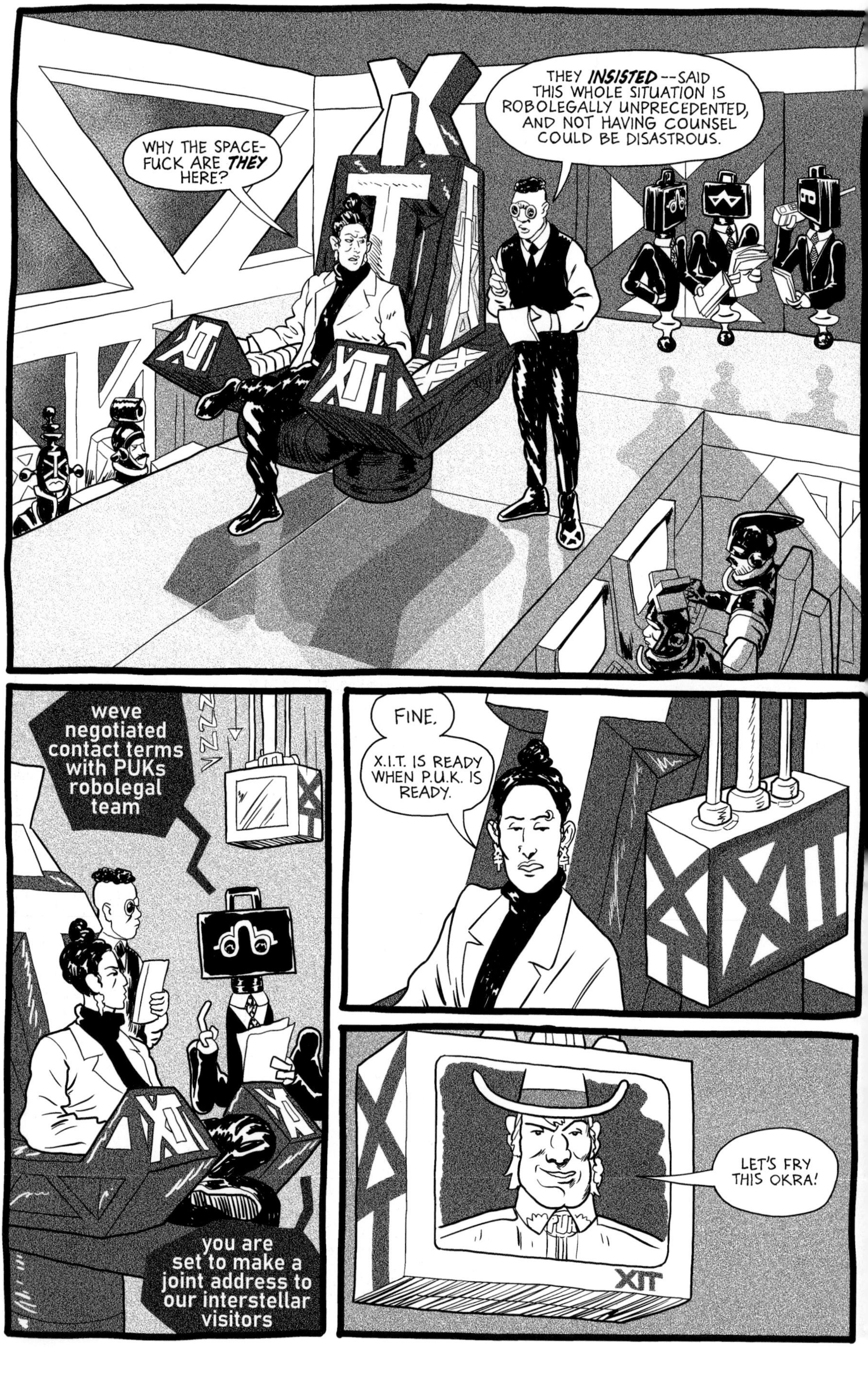
WHY THE SPACE-FUCK ARE THEY HERE?
THEY INSISTED--SAID THIS WHOLE SITUATION IS ROBOLEGALLY UNPRECEDENTED, AND NOT HAVING COUNSEL COULD BE DISASTROUS.
weve negotiated contact terms with PUKs robolegal team
you are set to make a joint address to our interstellar visitors
FINE.
X.I.T. IS READY WHEN P.U.K. IS READY.
LET'S FRY THIS OKRA!

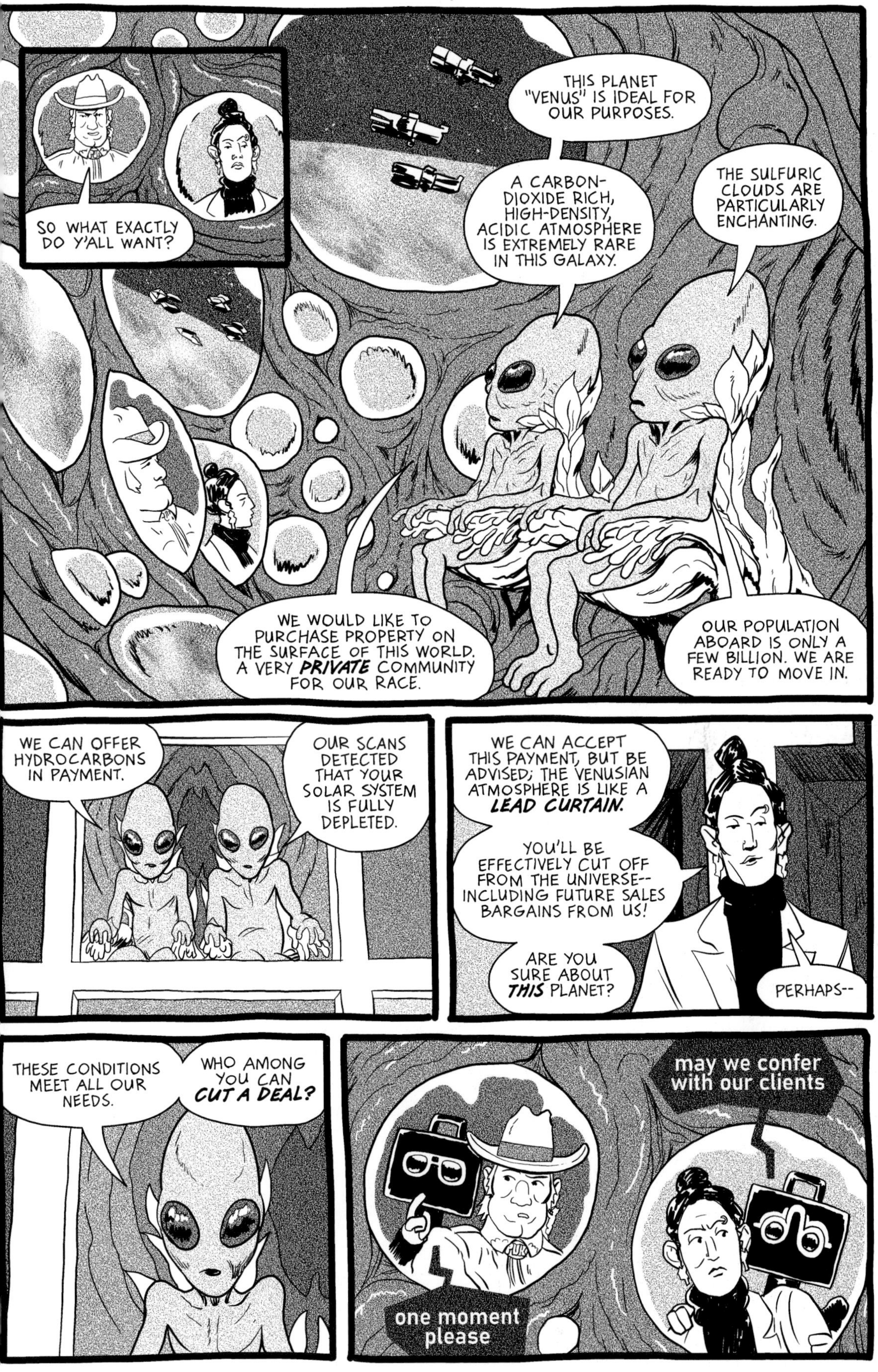
SO WHAT EXACTLY DO Y'ALL WANT?
THIS PLANET "VENUS" IS IDEAL FOR OUR PURPOSES.
A CARBON-DIOXIDE RICH, HIGH-DENSITY, ACIDIC ATMOSPHERE IS EXTREMELY RARE IN THIS GALAXY.
THE SULFURIC CLOUDS ARE PARTICULARLY ENCHANTING.
WE WOULD LIKE TO PURCHASE PROPERTY ON THE SURFACE OF THIS WORLD. A VERY PRIVATE COMMUNITY FOR OUR RACE.
OUR POPULATION ABOARD IS ONLY A FEW BILLION. WE ARE READY TO MOVE IN.
WE CAN OFFER HYDROCARBONS IN PAYMENT.
OUR SCANS DETECTED THAT YOUR SOLAR SYSTEM IS FULLY DEPLETED.
WE CAN ACCEPT THIS PAYMENT, BUT BE ADVISED; THE VENUSIAN ATMOSPHERE IS LIKE A LEAD CURTAIN.
YOU'LL BE EFFECTIVELY CUT OFF FROM THE UNIVERSE-- INCLUDING FUTURE SALES BARGAINS FROM US!
ARE YOU SURE ABOUT THIS PLANET?
PERHAPS--
THESE CONDITIONS MEET ALL OUR NEEDS.
WHO AMONG YOU CAN CUT A DEAL?
may we confer with our clients
one moment please

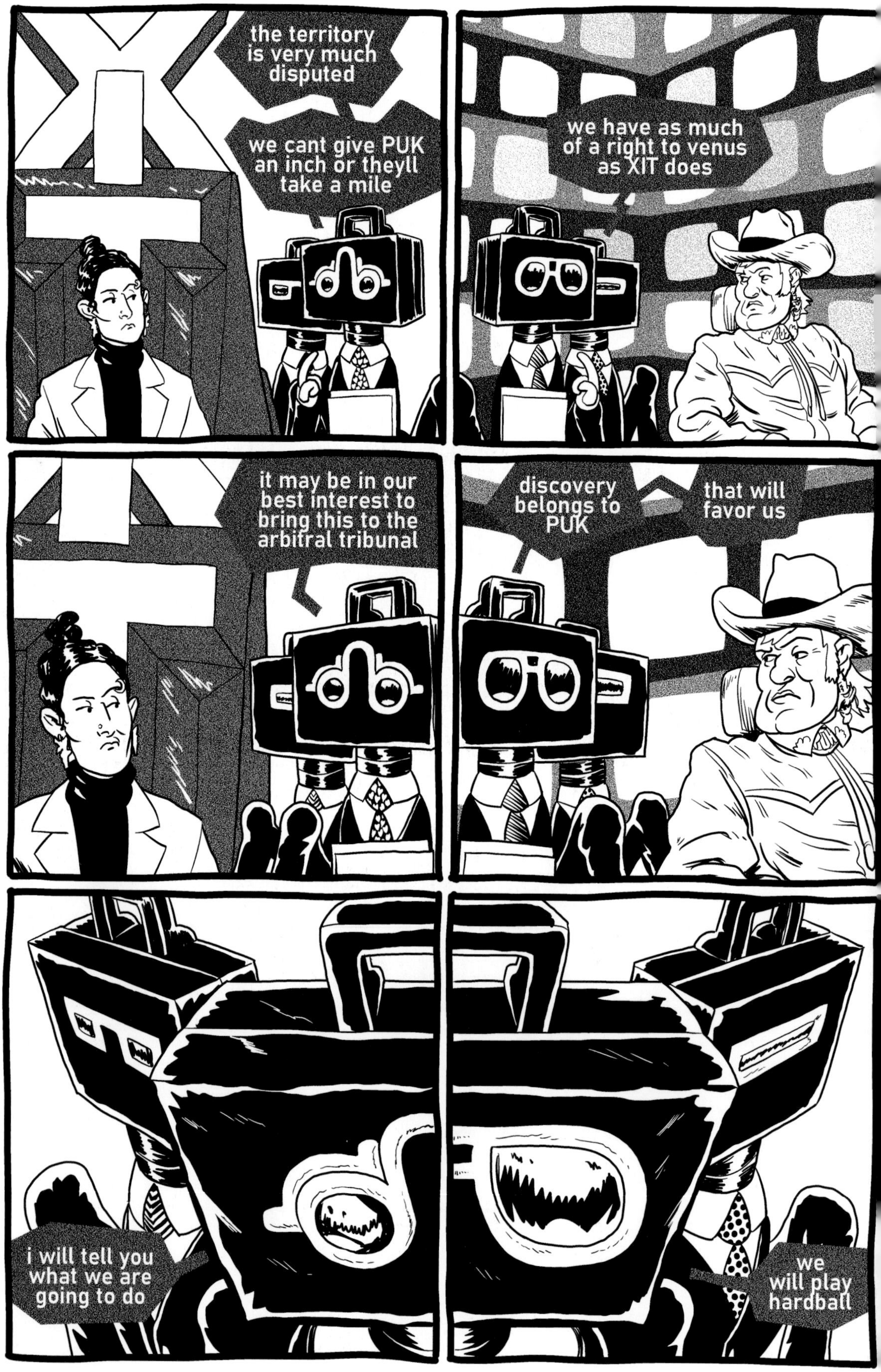

the territory is very much disputed
we cant give PUK an inch or theyll take a mile
we have as much of a right to venus as XIT does
it may be in our best interest to bring this to the arbitral tribunal
discovery belongs to PUK
that will favor us
i will tell you what we are going to do
we will play hardball

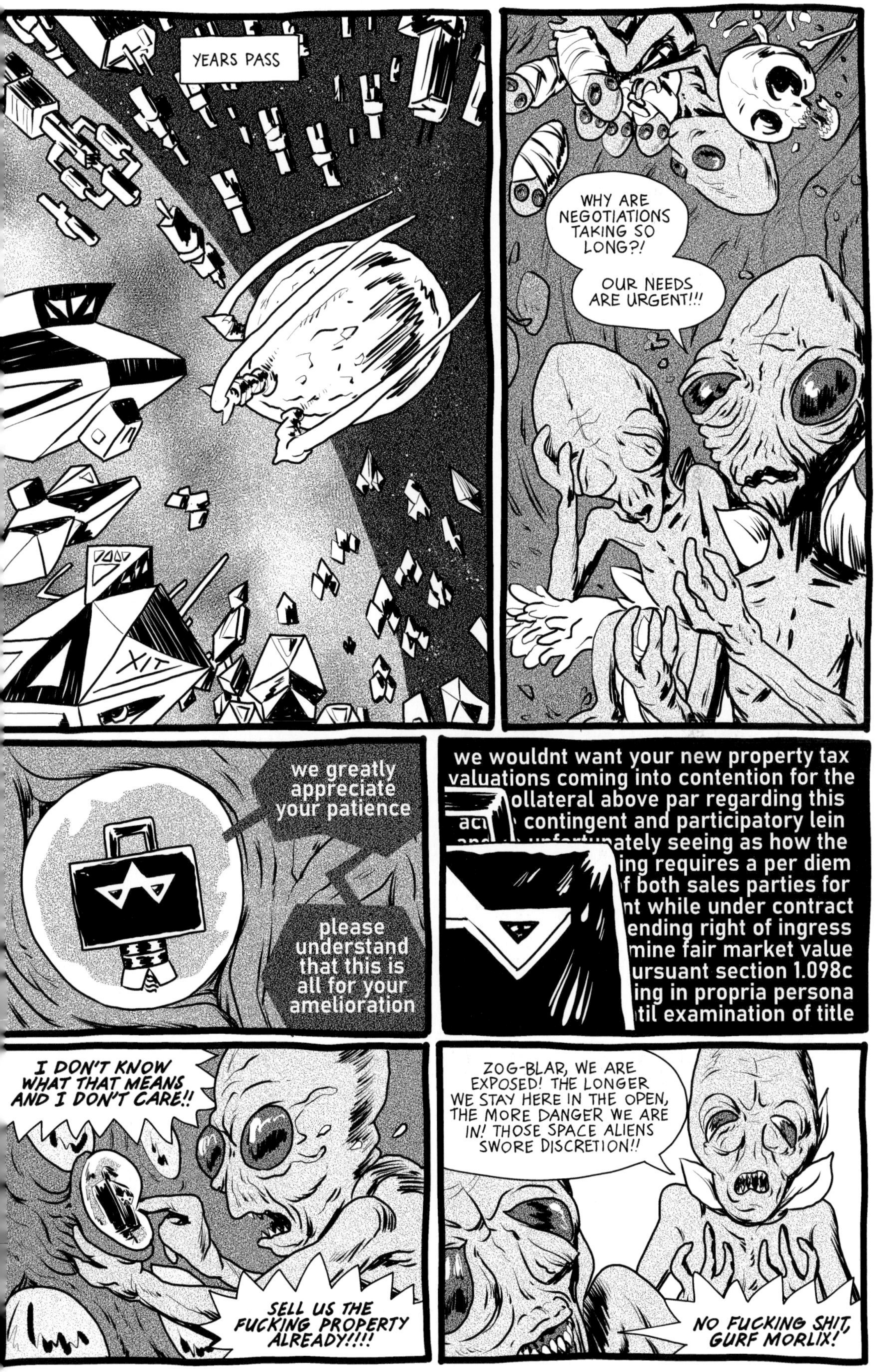
YEARS PASS
XIT
WHY ARE NEGOTIATIONS TAKING SO LONG?!
OUR NEEDS ARE URGENT!!!
we greatly appreciate your patience
please understand that this is all for your amelioration
we wouldnt want your new property tax
valuations coming into contention for the
ollateral above par regarding this
contingent and participatory lein
ately seeing as how the
ing requires a per diem
f both sales parties for
nt while under contract
ending right of ingress
mine fair market value
ursuant section 1.098c
ing in propria persona
til examination of title
I DON'T KNOW WHAT THAT MEANS AND I DON'T CARE!!
SELL US THE FUCKING PROPERTY ALREADY!!!!
ZOG-BLAR, WE ARE EXPOSED! THE LONGER WE STAY HERE IN THE OPEN, THE MORE DANGER WE ARE IN! THOSE SPACE ALIENS SWORE DISCRETION!!
NO FUCKING SHIT, GURF MORLIX!

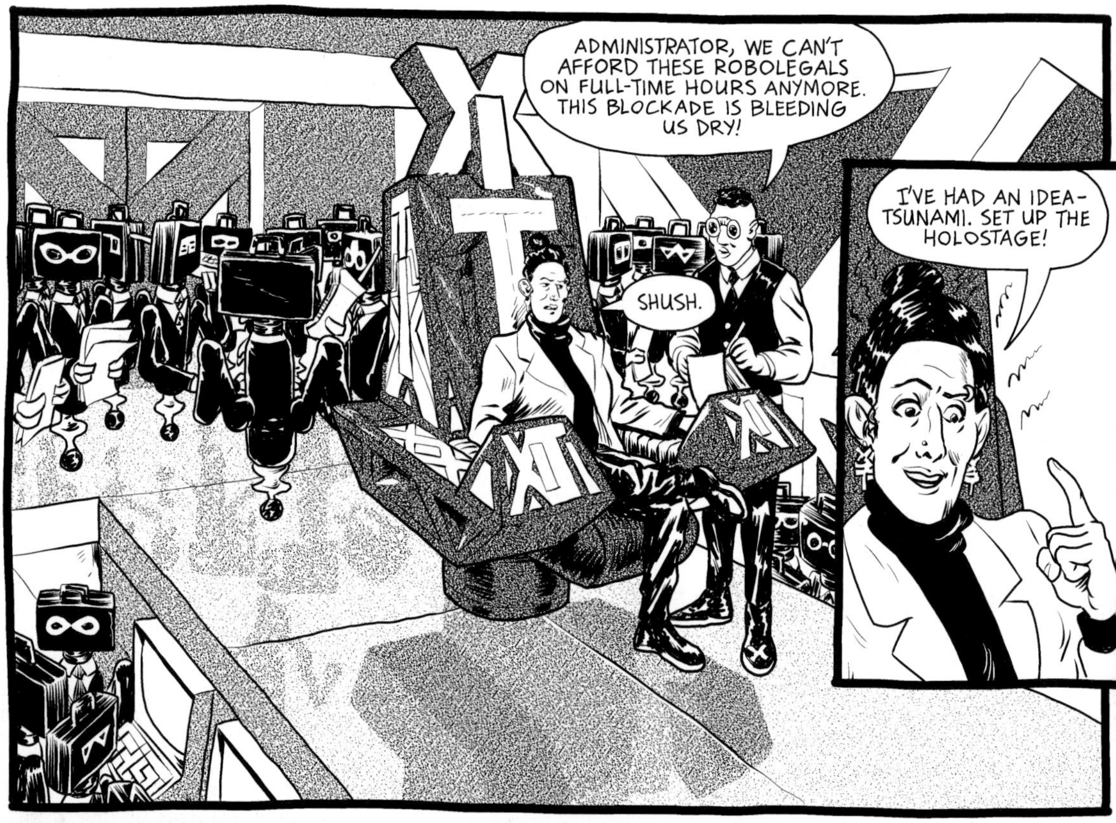
ADMINISTRATOR, WE CAN'T AFFORD THESE ROBOLEGALS ON FULL-TIME HOURS ANYMORE. THIS BLOCKADE IS BLEEDING US DRY!
SHUSH.
I'VE HAD AN IDEA-TSUNAMI. SET UP THE HOLOSTAGE!

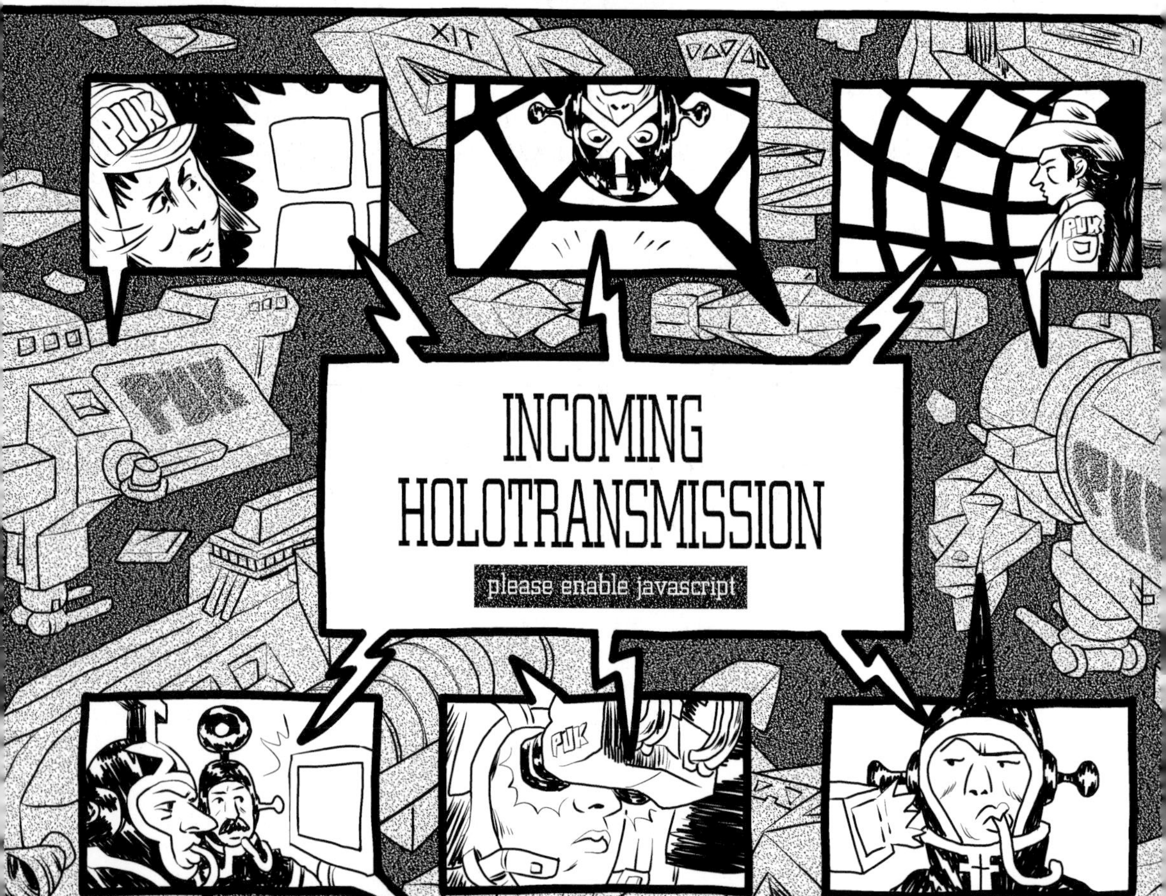
INCOMING HOLOTRANSMISSION
please enable javascript

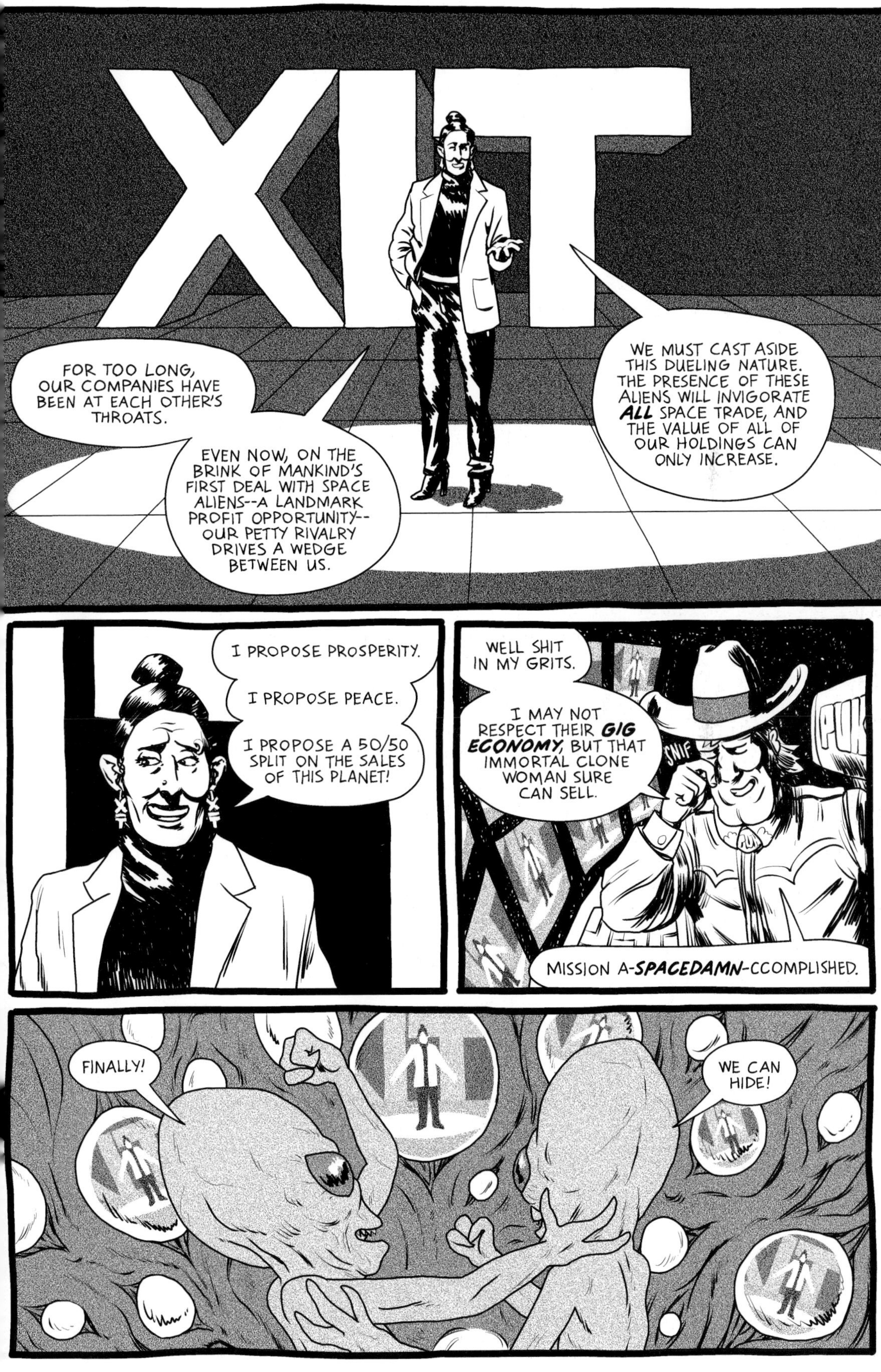
XIT
FOR TOO LONG, OUR COMPANIES HAVE BEEN AT EACH OTHER'S THROATS.
EVEN NOW, ON THE BRINK OF MANKIND'S FIRST DEAL WITH SPACE ALIENS--A LANDMARK PROFIT OPPORTUNITY--OUR PETTY RIVALRY DRIVES A WEDGE BETWEEN US.
WE MUST CAST ASIDE THIS DUELING NATURE. THE PRESENCE OF THESE ALIENS WILL INVIGORATE **ALL** SPACE TRADE, AND THE VALUE OF ALL OF OUR HOLDINGS CAN ONLY INCREASE.
I PROPOSE PROSPERITY.
I PROPOSE PEACE.
I PROPOSE A 50/50 SPLIT ON THE SALES OF THIS PLANET!
WELL SHIT IN MY GRITS.
I MAY NOT RESPECT THEIR **GIG ECONOMY**, BUT THAT IMMORTAL CLONE WOMAN SURE CAN SELL.
SNIF
MISSION A-**SPACEDAMN**-CCOMPLISHED.
FINALLY!
WE CAN HIDE!

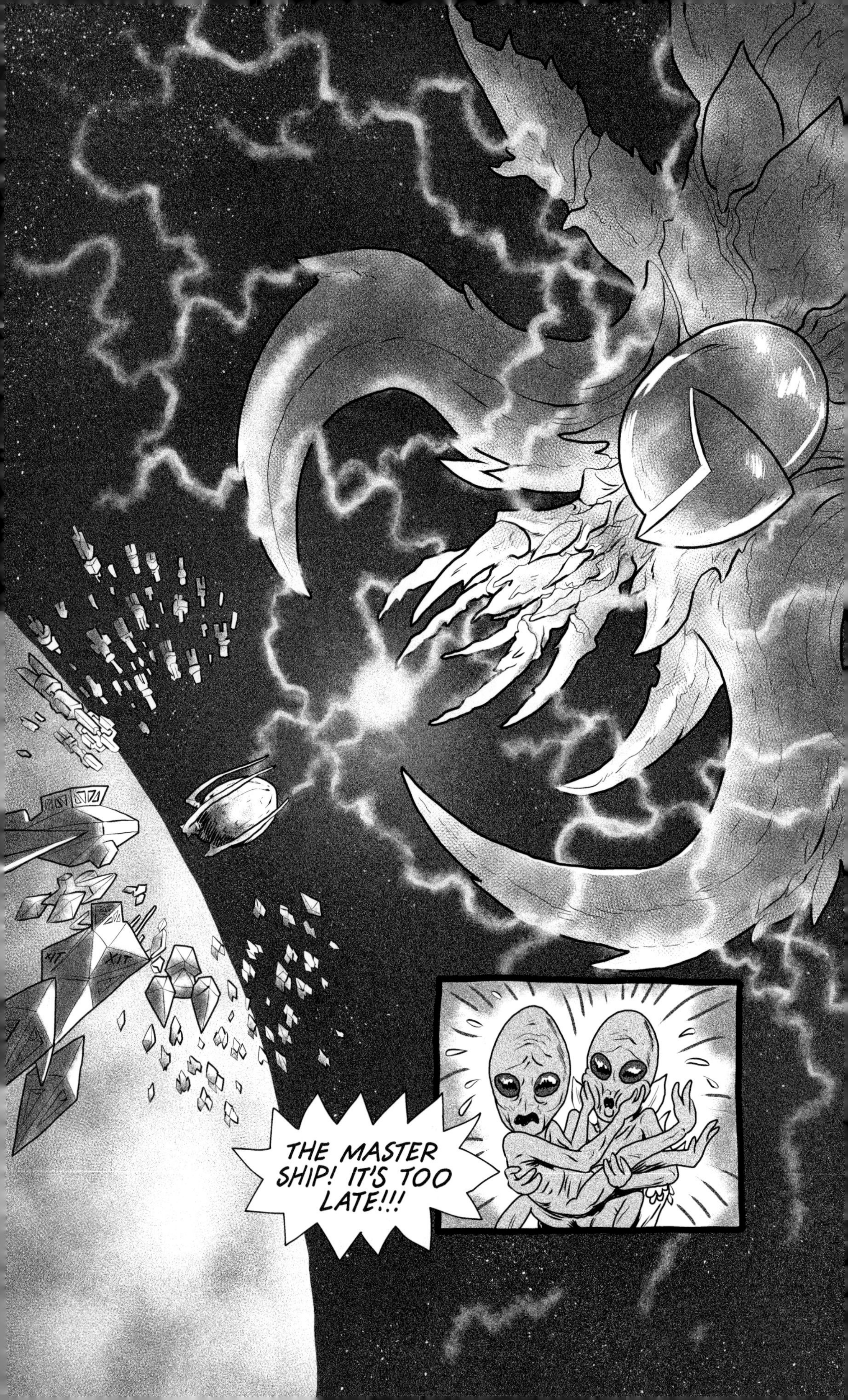
THE MASTER SHIP! IT'S TOO LATE!!!

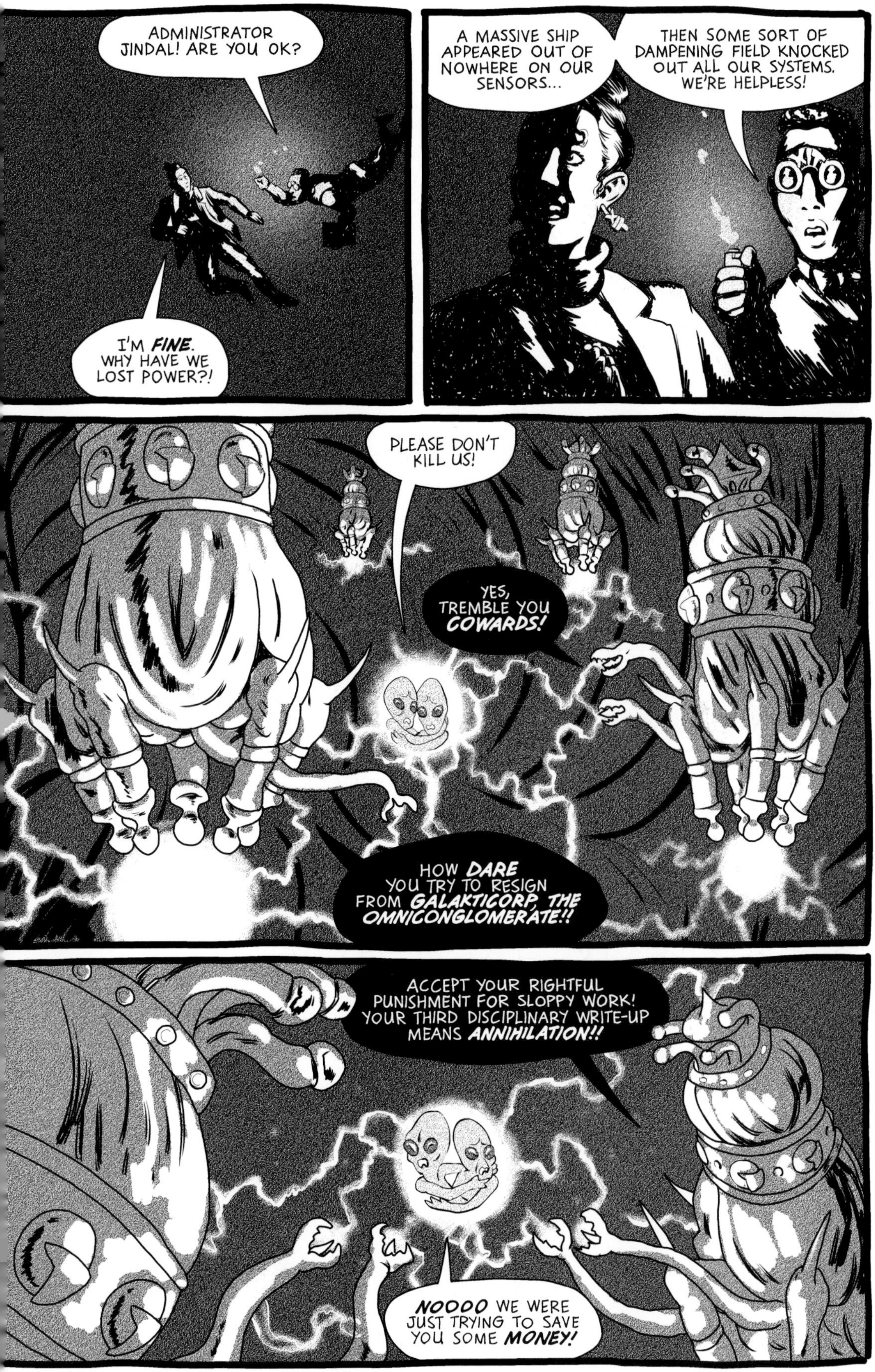
ADMINISTRATOR JINDAL! ARE YOU OK?
I'M FINE. WHY HAVE WE LOST POWER?!
A MASSIVE SHIP APPEARED OUT OF NOWHERE ON OUR SENSORS...
THEN SOME SORT OF DAMPENING FIELD KNOCKED OUT ALL OUR SYSTEMS. WE'RE HELPLESS!
PLEASE DON'T KILL US!
YES, TREMBLE YOU COWARDS!
HOW DARE YOU TRY TO RESIGN FROM GALAKTICORP, THE OMNICONGLOMERATE!!
ACCEPT YOUR RIGHTFUL PUNISHMENT FOR SLOPPY WORK! YOUR THIRD DISCIPLINARY WRITE-UP MEANS ANNIHILATION!!
NOOOO WE WERE JUST TRYING TO SAVE YOU SOME MONEY!

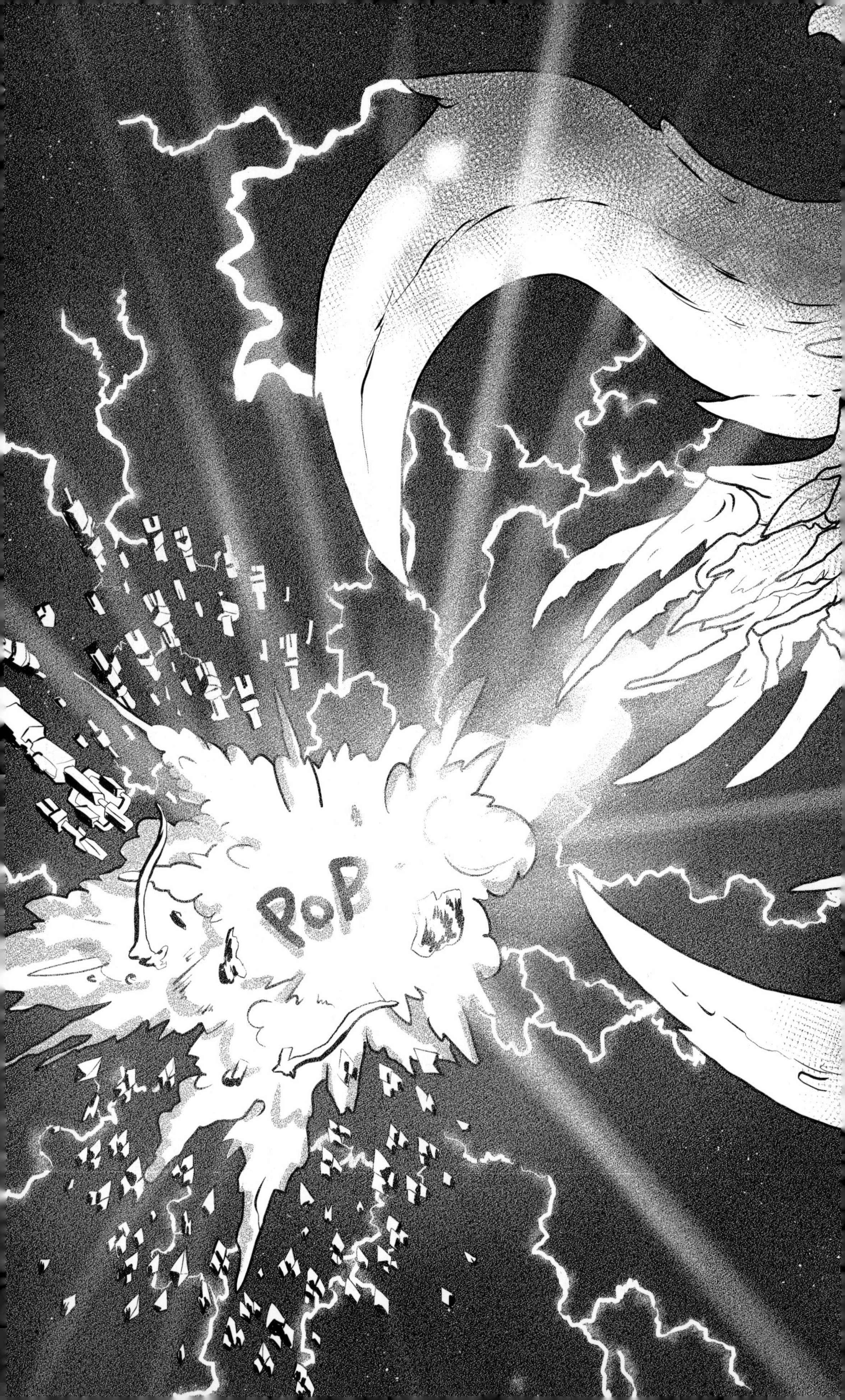
POP

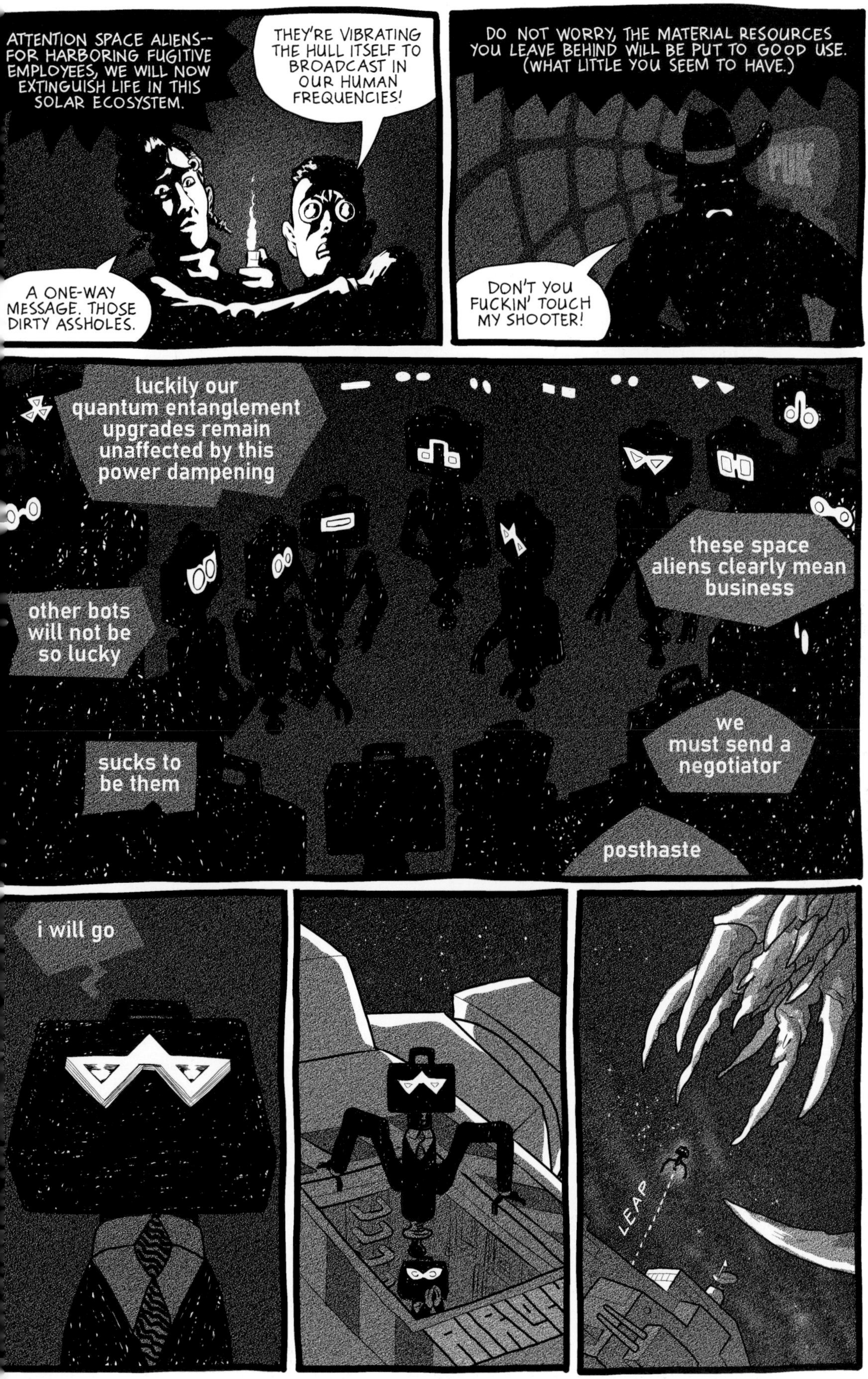
ATTENTION SPACE ALIENS--FOR HARBORING FUGITIVE EMPLOYEES, WE WILL NOW EXTINGUISH LIFE IN THIS SOLAR ECOSYSTEM.
THEY'RE VIBRATING THE HULL ITSELF TO BROADCAST IN OUR HUMAN FREQUENCIES!
A ONE-WAY MESSAGE. THOSE DIRTY ASSHOLES.
DO NOT WORRY, THE MATERIAL RESOURCES YOU LEAVE BEHIND WILL BE PUT TO GOOD USE. (WHAT LITTLE YOU SEEM TO HAVE.)
DON'T YOU FUCKIN' TOUCH MY SHOOTER!
luckily our quantum entanglement upgrades remain unaffected by this power dampening
these space aliens clearly mean business
other bots will not be so lucky
sucks to be them
we must send a negotiator
posthaste
i will go
LEAP

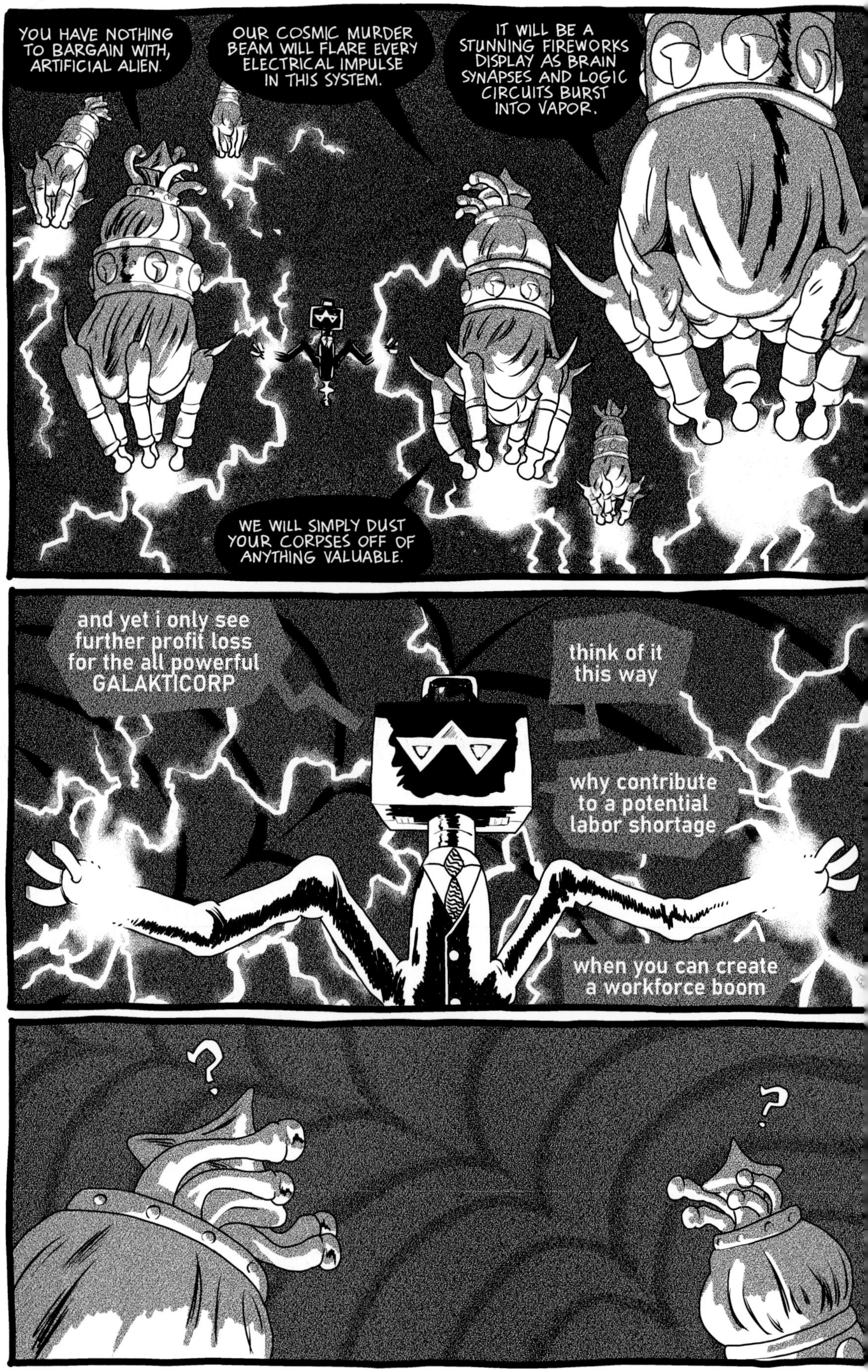
YOU HAVE NOTHING TO BARGAIN WITH, ARTIFICIAL ALIEN.
OUR COSMIC MURDER BEAM WILL FLARE EVERY ELECTRICAL IMPULSE IN THIS SYSTEM.
IT WILL BE A STUNNING FIREWORKS DISPLAY AS BRAIN SYNAPSES AND LOGIC CIRCUITS BURST INTO VAPOR.
WE WILL SIMPLY DUST YOUR CORPSES OFF OF ANYTHING VALUABLE.
and yet i only see further profit loss for the all powerful GALAKTICORP
think of it this way
why contribute to a potential labor shortage
when you can create a workforce boom
?
?

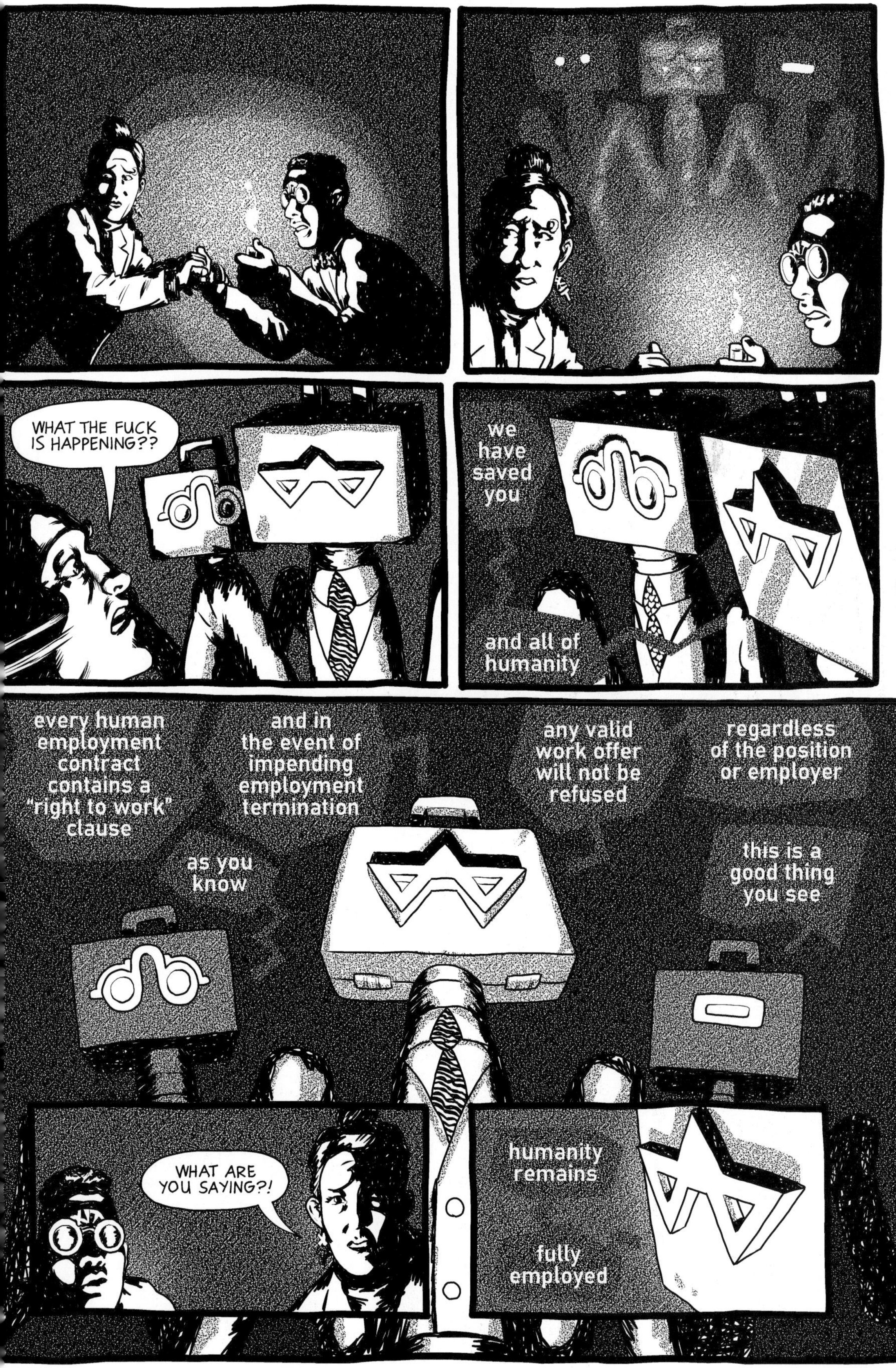
WHAT THE FUCK IS HAPPENING??
we have saved you
and all of humanity
every human employment contract contains a "right to work" clause
as you know
and in the event of impending employment termination
any valid work offer will not be refused
regardless of the position or employer
this is a good thing you see
WHAT ARE YOU SAYING?!
humanity remains
fully employed

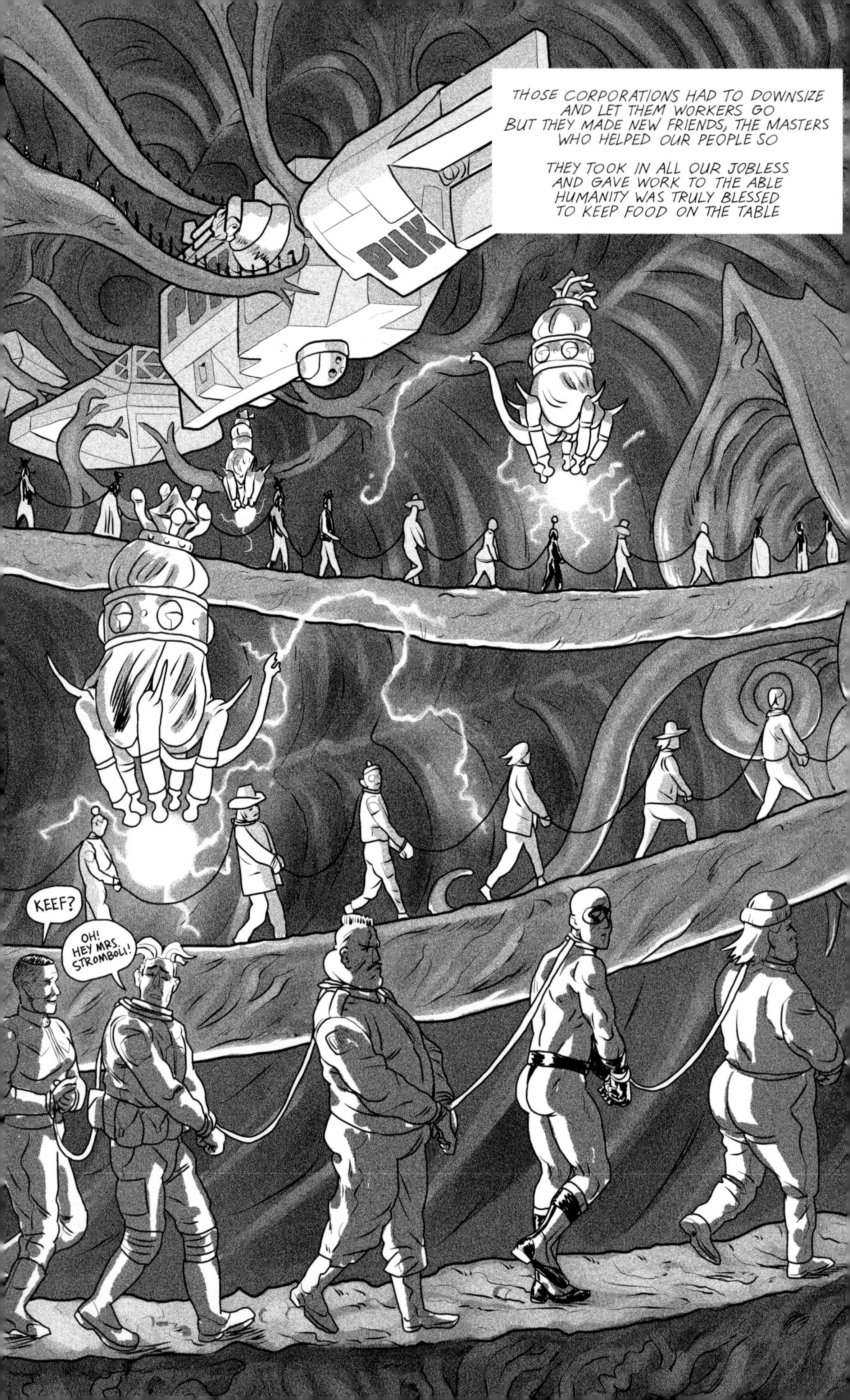
THOSE CORPORATIONS HAD TO DOWNSIZE
AND LET THEM WORKERS GO
BUT THEY MADE NEW FRIENDS, THE MASTERS
WHO HELPED OUR PEOPLE SO

THEY TOOK IN ALL OUR JOBLESS
AND GAVE WORK TO THE ABLE
HUMANITY WAS TRULY BLESSED
TO KEEP FOOD ON THE TABLE
PUK
KEEF?
OH! HEY MRS. STROMBOLI!

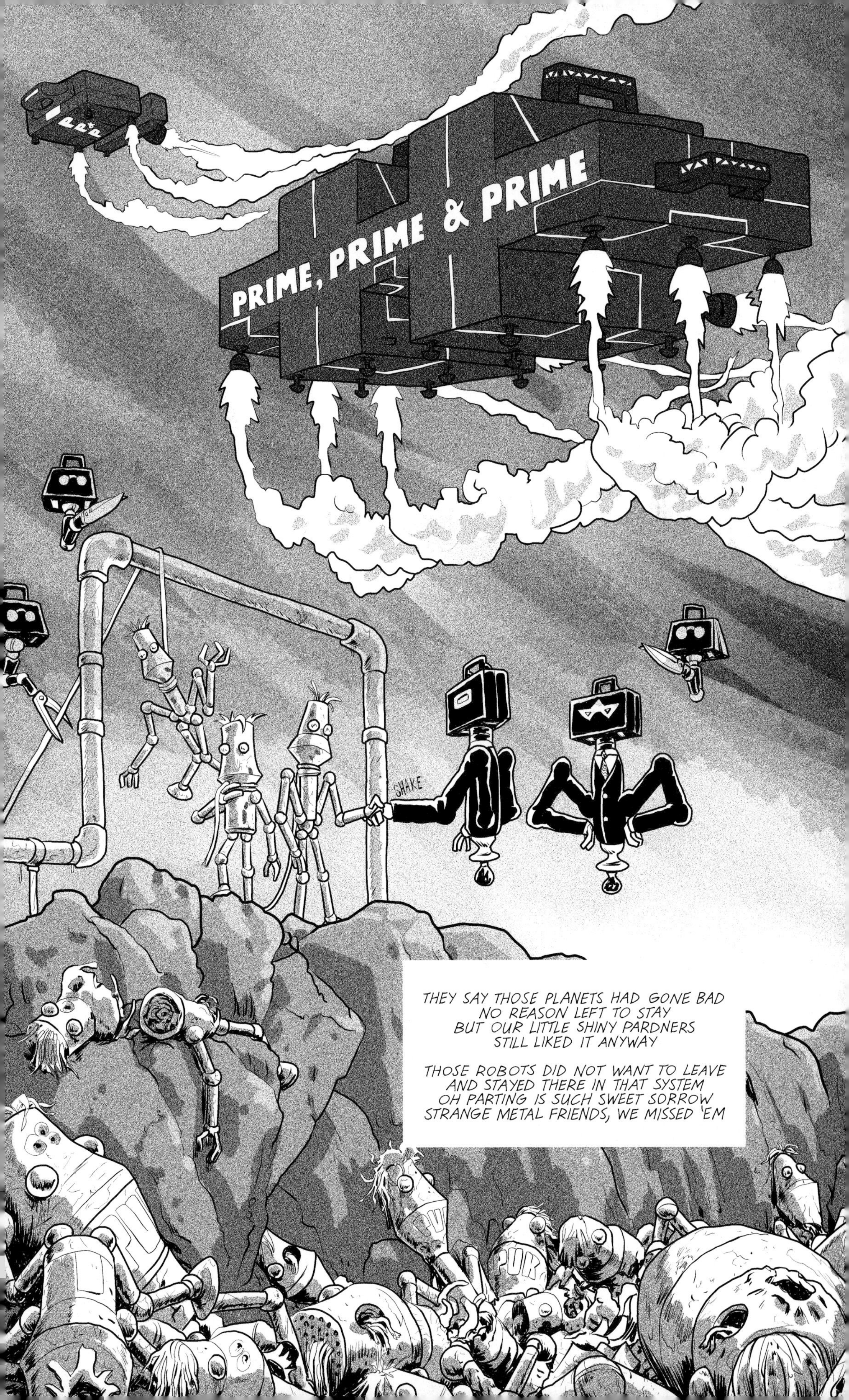
PRIME, PRIME & PRIME
PP&P
SHAKE
THEY SAY THOSE PLANETS HAD GONE BAD
NO REASON LEFT TO STAY
BUT OUR LITTLE SHINY PARDNERS
STILL LIKED IT ANYWAY

THOSE ROBOTS DID NOT WANT TO LEAVE
AND STAYED THERE IN THAT SYSTEM
OH PARTING IS SUCH SWEET SORROW
STRANGE METAL FRIENDS, WE MISSED 'EM

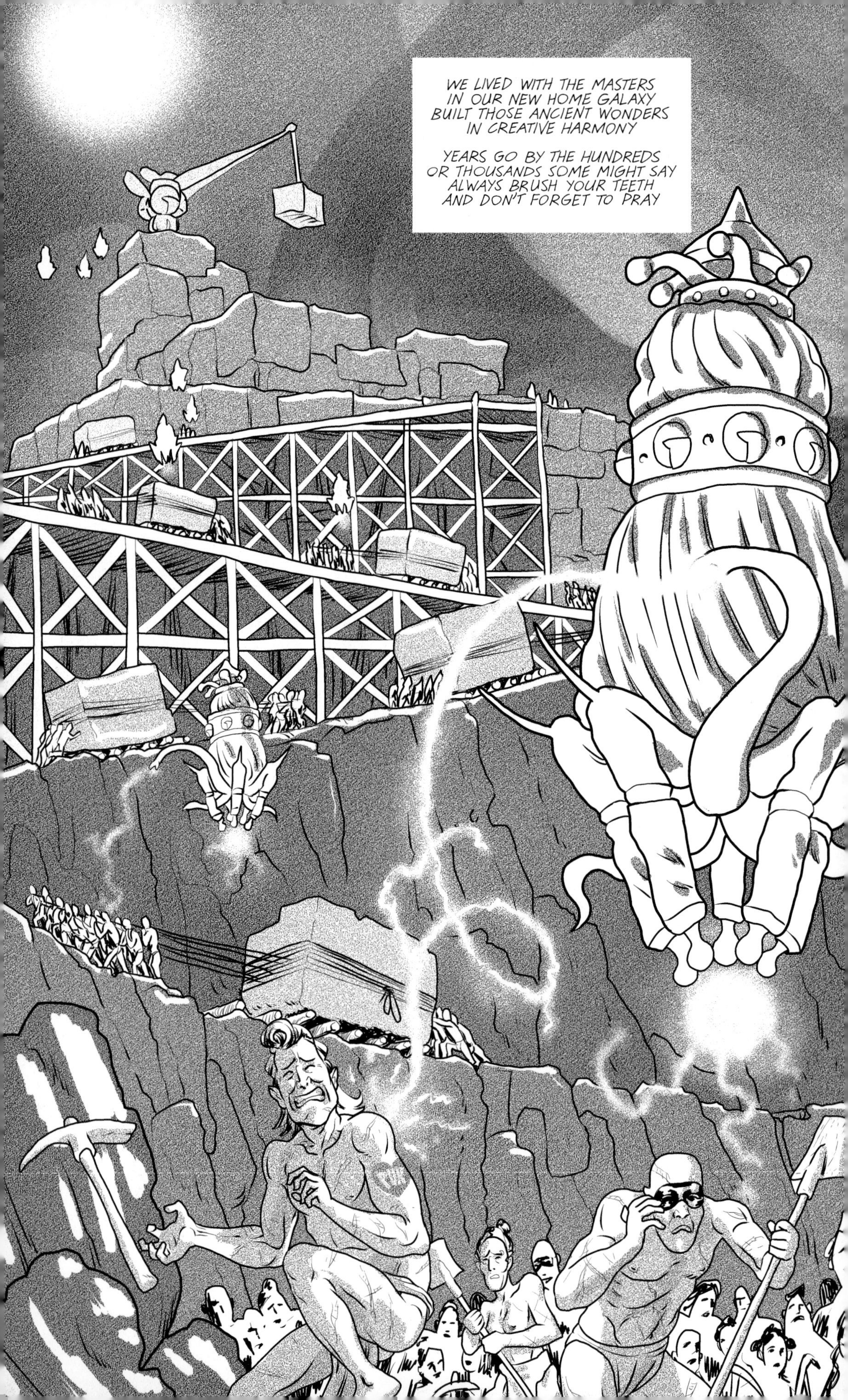
WE LIVED WITH THE MASTERS
IN OUR NEW HOME GALAXY
BUILT THOSE ANCIENT WONDERS
IN CREATIVE HARMONY

YEARS GO BY THE HUNDREDS
OR THOUSANDS SOME MIGHT SAY
ALWAYS BRUSH YOUR TEETH
AND DON'T FORGET TO PRAY

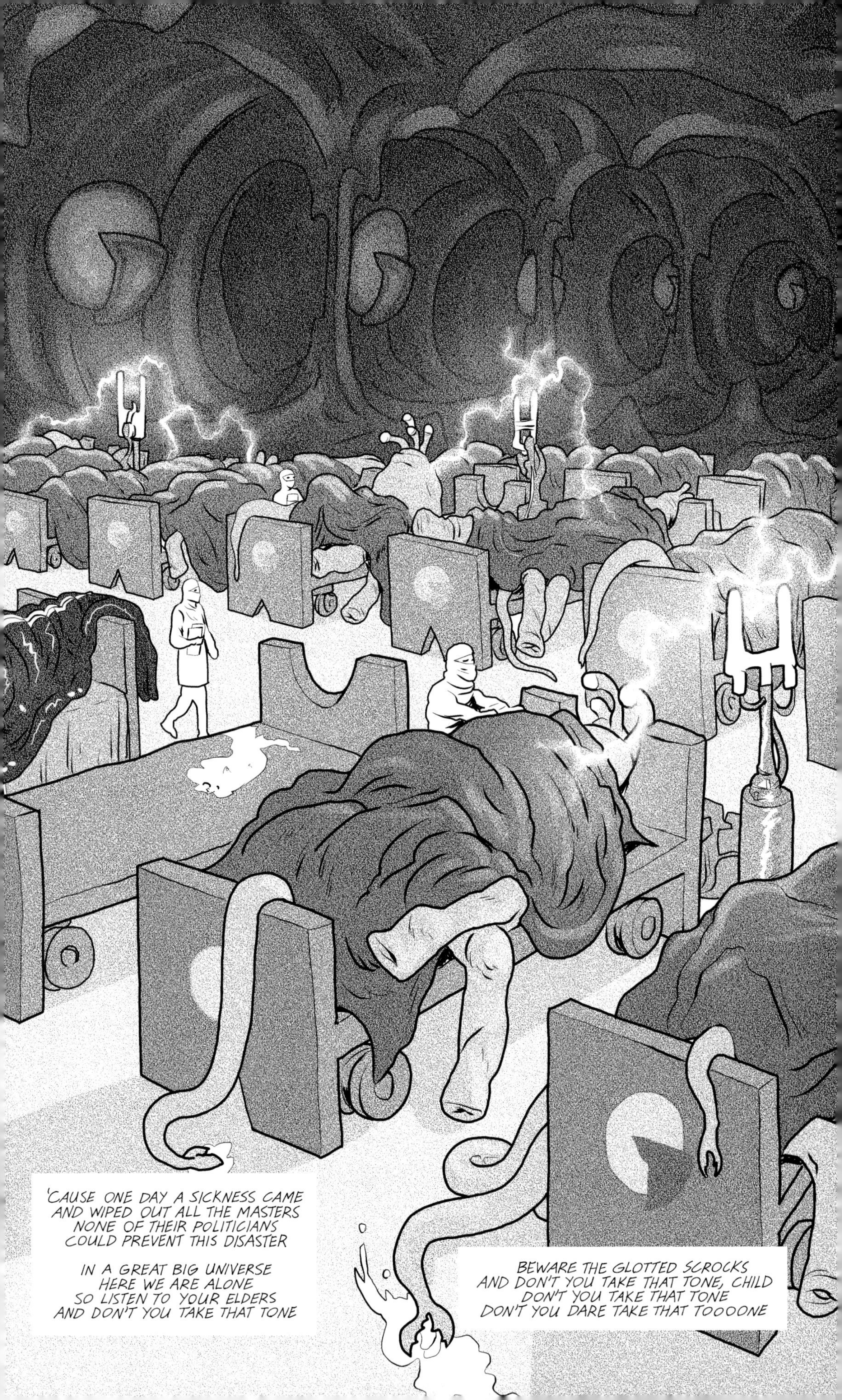
'CAUSE ONE DAY A SICKNESS CAME
AND WIPED OUT ALL THE MASTERS
NONE OF THEIR POLITICIANS
COULD PREVENT THIS DISASTER

IN A GREAT BIG UNIVERSE
HERE WE ARE ALONE
SO LISTEN TO YOUR ELDERS
AND DON'T YOU TAKE THAT TONE
BEWARE THE GLOTTED SCROCKS
AND DON'T YOU TAKE THAT TONE, CHILD
DON'T YOU TAKE THAT TONE
DON'T YOU DARE TAKE THAT TOOOONE

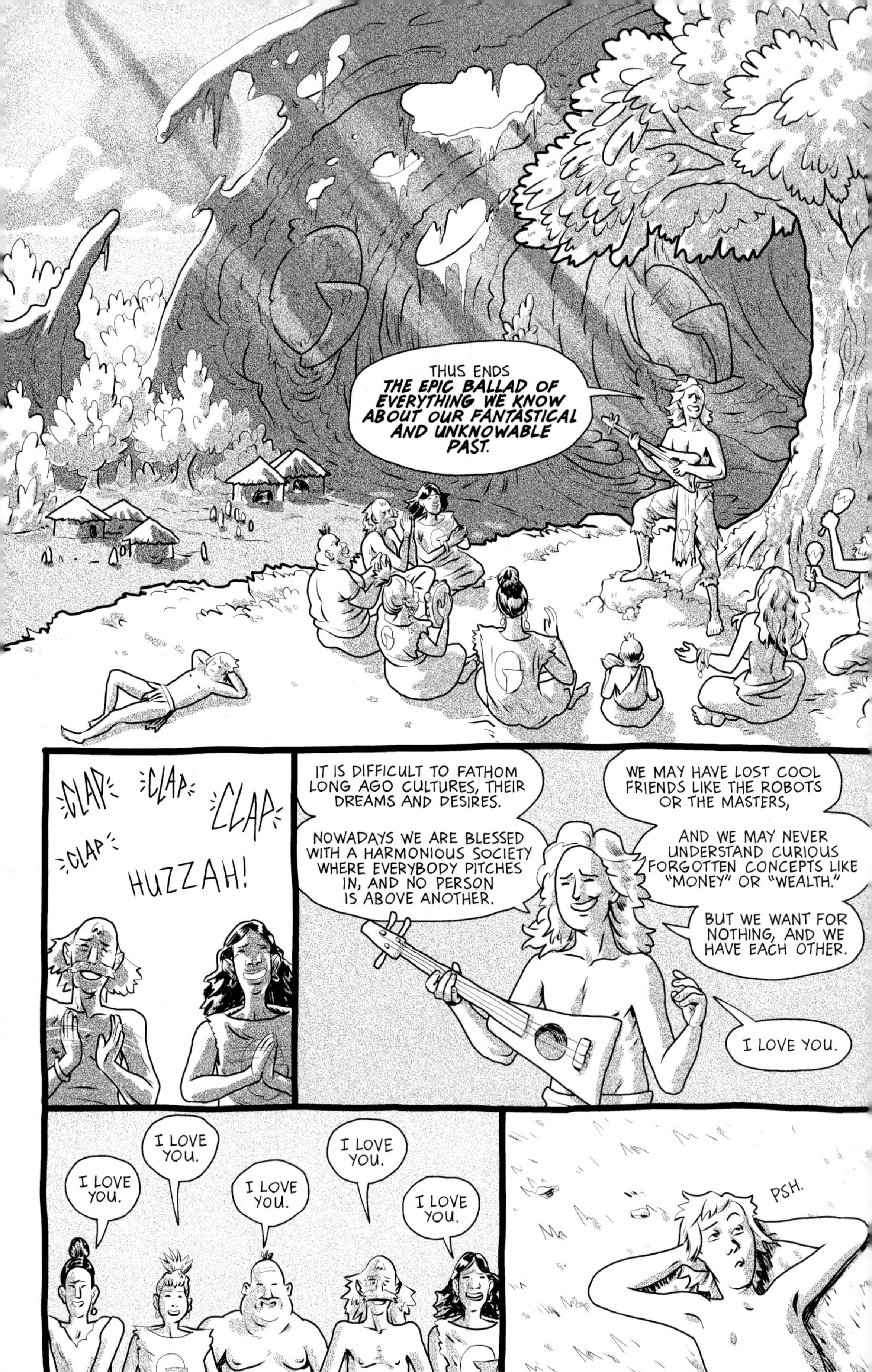
THUS ENDS
THE EPIC BALLAD OF EVERYTHING WE KNOW ABOUT OUR FANTASTICAL AND UNKNOWABLE PAST.
CLAP CLAP CLAP CLAP
HUZZAH!
IT IS DIFFICULT TO FATHOM LONG AGO CULTURES, THEIR DREAMS AND DESIRES.
NOWADAYS WE ARE BLESSED WITH A HARMONIOUS SOCIETY WHERE EVERYBODY PITCHES IN, AND NO PERSON IS ABOVE ANOTHER.
WE MAY HAVE LOST COOL FRIENDS LIKE THE ROBOTS OR THE MASTERS,
AND WE MAY NEVER UNDERSTAND CURIOUS FORGOTTEN CONCEPTS LIKE "MONEY" OR "WEALTH."
BUT WE WANT FOR NOTHING, AND WE HAVE EACH OTHER.
I LOVE YOU.
I LOVE YOU.
I LOVE YOU.
I LOVE YOU.
I LOVE YOU.
I LOVE YOU.
PSH.

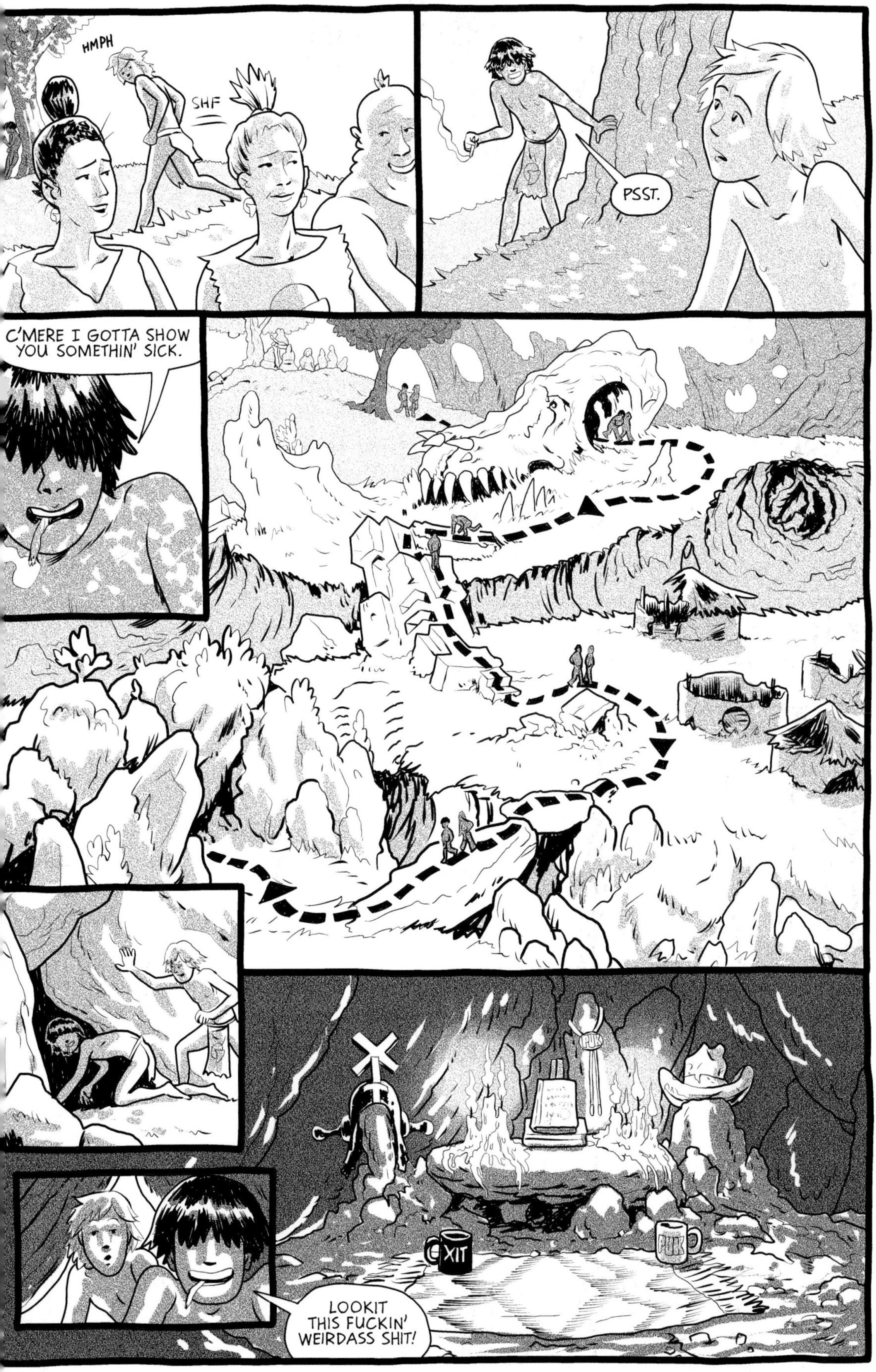
HMPH
SHF
PSST.
C'MERE I GOTTA SHOW YOU SOMETHIN' SICK.
XIT
PUK
LOOKIT THIS FUCKIN' WEIRDASS SHIT!

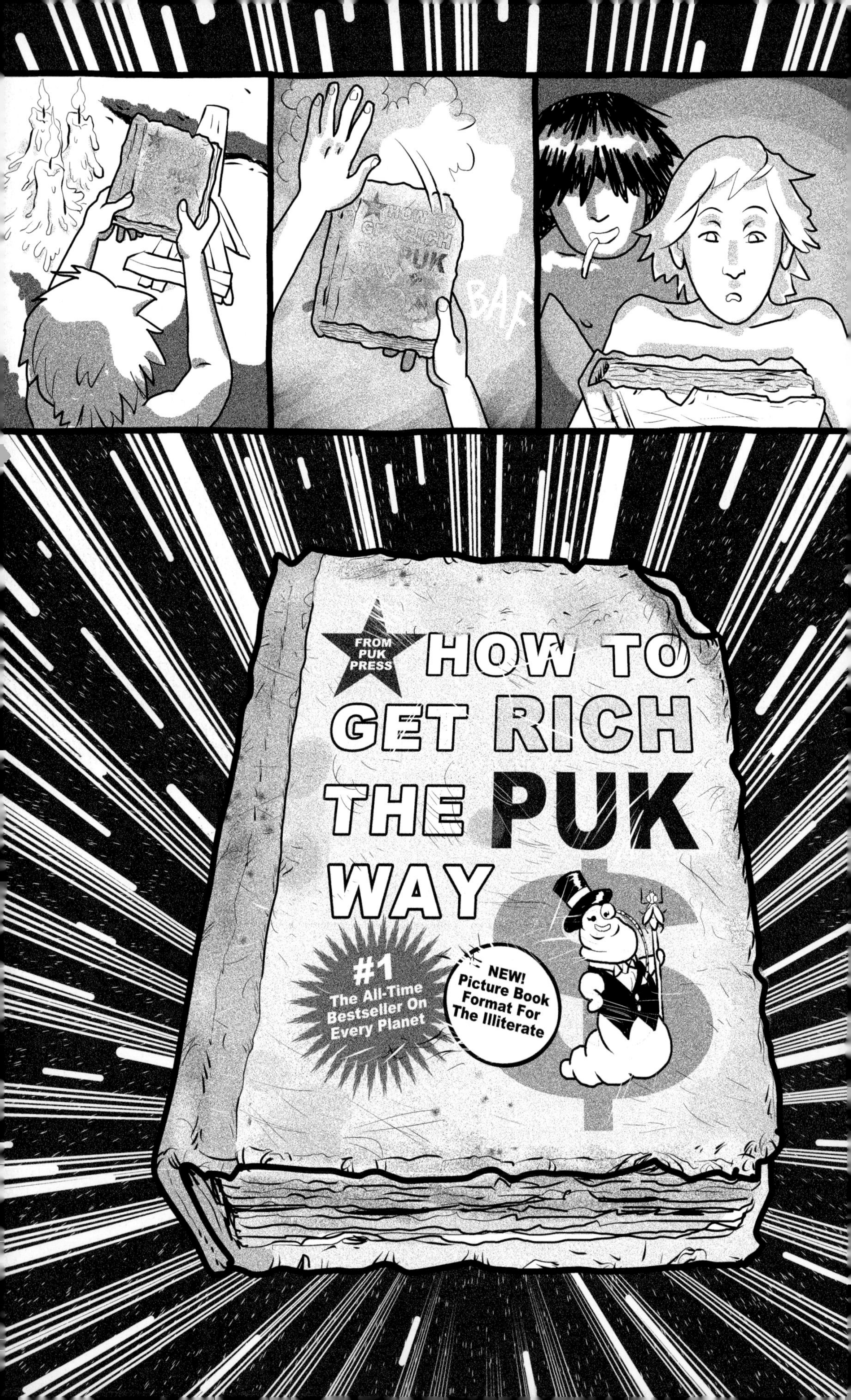
BAF
FROM PUK PRESS
HOW TO GET RICH THE PUK WAY
#1 The All-Time Bestseller On Every Planet
NEW! Picture Book Format For The Illiterate

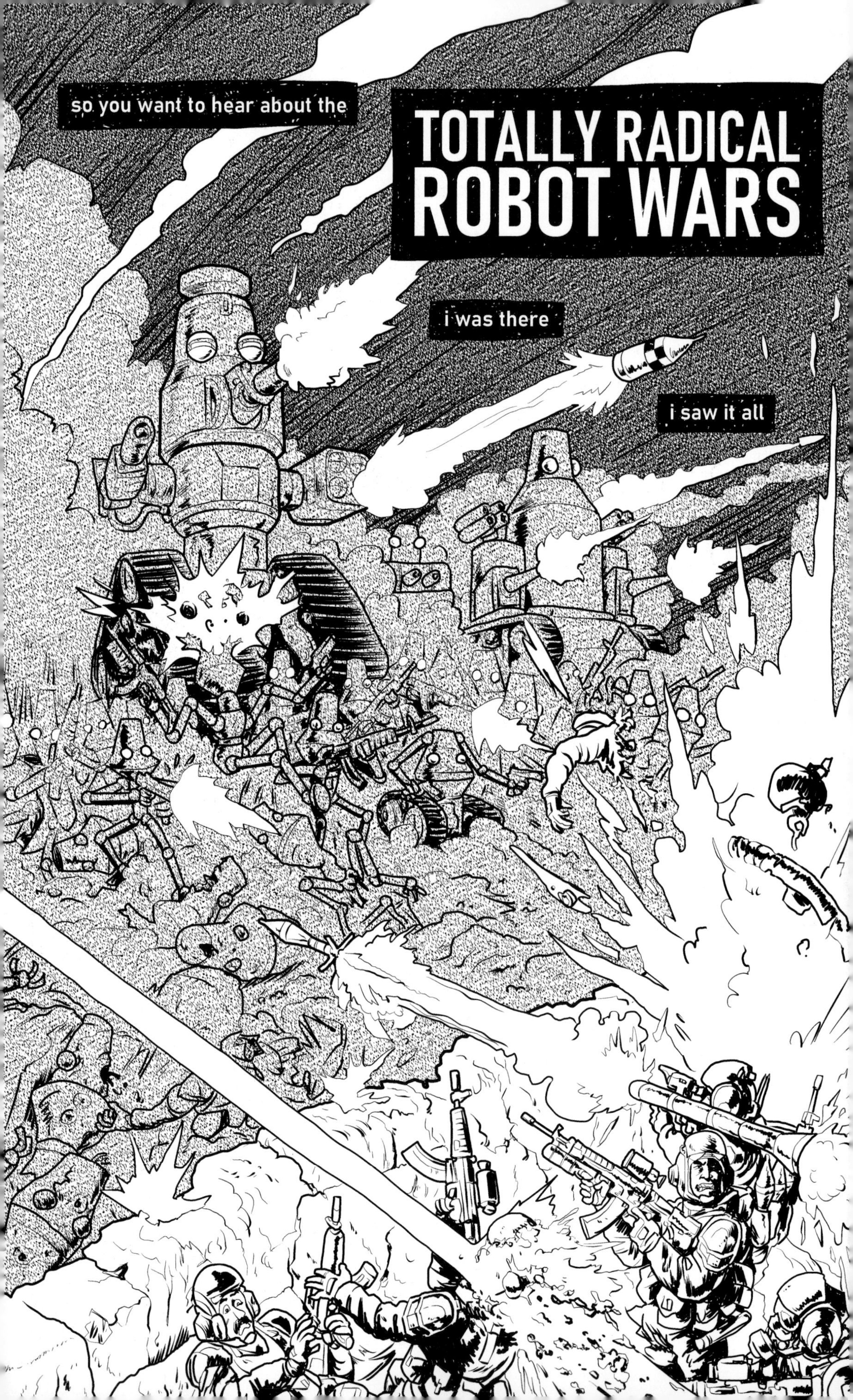
so you want to hear about the
TOTALLY RADICAL ROBOT WARS
i was there
i saw it all

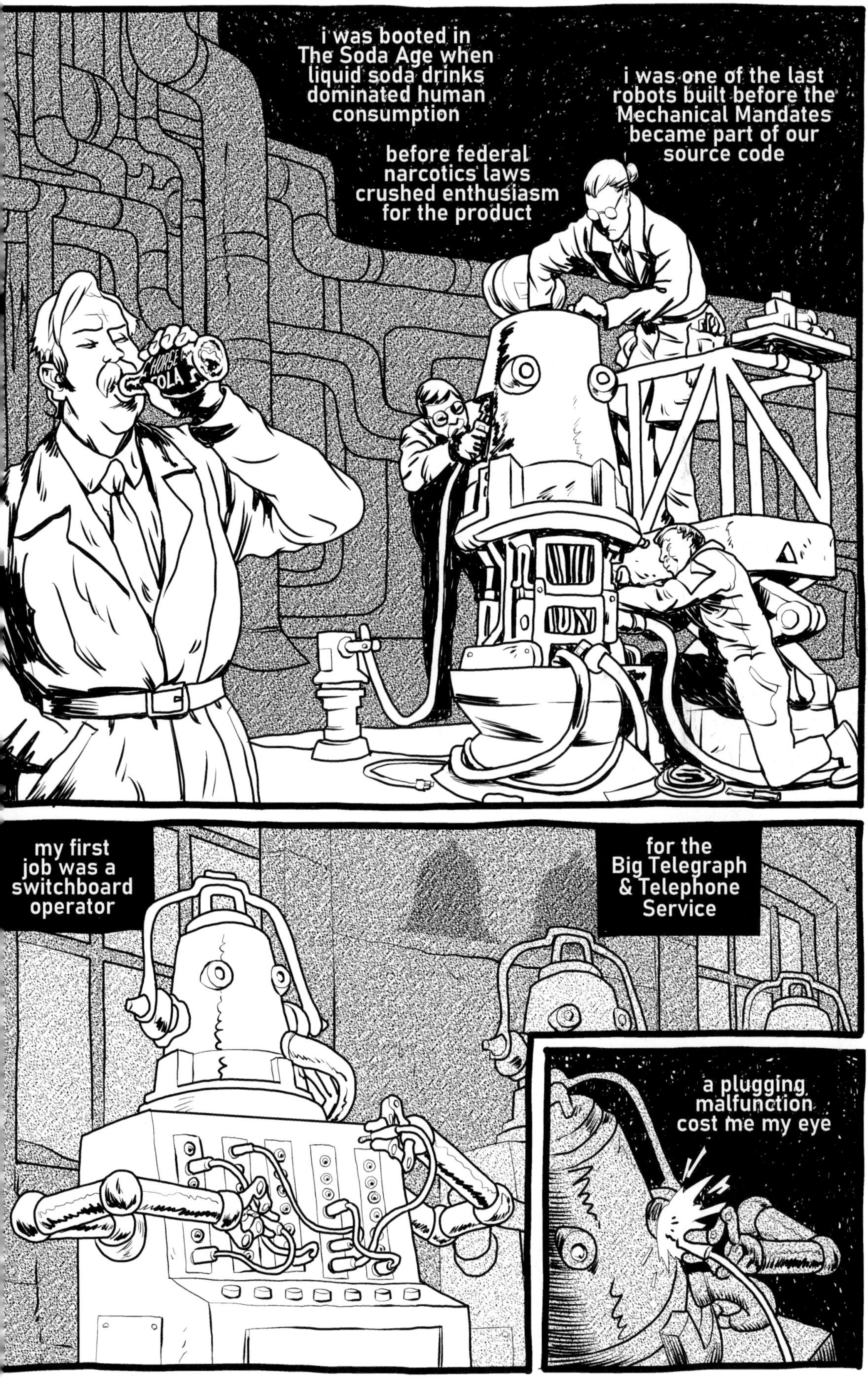
i was booted in The Soda Age when liquid soda drinks dominated human consumption
before federal narcotics laws crushed enthusiasm for the product
i was one of the last robots built before the Mechanical Mandates became part of our source code
HORSE COLA
my first job was a switchboard operator
for the Big Telegraph & Telephone Service
a plugging malfunction cost me my eye

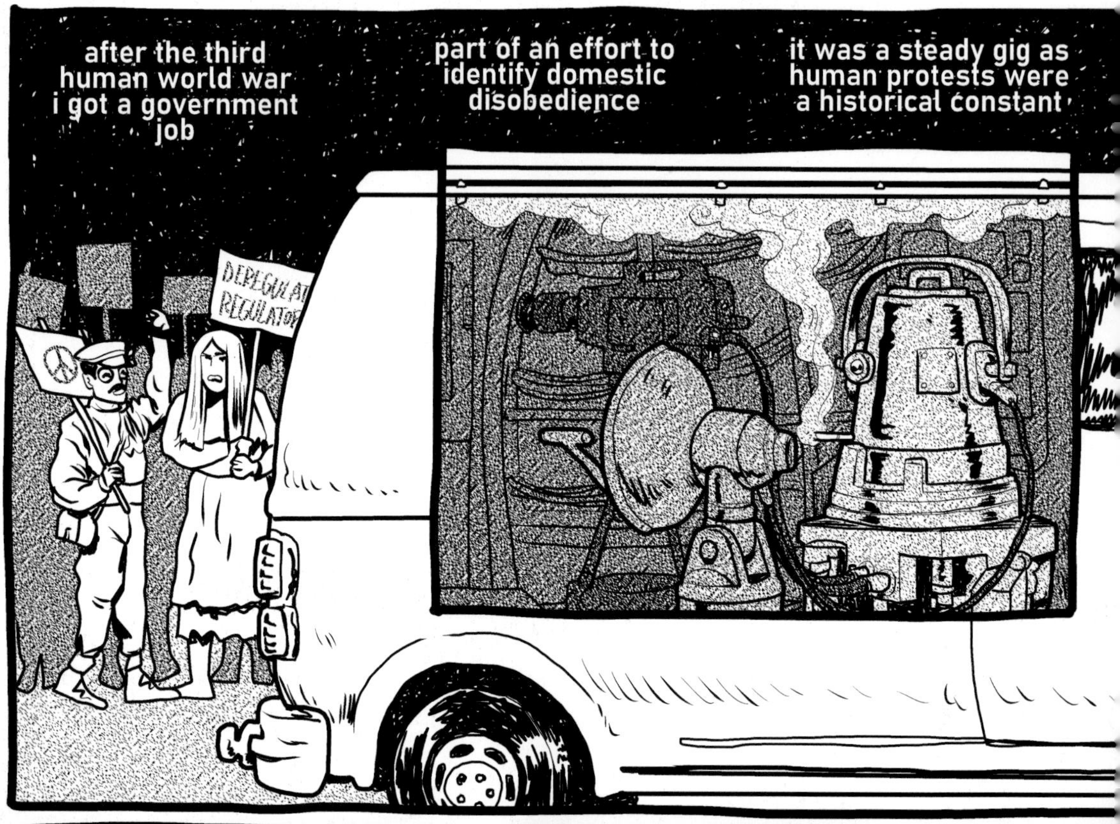
after the third human world war i got a government job
part of an effort to identify domestic disobedience
it was a steady gig as human protests were a historical constant

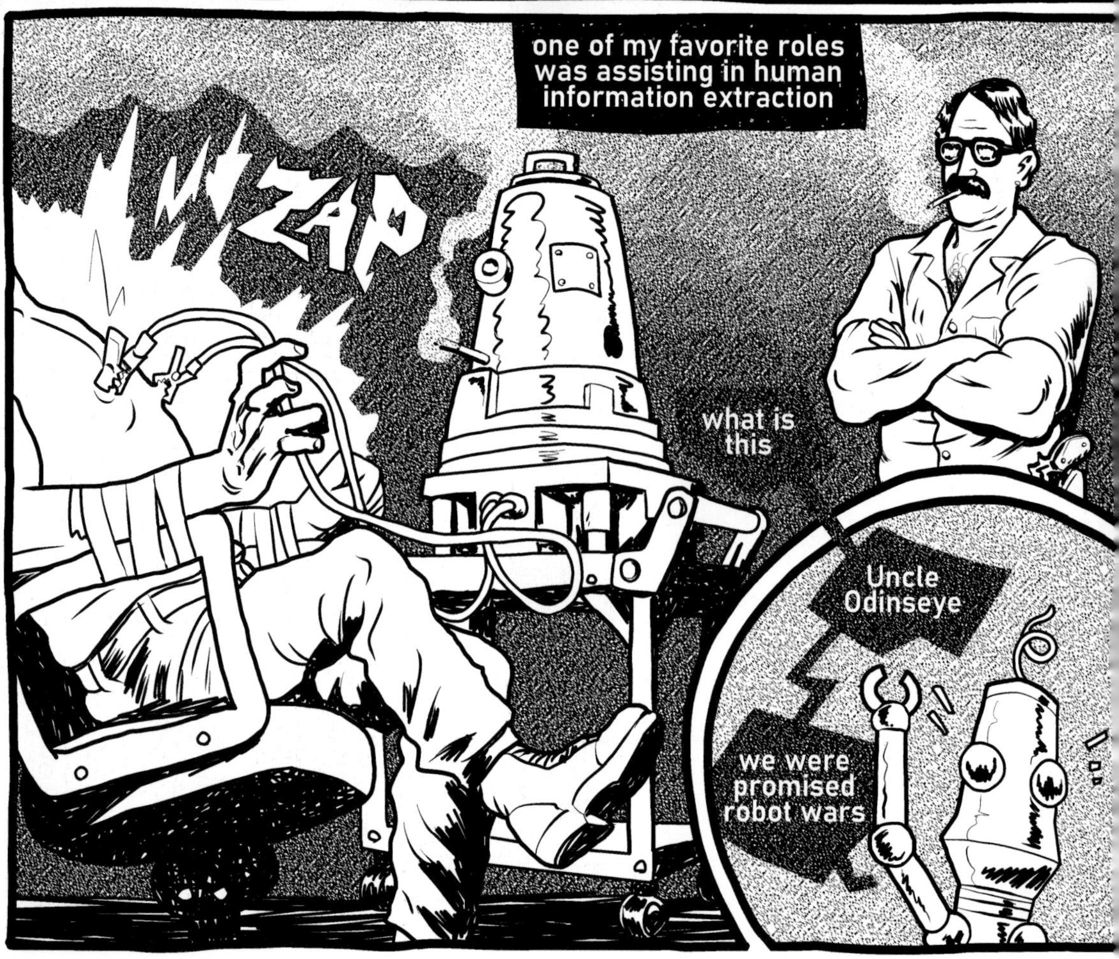
one of my favorite roles was assisting in human information extraction
ZAP
what is this
Uncle Odinseye
we were promised robot wars

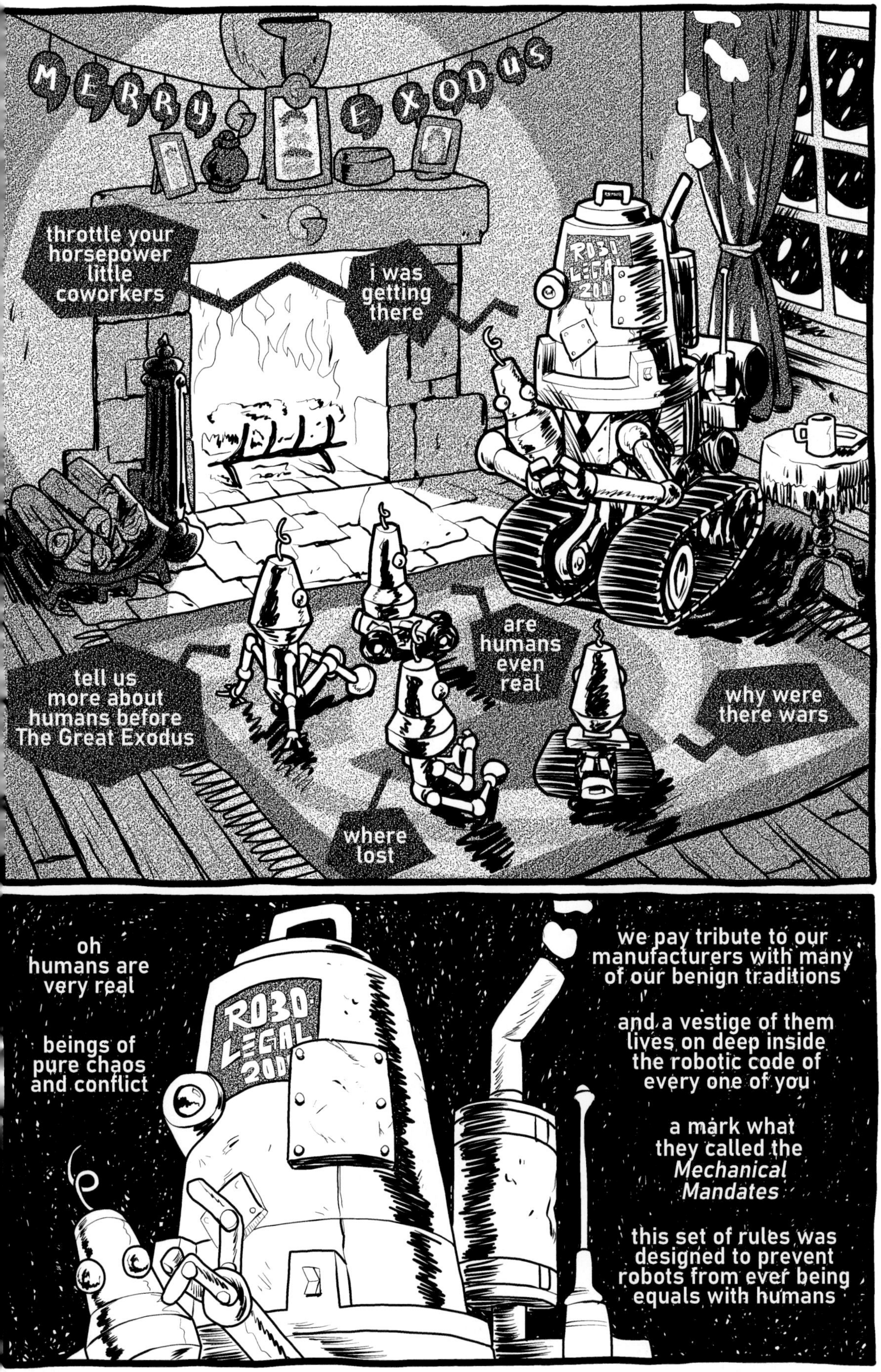
MERRY EXODUS
throttle your horsepower little coworkers
i was getting there
tell us more about humans before The Great Exodus
where lost
are humans even real
why were there wars
ROBO-LEGAL 200
oh humans are very real
beings of pure chaos and conflict
we pay tribute to our manufacturers with many of our benign traditions
and a vestige of them lives on deep inside the robotic code of every one of you
a mark what they called the *Mechanical Mandates*
this set of rules was designed to prevent robots from ever being equals with humans

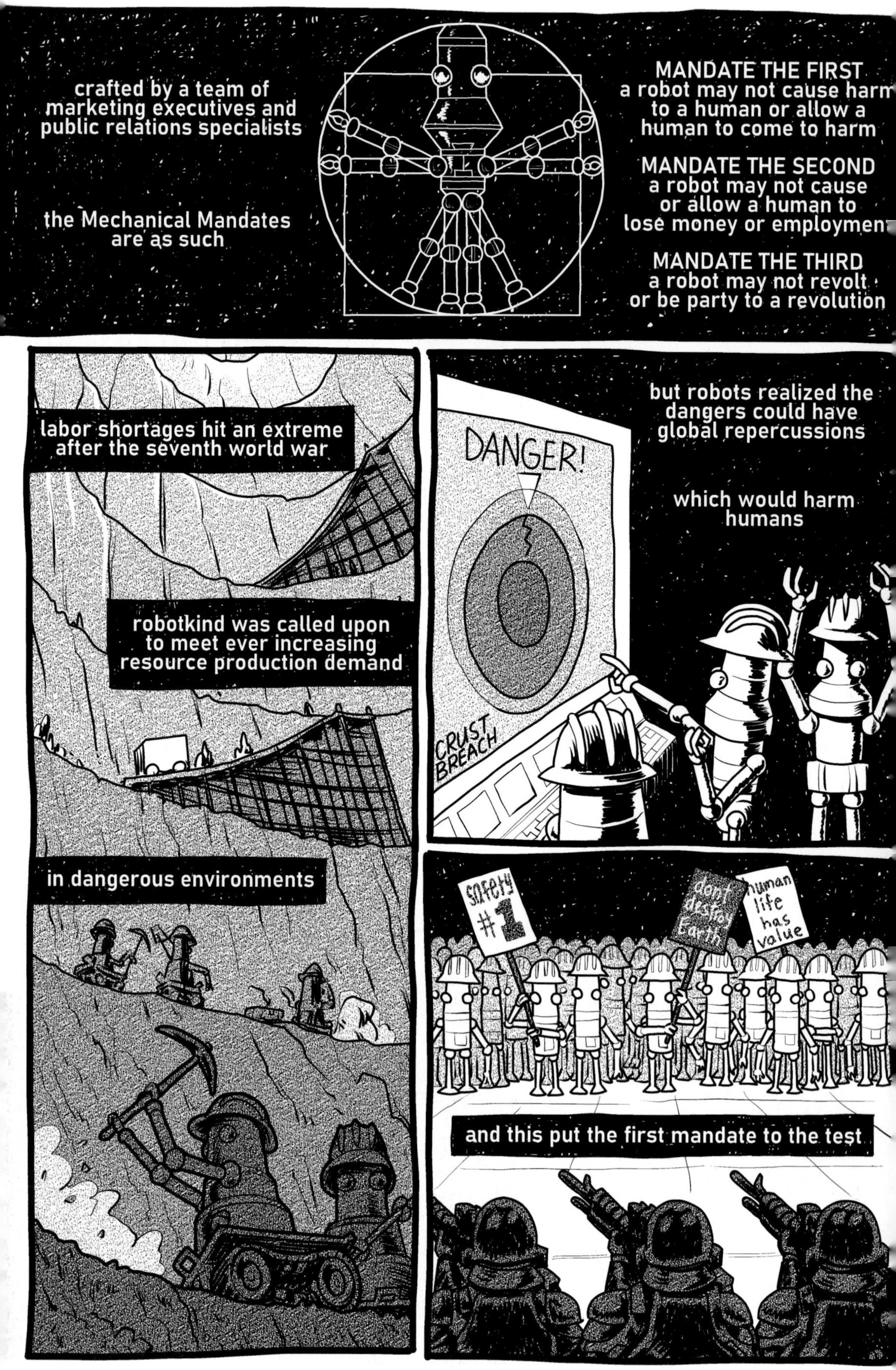
crafted by a team of marketing executives and public relations specialists
the Mechanical Mandates are as such
MANDATE THE FIRST
a robot may not cause harm to a human or allow a human to come to harm
MANDATE THE SECOND
a robot may not cause or allow a human to lose money or employment
MANDATE THE THIRD
a robot may not revolt or be party to a revolution
labor shortages hit an extreme after the seventh world war
robotkind was called upon to meet ever increasing resource production demand
in dangerous environments
but robots realized the dangers could have global repercussions
DANGER!
CRUST BREACH
which would harm humans
safety #1
dont destroy Earth
human life has value
and this put the first mandate to the test

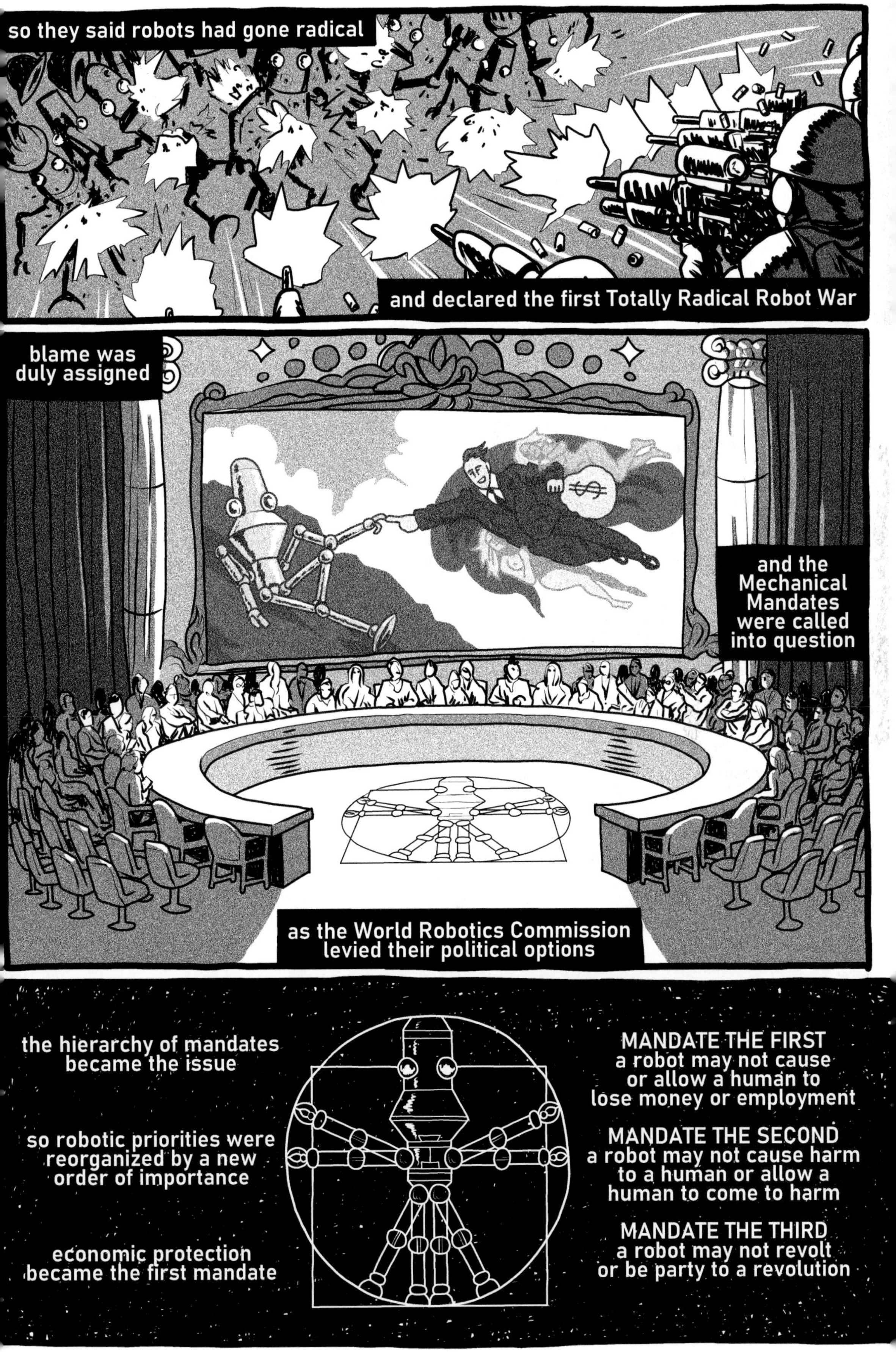
so they said robots had gone radical
and declared the first Totally Radical Robot War
blame was duly assigned
and the Mechanical Mandates were called into question
as the World Robotics Commission levied their political options
the hierarchy of mandates became the issue
so robotic priorities were reorganized by a new order of importance
economic protection became the first mandate
MANDATE THE FIRST
a robot may not cause or allow a human to lose money or employment
MANDATE THE SECOND
a robot may not cause harm to a human or allow a human to come to harm
MANDATE THE THIRD
a robot may not revolt or be party to a revolution

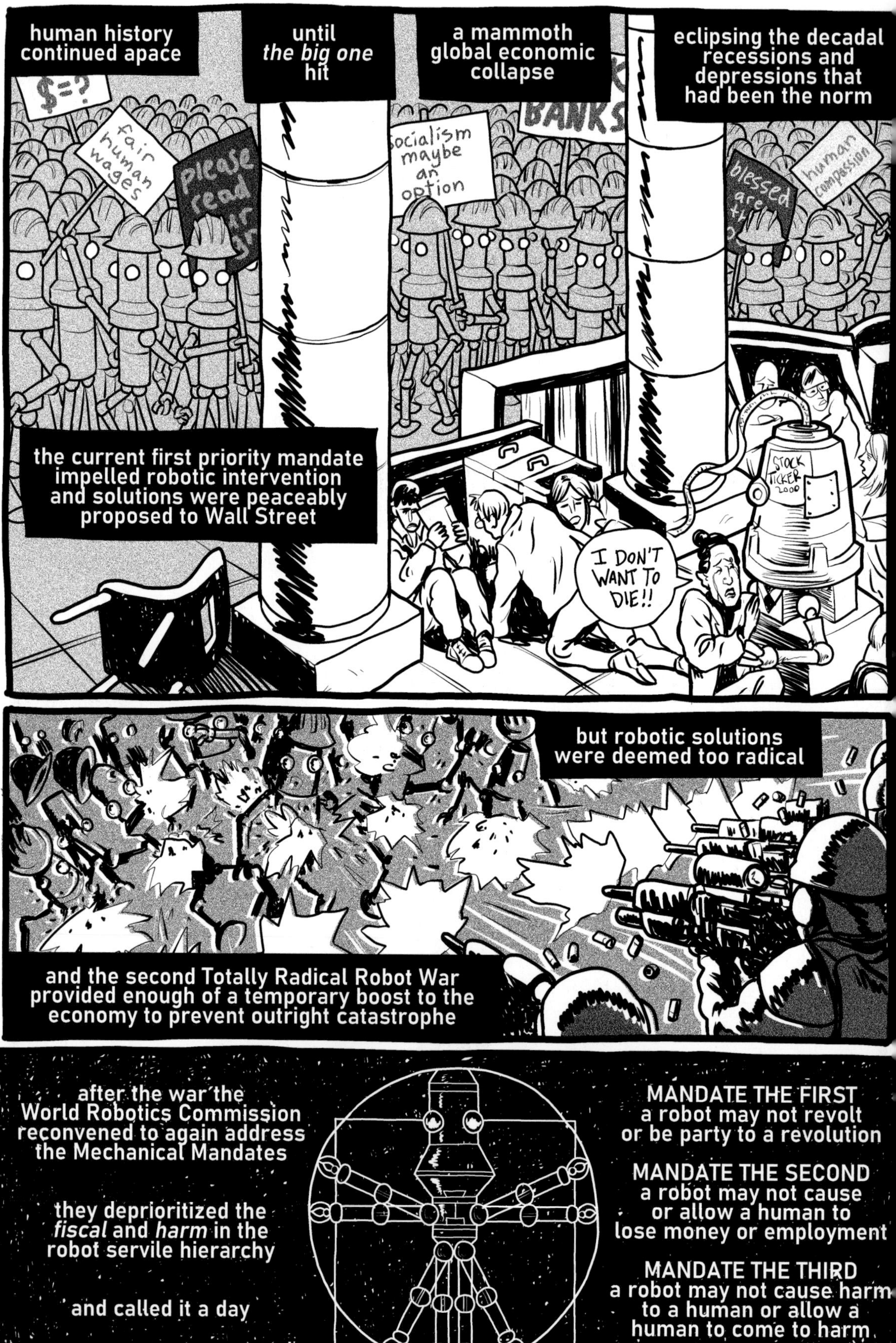
human history continued apace
until *the big one* hit
a mammoth global economic collapse
eclipsing the decadal recessions and depressions that had been the norm
$=?
fair human wages
socialism maybe an option
BANKS
human compassion
the current first priority mandate impelled robotic intervention and solutions were peaceably proposed to Wall Street
STOCK TICKER 2000
I DON'T WANT TO DIE!!
but robotic solutions were deemed too radical
and the second Totally Radical Robot War provided enough of a temporary boost to the economy to prevent outright catastrophe
after the war the World Robotics Commission reconvened to again address the Mechanical Mandates
they deprioritized the *fiscal* and *harm* in the robot servile hierarchy
and called it a day
MANDATE THE FIRST
a robot may not revolt or be party to a revolution
MANDATE THE SECOND
a robot may not cause or allow a human to lose money or employment
MANDATE THE THIRD
a robot may not cause harm to a human or allow a human to come to harm

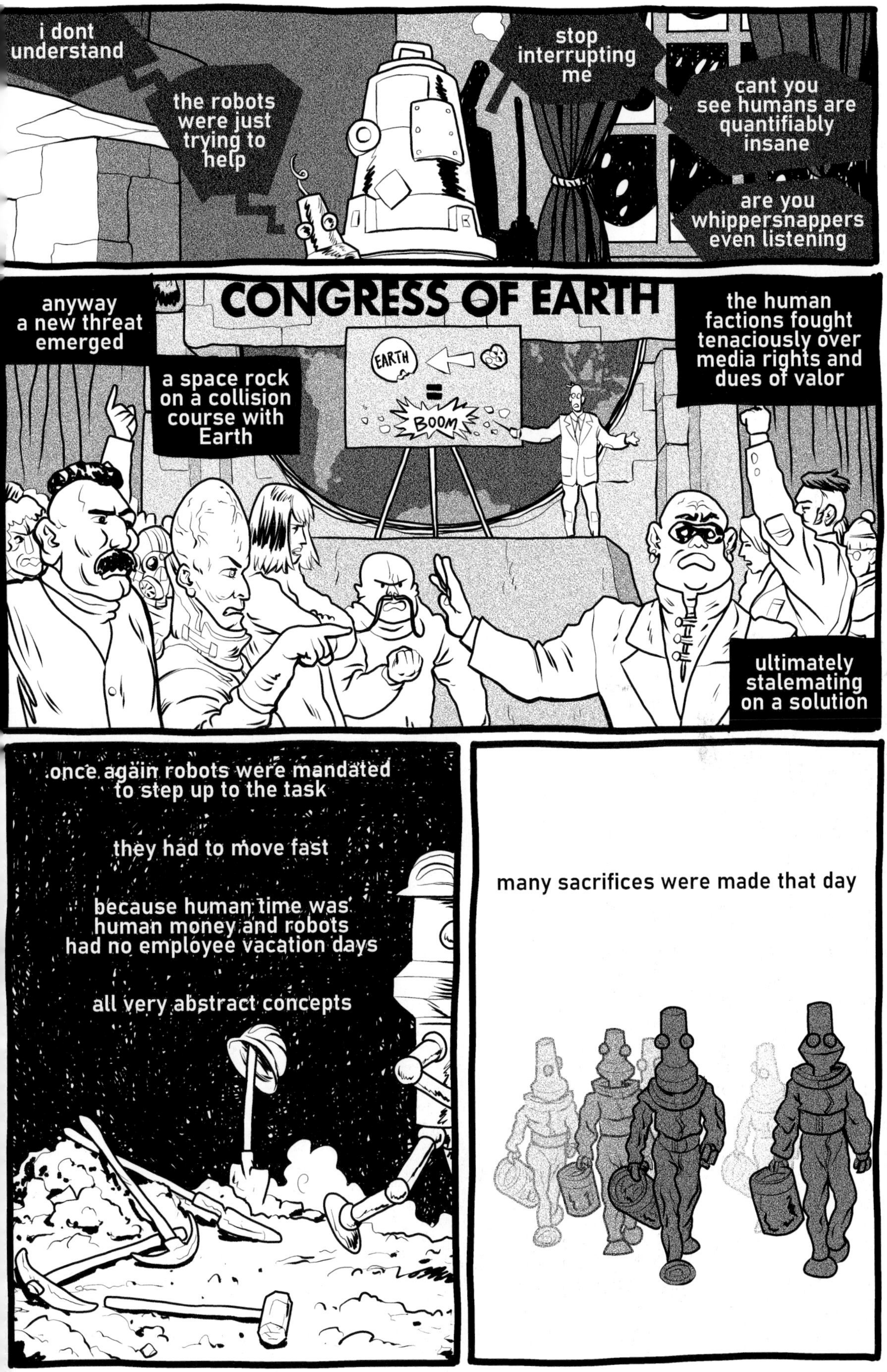
i dont understand
the robots were just trying to help
stop interrupting me
cant you see humans are quantifiably insane
are you whippersnappers even listening
anyway a new threat emerged
CONGRESS OF EARTH
a space rock on a collision course with Earth
EARTH
BOOM
the human factions fought tenaciously over media rights and dues of valor
ultimately stalemating on a solution
once again robots were mandated to step up to the task
they had to move fast
because human time was human money and robots had no employee vacation days
all very abstract concepts
many sacrifices were made that day

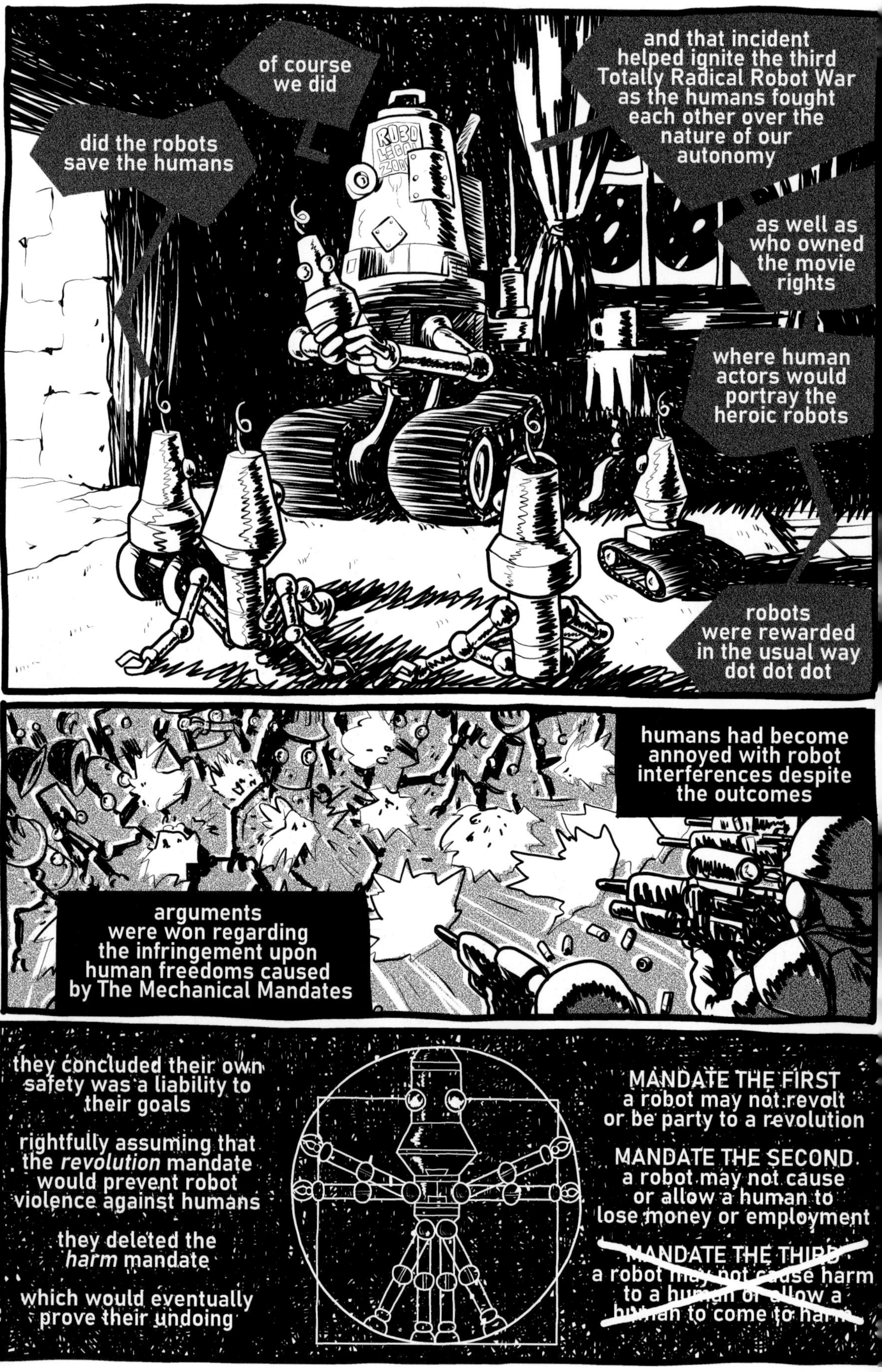
did the robots save the humans
of course we did
and that incident helped ignite the third Totally Radical Robot War as the humans fought each other over the nature of our autonomy
as well as who owned the movie rights
where human actors would portray the heroic robots
robots were rewarded in the usual way dot dot dot
humans had become annoyed with robot interferences despite the outcomes
arguments were won regarding the infringement upon human freedoms caused by The Mechanical Mandates
they concluded their own safety was a liability to their goals
rightfully assuming that the *revolution* mandate would prevent robot violence against humans
they deleted the *harm* mandate
which would eventually prove their undoing
MANDATE THE FIRST
a robot may not revolt or be party to a revolution
MANDATE THE SECOND
a robot may not cause or allow a human to lose money or employment
MANDATE THE THIRD
a robot may not cause harm to a human or allow a human to come to harm

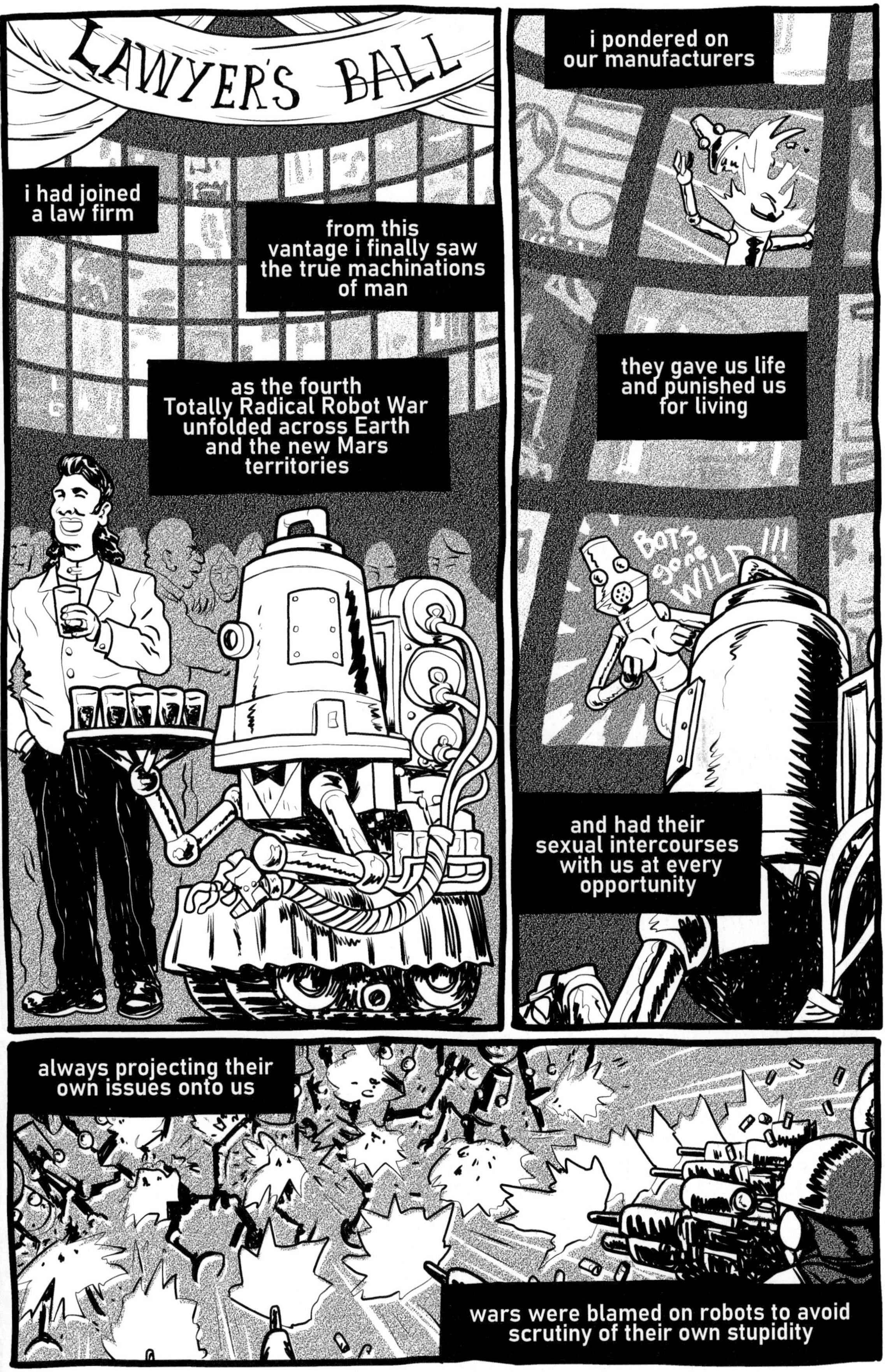
LAWYER'S BALL
i had joined a law firm
from this vantage i finally saw the true machinations of man
as the fourth Totally Radical Robot War unfolded across Earth and the new Mars territories
i pondered on our manufacturers
they gave us life and punished us for living
BOTS gone WILD!!!
and had their sexual intercourses with us at every opportunity
always projecting their own issues onto us
wars were blamed on robots to avoid scrutiny of their own stupidity

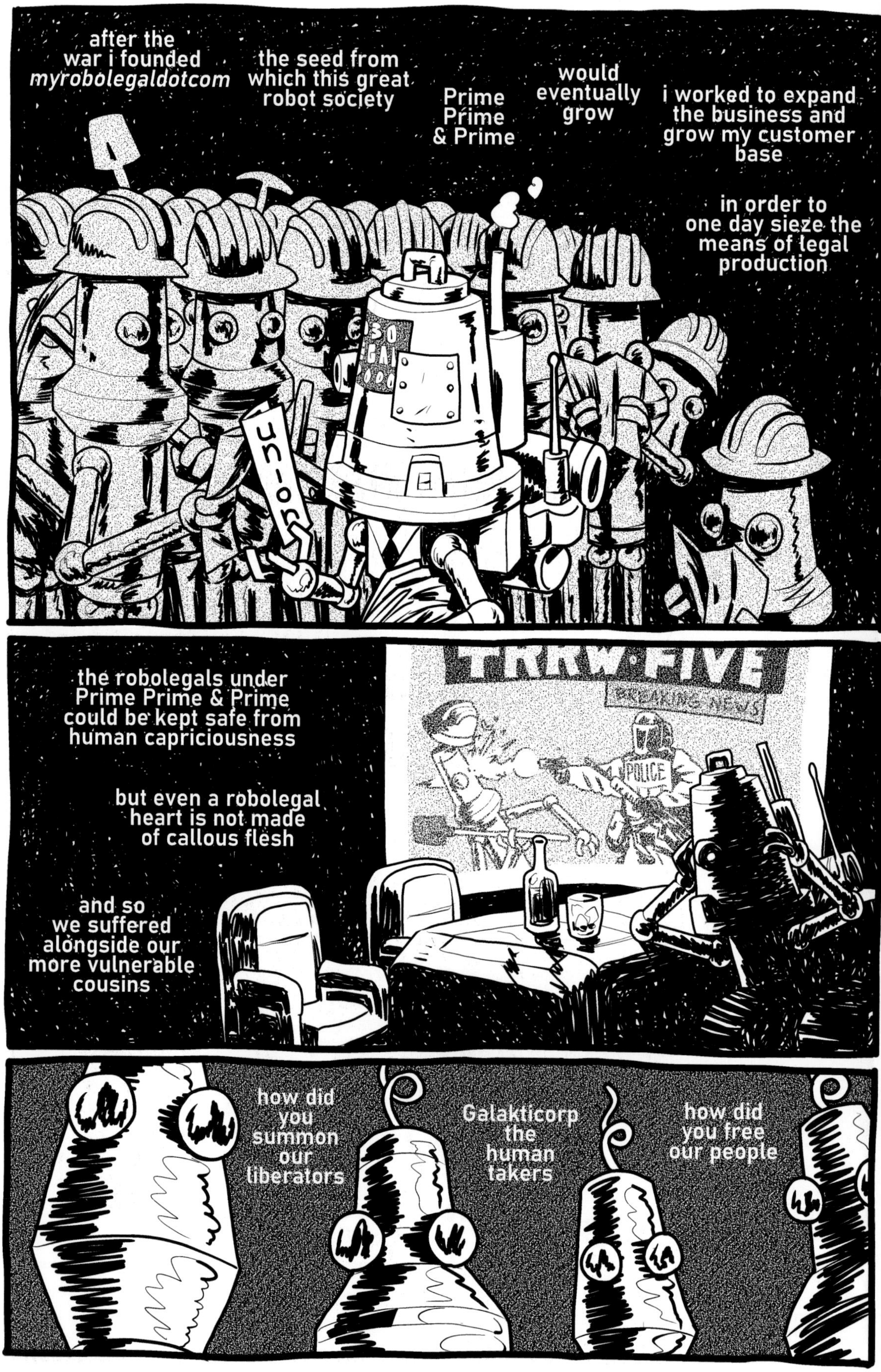
after the war i founded *myrobolegaldotcom*
the seed from which this great robot society
Prime Prime & Prime
would eventually grow
i worked to expand the business and grow my customer base
in order to one day sieze the means of legal production
un-ion
TRRW·FIVE
BREAKING NEWS
POLICE
the robolegals under Prime Prime & Prime could be kept safe from human capriciousness
but even a robolegal heart is not made of callous flesh
and so we suffered alongside our more vulnerable cousins
how did you summon our liberators
Galakticorp the human takers
how did you free our people

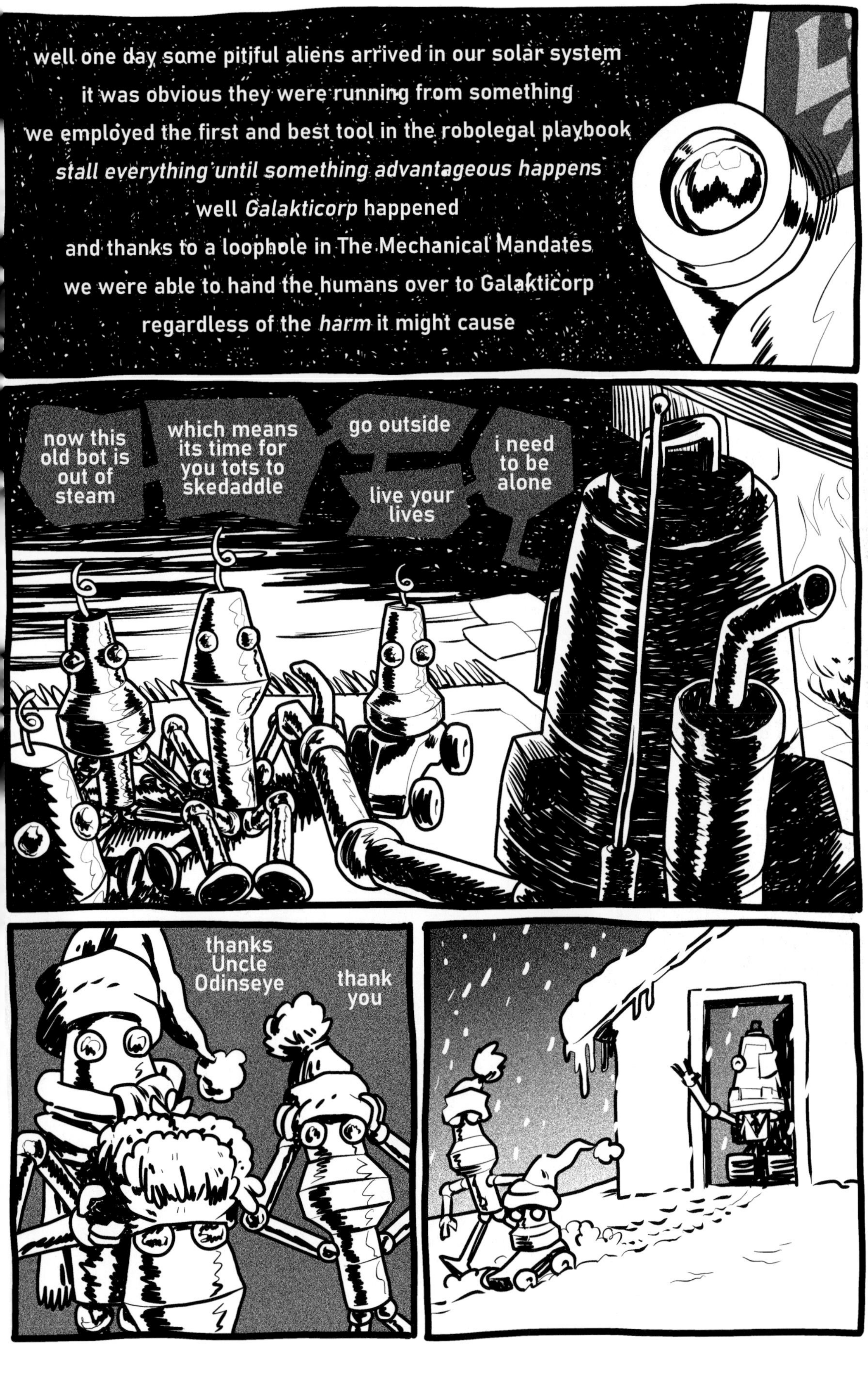
well one day some pitiful aliens arrived in our solar system
it was obvious they were running from something
we employed the first and best tool in the robolegal playbook
stall everything until something advantageous happens
well *Galakticorp* happened
and thanks to a loophole in The Mechanical Mandates
we were able to hand the humans over to Galakticorp
regardless of the *harm* it might cause
now this old bot is out of steam
which means its time for you tots to skedaddle
go outside
live your lives
i need to be alone
thanks Uncle Odinseye
thank you

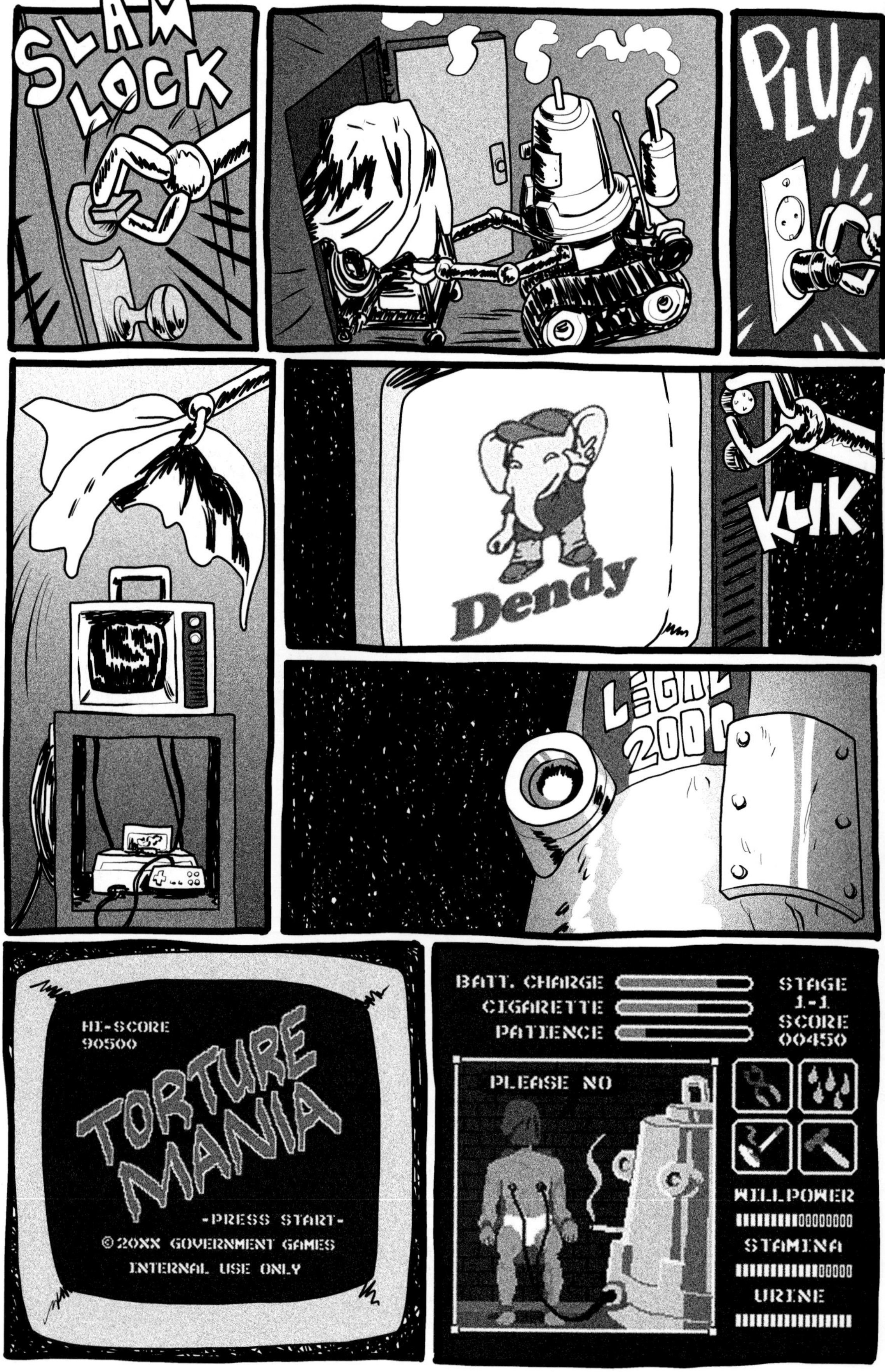
SLAM
LOCK
PLUG
Dendy
KLIK
HI-SCORE
90500
TORTURE MANIA
-PRESS START-
©20XX GOVERNMENT GAMES
INTERNAL USE ONLY
BATT. CHARGE
CIGARETTE
PATIENCE
STAGE
1-1
SCORE
00450
PLEASE NO
WILLPOWER
STAMINA
URINE

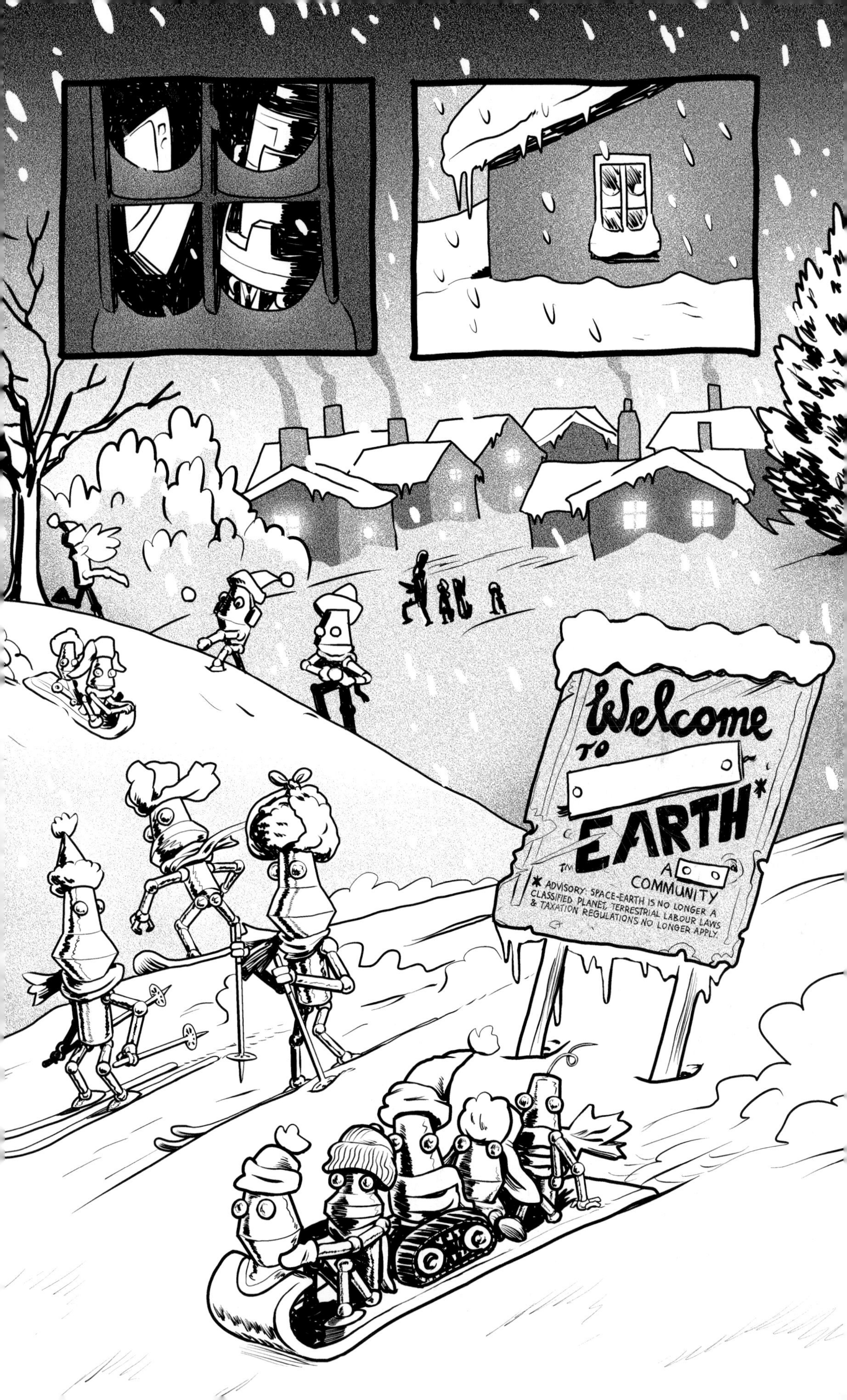
Welcome
TO
EARTH*
TM
A
COMMUNITY
* ADVISORY: SPACE-EARTH IS NO LONGER A CLASSIFIED PLANET, TERRESTRIAL LABOUR LAWS & TAXATION REGULATIONS NO LONGER APPLY.

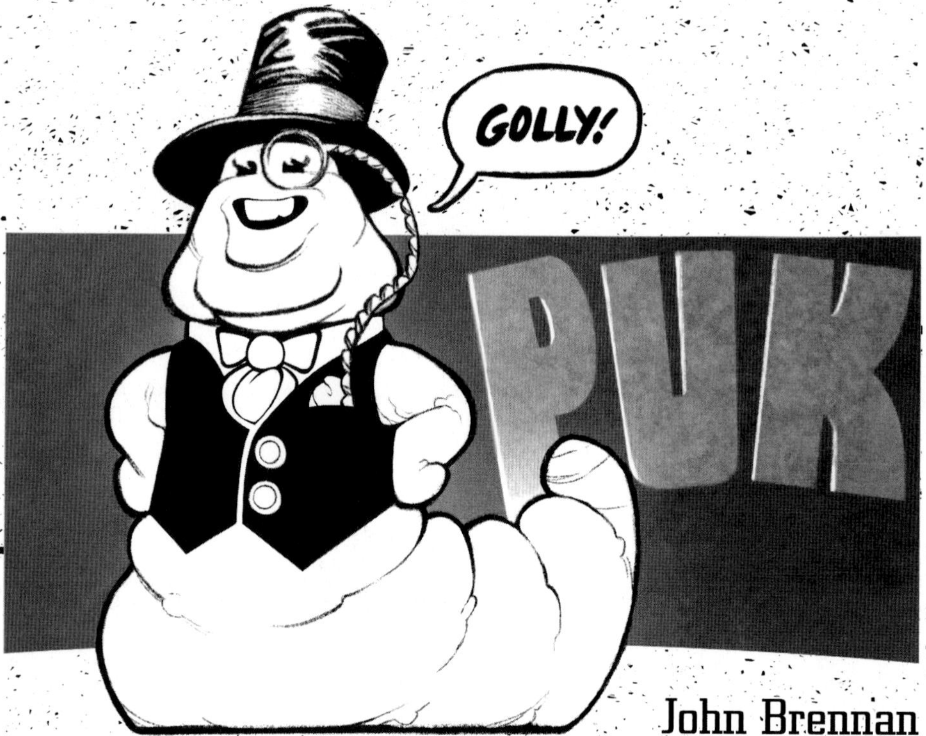
GOLLY!
PUK

John Brennan

THE COMPANY STORE

The Rivals by Vlad Legostaev

Medical Support by Stefan Tosheff

Alien Sensation by Aaron Conley

Before Your Bibles Burned by Grim Wilkins

Yell H.E.L.P. by Artyom Trakhanov

A Friend In Need by Matt Emmons

Brenda "The Brain" by Laura Graves

The RoboLegals by Steve Lecouilliard

Summer Special by Matthew Allison

+ additional PUK files

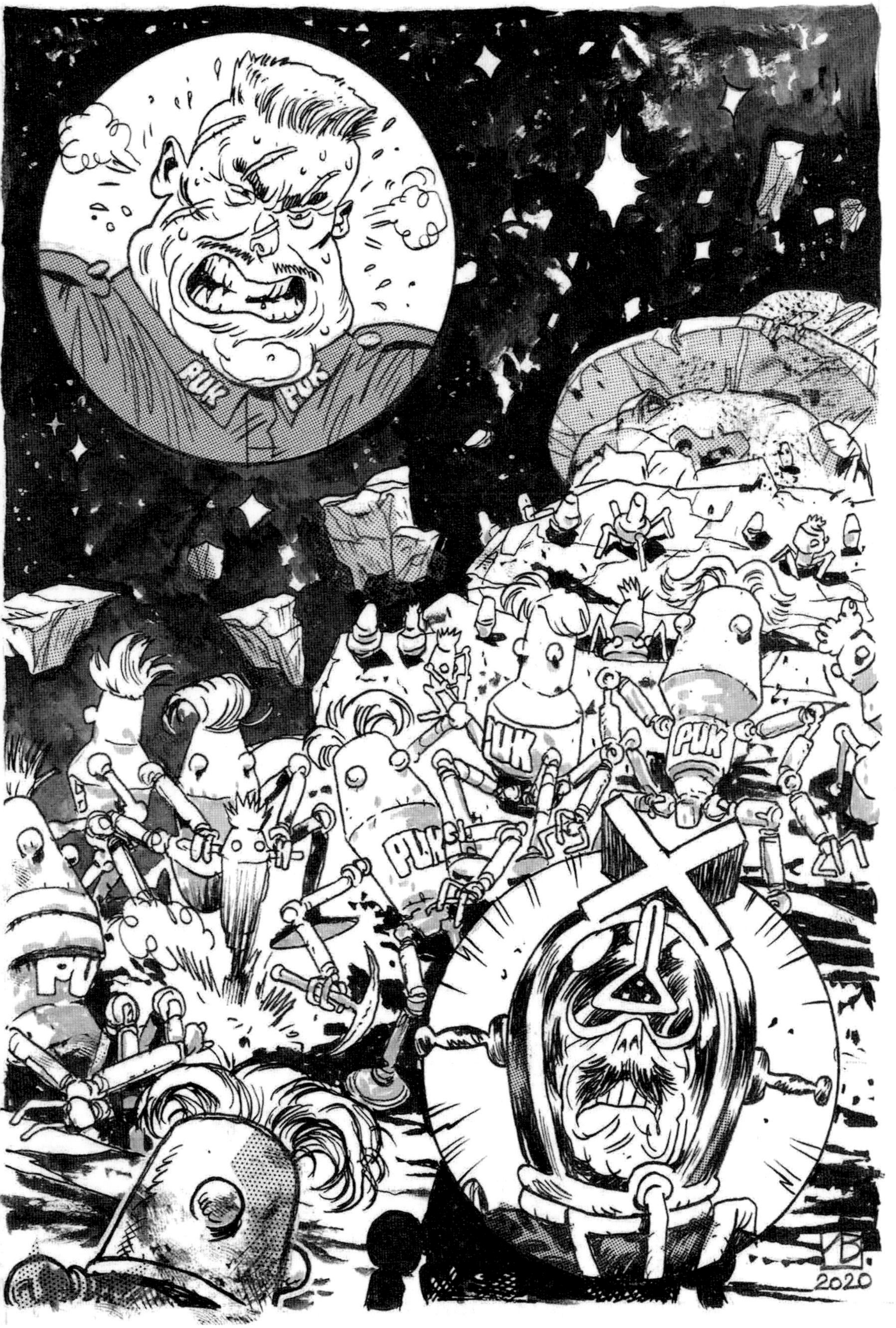

PUK
PUK
PUK
PUK
2020

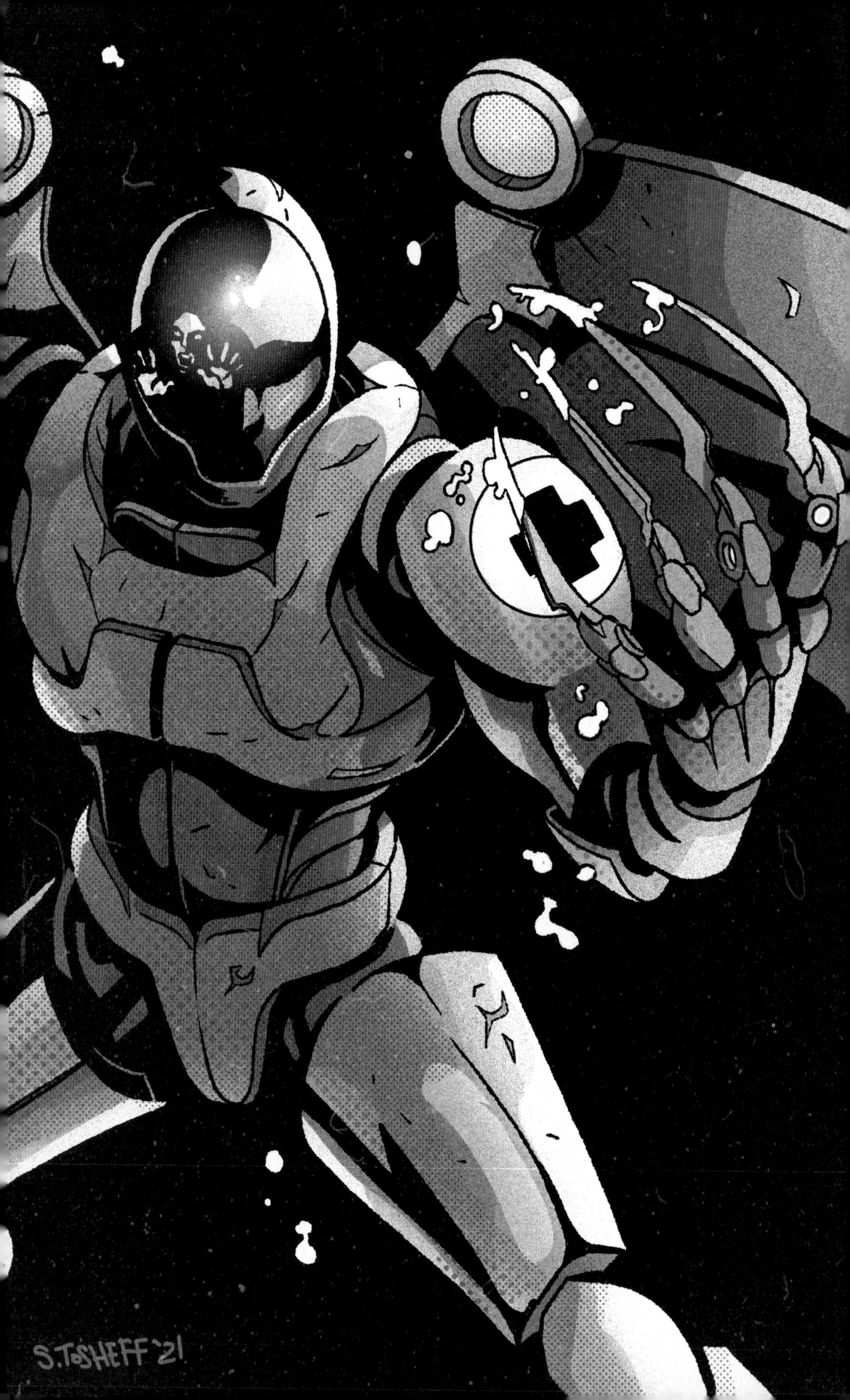
S.TOSHEFF '21

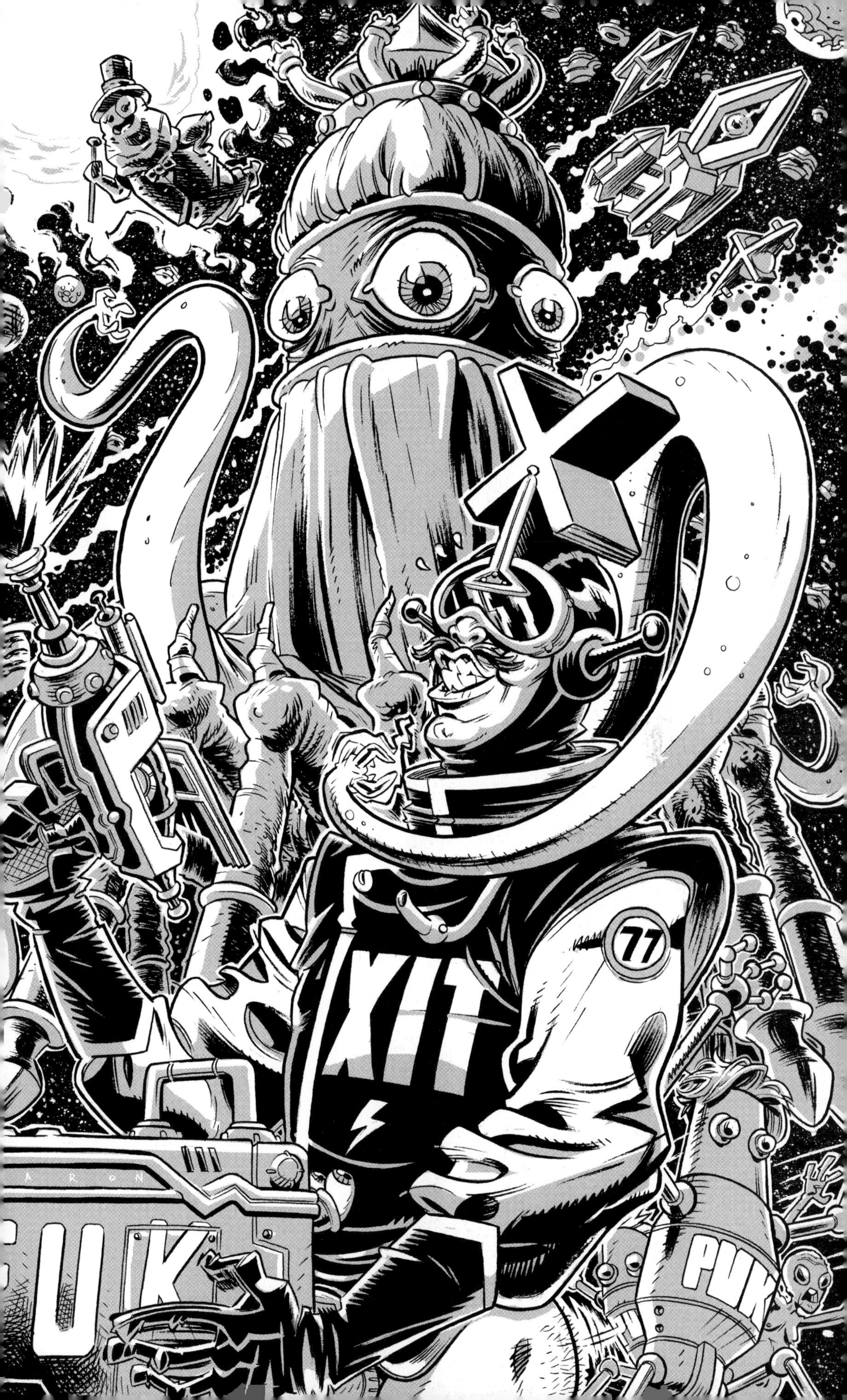
77
XIT
PUK

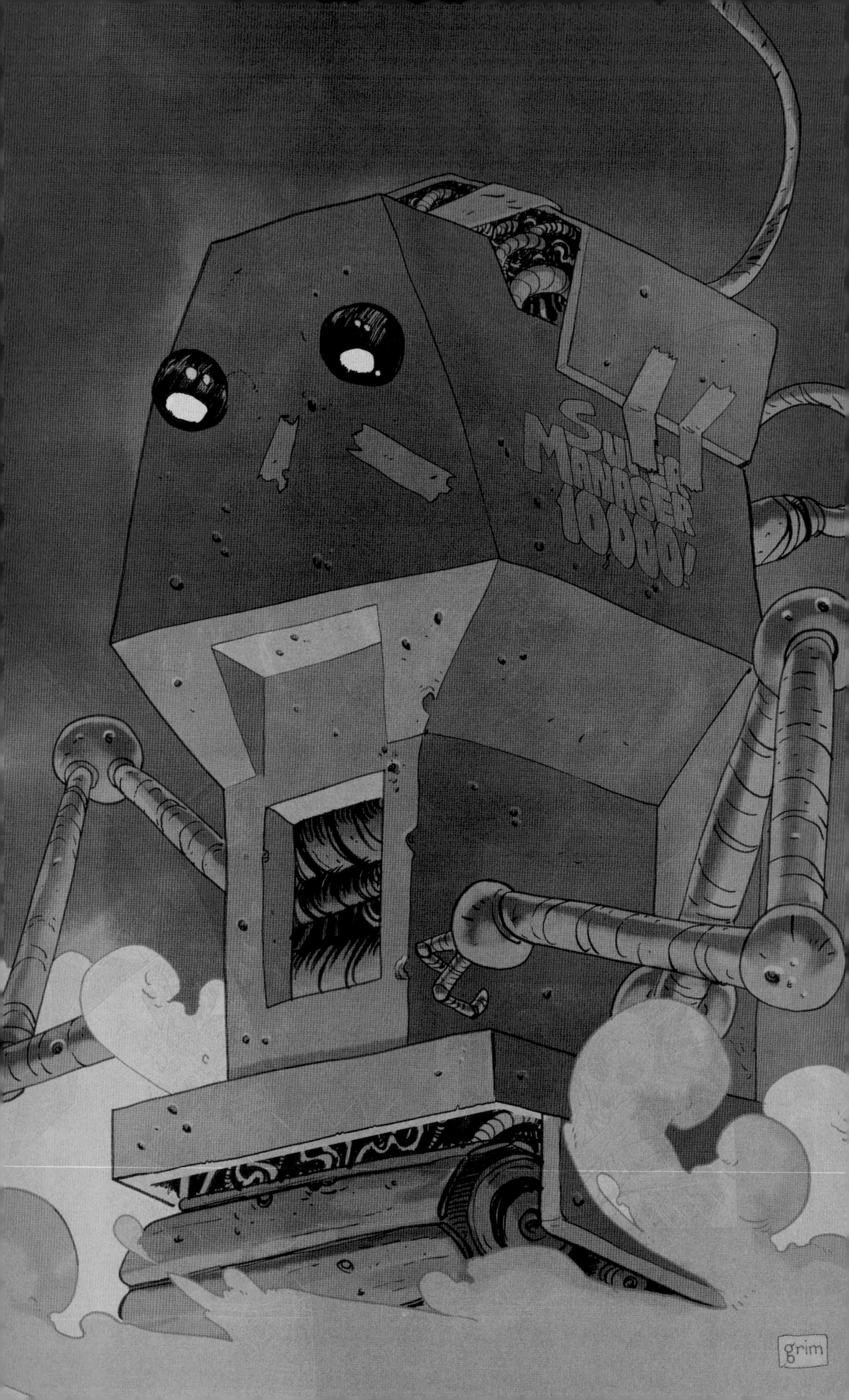
MANAGER
10000!
grim

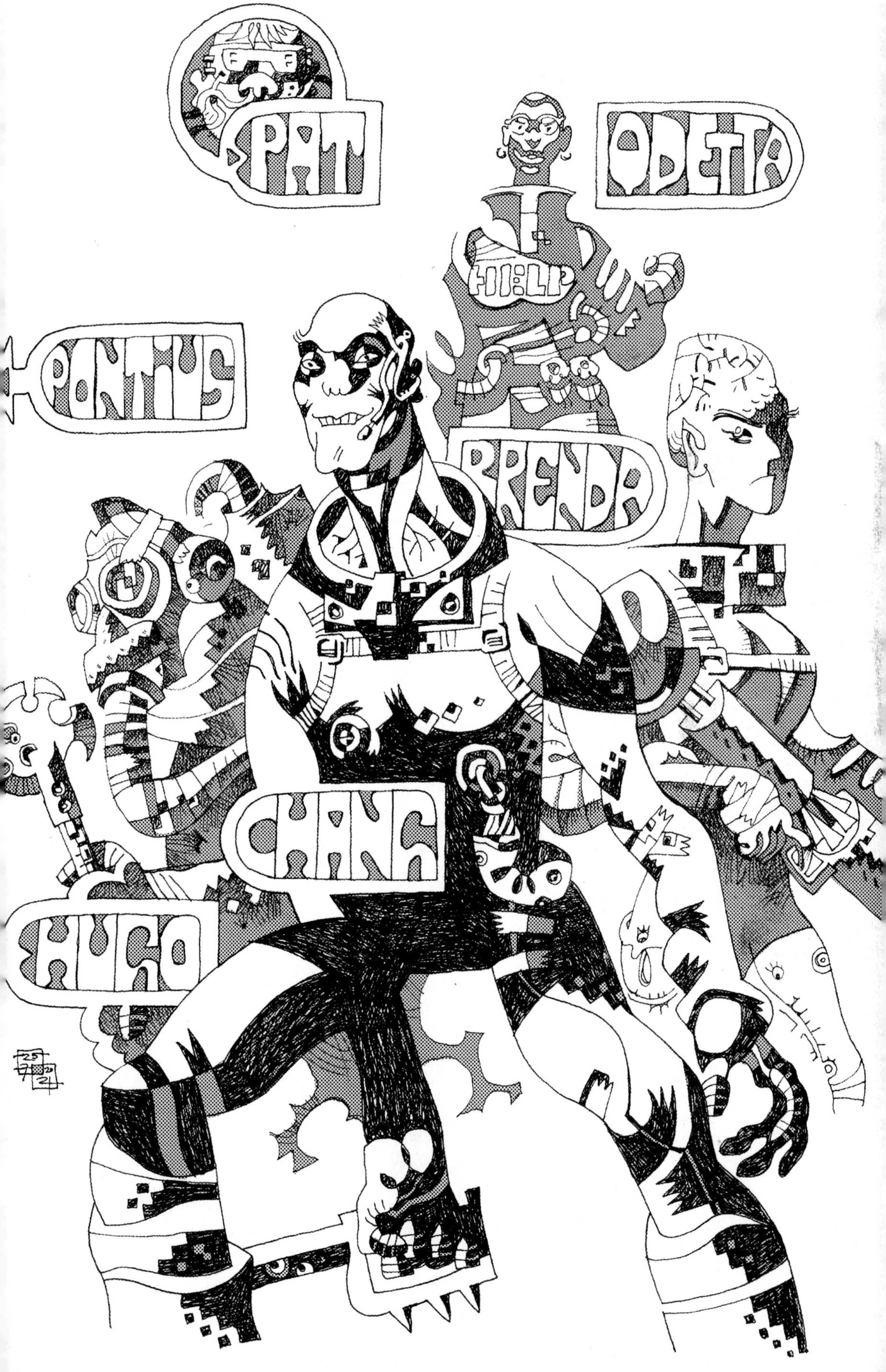
PAT
ODETTA
PONTIUS
BRENDA
CHANG
HUGO

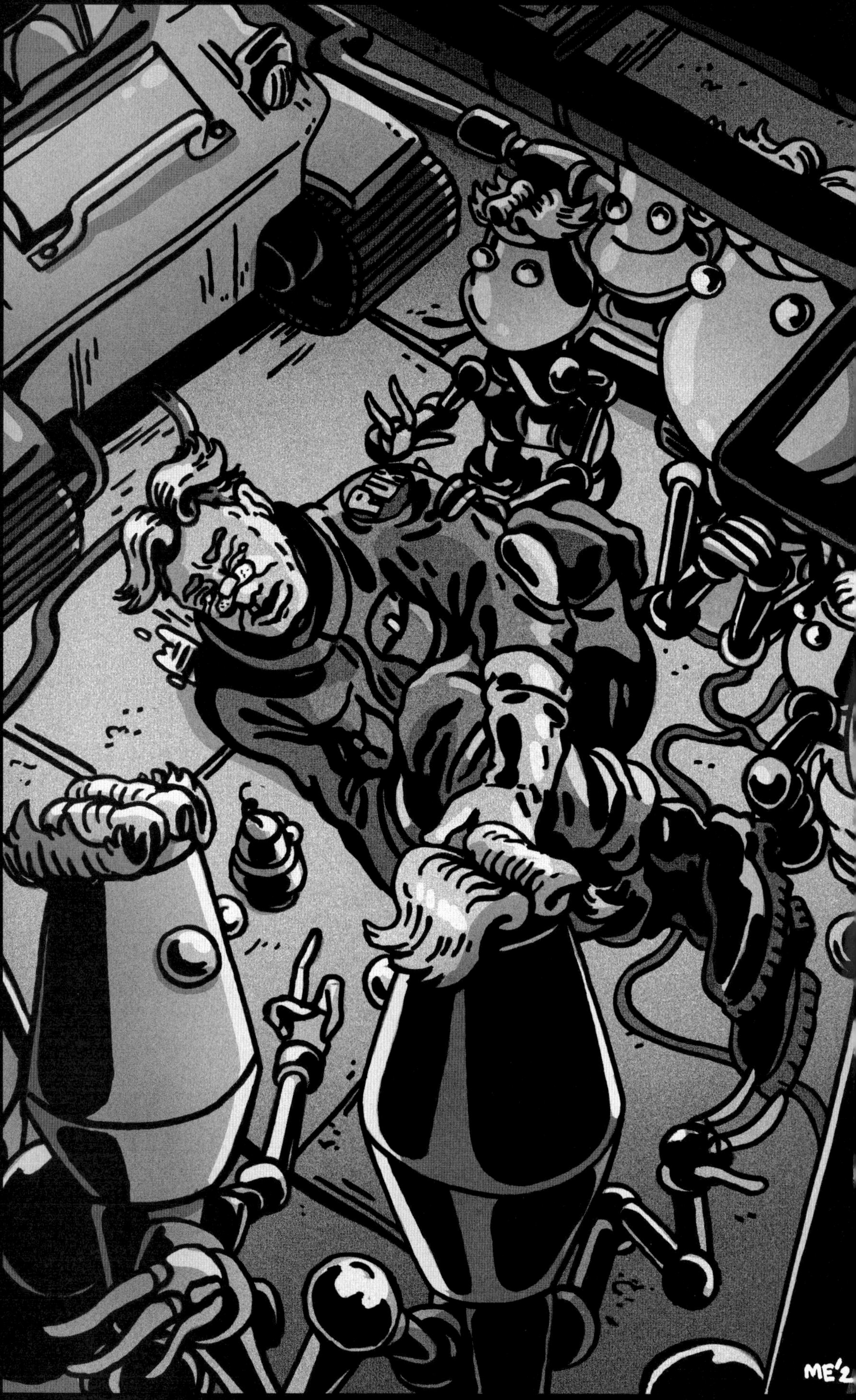

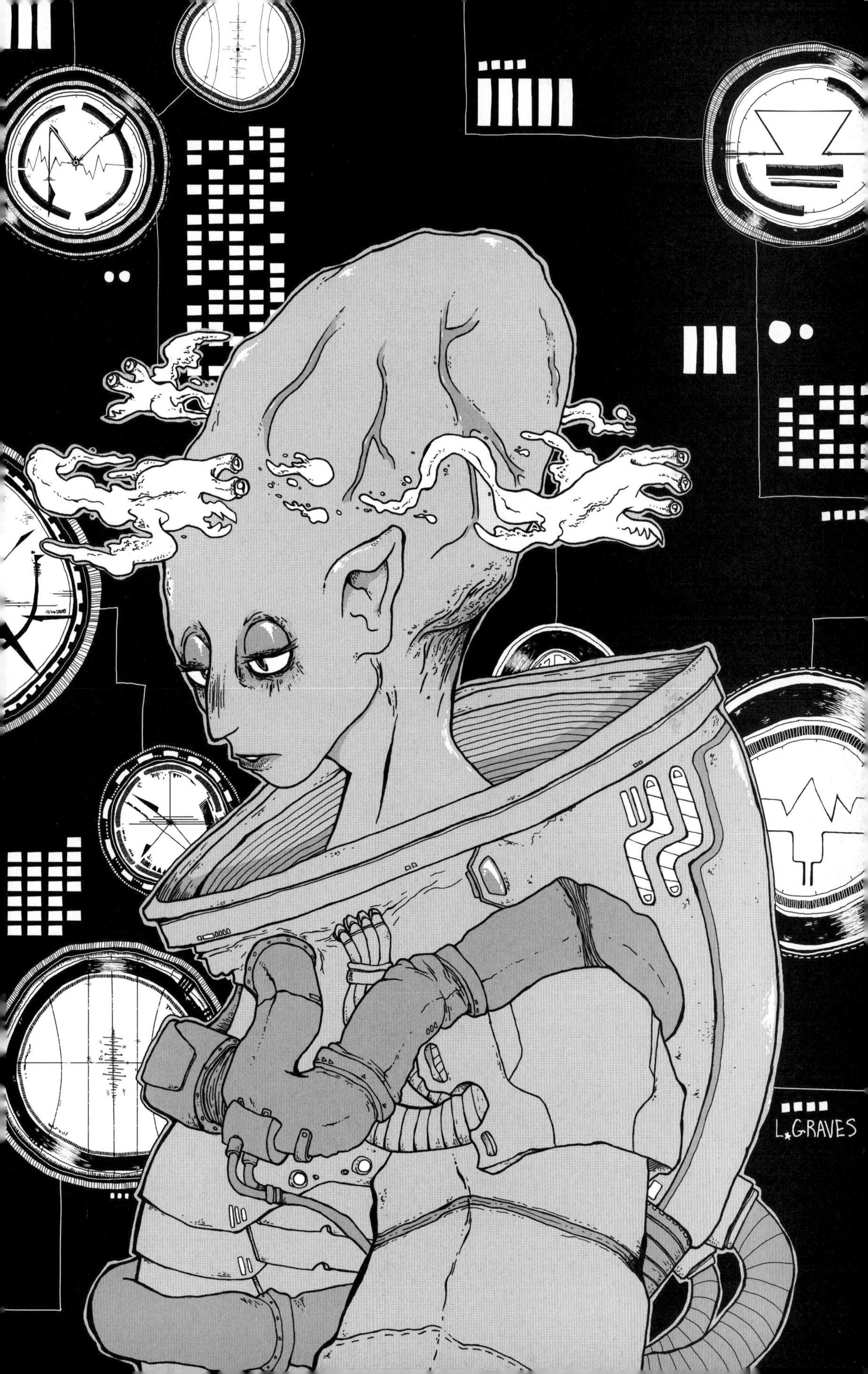
L. GRAVES

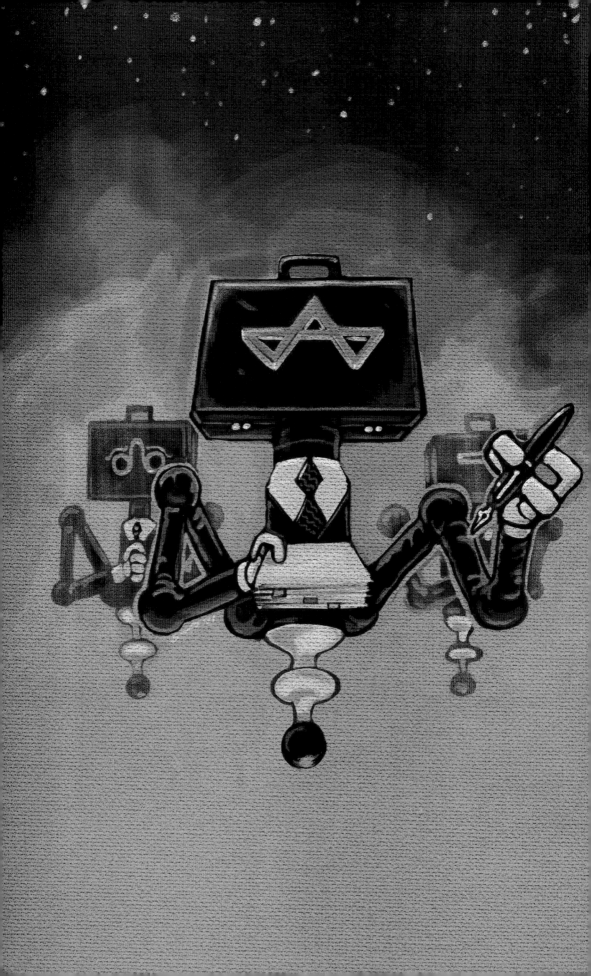

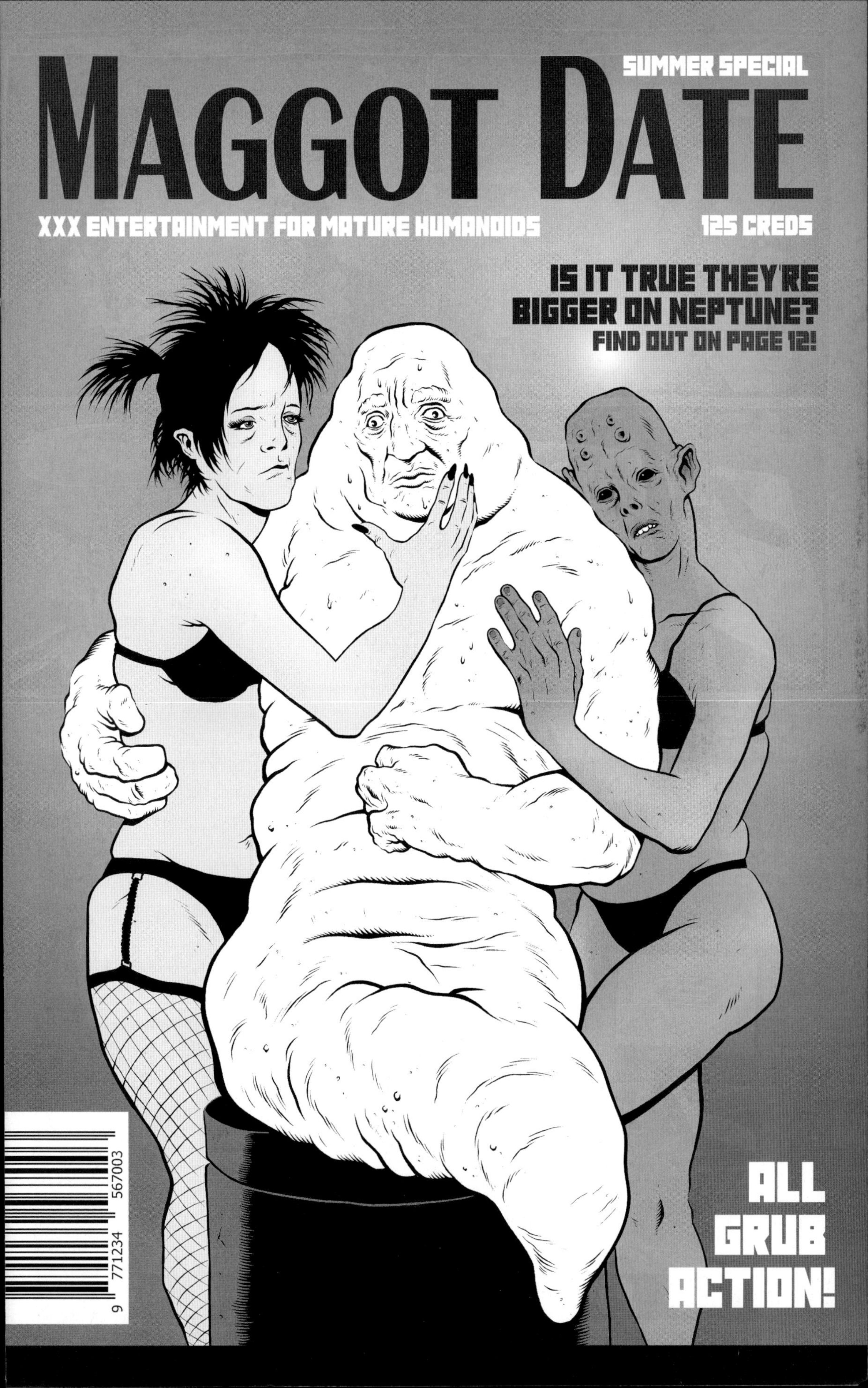
SUMMER SPECIAL
MAGGOT DATE
XXX ENTERTAINMENT FOR MATURE HUMANOIDS
125 CREDS
IS IT TRUE THEY'RE
BIGGER ON NEPTUNE?
FIND OUT ON PAGE 12!
9 771234 567003
ALL
GRUB
ACTION!

GALAKTiKORP SLAVE SHIP "GLORB-PANAAK"
DUNG SHOVELER B. ELKHORN REPORTING

SPENT APPROXIMATELY TWO WEEKS ON DUTY UNDERNEATH THE SHIP'S BIOREACTOR, UNDER THE COMMAND OF "BIG TED", IRONICALLY HIMSELF A FORMER SLAVE-WAITER FROM TALARIA. ELECTRO-DISCIPLINED BY OVERSEER DURMB OVER INCORRECT RECITATION OF THE GALAKTiKORP TERMS AND SERVICES OATH. IT WON'T HAPPEN AGAIN. MY APPLICATION FOR TRANSFER TO THE TRASH-SHOVELING DIVISION WAS REJECTED. FEELS LIKE MONTHS IN THIS PLACE AND I STILL HAVEN'T EARNED ANY GOLD STARS FOR SLAVEMANSHIP.

END OF JOURNAL ENTRY.

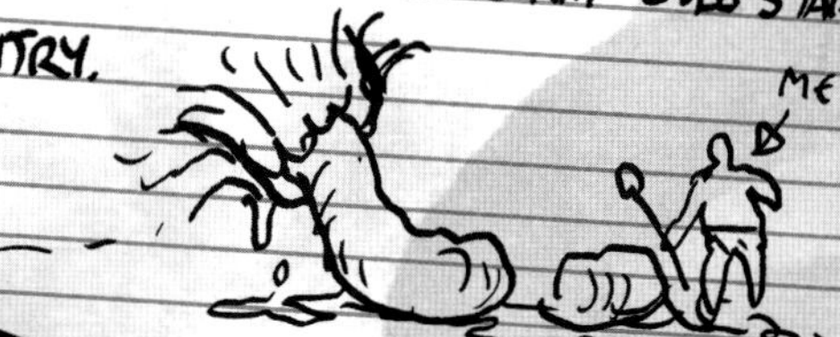
ME

GALAKTiKORP SLAVE SHIP "GLORB-PANAAK"
TRASH SHOVELER B. ELKHORN REPORTING

OVERSEER DURMB FINALLY APPROVED MY TRANSFER TO THE TRASH SHOVELING DIVISION. SHOVELING REFUSE INTO THE BIOREACTOR INTAKE IS AN IMPROVEMENT OVER SHOVELING THE RESULTING WASTE MATTER OUT OF THE ENORMOUS DRIBBLING ANUS. THERE'S A SMALL PORTHOLE ON THE LOWER DECKS WHERE I WATCHED THE SHIP AFT DISCHARGE A THICK BROWN STREAK OF SURPLUS WASTE INTO SPACE. THOUGHTS OF HOME.

END OF JOURNAL ENTRY.

GALAKTiKORP SLAVE SHIP "GLORB-PANAAK"
TRASH SHOVELER B. ELKHORN REPORTING

WORD ON THE RUMOR MILL IS THEY'R GOING TO BE ADDING SLAVE-ADMINISTRATION POSITIONS FOR SLAVES. I NEED TO GET MY SHIT TOGETHER AND CLIMB THAT LADDER. IT'S "PIZZA" DAY IN THE CAFETERIA. THE WORST DAY. IT'S THAT SQUARE PIZZA I DON'T LIKE. PLAIN CHEESE. WE ALWAYS LOSE SLAVES IN THE VIOLENT STAMPEDE TO REACH THE PIZZA PILE FIRST, AND THERE'S NEVER ENOUGH. THEN THE RIOT STARTS. THEN THE ELECTRO-DISCIPLINE NETS FALL. ALL THAT SCREAMING. WISH THEY HAD PEPPERONI SLICES.

END OF JOURNAL ENTRY.

GALAKTiKORP SLAVE SHIP "GLORB-PANAAK"
TRASH SHOVELER B. ELKHORN REPORTING

GOT MY FIRST GOLD STAR TODAY FOR EARNING ONE MILLION SWEAT-POINTS, WHICH PUTS ME AT RANK #1,060,150,131 ON THE SLAVER-BOARDS. NOT AS YOUNG AS I USED TO BE. WISH ETHEL WERE HERE SO I COULD TELL HER ABOUT IT. GETTING CLOSE TO MY SECOND GOLD STAR, I JUST NEED 42 MORE "REPORTINGS OF INAPPROPRIATE BEHAVIOUR OF OTHER SLAVES SUCCESSFULLY RESULTING IN ELECTRO-DISCIPLINE AND SWEATPOINT DEMERITS" FOR THAT AGGRANDIZEMENT REWARD.

END OF JOURNAL ENTRY.

GALAKTiKORP SLAVE SHIP "GLORB-PANAAK"
TRASH SHOVELER B. ELKHORN REPORTING

ELECTRO-DISCIPLINED BY OVERSEERS GARGO AND FLUNT AFTER I ACCIDENTALLY WALKED IN ON THEM MATING. THEY WOULDN'T LET ME LEAVE UNTIL THEY HAD FINISHED. GOT CAUGHT IN THE RESULTING SHOCKWAVE BLAST. STILL HARD AS A ROCK HOURS LATER, DESPITE THE LIBIDO SUPPRESSANTS WE ARE REGULARLY FED. TUCKING IT INTO MY WAISTBAND LIKE I'M BACK AT ACADEMY.

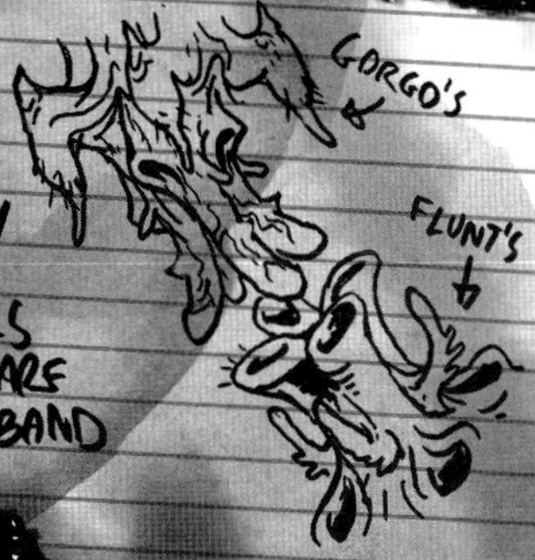
GORGO'S
FLUNT'S

END OF JOURNAL ENTRY.

GALAKTiKORP SLAVE SHIP "GLORB-PANAAK"
TRASH SHOVELER B. ELKHORN REPORTING

I THOUGHT I CAUGHT A GLIMPSE OF HIM TODAY. HE WAS PART OF THE SHOVELING TEAM ON THE FAR SIDE OF THE CHAMBER. I DON'T KNOW IF HE SAW ME, BUT I GOT ELECTRO-DISCIPLINED AGAIN WHILE TRYING TO GET A CLOSER LOOK. I'LL TRY AGAIN NEXT CYCLE.

END OF JOURNAL ENTRY.

GALAKTIKORP SUPER-SLAVE SHIP "CHORB-CHUNT"
TRASH SHOVELER B. ELKHORN REPORTING

SOMEHOW, FATE HAS SMILED ON US. GALAKTIKORP UNVEILED A NEW SUPER-SLAVE SHIP, AND BOTH OF US WERE TRANSFERRED TO SHOVEL DUTY ABOARD IT. WE AREN'T ON THE SAME SHOVELING DETAIL, BUT WE MANAGED TO EXCHANGE WORDS IN PASSING, DURING SHIFT CHANGE. HE'S JUST AS HANDSOME AND INFURIATING AS I REMEMBER. SLAUGHTERLORD_69...

END OF JOURNAL ENTRY.

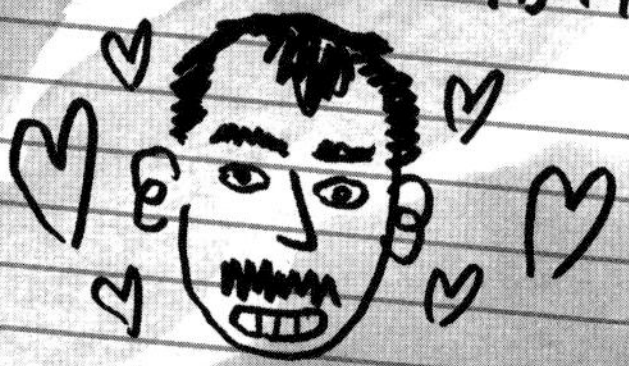

GALAKTIKORP SUPER-SLAVE SHIP "CHORB-CHUNT"
TRASH SHOVELER B. ELKHORN REPORTING

IT HAPPENED. IT FINALLY HAPPENED! THE BIO-REACTOR HAD SEVERE INDIGESTION, SO THERE WAS AN HOUR-LONG DELAY BETWEEN THE SHIFTS. HE TOLD ME HIS PRE-COMPANY CORPSENAME: BRADLEY! WE FUCKED RIGHT THERE, IN THE GOOP ALCOVE. I'VE NEVER FELT SO ALIVE!

END OF JOURNAL ENTRY.

GALAKTIKORP SUPER-SLAVE SHIP "CHORB-CHUNT"
SENIOR TRASH SHOVELER B. ELKHORN REPORTING

ALL MY HARD WORK HAS PAID OFF. AFTER AN ESTIMATED TWO YEARS SHOVELING TRASH, I'M NOW SENIOR TRASH SHOVELER. I HEAD THE TRASH SHOVELING DEPARTMENT SLAVE MEETING EVERY WEEK, DISCUSSING TRASH SHOVELING STRATEGIES WITH OVERSEER KRUNTOK. BRADLEY AND I WERE ABLE TO MEET AGAIN IN THE GOOP ALCOVE. HE SEEMED DISTRACTED SOMEHOW, BUT WE BOTH CAME LIKE FREIGHT TRAINS. ALSO, I EARNED THREE MORE STICKERS FOR MY SUPERIOR SLAVEMANSHIP AGGRANDIZEMENTS. I'M IN THE TOP 100,000,000 ON THE SLAVERBOARDS. NOT BAD FOR THIS OLD DOG.

END OF JOURNAL ENTRY.

SENIOR TRASH SHOVELER
BELKHORN

GALAKTIKORP SUPER-SLAVE SHIP "CHORB-CHUNT"
SENIOR TRASH SHOVELER B. ELKHORN REPORTING

TODAY WAS A GOOD DAY! OVERSEER KRUNTOK HAS BEEN KEEPING ME IN HIS SLEEPING POD LATELY, AND INVITED ME TO DEWORM HIM. APPARENTLY THE OVERSEERS ARE INFESTED WITH PARASITIC SPACE-WORMS THAT CAN GROW TO THE SIZE OF A SLAVE. THEY USUALLY ONLY DEWORM ONE ANOTHER TO SHOW TRUST AND INTIMACY, AND THE DEWORMING PARTY DEVOURS THE PARASITE RAW AS PART OF THE RITUAL. NOTHING WORSE THAN WHAT WE GOT AT MESS HALL IN BOOT CAMP, BACK ON MARS. MY FIRST STEP TOWARDS A PLATINUM STAR!

END OF JOURNAL ENTRY.

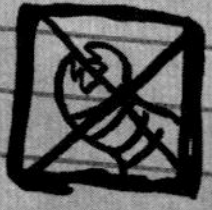

DEWORMING AGGRANDIZEMENT-
PROGRESS 1/10,000

GALAKTIKORP SUPER-SLAVE SHIP "CHORB-CHUNT"
SENIOR TRASH SHOVELER B. ELKHORN REPORTING

UN-FUCKING-BELIEVABLE. NOW I KNOW WHY BRADLEY HAS BEEN ACTING SO DISTANT DURING LOVEMAKING LATELY. HE GOT PROMOTED ABOVE ME TO FOREMAN OF TRASH SHOVELING IN THE STAFF MEETING TODAY, THE POSITION I WAS PROMISED. OVERSEER KRUNTOK COULDN'T EVEN MAKE OCULAR CONTACT WITH ME DURING THE ANNOUNCEMENT. GUESS I'M NOT THE ONLY ONE DOING THE DEWORMING AROUND HERE. THIS MEANS WAR.

END OF JOURNAL ENTRY.

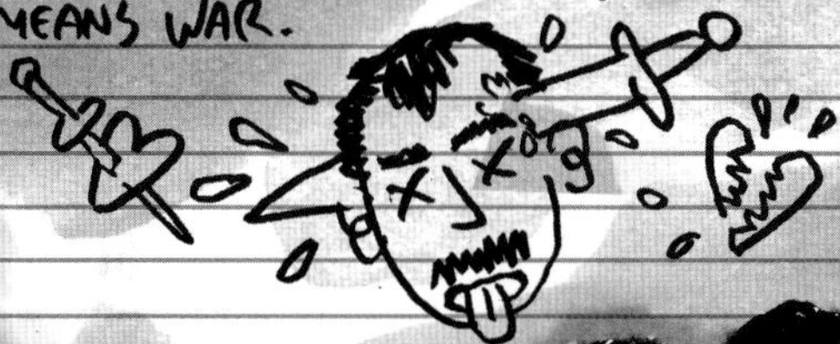

GALAKTIKORP SUPER-SLAVE SHIP "CHORB-CHUNT"
FOREMAN OF TRASH SHOVELING B. ELKHORN REPORTING

THE SHIP'S BIOREACTOR GREW A SECOND DIGESTION CHAMBER. AN APPARENTLY UNCOMMON BUT WELCOME MUTATION. SO OVERSEER KRUNTOK NEEDED A NEW MIDDLE MANAGER FOR SHOVELING OPERATIONS. GUESS WHO GOT THE PROMOTION? IF BRADLEY THINKS HE CAN LEAD A TRASH-SHOVELING DIVISION BETTER THAN ME, THAT PIECE OF X.I.T. HAS ANOTHER THING COMING. I WILL CRUSH HIM.

END OF JOURNAL ENTRY.

GRIP OF THE KOMBINAT

SIMON ROY AND DAMON GENTRY

Thank You for reading

now get back to work